Neptune's Trident

Published by Alpha Psi 1246 Publishing Co, Ltd.
1/9/2015
ISBN: 978-0-6923-6658-5 (sc)

Alpha Psi 1246 Publishing Co. Ltd.
P.O. Box 9422
Greenville, SC 29604

Cover by: Steven J. Catazone
Interior Design: Clare L. Dunning

*The views expressed in this work are solely those of the
author and do not necessarily reflect
the views of the publisher, and the publisher hereby disclaims
any responsibility for them.*

*This book is a work of fiction. Names, characters, businesses,
organizations, places, events, and incidents either are the
product of the author's imagination or are used fictitiously.
Any resemblance to actual persons, living or dead, events or
locals is entirely coincidental.*

Neptune's Trident

"Man is a history-making creature who can neither repeat his past nor leave it behind."

W. H. Auden

by

SCOTT WILLIAM

Alpha Psi 1246 Publishing, Ltd.,
P.O. Box 9422, Greenville, SC 29605

To Linda and to all readers equally possessed of such magnificent, loving, supportive creatures.

CAST OF CHARACTERS

Ken Hamilton - Nephew on sister's side of Senior Senator Cyrus Templeton

Cyrus Templeton - Senior Senator of Pennsylvania, Democrat. ProTempore of Senate.

Khalil - Arab pirate leader in Gulf of Aden.

Salah - Pirate in Khalil's band

Penny Hartwell - Daughter of "Chip" Hartwell survivor of pirate attack off Mexico's Yucatan Peninsula on *Constellation*.

Demetrio Salterez - Pirate leader operating near Cozumel, Mexico.

Emilio – Pirate in works for Demetrio Salterez band.

Dr. Pete Cadburess – Head U.N. Geologist of 1st *Constellation* mission off Yucatan Peninsula, Mexico.

Mr. Charleston - Deck Boss of the *Constellation*.

Captain Rusten - Captain of the U.N. chartered research vessel *Constellation*.

Andrew McLaughlin - U.N. General Secretary.

Royce Tillman - President of the United States.

Muriel - President Tillman's lead secretary.

Clayton Biggs - Chief of Staff for President Royce Tillman

Taylor Hutchinson - Secretary of State.

Tom Milby - Chief staffer of the Chief of Staff, Clayton Biggs, office.

Anthony "Tony" Castillas - U.S. Representative, Democrat House Whip, Godfather to Penny Hartwell.

Pete "Chip" Hartwell - Chief of staff for Tony Castillas.

Ambassador Moulton - U.S. Ambassador to Mexico

Ben Tarnsky - Senate Deputy Director, Republican Party.

Tom Blackwood - Senate minority leader, Republican Party

Cynthia Wellsworth - Democratic Majority leader of the Senate.

Clyde Tuvaris_- Deputy Director Democrat Senate minority party.

Owen Dorsett - Speaker of the House, Republican.

Tobias Sterns - National Security Advisor to President Tillman, Chief Point of Contact and Liaison for U.N. on Operation Neptune.

Tomba Mgashi - Head of security detail for Secretary General.

Admiral Tittinger - Four star Admiral, Chief of Naval Operations. Highest ranking naval officer in command of the Navy.

Jeremy Kohl - Wealthy industrialist, Brandt "Buck" Kohl's father.

Gloria Steinmetz - Colonel. Barrett's secretary.

Dr. Lila Melrony – Irish U.N. research scientist in charge of 2nd *Constellation* mission.

Dr. Miguel Espenoza - Venezuelan, Head of the U.N. Mineral Research Division.

Dolph von Bühl - Brazilian arms dealer servicing South American drug cartel, facilitator of illegal transactions.

OPERATION NEPTUNE

David Barrett - Head of Operation Neptune, retired British SAS Colonel.

Major Phillipe La Barré -French General Directorate for External Security-DGSE, the French external intelligence agency. Liaison officer to the DRM - Directorate of Military Intelligence which coordinates intelligence between the military and civilian anti-terrorism agencies.

Yoshi Kazahiro - Computer and communications specialist; hacker par excellence

STRIKE FORCE TRIDENT

<u>Strike Team Trident</u>

Brandt "Buck" Kohl - Lieutenant, Navy SEAL, Strike Force Trident Leader.

Steve "Rampage" Ramage - Lieutenant Navy, SEAL, Brandt Kohl's friend and second-in-command of Strike Force Trident.

Harold Brisbane - Sergeant, British Army SAS "Sassy."
Cooper Randall - Sergeant, Australian Army SAS "Coop."
Datan Ben-Moshe - Sergeant, Israeli Defense Force, Sayeret MATKAL "Rabbi."
Hubert Arceneaux - Special Agent, French National Police, Directorate of Territorial Surveillance - DST. "Striker" Served two years on SWAT Team member in Central Directorate of Public Security (DCSP) prior to DST.

<u>Agrippa</u>
Tadhg Ramsden - Lieutenant, British Royal Navy; Mk V.1 SOC *Agrippa* Boat Commander. Formally commanded Archer class patrol boat, the HMS Smiter. Second son of the Earl of Windum.
Grels Persson - Ensign, Royal Swedish Navy. Served aboard Swedish CB 90 Patrol Boats. Second-in-Command of *Agrippa,* weapons, navigation and communications officer.
Lenz Synder - Chief Petty Officer/Engineer, German Navy; Mk. V.1 SOC *Agrippa* crewmember.

1

"I've got a survivor," British SAS Sergeant Brisbane called on the comm link. "Lieutenant Kohl, you'd better take a look at this."

Moments later, a rangy built man of six foot one in combat gear and heavily armed jogged into view.

"Where is he?" he asked as he approached.

Sergeant Brisbane motioned to a hunk of rubble he was hovering over.

In the gathering light of the tropic dawn the newcomer's piercing gray eyes took in the situation. A set of legs disappeared under a large chunk of rubble that hours before had been part of a pirate stronghold they had assaulted. Circling around, he saw the upper torso of a man on the other side struggling to breathe. The man was whispering in Arabic and flailing his arms weakly, a trail of dried blood running from the corner of his mouth.

"I was afraid to move the hunk of rubble," the British SAS sergeant, who was also one of Strike Team Trident's medics, offered his dry synopsis. "It's probably the only thing keeping the poor bloke alive. His back and pelvis are probably broken. Most of the internal organs are crushed, the rest are pushed up against his diaphragm. The weight of the hunk has probably pinched off the blood supply to the crushed and torn organs in his midsection."

Brandt "Buck" Kohl, Lieutenant, US Navy SEAL and leader of the UN's anti-piracy unit known as Strike Force

Trident, eyed the weakly flailing man, accessing the options. "Yeah, you're probably right. The second we pull the chunk off, he'll start to hemorrhage. Probably bleed out in thirty seconds. If we leave him, he's sure to die; if we shoot him full of morphine to ease his pain, we might kill him anyhow. Six of one, half dozen of the other..." Buck fell silent.

"Well...what do you want to do?" Sergeant Brisbane probed.

"Let's shoot him full of morphine before we pull the chunk off. That's the best we can do for him. But before we do that, I want to find out who he is," Buck determined. Pressing a water-proof rocker switch on his chest to open his comm link, he spoke into the boom mike coming from under his helmet, "Rabbi, I need you at my position to translate. Rampage, I need you, too."

He heard two clicks in his earpiece from the strike force members acknowledging his order. Moments later, two soldiers appeared from opposite directions. The first to arrive was Lieutenant Steve "Rampage" Ramage, US Navy SEAL, Buck's second-in-command and his best friend since they were roommates at the US Naval Academy.

"What's up, Buck?"

"I wanted you to hear any intel we might get from this..." Buck paused to wave at the disjointed figure on the ground next to him, "suspect."

"Roger, that."

A fourth soldier, Sergeant Datan "Rabbi" Ben-Moshe, from the Israeli Defense Force's special forces unit, Sayeret MATKAL, joined the knot of men.

"Rabbi, see if you can get this man's name and any information about who was in the house," Buck ordered.

Rabbi swiftly knelt to whisper into the pinned man's ear

then put his ear to his mouth to catch the barely audible reply. After repeating the process several times, Rabbi stood to report to Buck and Rampage.

"He says his name is Khalil. No last name. All he kept saying was 'Please, please don't let me die. I can reward you, I have money; I'll give you anything you want, just don't let me die.' He just kept repeating it. I couldn't get anything else from him."

"Alright, if that's all there is…give him morphine, then Flexi-cuff his hands and feet so he doesn't do anything crazy when we pull that block off him."

Sergeant Brisbane knelt down and jabbed two ampoules of morphine into the man's shoulder then proceeded with the restraints. By the time he'd finished, the morphine had taken full effect so the soldiers gathered and gripped the chunk of rubble.

"On three. One, two, three," someone counted and the men grunted and lifted the stone before manhandling it to the side. They all turned to see the once pinned man writhing in agony that cut through the morphine. Unintelligible words formed on his mouth but got no farther. His writhing quickly subsided as the life drained from him until he was still. The men looking on silently bearing witnesses to the man's passing.

At that moment another call came over the comm link: "I've got another live one over here…"

Eight Months Earlier…
"*Allah uha akbar, Allah uha akbar,*" shouted the man wearing a red banded, white and black checked kaffiyet headdress of the nomadic Arab tribes. The praise for his god echoed off the crystal chandeliers that hung from the pilastered ceiling of the great hall. The long, heavy-bladed knife he held over his head looked out of place among the

opulence of fine bone china, white linen table cloths and cherry wood Queen Anne chairs upholstered in royal blue silk and monogrammed with the cruise line's emblem. The other men, holding AK-47s on the hostages and dressed in the flowing robes customary to the nomadic desert life called *jallabeebs*, nodded at the praise to God. Their filthy garb, rusted, worn guns and their violent demeanor seemed to collide with the room's elegant ambiance, giving it a surreal feel.

"Please, please, don't kill me. You don't want to kill me-- I'm valuable to you. My uncle is a U.S. senator. He can help you, whatever you want," Ken Hamilton begged from his hands and knees on the royal blue and red patterned wool rug that covered the luxurious dining room floor. It was hard for him to talk, his throat twisted by the crazed man with the knife yanking his head back by his hair to expose his neck.

The man with the knife, known as Khalil, heard the babbling of the fat, rich American pig below him and it disgusted him to hear the whining from this weak dog. *Probably begging for his life*, he thought. Just the sound of the American gibberish filled him with rage. "Salah, come tie this pig's hands and feet."

One of the pirates slung his weapon over his shoulder and advanced on the prone man at his leader's feet. From beneath his robes, he produced several feet of small cordage and proceeded to tie up the American, who kept up his continuous whimpering. The American was pulled to his knees, hands tied behind his back, legs crossed and tied at the ankles. Once he was done trussing up the man, Salah stepped back to examine his handiwork. Satisfied, he turned to Khalil and said, "He is ready to meet his maker."

"Watch this Salah," Khalil said. "The best way to get

these rich pigs to give us their money is to make an example of one of them." With that statement, Khalil stepped back behind Ken Hamilton, grabbed a fistful of the man's sandy blond hair and once again yanked his head down and backwards to expose his throat, prompting more of the American's sickening squeals. "Please, please, don't kill me! I'll give you whatever you want!" This only served to motivate Khalil. Sensing what was coming, the man fought him to turn his head so that he could lock eyes with one of the females in the crowd of hostages. *Probably the pig's adulterous wife,* Khalil thought. *If he wants to look in his whore's eyes as he dies, so be it.*

He swiftly brought the knife round to the front of the man's throat and began to draw it across the soft tissue as he pulled hard inwards, towards his body.

At the first touch of the stinging steel, the kneeling man let loose a high pitched scream. One of the women against the wall screamed. The other hostages either turned their heads away or stared in glassy-eyed horror.

Like everything else about Khalil, his knife was only sharp in a few places, so it did not part the man's throat easily. He had to saw several times through the neck sinew before he severed the windpipe and jugular vein. All the while, the man continued his high pitched scream, until Khalil had cut his throat sufficiently to sever his vocal cord nerves, turning his scream into a loud whoosh of escaping air and a wet gush of venous blood sprayed onto the surrounding tables, chairs and floor. Khalil's dull knife finally opened the carotid artery, spewing blood everywhere under high pressure. The man's attempts to scream finally stopped as the blood pressure to his brain zeroed, rendering him unconscious almost instantly, with death following only moments later. It took several more hard saws and wrenching of the partially severed head before Khahil was finally able to remove the head from the body that flopped over like a felled tree.

He held the head aloft towards the terror-stricken hostages to frighten them. He need not have. The civilized diners had already been transformed into a mewling mass of terrified animals reduced to their most primal instincts.

Khalil looked at the hostages, expecting them to already be throwing their wallets and jewelry at him. Instead all he saw was the fleeting, wild-eyed looks of terrified sheep looking for an escape. "Salah, grab that fat woman in the blue dress and cut off her finger with the ring," he ordered, pointing out the intended victim with his blood-drenched knife.

Salah stepped to the mob and reached in to grab the gray hair of an elderly matron who had a huge gold ring topped with a monstrous diamond on her right hand. The woman tried to resist, squirming as she tried to get away. The reward for her subconscious actions was two brutal punches to her face by Salah that sent her to her knees. Before he let her fall, Salah put all his weight into a vicious shot to her midsection with the butt of his gun. The woman, stunned and stupefied, did not see the blow coming. Through pain-glazed eyes, she buckled at the blow as several of her internal organs ruptured.

Salah grabbed his knife and wrenched the inert woman's right hand to a comfortable working height before he cut off her finger with the ring. Upon seeing this, both women and men started to desperately claw at their valuables. One man, whose ring finger on his left hand had fattened since the last time the ring had been removed, became desperate. He lurched to a nearby dining table to grab a pat of butter from a delicate china butter urn. He rubbed and massaged the butter over his ring finger, but still the ring wouldn't move.

One of the ragged gunmen looked on indifferently. He saw that the ring was not cooperating so he drew his knife and stepped forward to assist him in the same manner demonstrated by Salah. The man became frantic as he saw the knife leave its scabbard. In desperation, he strained, both arms horizontal across his chest, until a sickening crack dislocated his offending ring finger's second joint. Ashen, the man pulled the ring from his hand and tossed it to the floor as he tried to control the pain tremors from his mangled finger.

The guard sheathed his knife and joined Salah in picking up the remaining valuables from the floor, placing them in a cloth sack they had brought for the purpose.

"It's time to go!" Khalil shouted to his men. "The ship's crew is unarmed, but they may try something stupid if we wait much longer. Back to the boat!"

The six men turned their backs on their victims and retraced their steps to where Khalil had left one man guarding the small wooden boat they'd tied to the ship's rail. Below, the boat bobbed wildly in the twenty-four knot slipstream of the ship. Still attached to the railing were the grappling hooks used to scale the sides of the moving ship. Now, they used those lines to descend back to the boat below, weapons slung over their backs, disappearing one by one over the rail.

When all his raiders were back aboard the eighteen-foot boat, Khalil drew his blood-soaked knife and cut the bowline still tied to the rail. "Muhanna, get us out of here!" he shouted at the man operating the big outboard engine at the stern.

Khalil peered upward at the boat's rail to see if the ship's crew would try anything. As they pulled away, he saw the entire side of the boat was devoid of any signs of activity.

Feeling rich and full of himself, he turned to Salah. "That was easier than I thought it would be. We must do this again sometime," he said, his yellow teeth looking white against his olive complexion.

"We did well today," Salah said, holding the cloth bag aloft for Khalil to see. "We did very well."

"Yes, not only was it profitable, but we did the Prophet's work by killing an infidel." Khalil's smile broadened even more at that delicious interpretation. In Khalil's version of Islam, there was no sin attached to killing, as long as the life taken was not that of a believer of the Prophet; there was only reward. "I wonder how many wives will await me in heaven for that little deed," Khalil mused as he wiped the last remains of Ken Hamilton off his hands onto his white robe before he re-sheathed his knife.

2

"*Con permiso. Dondé está el capitán?*" The tall blond woman asked first one dock worker and then another while gesticulating at the nearest boat. The Texas twang of her imperfect Spanish was met with blank stares every time. Standing a head taller than the sea of Mexican locals that worked the commercial docks of San Miguel de Cozumel; she appeared as a blond bastion in the dock's current of activities swirling past her.

Penny Hartwell had the fine bone structure of which most girls dreamed. Leggy and narrow-waisted, she had athletic shoulders and was crowned with blonde, straight hair that framed a face of perfect symmetry and high checkbones. But for all the gifts of nature bestowed upon Penny, she was a rather plain girl, never more so as she worked her way down the dock without a stitch of make-up on in the tropical heat. Awash in her wide-eyed youth and naiveté to the backward leers of the workers she passed, she doggedly searched for a ship's captain.

"Excuse me, miss, but can I be of assistance to you?" Penny heard from behind. She turned to see an elderly gentleman dressed in khaki shorts, a buttoned tan shirt, and white socks bunched at the top of hiking shoes. His close-cropped white hair peeked out from beneath a floppy olive green bush cap, his faded, intelligent blue eyes framed by round brown glasses.

"Did you say something?"

"Yes, it sounded like you could use some help," the man said paternally, a slight crinkle coming to the corner of his eye. "It can be a bit intimidating on the docks here in Cozumel. They don't exactly hire workers for their congeniality."

Happy to have found someone who spoke English, Penny blurted out in frustration, "I'm trying to find the captains of these boats. I need to see if one of them will give me passage up the coast to the village of Canatas. There's no road to it; it's only accessible from sea. I'm going there for the next year to help the villagers learn modern farming techniques, sanitation, education, and stuff."

"Where, exactly, is Canatas?"

"It's on the west coast of Yucatan Peninsula. The Volunteer Aid Corps told me the best way to get there was to fly into Cozumel and then arrange passage on a local coastal freighter to the village." Penny cast her eyes downward and blushed before starting again, "But, I'm a flat-land girl. I've never been around boats before. I'm afraid I don't know the first thing about ships or where to find the captains."

This had been obvious to Dr. Pete Cadburess for the thirty-odd seconds he had followed her as she made her way down the dock. "I think I might know just where to find a captain who can help you," he said to her kindly. "But first, I think introductions are in order. I'm Pete Cadburess," he said, extending his hand.

"Nice to meet you...my name is Penny Hartwell," she said with two quick pumps of his hand.

"All right Penny Hartwell of Flat Land, U.S.A., walk with me down to the end of the dock. I know a ship captain that may be able to help you," he said as he brushed past her.

As Penny turned to accompany her elderly savior, she asked, "So what brings you down to the docks?"

"The research vessel I work on is in port for supplies and fuel. I had some free time while ship stores were being taken on, so I thought I would take the time to go buy a couple of t-shirts for my grandchildren," he said while lifting a small canvas bag that he had been carrying in his hand.

"The bag seems kinda full; how many grandchildren do you have?"

"I've got six--from five to thirteen years old. I'll probably have more, one day. My youngest son hasn't married yet, but we're hoping. So how 'bout you? Any grandchildren of your own?"

Penny laughed.

"No? Well good, then that means you're unattached. Maybe I should introduce you to my youngest son."

Still chuckling, Penny said, "Sure, bring him on down to Canatas sometime in the next year. I'll be there."

"That can be arranged."

While they were bantering, Penny noticed they were angling toward a blue hulled ship with white superstructure, with the word "*Constellation*" painted on the stern. The ship looked to be a couple hundred feet long, she figured as they headed for the set of stairs that hung from the boat's side midship.

"Is this the one?" Penny asked.

"Yep," Pete replied taking the lead up the stairs.

"Hi, Dr. Cadburess, how was the flea market? Did you get bit?" A ship's officer at the top of the stairs asked, smiling at his little joke.

"Only in my wallet, Albert, only in my wallet," he lamented. "Albert, this is Miss Penny Hartwell, I'm taking her to see Captain Rusten."

Penny had now stepped onto the deck behind Pete. "Hi," she said sweetly, accompanied by her best smile.

"Hello, Miss Hartwell, welcome aboard the *Constellation*."

"Thank you."

"This way, Penny," Pete said as he had already started up a nearby staircase.

Penny hurried after him. "Did I hear Albert call you *Dr. Cadburess?*" She asked of his back as they trudged up one staircase and then another.

"Yes, that's what they tend to call me when I'm at work," he replied off handedly.

"What kind of doctor are you? I've ruled out witch doctor. I'm sorry; you just don't seem to be the chicken entrails and incantation type," Penny said playfully.

"Oh, I'm a geologist--I study oil deposits. My youngest grandkids call me a rock doctor. They think that I heal sick rocks," he chuckled.

They had arrived at the bridge's outside deck platform. Pete waited for Penny to catch up before he opened the door, letting her enter the bridge first. Penny stepped in and surveyed a very modern bridge with computer screens everywhere, but oddly enough, no rudder wheel. There were three men present, all wearing white short-sleeved, open collared shirts with black pants, black shoes, and differently colored gold and black shoulder boards. Pete stepped toward the most elderly of the trio. "Captain Rusten, I'd like to introduce you to Miss Penny Hartwell. She has a problem that I think we can help her out with. Penny..."

Penny took her cue from the good doctor and dove right in: "I'm trying to find transportation to the village of Canatas on the western coast of the Yucatan Peninsula. I need to get ashore with my supplies and equipment. Can you help me?"

"We're certainly going that direction," Captain Rusten began in his scratchy baritone, "and provided that your supplies can be broken down into small loads, we can get that ashore for you, but ultimately, it's not my call. Dr. Cadburess is in charge of this expedition, since he's the senior U.N. researcher who chartered this vessel. It's up to him if he wants to lose the time on this charter. I just get him safely to where he wants to go."

"My supplies are just a couple dozen cases of medical and agricultural supplies and equipment like plows and shovels. Will that be a problem?"

"I don't think so. Can you have your supplies down to the dock in twenty-four hours?" the captain went on to say.

"I think so. I'll have to get right on it, though. So are we agreed?" She looked at both men.

"Yes, we are," said Pete.

Penny beamed, thinking *'How painless was this to find a ship? Now, if only the rest of my mission goes like this…'*

3

"I will make it perfectly clear for you. You must kill Dr. Pete Cadburess. Period. Finite," said the man, his tan linen tropical business suit stood in stark contrast to his surroundings. He was sitting in a dark, dirty, little flop bar just outside the dock area of Cozumel. It was like any other bar that serviced sailors and longshoremen; liquor and flesh could be had for the price of a few hours' wages. From his disdain, it was easy to see that the suited interloper was the kind of man that had never cared about fitting in. It was not just his fashionable haircut or his expensive tailored clothes that set him apart. It was his cold blue eyes, totally devoid of humor or humanity. Rather than take in the surroundings, they seemed to search for prey, and once found, locked on with intense, singular ferocity. And this bar had seen many a hard eye, including those of the man sitting across from the blue-eyed stranger.

"What of the boat and crew?" asked Demetrio Salterez.

"I don't care. This is your line of work, isn't it? You may keep whatever spoils you may take. All I care about is taking care of Dr. Cadburess. His ship sails tomorrow afternoon with high tide."

"Some of my customers have preferences about their victim's death. In the interest of customer satisfaction, do you want Cadbress's death to be fast or slow? Painful or painless? Any particular method that might suit your fancy, maybe?"

"None."

"Alright then, all I need is the money, in American dollars, as we agreed."

The suited stranger reached inside his breast pocket and produced a thick envelope that he slid halfway across the table. Demetrio eyed the envelope hungrily for several moments before he slowly started to reach for the money. With the speed of a mongoose, the blue-eyed stranger struck, driving the point of a switchblade knife that appeared out of nowhere, deep into the wood table between the fingers of Demitrio's outstretched hand. "I do not want to be disappointed, Salterez," the man hissed menacingly under his breath. "I do not want to come back here to finish the job. If I do, I will finish more than Dr. Cadburess. *Ja?*"

Demetrio had not been quite sure until the last question, but it was definitely clear now that there was something Teutonic about the stranger across from him, even though his Spanish was perfect with a hint of aristocrat added to the Portuguese accent. *'Maybe one of the Third Reich refugee families from World War II that immigrated to Brazil,'* he wondered. He also wondered if the man's strike was luck or skill to put the blade between his fingers. Looking into the man's eyes, he realized that the man did not care one way or another. *'Yes,'* Demetrio thought to himself, *'this was not a man who made idle threats or wasted effort.'* "I understand. This will be the last time we talk. That is, until you require my services again."

The well-dressed stranger sniffed at that idea while dropping a hundred pesos on the table before heading for daylight, leaving the knife in the table as a reminder of his threat. He walked outside and down the block to a rented Mercedes he had carefully parked in an unobserved location. Pretending to search and fumble for his car keys, he searched the surroundings for any surveillance or tails he might have picked up. Satisfied that he was not being watched, he pulled a satellite phone from under his coat and unfolded the antenna. When he saw he had satellite reception, he quickly stabbed a memorized number into the phone's keypad. Twenty seconds later, the phone connection went through several exchanges and an encryption device before it started ringing. After three rings, a male voice that was known to millions in South America answered.

"Go."

"Mr. Minister, it is done. The problem will be eliminated tomorrow when their ship sails."

A brief pause passed before the well-dressed stranger heard the click in his ear as the other party disconnected.

4

It had been hard work, but in the last twenty-four hours, Penny had gotten all her supplies delivered and loaded on to the boat. Exhausted, she adjourned to her stateroom, kicked off her shoes, and flopped down on her bunk for a little well deserved rest. She had just started to luxuriate in her accomplishments, drifting off to sleep when the ship's klaxon started wailing its warning. Jolted awake, Penny did not know if this was a drill or if there really was an emergency. Fearful, she re-donned her shoes and hurried for the bridge to find out.

On the way, she reasoned it more likely that this was only a drill. They had only just left Cozumel a little over two hours ago, and it made sense to her that they would drill early on in the trip to make sure all the crew knew what to do in case of an emergency. The closer she got to the bridge, the more she convinced herself that her apprehension was misplaced. That is until about halfway up the bridge's stairs when she heard Captain Rusten's voice come over the ship's P.A. system: "Man the stern fire hose. Damage control parties, man the starboard and port fire hoses."

Oh my God! We're on fire! Penny thought, sprinting the rest of the way up the steps. Arriving out of breath, she burst through the rear door of the bridge and nearly collided with Captain Rusten, who was striding across the bridge with a pair of binoculars in his hands. "What's wrong? Are we on fire?" she demanded breathlessly.

"Pirates," Captain Rusten replied calmly. "We're being chased from the stern by a boat of eight or nine waving guns at us."

"Oh my God! You have guns or something to shoot at them with, don't you?"

"No, this is a U.N. chartered vessel. As a research vessel, we're prohibited from being armed in any way." Captain Rusten explained calmly. "Don't worry, Miss Hartwell, I've dealt with these types of low-life bastards before. They're bullies mostly. If you put up enough of a fight, they'll lose interest and go find some other easier target to pick on. I've dispatched Mr. Charleston to the stern to man the fire hoses. It's hard to board a moving boat in the open sea when it doesn't want to be boarded, especially if they're getting hit with a high-pressure fire hose. Besides I have a few other tricks up my sleeve. Now, I want you to go back to your room and lock yourself in. Do not come out until you hear the all clear over the ship's loud speakers. It's the safest place for you. They can't hurt you if they can't get at you. Now, if you'll excuse me, I have business to attend to." With that, Captain Rusten headed out on to the port bridge wing and swung his binoculars aft.

Stealing a quick look out the port bridge-wing door, she saw what was happening. A couple hundred yards behind the ship was a small wooden boat powered by a big outboard engine, just like the ones local fishermen used, chasing the *Constellation* on the port side. One look was enough to tell that the armed men were gaining fast.

"Miss Hartwell," Captain Rusten stated gruffly from behind his binoculars, "I will not ask you again. Please leave the bridge and go lock yourself into your cabin."

A tickle of fear crossed the nape of her neck as she

exited. As the door was swinging shut behind her, she heard Captain Rusten shouting orders into the bridge from the wing. "I want maximum revolutions on the shaft. Call the engine room and tell them I want all safety checks disabled. I want all the revolutions this ship's got."

Penny hurried back to her cabin and locked the door behind her. All she could do was sit on her bed and hug her knees to her chest while fear's talons squeezed the air from her chest.

******

"Look at these stupid Americans, Emilio. They think sprinkling some water on us is going to stop us," Demetrio said to the pirate beside him. As Demetrio examined the boat, three fire hoses spat arcs of water at them. "Ernesto," Demetrio called to a man seated in the bow of the boat, cradling a long tube with a handle and bulbous head, "remember, use only the high explosive rockets until all the radio antennas are down."

"Yes, boss," he yelled back over the roar of the engine and the wind. They had been over this before. The weapon he was cradling was an RPG, or Rocket Propelled Grenade launcher of Soviet design that could be found in any Third World country arms bazaar. The weapon could fire different types of grenades depending on the desired effect. In this case, Demetrio wanted high explosive rounds fired first to take out the radio antennas on top of the bridge and destroy the radio equipment contained inside the bridge to prevent the ship from radioing for help.

After the radios were down, he would use the HEAT, High Explosive Anti-Tank, rockets on the bridge. They would burn a hole through two and a half inches of steel plate with a molten stream of copper spawling and project the liquefied metals at near supersonic velocities into the area behind the impact point. The liquefied metal had a devastating effect on flesh and bones and would kill anyone still alive on the bridge. With luck, they would kill Dr. Cadburess with the RPG rounds up front and get that business taken care of so they could get on with looting the ship.

On cue, the thug manning the big outboard engine started to angle into the bigger boat ahead of the bridge structure. This would be tricky. The man steering the outboard would have to keep a close watch on the *Constellation* to prevent the big ship from steering into their boat.

Emilio brought the RPG to his shoulder and sighted on the bridge. Just as the crosshairs in the aiming reticule settled on one of the front windows and he started to pull the trigger, the big boat turned hard away from the little boat. Emilio was nearly ejected out of the boat as the steersman turned hard to follow the larger ship. With the little pirate boat swinging hard into the *Constellation*, the ship turned hard back into the smaller boat, hoping to catch it inbound and smash it up on the flanks of its bow. But the steersman saw the maneuver and the little boat was too responsive. It narrowly missed smashing into the big blue boat's side.

"Son of a bitch!" Demetrio roared. "Emilio, get a round on that bridge now! It does not have to be perfect, just close enough to keep their heads down until we can get a better shot. Now, shoot, damn it!"

Once the little boat regained the proper position, Emilio launched a round that impacted below the windows, just left of center. As Demetrio guessed, the over pressure from the HE warhead detonation shattered the windows along most of the bridge's front and sent the glass flying inwards as thousands of razor-sharp pieces of shrapnel. The big ship immediately stopped its violent maneuvering and settled into a straight course.

"Now blast it with HE rounds to knock out the radios, Emilio!" Demetrio roared, fully engaged in the battle now.

The little boat was pitching and swaying in the ocean's swells, and it took four shots, two of which impacted on the sides of the bridge, before Demetrio was satisfied that the bridge and its radios were knocked out. "Now, put some HEAT rounds into the bridge," he commanded.

Emilio put four more shots into the bridge, and smoke began to roll from its shattered windows.

Demetrio ordered the steersman to bring the boat alongside so that they could board it.

******

Mr. Charleston had watched the attack on the bridge from the port side rail near the stern. His orders were to man the fire hoses and keep the pirates from boarding the boat. The bridge had taken heavy damage, and he knew that there had to be casualties. But, he reasoned, the immediate threat was the small boat loaded with men that was approaching the low deck section at the rear of the ship. Those on the bridge would just have to wait and fend for themselves while he battled the armed men in the small boat.

The fire hose under his right arm was a two and a half-inch line. The ship's pumps produced so much water pressure that he had to have one of the other deckhands stand behind him to help control the line from thrashing wildly about. He was a big man, but even so, he struggled to aim the hose's nozzle at the approaching boat. His concentration was on the hose, and the loud sound of its discharge completely masked the sound of gunfire from the small boat. It came as a great surprise to him, then, when three bullet holes stitched across his chest, one piercing his sternum. The fire hose kept him propped up for a moment before he crumpled. He was dead well before his head bounced on the deck with a thud.

The other crewmen saw their deck boss gunned down. A brave crewman rushed to take his place on the hose, but he was gunned down along with the second crewman on the hose. The other deckhands quickly saw that further resistance was useless and tried to find safe cover from the bursts of gunfire that were starting to rake them. One of them found a good hiding spot among lines, fenders, ropes and blocks in an equipment locker off the stern deck. The hose was left to flop wildly about the deck on its own.

******

Grappling hooks soon appeared on the deck, tossed over the rail in high arcs. Quickly, boarders clambered up the ropes and over the rails of the *Constellation*. One of the last to board was Demitrio, who started to shout orders at the others in Spanish.

"Jorge and Julio, go to the bridge and kill any still alive there," Demetrio ordered. "Don't shoot them in the heads. I need to be able to identify them in case one of them is Dr. Cadburess. Throttle down the boat to idle and disengage the prop. Now go!"

"The rest of you start rounding up the crew. If any give you trouble, shoot them and make your prisoners carry them back here to the stern deck. I want everyone, dead or alive, brought to the stern deck. Go!" The remaining pirates scurried off in all directions and disappeared through doorways and down hatches. The fire hose was still whipsawing around at the back of the deck. Demetrio fired a burst of bullets at it, puncturing the hose enough to stop it from thrashing around.

Minutes later, crewmembers with hands over their heads started emerging, pushed forward by pirates with AK-47s aimed at their backs. Demetrio felt the boat's engines go to idle as it started to coast.

The prisoners were herded into the middle of the deck while two pirates stayed to keep guard. The others returned to search for more prisoners.

******

Penny heard the explosions and gunfire that had lasted for ten minutes. Now that the ship was coasting, it became eerily quiet. Slowly, shouts in Spanish became distinguishable as pirates were going room by room in search of prisoners. Occasionally, there was gunfire. The shouts were getting closer to her room. Her fear blossomed into full fledged panic. She searched for a place to hide, but her room was too tiny. She slid under her bunk, which was supported from the wall by chains, hoping they would not look under the bed.

The door to her cabin was jerked heavily but did not yield. "Open up! Open up or we will kill you!"

Penny was immobilized by fear; she lay under her bunk; concentrating on breathing very quietly so the bandits would not find her.

The door was jarred again, followed by the sound of heavy gun butts being smashed against the door. After several strikes, the pirates stopped. A deafening roar of gunfire sounded from the door as the pirates blasted her lock with their guns. Wood, metal and bullets from the door sprayed across Penny's cabin. Then the door was kicked in.

Two of the criminals, short Hispanic males with faces that showed *mestizo* bloodlines, burst into the room waving their guns about wildly. Penny watched their knees and ankles move past the bed from her position jammed against the wall under the bunk. She thought they were leaving when a face suddenly appeared to look under the bed.

Caught!

Adrenaline shot through her system. A hand reached under the bunk, clutched a handful of her hair and yanked her out and to her feet. Terror stricken, Penny was shoved towards the door as the cutthroat yelled "Move!" in her ear. In the hallway, she saw other crewmembers being herded down the corridor. She was led outside to where the rest of their ship's company was grouped. She had been onboard such a short time that she didn't know many, though others she recognized by sight. Off to the side, several bodies were laid out. She recognized Mr. Charleston's body among them.

One of the crew in the middle of the huddle started to say something under his breath to the person standing next to him. A guard lurched into the crowd, parting the clusters of people with vicious gun butt swings and jabs of the muzzle until he reached the offender. The offending crewman was smashed in the head three times with the guard's gun butt, splitting the man's head open.

More crew arrived, carrying bloody bodies from the front of the boat. Penny recognized one as Captain Rusten's. The bodies were laid next to the others near the deck rail.

Finally, a heavyset ruffian that had been observing

everything moved forward. "Which one of you is Dr. Cadburess?" he shouted at the group in passable English.

"I am," called Dr. Cadburess from the middle of the huddle.

"Step out where I can see you."

Dr. Cadburess moved to the edge of the pack to face the speaker.

In one fluid motion, the speaker brought up his gun and placed it in the chest of the man standing next to Dr. Cadburess and shot him. The man dropped lifelessly to the deck while the rest shrank back in horror as far as the deck space would allow them. The heavyset pirate reached into the mob and pulled a small, thin man out by his hair and placed the warm muzzle of the barrel under the man's chin. "Which man here is Dr. Cadburess? Don't lie to me or I will kill you." Demetrio had learned a long ago that the threat of death was not credible if the victims didn't believe you, and the best way to get answers was to set an example up front by killing a prisoner.

From his awkward position, the man pointed at Dr. Cadburess and indicated, "He's Dr. Cadburess. He's the man you want."

Demetrio knew that no bond of loyalty or wish to protect Dr. Cadburess would be strong enough for a friend or colleague to lie after witnessing someone killed on a whim. Demetrio was now satisfied with the identity of Dr. Cadburess and turned to him, "Dr. Cadburess, come with me." He then turned and strode to the ship's rail.

Dr. Cadburess walked unsteadily behind the man to the rail and then stopped to face the murderer.

"I've been sent to look for you, Doctor," the pirate stated.

Confused, Dr. Cadburess stammered, "I don't understand. Sent by whom?"

"Oh, that really doesn't matter. Besides, I don't even know his name."

"Sent for what?"

"To deliver something to you," Demetrio said as he slung his gun back over his shoulder.

Seeing the gun being put away, Dr. Cadburess visibly relaxed. "Deliver what?"

Demetrio had calculated that putting the gun away would make the man stand easier and thus make it easier to accomplish his task. With a swiftness that belied the man's size, he stepped into Dr. Cadburess's guard and stabbed him in the heart with a knife. Dr. Cadburess's eyes bulged as he fell heavily into the pirate who caught him and held him up. As the life faded from his eyes, Demetrio said into his face, "Death, Dr. Cadburess, death."

Demetrio dropped the body to the deck and bent over it, placing two of his fingers on the late doctor's neck looking for a pulse. When he was sure that Dr. Cadburess was dead, he stepped away to admire his work. He left the knife, the black-handled switchblade his Teutonic friend had left for him in the table, in Dr. Cadburess's chest. *A nice touch*, he thought.

Then Demetrio walked back to the huddled captives. Having watched him kill two people in as many minutes, the prisoners parted before him, wanting to stay out of his grasp. He was searching for one of the prisoners, a blonde woman. When he saw her, he marched over and grabbed her by the hair, pulling her out of the mob. Once clear of the mob, he turned to Emilio and said in a voice devoid of interest, "Kill them all and throw their bodies over the side."

Penny, having understood what he said to the other pirate, moaned, "No, you can't do that!"

Demetrio shook his prize by the hair. "This one I think

we'll keep for a little fun and when we are done with her, we'll sell her to Ernesto for his whore house. I'll bet his customers will pay plenty to screw this blonde *gringo*. But first, I'm going to make sure that the merchandise is in working order," he said with smile that exposed his crooked, missing and stained teeth. "When you're done disposing of the crew, take everything of value that we can fit into the boat." With that, he turned toward the bow of the boat and shoved Penny toward the crew's quarters. Behind him the pirates' guns started to spit a dirge of death accompanied by the shrill vibrato of screams.

******

When he was done with the woman, he left her whimpering and tied to the bed, as he made his way back out to the aft deck. His band of pirates was nearly through looting the boat; the last items of value were being passed over the rail to their little boat. "I left our little prize all warmed up for anyone who wants to pleasure her," he announced to the crew who looked up at his approach. "But don't take too long, we need to get going. Oh, and," he paused for effect, "the last one to use her, bring her back to the boat. We would not want to forget the merchandise."

The pirates glanced hungrily at each other for a moment, then as one they started toward the crew's quarters. They fought each other on the way, elbowing each other, each wanting to be the first to have his way with the captive. By ones and twos, they passed through the hatch. Shortly after, a woman's scream pierced the air before it was suddenly muffled.

Demetrio stared at the blood on the deck; absent-mindedly he rubbed his sandal toe in the blood, making designs as he reminisced about the pleasurable last couple of hours he just had enjoyed.

A single eye watched the lone pirate through a crack in the door of an equipment locker, the one the pirates had failed to search.

5

"Thank you for meeting with me, Mr. President," Andrew McLaughlin said in a mellifluous Australian tenor, as he exchanged handshakes with Royce Tillman.

"My pleasure. The United Nations' Secretary-General is always welcome in the Oval Office of the People of the United States. Please, sit here by the fire with me, if you will," Royce said with a gracious sweep of his hand toward a couch opposite of him in front of the Oval Office's fireplace. The gray-templed, dapper Australian diplomat's short cropped, red curly hair highlighted the vibrancy that his eyes conveyed as he moved towards the indicated seat eyeing the fire gratefully. The ground-level view from the Oval Office's window showed January's accumulation of snow on the White House's south lawn outside the West Wing.

The staff had built a nice, cozy fire for this first informal meeting of the two leading diplomats of the world. While the occasion was informal, there was nothing informal about the polish these two accomplished diplomats brought to the conversation. Both men were old-fashioned poker players. Each was assured in his ability to read other players and their attainment of the highest office in their respective orbits bore evidence to their well-placed confidence.

"Muriel, will be in momentarily with coffee, tea, and some snacks. You know, since I've become president, I have more secretaries than I can count. Eight outside my door: clerical secretaries, travel secretaries, protocol secretaries, social secretaries, and that doesn't include the likes of the Secretaries of Commerce, Defense, State, et cetera, et cetera, et cetera. . ." His personal reflection was broken by a quick knock followed by a middle-aged woman in a conservative dress bearing a silver tray with coffee a hot water urn, cups, and condiments, as well as a small plate of pastries.

"But this," he said gesturing to Muriel, "is the one secretary I cannot do without."

The middle-aged woman looked up at the president as she set the tray down on the table between the two leaders, and she smiled the knowing smile of a woman who been with a man long enough to know his every mood and temperament.

"Muriel was the secretary assigned to me when I first became a State Representative in Colorado. She's been keeping me on track ever since."

Muriel poured the president his coffee and added cream and sugar before preparing Andrew's Earl Grey tea. She had checked with the Secretary-General's staff to learn that he liked his with a squeeze of lemon and sugar.

"Can she get you anything else, Mr. Secretary-General?"

"No, that is quite lovely. Thank you, Muriel."

"Thank you, Muriel. I'll call you if we need anything else," the president said as she bowed, every-so-slightly, while noiselessly backing through the door.

Andrew watched with appreciation the little choreographed court theatrics and interruption by staff. He had been here two minutes and already he was on a first name basis with the president's inner sanctum handlers and the topic of office help. As a politician, he understood the carefully crafted misdirection intended to distract him from his mission by humanizing the inhabitants of the office at the center of the most powerful economy and military of the world. It was said that the Oval Office was the single biggest home court advantage in the world of politics, and he was getting a lesson in that by a master.

"So how can the people of the United States be of assistance to the United Nations?"

Andrew noted that the president was already speaking in the third person, already setting up to stall or deflect any request.

"Mr. President, I wanted to get your feelings on a topic of great importance to the world community of nations and the United States. I wanted to get your opinion of the state of commerce upon the high seas. As you know, I am an Australian. And being born and raised on an island nation influences and tempers one's outlook on life, just as I am sure your upbringing in the state of Colorado influences your outlook on the way you view your country and the world."

"True, one can never completely divorce one's self of his upbringing."

"As a citizen and a product of an island nation, I am especially sensitive to the importance of oceanic commerce as the life blood of the Australian nation. The sea is our link to the world and its bounty. Likewise, international trade and shipping is a cornerstone of the United States' economy. Grains, electronics, foodstuffs, timber and the like must freely flow to and from the United States ports in order to keep the global economy and yours vibrant."

"We certainly agree on the importance of oceanic shipping and the intertwined relationship of our economies with the other nations of the world," President Tillman confirmed, nodding in agreement.

"Good. Then, I would expect you to share the same concern that I have about a growing problem that threatens this vital link to the peoples of the earth. Piracy upon the high seas has been growing since the collapse of the Cold War. One of the unforeseeable outcomes of the end of the Cold War has been the demise of the Soviet fleet. During the Cold War, when both NATO and Soviet Bloc navies vied for supremacy of the oceans, it had the side effect of suppressing piracy.

"But now, the ex-Soviet Bloc countries aren't interested in pursuing blue-water navies; they're focusing primarily on coastal defenses. What remains of their blue-water navies still seaworthy sit in ports because they lack the money to send them to sea. The Law of Unintended Consequences is alive and well. With the easing of East/West tensions, the United States has spent its peace dividends in other areas, creating an opportunity for the scourge of pirating to reemerge.

"This rise of pirating is creating tensions among neighbors previously unaffected by conflicts. Most of the tension is arising in third world countries that are unable to afford navies or patrol craft to police their waters. In locations where patrol craft are available, the pirates escape into another's territorial water and are unable to pursue the pirates without invading a sovereign country's territorial waters, which is an act of war. Or they escape to sea, beyond the twelve mile limit of territorial water claims.

"Under the United Nations Convention on the Law of the Sea, UNCLOS, piracy is the responsibility of individual nations. But it's unclear which nation has the right to act. Is it the nation closest to where the piracy act occurred, even though it may have been outside their jurisdiction? Is it the responsibility of that nation to which the pirates may have returned, even though those individuals may not have broken any laws in territories of their jurisdiction? Is it the responsibility of the nation of the attacked owner? Is it the nation under which an attacked vessel is flagged? Is it the responsibility of the nation of the crewmen threatened, killed, or injured in an attack, or whose cargo may have been stolen?

"Because so many nations have grounds to act, no one acts. Each expects others with stronger claims to accept responsibility. Consequently, nobody is taking action to reduce the threat.

"Pirates are robbing, murdering and kidnapping with impunity on the high seas. Why, it is my understanding that the nephew of one of your senators was killed by pirates recently. The crew of one of the UN's research vessels was recently slaughtered by them. All that and more is why I came today to ask the United States for help."

"What exactly are you seeking, Mr. Secretary-General?" President Tillman inquired skeptically. "Are you asking that the U.S. grant the use of its warships to foreign commanders to patrol areas of the ocean? I can tell you right now, we tried that with Kosovo and that dog won't hunt with this administration. I still have major parts of U.S. Naval command still grousing about the Kosovo experience. Half my admirals would resign if I tried that stunt under the present circumstances. As you know, the U.S. is committed to an aggressive policy of democratizing the Middle East. U.S. Armed Forces are committed currently in Afghanistan and Iraq, not to mention our nearly fifty-five year commitment to Korean sovereignty, which as you know was a U.N. policing action. With the antics of China in the Straits of Taiwan and the Sea of Japan, plus Iran in the Gulf, the U.S. Navy has no idle assets available for U.N. patrolling actions.

"I agree that piracy is a growing problem. My own intelligence agencies have been briefing me on the rise of pirate activities around the world. But I'm not sure that it has risen to a level critical enough for me to commit the U.S. Navy and for me to expend the political capital necessary for such a commitment. The American people are still behind the War on Terrorism, but only because the war was brought to our shores and took the lives of two thousand nine hundred and ninety-nine or our citizens. The probability of pirates coming to our shores and taking the lives of U.S. citizens is near zero. Without an immediate threat to a vital national interest, the American people won't support the expansion of armed action and the expenditure of either the US's treasure or the lives of our young soldiers and sailors."

"Please, Mr. President, before you say no, let me reiterate that my goal was mainly to seek your feelings on the matter. And I believe that we have discovered common ground in that we both believe that piracy is a growing problem that can impact both international stability and the global economy. I would like to ask you to consider your options for support in both diplomatic and military terms. Surely there can be some way in which the world's lone superpower can contribute to increasing the security on the world's waterways and trade routes."

"Mr. Secretary-General, this is a complex problem strewn with many legal, military, and international considerations. I will need to consult my team to get their opinions and to develop options that my administration can support. If you will give me some time, I'd like to explore the possibilities and get back to you."

"I'm certainly pleased that you are taking this problem into consideration. It is more than I could have hoped for today at such an early stage of discussion. I just want to reiterate that I believe that this is a problem of significant proportions and I have dedicated my administration to addressing this problem. I am open and thankful for any assistance that the People of the United States can offer. I thank you again for your consideration."

******

As the President slowly shut the door behind his parting guest, his chief of staff, Clayton Biggs, came hustling in another door on the other side of the Oval Office, his usual look of inquisitiveness and intensity upon his face.

"You heard?" the President said by way of greeting. Clayton was the man that put into motion all of President Tillman's vision and programs. As his title implied, he was the person responsible for the hiring of all presidential appointments, from the Cabinet Minister down to the kitchen staff. While on paper the various secretaries of agencies reported to the president, in actuality, they reported to him. He had been President Tillman's first campaign manager when he spotted something extraordinary in the then polished, but green, politician, and he volunteered to run his election campaign for State Congressman. Since that time, Royce and he had been politically inseparable. He was happy to work behind the scenes. He was a brilliant political strategist, but he knew he lacked the political charisma to ever run for office.

"Yeah, I watched on the video monitor in your office. On the surface, it's a simple request. There are problems on the high seas, so the Secretary-General seeks assistance from us, the biggest navy in the world. But this has more prickly spines on it than a porcupine. As you correctly pointed out, there's no way we're going to put U.S. warships under U. N. Security Council control. Besides being a colossal waste of the taxpayer's money for a leadership-by- committee approach, very few countries know how to project power via a blue water naval fleet or how to fight our ships. They would come up with rules of engagement that would be contrary to the way our ships and crews are trained to fight, and that would ultimately endanger the ship and crew needlessly.

"The thing is, the problem of piracy is really penny ante stuff to our fleet. Our fleet is designed to destroy other large massed navies, project air power inland, neutralize sea-based nuclear missile threats, and land large contingents of Marines and soldiers ashore. In fact, the Navy and the Air Force have become the premier offensive weapons of this nation based on power projection capabilities and budgetary expenditures.

"The U.S. Air Force can destroy any target in the world, usually with only one bomb, provided somebody has spotted the target and identified its coordinates. Likewise, the Navy can wipe the seas of any nation's capital ships.

"But frankly, using any of those approaches would be like using a sledgehammer to kill an ant. And none of these is suitable for hunting down a handful of boats loaded with ruffians toting AK-47s and RPGs. This action would be more suitable for the U.S. Coast Guard, except their mission is safeguarding U.S. territorial waters, and they're not really suited or structured for overseas deployment or force projection. Besides, they're already tied up with missions of drug and illegal immigration interdiction, as well as ship and cargo inspections. The U.S. Navy is just not set up to fight guerrilla pirates in small, outboard motored boats.

"But we can't be seen as not caring about this issue

because it *is* impacting the economy. The problem is that we just don't have anything small enough to effectively deal with the problem."

"Maybe we're looking at it from the wrong angle, Clayton," the president said in thoughtful way. "Maybe we should let the boys at the State Department handle this. We could provide patrol boats and training for pirate suppression. Hell, we're only talking the cost of a couple dozen patrol boats and training. The State Department's Foreign Aid Budget wouldn't even notice something that small. And besides, it would have a direct benefit to the U.S."

"Good idea, Royce. I'll get Secretary Hutchinson at State on it right away." Clayton smiled at the thought of finding an inexpensive solution to a problem of international importance, especially if the Secretary-General of the U.N. was doing the asking. And then his smile faded.

"Ah, Clayton – don't give me that look," Royce groaned.

"I know, I know...look, I think the aid of patrol boats and training is a good step, but it's a passive, indirect response to a problem brought to us by the international community. It would make us look like the only time we use our military might is when we want to act punitively. This is an opportunity for us to put a different light on ourselves, to show that we can be sensitive to the needs of the international community, that we're not just some big bully. The problem is too small to 'declare war on' but too big to ignore. I just think that there has to be another option somewhere that's a bit more direct. I can feel it."

President Tillman had learned long ago to believe in Clayton Biggs's intuition. It was a major contributor in propelling him to the White House. "Well, we'll keep our eyes and ears open. Something will present itself, it always does," he said glancing at his watch with a sigh. It was

time for the president's next appointment, a brief picture
ceremony with this year's National Spelling Bee
Champions. On cue, there was a soft knock at the door
that he recognized as Muriel's letting him know that his
discussion with Clayton was up for the time being.

******

Back in his office, Clayton called in his chief staffer, Tom
Milby, and brought him up to speed on the president's
directions on the UN's piracy request. Tom was just a
crackerjack policy wonk, a master of the minute and
genius creative thinker who thrived in the back offices of
the nation's capitol. When he was done with the update,
Clayton asked about his messages.

"There was a call from Senator Cyrus Templeton. He
said he had a personal matter to discuss with you."

This made Clayton Biggs's eyebrow rise. "Did the Pro-
Tem happen to mention what it pertained to?"

"All he would say was that he wished to get the
president's assistance in the matter of his nephew's death
by pirates a couple of weeks back."

"Ooohhh reeeally?" Clayton Biggs said, his political
nose starting to quiver at the smell of opportunity and
coincidence even as his phone started to ring in the
background.

6

"Damn it, Chip, I know Penny has been missing for almost two weeks now. If there is any one on this earth as worried about her as you and Louise, it's Kathy and I. She's the closest thing to a daughter that we have in this world." Congressman Anthony "Tony" Castillas, Republican Majority Whip, was on the phone, pacing behind the large mahogany desk of his office in the Cannon House Office Building in D.C. He and Pete Hartwell had been best friends since their freshman year as roommates at Texas A&M, but he had always called him by his nickname, Chip.

Normally, Chip managed the Whip's affairs from their Washington, D.C. office as his chief of staff, but since his daughter had been kidnapped off the coast of Mexico, he'd returned home so that his wife could be near family during the crisis. Cut off from the levers of power in the nation's capitol, he was now totally reliant upon Tony's efforts alone.

"I've called the Mexico's ambassador to the U.S. twice a day since she went missing," Tony continued. "He's been very polite and concerned about the situation, but utterly worthless. All I get are vague promises to help the investigation along and to keep me informed, but all I really get is squat."

"Of course," Chip retorted from the other end of the line, "what he's really interested in is damage control. His problem isn't your missing goddaughter. But the fact is that a U.S. congressman from a border state to Mexico had a family member carted off by pirates in Mexico. Except for one that managed to escape, these pirates killed the rest of the crew, including several notable scientists off a U.N. chartered ship. And he knows that the local police force has a snowball's chance in hell of finding who is responsible. Hell, the local police department is probably in cahoots with the son-of bitches more than he'd care to admit. How about Ambassador Moulton and the U.S. Embassy in Mexico City? Has he been able to do anything for us?"

"Again, helpful and concerned, but he doesn't have any real juice in that area. America has only a small consulate in Cozumel. Primarily, all they do there is replace lost or stolen passports for U.S. tourists. They're not really set up for a major investigation. The best that he can do for us is to ask some of his business contacts from the older, wealthier families of Mexico to reach their tentacles into the seamier side of the Cozumel waterfront. Everybody has a vested interest in Penny, it seems. They don't want pictures of another disappeared blonde tourist splashed across U.S. televisions every night like the Natalee Holloway thing in Aruba. The negative publicity killed Aruba's tourist industry. And nobody wants Mexico's tourist industry to get the same black eye. Ambassador Moulton tells me that the old families of Mexico's capital have major holdings in the Cozumel tourist trade. He said he would get back to us if his contacts hear anything.

"I also called the U.N. Secretary-General's office to see what steps they're taking in the matter. The Secretary-General himself returned my call to outline their plan. Of course it's totally reliant upon the local Mexican law enforcement to run the investigation. I asked him if it would be helpful to the local law enforcement if investigators from the FBI assisted them, since several U.S. citizens were killed or are missing, and if so, would he assist in easing the way with the Mexican authorities. He told me that would be greatly appreciated. He also told me something very interesting -- he had been to see President Tillman that very morning to ask for U.S. assistance in curtailing pirate activities around the world. He said the President is examining options and will be getting back to him.

"I was planning on calling Clayton Biggs at the White House tomorrow to see if he can get the Justice Department to send some FBI investigators to Mexico to help in the '*Constellation* Massacre' as the press has dubbed it. We've worked with him on several pieces of legislation that the President wanted, so by God, he owes us a favor or two, or three. I'll continue to pull in every favor I can that will help us get Penny back, Chip, I promise."

"I know you will, Tony, and I don't mean to sound ungrateful. I know you're kicking ass on this and taking names. It's just that...I feel like the hind tit on a bull out here in Houston. There's nothing for me to do except pat Louise's hand. I'd rather be doing something useful."

"Well, hold it together and I'll let you know what Clayton Biggs has to say. Clayton's a good egg, political as hell, but still a good person. And this isn't a political issue, so I don't think he'll try to leverage this situation. If he does, God help him because I will fry his ass for the rest of the president's term."

7

Cyrus Templeton, senior senator from the state of Pennsylvania paced around his desk waiting for his call to go through. This was the second time that he had to call Clayton Biggs, which chapped his ass. As Pro-Tem of the Senate and member of the Democratic Party majority, he was used to prompt response when he called. He did not sit on hold. The speakerphone continued to beep occasionally to let him know that he was still on hold, which only served to stoke his anger.

Why did I let Ken go on that cruise? He wondered for the thousandth time. It seemed like such a good idea at the time, so innocuous, so well meaning. So how did it end up with his sister's boy coming home in a coffin with his head rolling around in a plastic bag and his wife a mental wreck so whacked out on tranquilizers as to be almost dead herself?

"Senator Templeton, I have Clayton Biggs on the line for you," the speakerphone announced. Cyrus snatched the phone from the cradle and squared his shoulders as he said in his silkiest tone, "Clayton, thank you for taking my call at such a late hour."

"I'm sorry that I wasn't available for your call earlier, Cyrus. But the Secretary-General of the U.N. had requested an informal meeting with the president. I just got back to my office."

"And what did the good Secretary-General want to

discuss, our delinquent U.N. dues?" he bantered lightheartedly, hoping to soften the moment before he got to the heart of the matter of his call.

"No. Actually, he wanted to talk to the President about the same thing that you do, if the message you left earlier is accurate."

"He wanted to discuss piracy?" the Senator probed, thrown off stride by this unexpected announcement.

"Yes. The recent massacre of the U.N. researchers aboard the *Constellation* has brought the issue of piracy to the forefront in international circles. He was seeking U.S. support in an effort to eliminate the threat to the world's commerce routes."

"Was he trying to push the ratification of the Law of the Sea Treaty? I hope not, because there's no support for that in the Senate. It'll be dead on arrival. The citizens of the U.S. will skin us alive if the Senate ratifies that clunker. We will never subject our military personnel to the Tribunal Court of the UNCLOS unless the treaty is modified to expressly recognize the U.S's right to pursue terrorists on the high seas in 'extraordinary circumstances,'" Cyrus said gruffly.

"Never mentioned a word about it. He was primarily looking for U.S. military assets to patrol and pursue pirates."

"That's rich," Senator Templeton groused, "coming from a bunch of dictators and socialists looking to hamstring the U.S. Navy's ability to roam the seas and protect America's interests." He paused to catch his breath before taking a different tack. "Well, I guess it does make sense in a certain kind of way. Third world countries have tried to use the U.N. Convention of the Law of the Sea as a method to take the wealth of the developed countries and superpowers and redistribute amongst them. Now, I guess they're still playing the same game, trying to redistribute our military resources for their benefit. Still," he paused for reflection, "this new Secretary-General McLaughlin seems to have his head on straight. He's on record saying he wants to restore the century old tradition of 'Freedom on the High Seas' that was the operating principle before the UNCLOS treaties. He has been very pointed about his desire to clean up the lawlessness of the seas. The question is whether he can control the zoo that passes as the U.N. enough to restore freedom to the high seas."

"I agree with everything that you've said, but I'm sure you did not call me up to discuss a DOA turkey of a treaty that was never mentioned. What's on your mind?"

"Listen, Clayton, it's no secret that my nephew was killed by pirates in the Middle East a couple of weeks ago. I'm getting ready to introduce legislation that would broaden America's response to this murderous trash. I wanted to get the White House's position on the issue. I'd like to work with the administration in crafting tools for America to pursue and bring justice to those who think that cutting off people's heads for profit is the path to a long and healthy life.

"I know that it's the president's prerogative to set policy, but I believe that the Senate would like to be part of solving the pirate issue."

"Cyrus, I really appreciate your enthusiasm for the topic, but right now, I have my staff working up possible options based on the conversation between the Secretary-General and the President. I don't want to change their task direction in mid-stream, so when we have a list of options, I'll send them over to your office. I think that this problem is best solved by Congress and the administration working together to give the U.N. enough rope to hang themselves if they're not serious about fixing the problem;

then we will have already laid the ground work for a more comprehensive approach. But I can tell you right now that a military solution will not be in the cards. So anything you can think of short of that, communicate it to Tom Milby on my staff and we'll see if we can work it in."

"Thanks for your support, Clayton."

"Anything else I can do for you today, Cyrus?"

"Yeah. Don't be afraid to pick up your phone to return calls."

8

"I certainly understand your point of view, and it is well supported by the situation, Congressman Castillas. I will personally see that your request gets forwarded to Mr. Biggs. And if you would follow up the request with a formal letter, we can use that as a platform upon which to build." After a pause, Thomas Milby concluded, "All right, thank you for calling," he said before returning the handset to its cradle.

"Forward what to me personally?" Clayton asked as he walked into his subordinate's office. His office received dozens of requests daily. It was a little unusual for Thomas to guarantee personal action.

"That was House Republican Deputy Director Castillas on the phone. He was calling to enlist the FBI's help in the case of the '*Constellation* Massacre' in Mexico. There were several U.S. citizens killed in the incident. The daughter of his chief political advisor, Chip Hartwell, who is also his goddaughter was on board and taken by the pirates. I thought that the dispatch of FBI investigators would be an option that you would want to take up with the president, since he would have to have Ambassador Moulton pave the way with the Mexican government."

"That's a good idea; I'll discuss it with the president later on today. You know…" Clayton's voice trailed off in contemplation, "I came in to tell you about a conversation that I just had with Senator Templeton concerning piracy issues. He wants to draft legislation to support our response to this problem, and now I walk in to find you on the phone talking to the House Democratic Whip on the same subject. The U.N. Secretary-General pays the President an informal visit just days before to discuss the same thing...it seems like the issue of piracy on the high seas is going critical. It jumped up out of nowhere and we've been caught flat footed. What the hell is going on?"

"Piracy has always been around" Thomas replied, "it just kinda ebbs and flows with the times. You never hear about it because the shipping companies don't want you to. They bribe reporters to not cover the stories, and they spread a lot of hush money around to keep it quiet. Pirates are getting seventy to one hundred thousand dollars ransom for captains and sixty to eighty thousand for chief engineering officers. And what's more, the shipping companies are paying it, quietly. They're afraid that if the ransoms became publicized, their stock price and shipping business would be hurt, which ultimately would encourage more copycat piracy."

"But it all seems so medieval, Thomas. I mean for Christ's sake, this is the age of the internet, and we're having to deal with the world's third oldest profession."

"Actually, the internet makes it easier for the pirates to pick their targets. They can get on the web and pull up a ship's cargo manifests, schedule, and GPS position with a click of a mouse. It also makes it easier for them to dispose of stolen cargo. Buyers can be found and transactions accomplished without ever learning the real identity of either buyer or seller," Thomas explained.

"No modern presidency has had to deal with pirates, not since the Marines landed at Tripoli to deal with the Barbary Coast pirates at the end of American bayonets and bullets. That's all I know about piracy other than what I've seen in old movies. How have we historically dealt with the issue?" he mused to the walls as much as Thomas.

Thomas slapped the desk, which snapped Clayton out of his reverie. Shoving himself back from his desk forcefully, he vaulted from his seat, his chair banging into the wall as he charged a nearby bookcase.

"What?" Clayton asked, focusing on Thomas, who was skimming row after row of books, ignoring his boss as he intently searched for a title. When he found the book he was looking for, he whipped it from the shelf and started scanning the text. After quickly scanning a dozen pages, he gave a little shout of success and rapidly started fingered the text rapidly. Just as quickly, he snapped the book shut tossing it on his desk. Next, from the bureau behind his desk, he pulled a small black bound book entitled *The United States of America Constitution*. Cracking the book open, he rapidly started to scan the script, while absentmindedly replanting himself in his seat.

"What?" demanded Clayton again.

Thomas looked up at Clayton with a strange look in his eye. "I've got an idea, boss." He then went on for the next twelve minutes to explain his brainstorm before finally pausing for Clayton's his reaction.

Clayton stared at his subordinate for what felt like twenty seconds before his face cracked into a smile. "Thomas that has got to be the biggest, most hare-brained …craziest… best goddamn idea I've ever heard. When will you be ready to brief the president?"

9

"Representative Castillas, thank you for coming this evening," President Tillman welcomed the last arrival. "I believe you know my Chief of Staff and Senator Templeton. This is Thomas Milby, one of Clayton's staffers."

After handshakes had been exchanged and everyone had settled into the cushions of seats and sofas by the fire, the President started, "Gentlemen, before we get to the meat of the discussion, I want to make sure that we all have the same information." He went on to recap the beheading of Senator Templeton's nephew and the abduction of Representative Castilla's goddaughter as well as the massacre of the crew of the *Constellation* by pirates.

The president paused while the representative and the senator eyed each other with a new appreciation.

"Three days ago, the new U.N. Secretary-General, Andrew McLaughlin, came to me seeking assistance from the United States to help rein in pirates terrorizing the shipping lanes of the world and restore freedom on the high seas. He came to us because we are probably the only nation in the world that has a navy big enough to patrol the oceans of the world.

"Cyrus has approached my administration to seek cooperation in writing legislation that would allow the United States to better respond to the threat that pirates are posing to U.S. citizens, our vital commercial concerns abroad, and our ability to conduct business with foreign countries. Tony also approached my office seeking the assistance of the FBI in investigating the massacre of the *Constellation's* crew and his missing goddaughter." He paused to let the others in the room deliberate these facts. "Have I missed anything, gentlemen?" he asked as he looked to Clayton, Cyrus, and Tony.

"No," came a trio of responses.

"As you can see, each of us in this room represents different perspectives, and we all have a vested interest and motivation for solving the piracy problem, whether professional or personal.

"The rub is that this problem is too small for the use of U.S. armed forces to fix, yet too big to ignore. From my perspective, gentlemen, politically, putting U.S. Naval forces under the command of the U.N. Blue Hatters is a no-win for me. I don't have the political capital to add a new front to the war on terror in addition to Afghanistan, Iraq, and all the other hots spots. My learned colleagues of the Democratic Party have made it impossible for me to respond militarily to this problem at this time."

Senator Templeton started to sputter a response to this challenge but the President shushed him down, "Cyrus, I'm not here to debate past policies, nor am I here to hammer you down for your party's misguided actions. The plain truth of the matter is that even if we *had* the surface ships to take on this task, the mood of the American people would not allow us to spill the blood of our sailors and spend our tax dollars to correct somebody else's problems. Clayton, why don't you take it from here?"

"Thank you, Mr. President," Clayton started, "The U.S. Navy has become a victim of its own success. Since the end of the last World War and the Cold War, America has concentrated its industrial and technical abilities on developing weapons systems that make our armed forces more lethal, pound for pound, than any other nation's in the world. Our armed forces are built to fight and destroy other nation-states' forces which they're more than capable of doing so. As a result, our armed forces are more lethal, vastly more expensive to operate, and fewer in numbers. But what it boils down to is we simply don't have enough *low-tech* assets to patrol the world's oceans, and it would be in direct contradiction to the arms development aims of our military for the last fifty years to try and develop a solution."

"Well, what about all those unmanned surveillance drones that we've been spending billions on developing? This sounds like it would be the perfect solution," interjected Senator Templeton.

"In theory, yes," Clayton responded. "But the problem is that all our UAVs and UUVs have limited range and require U.S. support personnel nearby to keep them operational. The state of the unmanned vehicle surveillance is more suited for theatre tactical support rather than large area surveillance. Satellite surveillance is the only thing that could come close enough to watch the earth's oceans and waterways, but even then, if we devoted all our orbital surveillance assets, there would still be large gaps that could be exploited by pirates. And that's *if* we had satellites to spare."

"Well, what about Special Forces?" Representative Castillas asked. "Isn't this exactly what they are supposed to be experts in, low intensity conflicts?"

"Yes," Clayton answered, "they would be perfect to handle the matter. But there are two problems with that strategy. Firstly, the president, in order to employ them in any meaningful way, would also have to deploy substantial support units, which again would require him to mount a political campaign to build the necessary coalitions within the U.S. political realm. Secondly, the bulk of our special forces are land-based warriors not suited to maritime patrol and low-intensity littoral combat. To strike pirates on land with ground based Special Ops units would mean that the U.S. would have to invade a sovereign nation, which would be an act of war; again, not a viable option."

Tiring of all the negatives, Senator Templeton cut to the chase. "With all due respect, Mr. President, I hardly think you invited us up here to cry on our shoulders about what you can't do. I'm more interested in discussing what *can* be done."

Congressman Castillas nodded in agreement.

President Tillman had been waiting for such an opening. "You're right, Cyrus. Clayton was only laying the foundation for a proposal that we have in mind. If you've been following the conversation, we've been careful to outline the limitations I have on using military force to solve this problem. However, when it comes to the application of military force, *you* have more options than I do."

This time Representative Castillas took the lead, "I don't understand. Under the Constitution, the president directs the armed forces. Congress," he waved at Senator Templeton and himself, "only has the ability to declare war and fund the troops."

"Not necessarily," Clayton said in a well-oiled tag-team on the congressmen.

"Explain," Cyrus demanded.

With a nod from Clayton, Thomas got up and passed out a piece of paper to each of the congressmen.

"I call your attention to Article I, enumerating powers of Congress in the U.S. Constitution, Section 8, Paragraphs 10 and 11 which state:

> *To define and punish Piracies and Felonies committed on the high Seas, and Offenses against the Law of Nations;*

> *To declare War, grant Letters of Marque and Reprisal, and make Rules concerning Captures on Land and Water;*

"It seems that the solution to this problem, according to the framers of the Constitution, sits squarely in the hands of Congress," Clayton finished as the two congressmen studied the lines given them.

"I don't understand," Tony said with a frustrated sigh, "this still doesn't give us the authority to use the armed forces."

"No, but it gives you something almost as good," Clayton purred. "Congress and *only* Congress has the authority to grant Letters of Marque and Reprisal."

Neither congressman wanted to look stupid, so he waited for the other to ask the question. Tony blinked first. "Okay. Just what exactly is a Letter of Marque and Reprisal?"

"Put simply, Tony," President Tillman explained, "it's a license to kill."

10

Both Congressmen stared at the President with open incredulity. Finally Senator Templeton broke the moment. "You're telling me that we grant licenses to kill? I've never heard of this. Aren't the British the only ones who go for that 'licenses-to-kill'? James Bond-007 nonsense."

"Maybe. I've never asked the British prime minister if MI-6 really issues licenses to kill. But here's what I *can* tell you; Letters of Marque and Reprisal are as real as our Constitution. I think now would be a good time for a little historical background. I'm going to let Thomas here give you a quick brief, and then I would like to discuss a couple ideas on how we can make this work. Thomas, if you would, please."

"Thank you, Mr. President. Letters of Marque and Reprisal initially arose out of France. Prior to large navies sponsored by nations, entrepreneurs built and sailed ships for profits with each considered to be a floating island or sovereign piece of the flagged country. During times of tension and war, or in events of theft and piracy, ships were seized and robbed on the high seas. The injured owners of the boat would appeal to their sovereign for diplomacy on their behalf for relief. If the sovereign didn't have the means to force the return of the stolen ship or cargo, they would grant a Letter of Marque and Reprisal to the party seeking relief. "Letter of Marque" comes from the French "to go beyond the markers or border."

"Historically *the United States* has used Letters of Marque and Reprisal to augment the Navy, when it did not have the necessary assets to resolve waterborne issues of contention.

"The right of reprisal was granted as a tit-for-tat. If citizens of a flagged country were killed in the taking of a ship, then the right to retaliate in-kind was granted against the offending country. It was a way of saying to other countries, 'If you kill my subjects or take my sovereign ships on the high seas, I'll allow my subjects to kill yours to even the score.' The authorized agent would face no penalty or trial for any infraction that would normally be administered when they returned home.

"By authorizing this kind of action by proxy to a third party, the rulers of countries avoided direct conflict and lessened the possibility of war. They did this by narrowly drafting the Letter of Marque by specifying everything from the number and size of the ships to be used, the number of crewmen that could be used, specific time frames, number and size of cannons, where they could execute their reprisals, and any other conditions, such has how to handle prisoners and nationals not involved in the conflict. All in all, it was a very specific and limited response to provocation. It was an effective way of sending messages amongst rulers of nations, rectifying problems, and righting wrongs without declaring war.

"In 1859, at a convention of the world's leading powers in Paris, a treaty was drafted and signed outlawing the practice and use of Letters of Marque and Reprisal. Every country signed the treaty, with one notable holdout." Thomas paused while a 'cat ate the canary' smile spread across his face. "The only country that did not sign the treaty was the United States of America. Essentially, we could not sign it without the modification to our

Constitution, which expressly grants that right of Letters of Marque and Reprisal to Congress. A treaty that nullified a portion of our Constitution would not be legal. But in deference to the world's opinion, the U.S. has not issued a Letter of Marque and Reprisal in almost a hundred and fifty years. Any questions so far?"

Tony was the first to fire off a salvo. "So what are you advocating here? Are you saying we should grant a Letter of Marque to Cyrus and me to go deal with pirates?"

"Ah," the President exclaimed, "actually I had another idea in mind." He now had the rapt attention of both congressmen. "I recommend that we use the incident of the '*Constellation* Massacre' as the foundation of our actions. U.S. citizens were killed aboard a U.S. flagged research vessel. I am recommending that Congress grant the U.N. a Letter of Marque and Reprisal. But rather than making it specific to the *Constellation* incident, we fall back on Art.I, Section 8, Paragraph 10 and grant them a Letter of Marque and Reprisal that allows them to deal with piracy on all the world's seas. This is perfectly in fitting with the past use of Letters of Marque and Reprisal. By allowing the U.N. to do the policing, we would be augmenting our naval capabilities.

"Even more importantly, the Constitution grants the power of punishment for piracy and crimes upon the high seas specifically to *Congress*, not the judiciary. In one of the flukes of our legal system and Constitution, the Founding Fathers were very clear that Congress was to punish crimes committed on the high seas.

The President continued, "The only portion of the Constitution that could allow judicial intervention is in Paragraph 11, which grants Congress the ability to 'make Rules concerning Captures on Land and Water.' If you decide that you want to bring captured pirates to our shores and give them habeas corpus with full access to our judicial system, to a tribunal created by you specifically for dealing with pirates, or if you wish to abdicate your responsibility to the World Court in The Hague, that's your decision. But habeas corpses isn't specifically guaranteed to them.

"If you want my opinion," President Tillman paused, "given what my predecessors learned about battlefield detainees from the Iraq and Afghanistan, whatever you decide, I would keep them off American soil. I will make Guantanamo Bay's prison, which falls under my jurisdictional control, available to you as either a temporary holding pen or permanent incarceration if that is the punishment you want meted out."

Both men were stunned by these revelations. Both had been in politics most of their adult lives and they had never heard of these powers.

Tony started to think out loud, "There is no way in hell I would advance this sort of Constitutional authority to the Blue Helmets of the U.N. Security Council. That would be like giving the keys to your new pick-up to your mentally infirmed grandmother. She wouldn't know what she was doing, while throwing around three tons of rolling death."

"I couldn't agree with you more, Tony," the President replied smoothly.

Now Tony and Cyrus were really confused. "Didn't you just recommend giving a Letter of Marque and Reprisal to the U.N.?" Cyrus demanded.

"Yes I did. But, I didn't say anything about the U.N. Security Council. I recommend granting the Letter of Marque to Secretary-General McLaughlin. Make him personally responsible for policing the seas. You can give him access to use all of our military assets, except uniformed military personnel. That way the United States can be left at arm's length in case anything goes wrong."

Cyrus voiced another concern that had been nagging him, "But wasn't the use of Letters of Marque outlawed a century and a half ago? Wouldn't this fly in the face of international convention? It could make our situation and reputation among nations more volatile."

"Possibly, but I doubt it," President Tillman soothed. "For starters, times have changed. Our research has shown that almost every nation in the world has stated for the record at the U.N. that piracy is a major concern that needs to be addressed. They're calling out for a solution, and Congress has it. Hell, they'd thank you for it. And besides, who embodies the voice and opinion of the world more than the Secretary-General himself? If he accepts the Letter of Marque, it would be the U.N., through him, doing the policing; we're just granting him authority to do it on our behalf in addition to funding them with equipment and facilities."

******

Cyrus was calculating the resistance of his party in the senate to such a concept. The political geometry of this solution was shaping up very nicely: the possibility of credit for positive action with insulation from blowback if things should go wrong. This had all the earmarks of a winner. The Democrats had always been seen as weak on national defense. With a Letter of Marque, the Democrats would be taking the initiative on national defense. The wing of his party that was highly focused on the U.S.'s reputation abroad would be ecstatic that this action was being conducted through and by the U.N. sans with world blessing. It had all the attributes that declaring war did not. It was specific in focus. Timetables for withdrawal and cessation were built in from the start. It had a beginning, middle, and end that could all be controlled from the outset, and best of all, there would be no flag-draped closed caskets arriving home to give rise to protesters. The human rights activists within the party could be managed with the proper set-up of tribunals to deal with captured pirates. But it was clear that Congress could control the whole issue without getting involved in some inter-governmental branch squabble of jurisdiction.

******

Tony's calculations were a little more straightforward. America's interests were being threatened abroad, and its citizens were subjected to cruelty and death. Any aggressive action was good action. This case was especially straightforward: Americans were getting killed, and Americans were demanding that this be stopped and that those doing the killing be brought to justice, preferably at the business end of a smoking, large-caliber gun. And the bonus was that all this could be done at arm's length, without killing any American servicemen and the cost was inconsequential.

The only drawback that he could see was the issue of what to do with the captured pirates. The British used to hang them at the entrance to their ports and leave their bodies to rot on the rope. They had the right idea. Though he was highly doubtful the Democrats would go for that, he was sure that he could negotiate this point in a satisfactory manner for the Republican constituency. The only other possible problem he could see was depending on Andrew McLaughlin, the new Secretary-General of the U.N.

******

"Have you spoken to Andrew McLaughlin about this yet, Mr. President?" Cyrus asked as he continued to percolate on the idea. "It seems that we would be putting a lot of faith into an organization that has demonstrably preferred dialogue over action, and consensus over confrontation. If we gave him a Letter of Marque, how can we be sure that he won't just sit on his hands and placate the dictators and juntas that constitute most of the U.N.?"

"I haven't talked to the Secretary-General yet, Cyrus. Quite truthfully, it was not my place since this matter is clearly the domain of Congress. But I can tell you that the Secretary-General seemed very earnest in doing whatever was necessary to bring piracy under control. If we can agree tonight on a basic plan of moving this forward, then the next step would be for all of us to sit down with the McLaughlin and see if he is willing to be a man of his conviction and a man of action."

"I totally concur," Tony affirmed. "There is no reason to start making motions in our respective houses if the end product won't be received or acted upon."

"Here, here." Cyrus rejoined.

The meeting adjourned on that note and the men filed out. As soon as they were in the hallway out of earshot of the President's Office, Tony grabbed Cyrus's arm and held him back.

"Listen, Cyrus. If we are going to do this, I don't want to mamby-pamby around. My goddaughter is out there. This girl is the closest thing to a daughter that my wife and I have in this world. We've changed her diapers, and we've been to every birthday party since she was born. We helped take her off to college. But there is information about her disappearance that has been kept out of the

news. The one surviving crewman that managed to escape
said that the pirates raped her for hours and then took her
to sell into slavery. She's alive out there somewhere, and
we need to rescue her. So every moment lost is a moment
she suffers in hell. I mean to ram this thing home in record
time. I need to know if you and I are on the same
wavelength."

"I had no idea, Tony." Cyrus, after thirty-five years of
public service, had become jaded to human suffering. But
the intensity of Tony's revelation, coupled with his rage at
his nephew's death, caused the ember of his emotions to
flare, then burst forth from their restraints. This was no
longer about constituencies. This was about people
connected to families. "Tony, if you can handle the
Republicans in the House and the Senate, I know damn
well I can get this through on my side of the aisle."

"Thanks, Cyrus." Out of nowhere Tony let loose a little
sob and catch of breath; for the first time he let himself
have real hope that they still might find Penny alive.

Cyrus was caught off balance by the momentarily
unguarded emotions of the other politician, something
one never showed on Capitol Hill. "What's she like,
Tony?"

"Sweet...a little shy; between her father and me, led a
sheltered life. Just your normal naïve, bright-eyed, young
twenty-something, who only sees the good in the world.
Very girly...we were surprised when she announced that
she was going to rough it for a year in a Third World
country as a peace volunteer. But now evil has snatched
her up in its claws."

After a moment's silence the two approached the door to
outside. Tony continued, "If you really want to know
what I fear, I'm afraid of what we'll get back when we find
her. She could be so damaged, physically and mentally,

that she may never be right. I don't know what would hurt more, that or finding out she's dead."

11

Senator Templeton had called his chief of staff last night from the back of his armored Secret Service limousine to get him going on a plan to produce a Letter of Marque and Reprisal. Next he called the Senate Legal Counsel to start research verifying viability of and use of a Letter of Marque. By the time he swept into his office at nine-thirty the next morning, he had several answers waiting for him. Per usual, there were several members of his staff vying to get his attention. He waved them off and went straight to his chief aid, Theodore Bernstein, "Teddy, what have you got for me?"

"I'll tell you, Cyrus, it's been a real stumper you threw me last night. You know that the U.S. hasn't issued one of these in over a hundred and fifty years, don't you?"

"Yeah, I know."

"I got to chewing on it, after you called, and got so wound up that I couldn't sleep a wink. I ended up sitting at my computer until two this morning. I'm not sure how one would even go about the process of enacting a Letter of Marque. I think that the best method would be to do a Joint Resolution between the Senate and the House. But that would mean that it would have to go to the floor for debate, and from what you told me last night, that might take too long since there are lives hanging in the balance. I suppose that we could strong-arm this through the Rules Committee and insert a rule specifically for Letters of

Marque."

"That was kind of what I had in mind," Cyrus agreed. "I think we can do something like a Letter of Marque that would need the signature of the majority and minority party leader and their deputies. That way, we can keep it short, sweet, contained, and manageable; the fewer the signatures, the quicker that we can get into this. And, more importantly, we can get out of it if it goes south on us."

"Technically, that could be done. But I think that it would step on a lot of toes. You know that senators want to be on record with this sort of stuff for election purposes. If you take that opportunity away from them, you may cause a lot of unwarranted friction."

Thinking back to last night's conversation with Tony Castillas, he re-affirmed his decision to ram this through at any cost because it was the right thing to do. "I know, Teddy, but I think I can sell it to the senators by telling them it's for their own protection. If it goes south, they can be insulated from any fall-out and leadership takes the hit. And, I will promise to bring this to the floor for full debate when it comes time to re-issue the Letters after the first one expires. That way, if it *is* a success, everyone can claim paternity in supporting leadership the first go around. If it doesn't pan out, I don't think that we will really hear a whole lot from the other side of the aisle, since their leadership's signature will be needed also. No one will be able to hold up the other party and point a finger."

"This is looking better by the minute," Theodore smiled to himself. "This is almost like political détente: credit to spread around by showing the American people that we can reach across the aisle and work with Republicans and silence by Mutually Assured Destruction if they want to play the blame game if it goes bad. Beautiful, man, beautiful…"

"It *is* a thing of beauty, isn't it?" Cyrus beamed. "Give Ben Tarnsky a call. It's time to take this to the next level and get the Deputy Director of the Senate involved. I want to move on this."

"You got it, boss."

"Oh, and one more thing, Teddy. I want to bury this rule change in the omnibus bill coming up. I want to keep this as quiet as possible until the deed is done. Bury it deep."

That afternoon, the Legal Council called Cyrus's office with his legal opinion that despite the Letter of Marque's historical absence, it was still very much a working legal concept in the U.S.

Later that day, the President's office called to let Cyrus know that the U.N. Secretary-General's schedule allowed for him to come down to D.C. for a meeting the first of next week. They had taken the liberty of scheduling a meeting at the White House with the same players as last time. During that time Cyrus and Tony worked together daily to come up with a first draft of a Letter of Marque and Reprisal to present to the Secretary-General.

Tony had arrived at pretty much the same strategy and reasoning, independent of Cyrus for the House of Representatives' side of the Letter of Marque. As the two conferred, they both realized that this issue was an American issue. There was no left or right of the issue, only pros and cons. America's interests were in jeopardy, and the setting was the high seas, which was neutral compared to land campaigns.

Monday night seemed forever in arriving for Tony. The constant immersion in drafting the Letter of Marque kept his emotions and fear for Penny in the fore. Fortunately, Chip Hartwell arrived from Texas to help Tony with the project. He was happy to be out of the emotional cauldron stirred by his wife's bipolar, emotional response to the abduction of their daughter. If felt good for him to be doing something constructive. He and Tony leaned on each other for support when the work wore them thin or when the sudden rush of panic would overtake them. Shortly, a pattern emerged, keeping them focused, positive that they were doing something to get Penny back.

Monday night arrived with a break in the cold, rainy weather typical of fall in D.C. A warm, clear night lit by a large harvest moon beckoned the members of a historic cabal as they made their way to their appointed meeting. Tony and Cyrus were the first to arrive at the White House, which allowed President Tillman some time to confirm many of the points to be discussed that night before Secretary-General McLaughlin arrived. Shortly, there was a knock at the door and Andy McLauglin was ushered in.

After introductions were made and everyone was settled into the couches in front of the fire, President Tillman took a few moments to use the fire poker, prodding the logs to get them burning nicely for the occasion. It was times like this that he wished that he smoked a pipe. The words of Anwar Sadat, former president of Egypt, came to mind: "A pipe gives a wise man a few moments to think, and fool something to stick in his mouth." Tonight's meeting would either be a moment of historic proportions or a dud to be swept under the carpet and dismissed from living memory. *Where to start? This must be handled delicately,* President Tillman thought to himself. Intuitively, he knew that this might be one of the moments that would define his presidency and change the course of his nation. Not that the actions to be discussed were all that large. In fact, they were here to discuss the actions of only a dozen or so men. No, the real import was how this handful of men would go about their mission, if accepted. He had tossed and turned the last couple of nights, restless with the thought that he was about to take a departure from his country's history by turning over an issue of security to a third party entity with an abysmal record of success. But, still, he had faith in this man, Andy McLaughlin, and if he accepted, it would certainly change the way the world viewed the United States. It would send a message to the world that the U.S. was willing to work with the world, if the world would get off its ass and take action for the betterment of the global community.

President Tillman finished with the poker and replaced it before turning to the assembled leaders of his country and the world community. "Thank you for coming back to D.C., Mr. Secretary-General. Last time we talked, you were seeking assistance to issues with the issue of piracy on the high seas. There is a one particular option that we wish to discuss with you tonight, a rather *unique option*."

"Thank you, Mr. President, and if you like, please, call me Andy. I was certainly surprised to hear from you so quickly. I'm truly looking forward to hearing about this unique option."

"Very well, and, please, call me Royce. As a basis of understanding for the purposes of this conversation, Andy, I need to cover some background that you're surely aware of to some degree or another, being a citizen of a democratic nation yourself." President Tillman then went on to give Andy a recap of the historical and legal precedents behind Letters of Marque and Reprisal that he had learned in the days just prior.

"A very interesting bit of history..." Andy observed.

"I quite agree." Royce nodded in agreement. "But to the point then. The United States Congress would like to issue a Letter of Marque and Reprisal to you, Andy, as the U.N.'s Secretary-General to pursue, capture or kill pirates on the high seas. The United States would grant you full authority to hunt these criminals down, essentially making you the enforcer of the laws of the seas on our behalf."

There was a stunned silence in the room that hung pregnant. Andy was a very seasoned diplomat, used to controlling his poker face, and while nary a tick or twitch escaped his countenance, even *he* could not control the drain of color from his face, nor the flush that replaced it. Finally, he sputtered, "But I have no ship or navy. This would be a matter for the Security Council."

"Ah, but you wouldn't need a navy, and we'll provide you with a ship," the president countered.

"Mr. Secretary-General," Cyrus opened, "what we envision is this: The U.S. would grant a Letter of Marque and Reprisal that would authorize you to bring pirates to justice on our behalf using one boat, with somewhere between ten and twelve personnel to use as you see fit. We would supply you with all the material resources you need, including funding and access to all of America's military and law enforcement resources to assist you. The only thing that we cannot directly supply you with is personnel. We feel you should have a free hand in selecting your operational personnel; that, and we feel doing so will also put the stamp of the UN's imprimatur on this project."

"But, we will only grant this to *you*," Tony interjected, "not to the Security Council. There is no room or time for debate. Lives are being taken daily, and if the Congress is going to grant you this authority, it must do so with the expectation that it will be used, and used with discretion. The U.S. has been a permanent member of the Security

Council since its inception. We know full well that the timely and discretionary use of a Letter of Marque is something that the Security Council cannot promise or deliver. The job of enforcing the intent of the Letter of Marque is a one-man proposition. We need to have someone that we can look in the eye and take his measure, to see if he is the man for the job before we grant such enormous authority. We are here tonight to see if you are that man."

"But U.N. officials and peacekeepers,' Andrew countered, "already enjoy diplomatic immunity while performing their duties in foreign countries. I'm not sure what additional value the protection of a Letter of Marque and Reprisal would give. Besides, the United Nations is an organization of peace dedicated to using diplomacy to resolve issues. Traditionally, the U.N. doesn't fill the role of law enforcement that this Letter of Marque would put us in."

"Well, maybe it's high time that *you* did," Cyrus countered. "The U.N. legislates laws like the U.N. Convention on the Law of the Sea, which states that piracy is the responsibility of each country. The U.N. adjudicates laws at the Hague in the International Court of Justice. Why should the U.N. not be involved in the process of law enforcement between legislation and adjudication? That just makes no sense at any level. This is something I know from personal experience: if you are willing to make the laws, then you better be ready to enforce them or your constituents will think you a joke. You'll soon find yourself irrelevant, mocked, and removed from office if you are not willing to stand behind the laws you make. If the U.N. wants to be a relevant force in the world, then it had better be able to assist in the enforcement of its laws.

"As for additional legal protection, that's tertiary. The

goal is to squarely put the legal responsibility of the actions of the proposed force on the United States as well as the responsibility for prosecuting those they capture.

"Besides, the responsibility for your actions will still rest with the men in this room. We are only asking you to be the impartial agent of enforcement of the laws on our behalf. The American people have grown to distrust and mock the U.N. for the very reasons that I just mentioned. As the lone superpower of the world, it would behoove the U.S. to work more closely with the U.N.; but this won't happen until the U.N. can demonstrate that it can take action in a timely manner - when needed and necessary - rather than just condemn the U.S. at every turn. This is a terrific opportunity to change the dynamics of our relationship with the U.N. and the world. But it will take a man of action as well as words to make that change. The question before you, Mr. Secretary-General, is: are you a man of action, or are words the extent of your commitment to the principles of the U.N.?"

The room fell silent as Cyrus's challenge floated in the air above their heads.

Andy McLaughlin put his chin in his chest, as he contemplated the opportunity before him.

'To bring the United States into a closer orbit at the U.N. would be historic,' he thought. 'But, the difficulties of taking such action would not only affect me, but also future U.N. Secretary-Generals by setting the precedents of using the Office of Secretary-General as a law enforcement vehicle.' "Just how exactly would the Letter of Marque and reprisal read?"

Tony pulled a couple of sheets of paper from a satchel at his side and pushed them across the coffee table to Andy. He read them briefly but thoroughly, looking up at the expectant faces of the men awaiting his decision when he finished. "This would be acceptable except for one small change I would ask. I will *not* become the head of a hit squad for the U.S. This needs to be changed to emphasize that the objective of the Letter of Marque is to pursue and apprehend pirates and those committing violent crime upon the high seas and then turn them over to the U.S. for trial."

"Agreed," both Tony and Cyrus answered.

"However," Tony rebutted, "you must be aware that pirates by their very nature will resist apprehension with violence and deadly force. The chances of apprehending them without bloodshed will be a very rare occurrence."

"Still, one must try," sighed Andy.

"Then we are agreed?" the President asked rhetorically.

"Yes," Andy replied with conviction.

"Absolutely," from Tony.

"Agreed," answered Cyrus.

12

As Secretary-General of the U.N., Andrew McLaughlin carried a small security contingent. Their main function was to coordinate safety measures with the security forces of the countries on the SECGEN's travel itinerary. Although not a true head of state, he was accorded such honors because the small piece of land the U.N. owned in New York was deemed to be that of an independent country much like an embassy. The U.N. was a legislative body, a clearinghouse, of common issues for the countries of world. It had no authority other than that which was lent it by the community of nations.

Still, the status of a separate nation-state within New York City remained, and with it the need for security of its titular head, the Secretary-General, when he traveled. The head of his security detail, David Barrett, was waiting for him as he emerged from the President's office and accompanied him to his waiting limousine outside the West Wing. Tonight's plan had the secretary-general spending the night in Washington D.C. and returning to New York and U.N. Headquarters in the morning. The two rode in a well practiced silence, facing each other in the back of the limousine; Andrew was studying the salt and pepper haired man across from him with unfocused eyes. Davids's bright, intelligent eyes seemingly underscored by his big bushy mustache that matched his close cropped hair. His short, wiry stature belied his fierceness.

As Andrew McLaughlin's mind turned over the political implications and opportunities, a small portion of his conscience started working the problem of who he would need to run this operation. This person would be crucial to the success or failure of this venture. As more and more of his concentration moved to this aspect of the concept, he slowly started to focus on the man sitting across from him. He put his life in this man's hands daily. He trusted David Barrett, and in the end, trust was the most elusive and valued commodity in the world of silver-tongued diplomats. He realized that the very attributes and skills that he had used to select David Barrett for the head of his security detail were also ideal for the person to run this operation.

"David," Andrew McLaughlin spoke into the dark interior of the car, the tinted glass of the windows muting the strobe flashes of lights from the passing businesses on the street, "it seems that the Americans want me to hunt pirates for them. They are willing to provide material and financial support if we put the program together. I'd like you to draft a report on the types of assets, material and personnel, organization and operating procedures for no more than a dozen people in the unit. And I am going to need that report in a week."

"Why a dozen, sir?"

"Because that is all to whom the Americans are willing to grant immunity from prosecution."

"Right-oh, then. Let me ask this: is this to be a military operation or law enforcement action?"

"Both. Taking armed men on the high seas will require a military approach, but the aim of the program will be to bring them to justice."

"That will be a bit of a problem, sir. You see, the military does things one way, and law enforcement does things another way. A military approach would be to deal with the problem using the necessary force to neutralize the threat while minimizing your own force's casualties. Law enforcement's goal is to neutralize the threat while taking equal consideration of the perpetrators, minimizing collateral damage and the overall loss of life. Military deals with organized military and militia units, while law enforcement deals with civilians. To put it bluntly, the military is trained to use the biggest tool available to get the job done quickly and efficiently while law enforcement is trained to use the smallest force necessary. The rift's just too big between their views of the world.

"Pirates are a para-military organization because they use boats and ships, both of which require someone to command while others perform those commands. That places them much closer to a military threat than a civilian threat. For that reason, I think it would be best to treat pirates as a military threat and organize accordingly."

"That won't do, David. In order to have legitimacy, this unit must have a law enforcement element to it. Otherwise, it might be seen by the world as an assassination squad being run for the United States. No, the ultimate goal must be to bring them to justice and a law enforcement end. The environment that these criminals operate in does make it a lot harder a nut to crack than the typical law enforcement situation, but that's just the way it has got to be."

"Alright then…but would it be permissible to shade the operation towards the military side?"

"Yes, as long as it has credible law enforcement cover," Andrew instructed his subordinate.

"I can make do with that. You said the Americans would provide money and materials. Does that mean they won't supply personnel?"

"Correct. They were pretty emphatic about not using U.S. Military personnel. They felt that doing so would make any territorial transgressions look like another invasion or war mongering. They want to avoid that all costs."

David rubbed his chin and pondered the floor as he considered his next obstacle. "That also is another sticky wicket. If you're going to assemble a unit based on American material, equipment and technology, the best choice of personnel are those with the most experience using those resources, a la American military personnel. It would be really helpful to have just a few kernels of their personnel to anchor a team around. That will really speed the process up of bringing the operation online.

"Besides, if you're really going to take on pirates, you're going to need people who can operate in land and sea operations. There just aren't that many Special Forces organizations that train for both environments. The U.S. Navy SEALs are the most ideal, followed by Marine Force Recon. Would you be able to see if perhaps they could temporarily detach a couple of their operators to assist in the formation of a team? And maybe get me access to personnel records so that I can select and recruit the right people?"

Andrew was pleased to see David's mind starting to work the problem and organize the solution. "Sure. I'll ask next time I talk to the President."

"If done right, this could be downright sporting: hunting pirates with your own dedicated task force, and with the American arsenal at hand...now that is a command to be envied."

The car fell silent as both men's minds started cataloguing the opportunity.

13

With the groundwork in place, Tony and Cyrus worked
all hours of the day to bring the necessary legislation
forward. But first, it was time to bring other congressional
leaders up to speed and on board. This was done in an
informal setting one night in Cyrus's office. Because of the
possible likelihood that Cyrus could be, in the next
election, called to be in line for president someday, both
parties now paid tribute to his ideas, legislation and
opinion well beyond the measure of a normal senator.
And this time, Cyrus was going to use every bit of
leverage that his seniority had garnered to avenge his
nephew and return Penny Hartwell home.

The meeting started cordially enough. Tom Blackwood
and Ben Tarsky, his Party's leader and his deputy, were
joined by the senate Republican leadership, Cynthia
Wellsworth and Clyde Tuvaris. The sale presentation was
not even complete before objections started to fly from
Wellsworth and Tuvaris. They surmised early on that the
Democrats were fishing to give more war powers to the
President. They were highly suspect of anything remotely
approaching this due to a long history of his party using
the military for things not of a military nature. Opposing
parties had been so conditioned to discount ideas from
across the aisle that it was just second nature for the
Republicans to start sniping at the concept before it even
took shape. It took all the diplomacy that Cyrus possessed

to wrangle the meeting back into order.

"My dear Cynthia, I could not agree with you more. The United States of America does not need to throw its military weight around the world any more than it already is," Cyrus purred his retort back at Cynthia's objection. "That is why I have gone to great lengths to explore and communicate the history of Letters of Marque this evening."

"If you aren't trying to expand our military's footprint in the world, then just what exactly are we doing here?" Cynthia fired back, still in contradiction mode.

"I am laying the legal foundation for us, here in this room, to take action against a problem that does not care if you're conservative or liberal. Blood is blood. Pirates are spilling American blood the world over. I am not here to sell you on the idea that we should be the world's ocean cops. Fortunately, the U.N. through the Secretary-General, Andrew McLaughlin, has already agreed to take on that responsibility. We just need to provide him with authorization to do it on our behalf and to supply him with the resources to do so.

"Let's put this into historical perspective with brutal honesty, shall we? President Clinton treated terrorism as a law enforcement issue. The result was that there was no legal cause to detain Bin Laden when the Ethiopians presented him to Clinton early in his Presidency. That led to the tragic death of thousands of Americans on 9/11. We retained our world standing and reputation among the countries of the world by not being a bully. But the impact to Americans, and our society, will be manifested for as long as the generation who saw the hole burned into the side of the Pentagon, my state's countryside, and the Twin Towers collapsing into rubble is alive and able to infuse that memory into the next generation - altogether, an unsatisfactory outcome."

Both Wellsworth and Tuvaris started to sputter rebuttals at the same time, but Cyrus just waved them down and continued on.

"President Bush went the military route by invading Afghanistan and Iraq, while waving the proverbial 'Big Stick' around the globe. The result: no new attacks on America, but our standing and prestige among the nations of the world took a nosedive. This led to the loss of over four thousand military lives while other countries have shunned American business ventures because of the heavy hand that we utilized with military intervention. The trade off? No more attacks upon American society, but the impact on our economy has been significant due to loss of foreign business -- also, an unsatisfactory outcome.

"If we have learned anything from these two approaches, it is this: commerce, markets, individuals, and governments the world over abhor the large scale disruption of peace and tranquility that the use of our military brings, and terrorists of every stripe must be stopped.

"What I am doing tonight is proposing a middle ground approach. By authorizing a small unit combining the best aspects and outcomes of military and law enforcement administered on our behalf of by the world's voice, the U.N., I believe we can achieve the best of both worlds: American participation and cooperation in a world-wide problem within the spirit of UNCLOS.

"In the past, Congress has been shunted to the side lines while presidents have dictated the course of action, seeking only the most basic approval from congress for our nation's treasure, with little or no input from us. History has shown that the Presidency, as an institution, has not the scope or authority to solve the problem by itself. The problem needs the cooperation and tools of Congress, the Presidency and the world, through the U.N., to handle this new type of disruptive force to our country, and the world order, and peace.

"Tonight is an historic event," Cyrus continued. "History will judge us by whether we recognized not only that a new paradigm shift has occurred but also that terrorism is not the realm of the nation-to-nation diplomacy that has dictated our country's affairs for the first two centuries of our existence. Transnational threats, as the military is so fond of calling terrorists, require an approach beyond the demarcations of national boundaries and the narrow confines of nation-state diplomacy. The Presidency controls the military and diplomacy of our nation. Yet only Congress can grant the authority needed for persons to go beyond our borders to seek out these water-born terrorists. By taking this first step into dealing with piracy, we are forging a new role that Congress will take in shaping the world order. And what more deliberative body can you name that would be better suited for this role?"

Cyrus could see that his rhetoric had hit that mark. Wheels were visibly turning behind Wellsworth's and Tuvaris's eyes. Cyrus had known that the idea of shaping and molding America's foreign policy was more than any senator or congressman could resist. In his long tenure, Cyrus had learned that every senator thought that he was smarter and better at foreign policy than the President, and the House of Representatives felt the voice of the people, as expounded by them, should take precedent over all else. Yet Cynthia Wellsworth's eyes clouded over with doubt.

"That is all good and well, Cyrus, but this authorization would require the House of Representatives as well. While

I agree that I like the whole concept, I'm not sure how far I can go with this until I have some time to confer with my counterparts in the House."

"Oh. Well, let me put your mind at ease then, Cynthia. As we are speaking, my co-sponsor in the House on this action, Tony Castillas, is meeting with your party's leadership, which fully supports this action and is also presenting this legislation to my party's leadership."

"Oh, this has already been embraced by House Republicans?"

"Most assuredly. Tony tells me that the Speaker of the House, Owen Dorsett, has instructed the chairman of the Rules Committee to see to it that the rule changes necessary to authorize the Letter of Marque are put on at the top of the agenda. The same thing we need to discuss if you believe that this is a direction that we can jointly work in."

What little resistance Cynthia Wellsworth had vanished when she learned that the co-sponsor of the concept was House Whip Tony Castillas, someone she had worked with many times before on legislative conferences to reconcile House/Senate bills. She could feel a vague sense of panic beginning to set in. She knew the American people would be on-board since no American servicemen's lives would be jeopardized, and she didn't want to be seen in the press as the person or party gumming up a perfectly crafted piece of legislation. If the Speaker of the House, the President, the Secretary-General of the U.N., and the Senate Majority leadership were already on board the bus, she'd better find a seat on the bus it before it left the station.

Still the urge to nit-pick died hard. This time it was Senator Tuvaris's turn. "All we have discussed is the concept in general, which sounds reasonably agreeable.

But my pappy," he said, switching into his best Missourian brogue, "always told me the devil is in the details. I need to see the exact verbiage of what you want this Letter of Marque and Reprisal to confer."

"Certainly. I was hoping you would be interested enough this evening to actually see the letter's contents." While speaking, he had produced a couple documents that he handed over to Senators Wellsworth and Tuvaris.

LETTER OF MARQUE AND REPRISAL

THIS LETTER SHALL AUTHORIZE THE SECRETARY-GENERAL OF THE UNITED NATIONS TO USE DEADLY FORCE, IF NECESSARY, AND ANY OTHER MEANS NECESSARY, TO PURSUE, CAPTURE, OR DESTROY ANY PERSON, PERSONS OR VESSELS COMMITTING ACTS OF PIRACY OR CRIMES UPON THE HIGH SEAS, AS DEFINED BY U.S. STATUTES AND FOREIGN OR INTERNATIONAL STATUTES, AGAINST CITIZENS, PARTIES, COMPANIES, STATES OR ENTITIES OF THE UNITED STATES OR ANY CITIZENS, PARTIES, COMPANIES, STATES, GOVERNMENTS OR ENTITIES OF FOREIGN DOMESTICATION WHO MAY BE ENGAGED IN LEGAL COMMERCE WITH ANY OF THE AFOREMENTIONED ON BEHALF OF THE UNITED STATES OF AMERICA. PURSUIT AND ENGAGEMENT PURSUANT TO THIS LETTER IS AUTHORIZED UPON ANY BODY OF WATER, INCLUDING INTERNATIONAL, TERRITORIAL OR ANY WATERS UNDER CONTROL OR AUTHORTITY OF ANY SOVERIEGN STATE OR ON FOREIGN LANDS IN WHICH SUSPECTS MAY SEEK SHELTER OR REFUGE, EXCLUSIVE OF UNITED STATES OF AMERICA'S LAND AND ITS TERRITORIAL WATERS. DURATION: THIS LETTER OF MARQUE WILL BE IN

EFFECT FOR TWO YEARS FROM THE DATE OF AUTHORIZATION. NO EXTENSION OF AUTHORITY OF THIS LETTER, WHETHER STATED OR IMPLIED, SHALL HAVE ANY EFFECT UPON THIS LETTER. THEREAFTER, ADDITIONAL LETTERS OF MARQUE AND REPRISAL MAY BE AUTHORIZED IN WRITING BY THE CONGRESS OF THE UNITED STATES ON A YEAR BY YEAR BASIS AS THE NEED ARISES. CONGRESS RESERVES THE RIGHT TO CANCEL THIS LETTER OF MARQUE AT ANYTIME IT DEEMS NECESSARY OR PRUDENT WITHOUT PRIOR NOTICE, WRITTEN OR OTHERWISE.

PERSONNEL: THIS LETTER AUTHORIZES THE UNITED NATIONS SECRETARY GENERAL TO DESIGNATE UP TO TWELVE PERSONS AT ANY ONE TIME TO ENGAGE IN ACTIVITIES AUTHORIZED BY THIS LETTER.

ASSISTANCE: NO PERSON, NOR PART OF THE U.S. GOVERNMENT OR MILITARY MAY BE USED OR ASSIST IN THE ACTIONS OR ACTIVITIES PURSUANT TO OR AUTHORIZED BY THIS LETTER AND MAY NOT VIOLATE THE SEAS, LAND OR AIRSPACE OF A RECOGNIZED SOVERIEGN STATE. AS AGENTS OF THE UNITED STATES OF AMERICA, MILITARY ASSISTANCE WILL BE RENDERED ONLY IN INTERNATIONAL WATERS, THE STATES AND TERRITORIES OF THE UNITED STATES AND ALL WATER UNDER ITS AUTHORITY, AND ANY MILITARY BASES RECOGNIZED BY TREATY, AGREEMENT OR CUSTOM. FURTHER, THIS LETTER AUTHORIZES ACCESS TO, USE OF AND REQUISTION OF ANY MATERIAL, ASSETS OR EQUIPMENT WITHIN THE U.S. MILITARY AND LEGAL DIVISIONS OF THE U.S. GOVERNMENT AS DEEMED NECESSARY AND

PRUDENT BY THE PRESIDENT OF THE UNITED STATES.

<u>SCOPE</u>: THIS LETTER AUTHORIZES ONE SHIP OR BOAT, UNDER FLAG OF THE UNITED NATIONS, AT ANY ONE TIME, NOT TO EXCEED EIGHTY FEET IN LENGTH AT THE WATER LINE, AND ANY SUBSEQUENT AUXILLIARY BOATS THEREOF, TO ENGAGE IN ACTIVITIES AUTHORIZED BY THIS LETTER.

<u>CAPTURES AND PRIZES</u>: ALL DETAINEES AND PRIZES CAPTURED WILL BE RENDERED MEDICAL ATTENTION AND ASSISTANCE, IF NEEDED AND PRACTICAL; AND ACCORDED SAFE AND HUMANE TREATMENT UNTIL SUCH TIMES AS THEY CAN BE DELIVERED TO THE PROPER, DESIGNATED AUTHORITY OF THE GOVERNMENT OF THE UNITED STATES. ALL PRIZES TAKEN PURSUANT TO THE ACTIVITIES AND ACTIONS AUTHORIZED BY THIS LETTER WILL BE THE PROPERTY OF THE UNITED STATES AND DELIVERED AT THE LOCATION AND TIME DEEMED APPROPRIATE BY THE PRESIDENT OF THE UNITED STATES.

"That's an awful lot of power and authority to be giving somebody," Clyde murmer as he continued to stare at the document after reading it. "A couple questions, though. First of all, why is this Letter for two years, and thereafter, they're only good for one year? Secondly, this Letter, if I understand it correctly, authorizes action anywhere in the world except the U.S. and Cuba, right?"

"In answer to the first part of your question," Cyrus began, "we anticipate that there will be a ramp up period of six months to a year necessary to pull together the personnel and equipment and get them trained into a cohesive unit. We want to give this program at least one year of action to assess whether it will work and if any subsequent Letters need to be modified in any certain way.

"As for your second question, you're correct. The Letter permits actions against people who are committing acts of piracy and crimes against those that the U.S. is doing business with. That would just about cover the world, except Cuba, which the U.S. does not recognize diplomatically and has a trade embargo against, at least on the surface anyhow. If a criminal act is perpetrated against Cuba, a Cuban national or company, no, this Letter would not authorize response. However, on closer examination, you will note that it is worded that if any acts of piracy or a crime is committed against a trade partner, like Canada for instance, in Cuban waters, the Letter would authorize action. Also, if the acts of piracy against Cuban nationals violated international law, the Letter could authorize action. But we will make it clear that any action on behalf of Cuba will need to be discussed with us first."

"This could work in our favor, too," Ben Tarsky piped in. "Defending Cubans against piracy and high seas crimes by proxy, through the U.N., could have very positive results at the ground level for us in Cuba. The Castros may control the media, but they have never been able to control the rumor mill among the populace. If the U.N. is doing this on our behalf, it may add pressure to the Castro regime. Fidel and Raul are getting long in the tooth. Who knows? Maybe just the slightest push might topple them, and Cuba could rejoin the nations of North America. Besides, Florida has scads of Cuban exiles. Going after pirates operating in Cuba could go a long way with that political constituency for both parties…just a thought."

Silence filled the room as everyone pondered the ramifications of the proposal. "So are the Republicans onboard with this?"Cyrus finally asked, looking directly at Cynthia.

"Two more questions. What are we going to do with detainees captured by the U.N.?" she asked holding Cyrus's gaze.

"Totally negotiable...the Letter of Marque and Reprisal is only designed to create a mechanism to stop and capture high seas criminals. What happens after that is a separate issue. The goal here is to begin the process of reigning in these thugs – we can wrangle over where to try them and what rights, if any, to grant them separately. No, we learned our lesson from the illegal immigration legislation package that Congress tried to pass in '06. We want to keep it small, keep it specific and allow a la carte follow-on legislation to sort out the rest according to the American people's wishes. And your last question?"

"Just how exactly does Congress issue a Letter of Marque and Reprisal?"

"Yeah, I've been kinda curious about that myself," chimed in Clyde Tuvaris.

"Research of the Library of Congress shows a mixed bag of ways to do it. Almost every Congress that used Letters of Marques did so in different ways, depending on the needs of the moment and the political exigencies. The bottom line is there is no prescribed way to issue a Letter. It is totally up to us how we want to accomplish it. The one thing that has changed though is the structure of Congress. Most of the Letters of Marque were issued between the seventeen hundreds and the early-to-mid eighteen hundreds. Back then, they had less than a couple dozen states and very few U.S Representatives, so it was possible to get everyone's signature on a Letter. Hell, when Abe Lincoln signed the last Letter during the Civil War, he only had half the Congress to deal with due to the Southern secession.

"I think that it would be impractical to try and get the signature of every senator and representative to authorize a Letter. What *I am* advocating is a simple rule change to both houses. This would allow the issuance of a Letter of Marque by signatures of the elected leaders of both parties in both houses, so long as those leaders represent a combined total of ninety percent of their body's membership. That way, the majority party cannot just go off and issue Letters anytime it wants. It will only take eight simple signatures to get things in motion. If you think that's fair, can I count on your two signatures?"

After a few moments' pause, both Cynthia's and Clyde's heads started to bob affirmative in unison followed by verbal acquiescence. With their commitment made, the conversation then turned to how best to structure the rule change and punch it through Committee.

Tony's evening had gone pretty much the same way. After some initial hemming-and-hawing, the Democrats saw the light when they realized that they might be the only ones on the outside of a low risk, high voter support program sponsored by all the major players.

When Tony and Cyrus spoke an hour later, they were delighted to find that each had only met with minor resistance before sealing the deal.

The Letter of Marque and Reprisal was going to become a reality.

Tony was the first to volunteer to call and let the President know. However, Cyrus pulled rank using the seniority card. Tony folded, but only because he was more interested in calling Chip Hartwell back in Texas. He, along with the President, looked forward to the next morning and disseminating the good news.

14

President Royce Tillman came strolling in the side door that led from the covered portico walkway between the family's residence in the White House to the West Wing with a beaming smile upon his face. He was greeted immediately by a phalanx of secretaries, advisors and his Press Secretary wanting to update him. He listened patiently, giving brief directives to keep things moving in the direction of his choosing. When everyone had expelled their mental loads, he told Muriel that he needed to talk to the U.N. Secretary-General at his earliest convenience.

He had just finished reading his morning intelligence and threat brief when Muriel rang through.

"I have the Secretary-General for you, Mr. President. Would you like me to put him through?"

"Please. Thank you, Muriel."

"Andrew," Royce Tillman boomed into the hand set as he picked it up, "how are you today?"

"Fine, thank you, Royce...and yourself?"

"Just could not be better today, Andrew. I wanted to call you first thing this morning to give you the good news. The leadership in both parties in the Houses of Congress reached an accord last night on issuing the U.N. a Letter of Marque and Reprisal. They estimate that they should have it in your hands sometime next week. So it's time to start staffing and pulling together your team."

"After our last conversation, I put the head of my security detail, David Barrett, on the job of drafting a preliminary report on organization and materials needed to get the job done right. He's a retired British SAS Colonel, a real professional. He did bring up one good point, though. Because the technology will all be American based, he thought that, in order to integrate and organize the team in the fastest manner, the team leadership should be either retired U.S. Special Forces or detached temporarily from their units to serve on this team. If you agree that this will give us the best possible chance to bring this project up to speed in the most efficient manner possible, then he'll need to have access to personnel jackets of SEAL officers. I know that this runs contrary to the stipulation of no American personnel are to be used, but surely, there's got to be a way for us to use one of your officers and still give you the political distance you need."

"I can make that happen. Have your man Barrett coordinate with my National Security Advisor, Tobias Sterns. He'll serve as the liaison between your team and my administration – he'll see to all your team's needs and requests."

"Good. By the way, we're calling this Operation Neptune, after the Roman god who ruled the seas; and the strike team will be called Trident, which he used to meter out order and justice. I have decided to appoint Colonel Barrett to run Operation Neptune. He wrote the preliminary organizational needs and this is his area of expertise, so it was only logical for him to carry it out. He says he'll need to have access to the files of U.S. Special Forces personnel to find the right candidate."

"Just bring up the request with Tobias -- I will let him know I've approved the request."

"Very good, Royce, I am looking forward to working with you, and I am eager to get started."

"As am I."

15

Good to his word, President Tillman had the name and number of the person at the Secretary of the Navy's Office waiting for Colonel Barrett the following day.

Four days later, Colonel Barrett found himself in a little office next to the U.S. Navy's Chief of Naval Operations looking through SEAL officers' jackets. The admiral in charge, a stern four-star Admiral by the name of Tittinger, was one of the highest-ranking admirals in the Navy and was in charge of its day to day operations.

After reviewing heavily redacted files for seven hours, he had identified several good candidates when one jumped out at him. As he reviewed this particular file, he knew this was the man he needed to lead his team. An Annapolis graduate that had arrived at the Naval Academy with a Black Belt in Ju Jitsu, he had joined the boxing team, and graduated in the top twenty percent of his class. He chose Surface Fleet Operations straight out of the Academy and was assigned to the Special Boats Squadrons where he operated and then commanded Mk. V Special Operations Boats before applying to the SEALs. His file was scant on detail and heavy on redaction, which indicated he had numerous opportunities to perfect his craft in the field. But his file also showed that his wife and three year old daughter were killed in an automobile accident fourteen months ago. Co-incidental to the deaths, he had been assigned to a shore based command in Special

Operations HQ logistics.

If he was any measure of fighting men, and Colonel Barrett prided himself on being an expert judge, this man would be itching to get back into action. His jacket indicated that he was a fighter, a scrapper, someone who overcame and adapted. After the loss of his wife and child, reasonably, he had been pulled from active duty while he grieved and sorted out his personal life. Special Operations was no place for an operator whose head was not totally in the game. But once out of the active loop, it was tough in any Special Operations Group to get back into the game. He was sure that this officer would jump at the chance to get back to the familiar warrior's way of life, where trigger time mattered more than forms filled out or reports completed.

This officer had the skills, talent and expertise to run this program in all phases from boat operations to logistics to combat. The question was: did he still have the fire in his belly?

"Well tomorrow, Lieutenant, Junior Grade Brandt Kohl, we'll see if you still have your warrior's spirit."

******

"Where do we stand, David?" Secretary McLaughlin inquired.

"I've made contact with Tobias Sterns, President Tillman's National Security Advisor and given him a brief overview of the program. He set me up to look at SEAL files yesterday, and I think I found our man. I'm going out to the Virginia Coast to talk to him later on this afternoon. I'll know then if he's right for the job.

"The other thing I'm concerned about is being able to sell this Navy SEAL Officer on the notion that his career would benefit from a tour with us. This is more than a little outside normal channels, even by Special Forces standards, and I would like some assurances that the military won't derail or curtail an officer's career for lending his talent to us."

"What's his name?"

"Lieutenant, Junior Grade, Brandt Kohl."

"I will talk to President Tillman and the Congressional leaders tomorrow about that. I'll be in Washington tomorrow to formally receive the Letter of Marque and Reprisal. It's in the Capitol Building, but the President has informed me that he will be in attendance too. "

"Good, I'll have a final draft of our materials request to them tomorrow. I should be able to tell you tonight about the disposition of Lieutenant Kohl. I would suspect that it will take several weeks for them to collect, modify and deliver the first of materials and equipment I've requested. It will probably take more time for some of the more exotic equipment to be rounded up. I'll use that time to train the Strike Force using standard equipment."

"Just what do you mean by 'exotic,' David?"

"Well, due to the limitation of personnel being set by their Congress, I've had to reach deep into the haversack of their technology to combine and integrate systems that are being developed separately or combine current systems technologies, that's all...plus a few little surprises."

"Surprises? Surprises for whom?"

"The bad guys, of course."

16

It took longer to go through security and ticketing than took to make the short flight from New York City to Norfolk International Airport, Virginia. It was late afternoon before Colonel. David Barrett, cleared security at the front gate of Little Creek Naval Amphibious Base and another twenty minutes before he found himself in a nondescript waiting room waiting to be escorted to the Special Operations area of the base.

He barely had time to take note of his surroundings before a fit and trim third class petty officer strode through the door. Barrett noted the confident, unfazed, alert inquisitive eyes that were unique to all Special Forces.

"Colonel Barrett, would you follow me, please?" the chief petty officer asked in a neutral tone.

"Certainly," David said getting up from his chair. As he followed the young enlisted man, he pondered his dilemma to this whole operation. Operation Neptune was designed as, and would be at its most effective as a clandestine operation. Yet, it answered directly to a politician, the Secretary-General. Although a good man, the SECGEN worked in a fish bowl of transparency on the world's stage and had no concept of operational security. Every aspect of his operation, his successes and failures, would be revealed for all the world to see and critique. *A bloody awful way to run a covert program*, he thought to himself, shaking his head, as he followed the petty officer in front of him. *Well, at least for the moment, I had some anonymity; best take advantage of it until it dissipates.*

The chief petty officer turned sharply towards a large building with the word GYMNASIUM printed on the building's placard. The enlisted escort held open the door to the building for Colonel Barrett.

"I took the liberty of calling Lieutenant Kohl's C.O. to ascertain his whereabouts," the CPO explained unprompted. "He said that Lieutenant Kohl could usually be found here at this time."

Once inside, the escort indicated which of the sweaty athletes Lieutenant Kohl was and then discretely backed away to an unobtrusive spot along the wall to observe. Colonel Barrett recognized Lieutenant Kohl from is file's photo and took a few moments to watch him spar on the mats in hand to hand combat. He looked every bit the six foot and a half that his file stated. His build was slightly more than rangy, but not quite that of a bulky bodybuilder. He wore his sandy brown hair longer than regulations allowed, typical of special operators because it helped them infiltrate and blend with indigenous populations. His bright blue-gray eyes were locked on his opponent, watching with all the passion of a praying mantis right before it snatched and devoured a fly. His opponent was very good, but Kohl was always two moves ahead. After several scrambles and restarts, with Kohl always getting the upper hand, his opponent bowed out and headed for the shower.

"Thanks for the match, Kirby. I'll see you in the Officer's Club later tonight. The first two beers are on me," Lieutenant Kohl said before moving to a heavy bag suspended by chains, ducking and weaving while delivering powerful blows to the bag that soon had it swinging and jiggling on its tethers.

Colonel Barrett moved to introduce himself. "Lieutenant Brandt Kohl?"

The Lieutenant stopped and turned to face his speaker. "Yes. But nobody calls me Brandt. Just call me Buck."

"Alright, Buck. My name is Colonel David Barrett-formally of the British SAS, now retired." The men shook hands in an informal manner.

"British SAS, huh? Nasty operators you, Brits. I've worked with a few; about as cool-headed operators as I've ever seen. What can I do for you, Colonel?"

Colonel Barrett instantly liked this brash young American naval officer who looked him straight in the eye. "I've got a proposition for you I'd like to discuss. Is there somewhere we can talk? Maybe over dinner? My treat."

Buck eyed him for moment, making a quick appraisal. "Sure. Dinner sounds good. I won't get finished at my desk 'til around eighteen hundred. Let's say dinner at eighteen thirty? That work for you?"

"Indeed. Is there an upscale watering hole you can recommend that might have a good collection of fine American Bourbons?"

"I know just the place." Buck gave him the name and location.

"Perfect. Alright Lieutenant, I'll let you get back to your exercise. See you tonight," Colonel Barrett said as he took a step backwards and pivoted to the gym's door.

Buck watched the back of the mystery Colonel recede four paces before he turned back towards the bag and began again to pummel it, this time mixing in some kicks.

17

At precisely the appointed time, Lieutenant Brandt 'Buck' Kohl strode through restaurant's front doors wearing his tan naval officer's uniform with all his breadboard trimmings. Not seeing his dinner partner in the foyer, he quickly scanned the dining room, spotting Colonel Barrett seated with a small tumbler of amber liquid pressed to his lips. A young, comely hostess approached Buck with menus crooked in her elbow. Flashing a winning smile, before she could speak, Buck told her that he just spotted his table and would just mosey on over there himself. Obviously responding to the attractive figure he cut, she gave him a disappointed smile while waving him on and watched the handsome officer recede.

Buck joined Colonel Barrett at the table and ordered himself a beer from the waitress as he settled in. "I see you wasted no time in sampling the bourbon," Buck observed.

"American whiskies and their derivatives are one of the many perks that I've come to enjoy in my retirement here in the States. I guess it's my Irish upbringing."

"If you don't mind me saying so, Colonel, you don't particularly strike me as a man retired from much of anything."

"Quite right. It's just a useful illusion that I use on myself from time to time to impress upon my psyche that I'm too old to go around smashing in doors or jumping out of helicopters and the like."

Buck's beer arrived, and he took the occasion over a long pull of beer to really scrutinize his host for the evening. The man's once lively red hair was now faded to almost blonde from years in the outdoors, graying at the temples. Deep cracks around his eyes indicated years of squinting in the bright sunlight. The man was rather small, standing no more than five foot nine with a slight build; Buck guessed he weighed about ten and a half stone, as the British would say, or about a hundred and fifty five pounds. But if there was one thing he had learned in Special Forces, it wasn't the size of the dog in the fight that counted, it was the size of the fight in the dog. Neat and trim, Buck surmised that in his day, the Colonel had probably been a steely-eyed killer and was now probably a formidable officer.

"So tell me, Buck, what to do you know about pirates?"

"Well, they have eye-patches, parrots as shoulder epaulettes, usually have really bad teeth and they say 'Aaargh.'"

"We'll that would be accurate of the fictional version. But what do you know about today's real-life pirates?"

"Not much, really…just what I hear on the news."

"Then let me give you a brief primer. Today's pirates range from local hoodlums in leaky boats to sophisticated criminals using the latest electronics, equipment and firepower to accomplish their nefarious deeds. With the cessation of the Cold War, pirate activities have bloomed. The problem is: no one knows just what exactly to do."

The waitress interrupted them momentarily to take their order and see if their drinks needed refreshing, which they did. Barrett waited until she finished and moved out of earshot before continuing.

"In a joint operation, the United States Government and

the United Nations, under a Letter of Marque and Reprisal granted by your Congress, are setting up a small task force called Operation Neptune to hunt down and capture or kill pirates. Dead or alive, their choice. The Secretary-General of the U.N., Andrew McLaughlin, is ultimately responsible for Operation Neptune, but I run it for him. We have the full backing of your government, anything we want, carte blanche, with two caveats: 1) no U.S. military craft will transgress national boundaries in pursuit of Operation Neptune activities, and 2) no U.S. Military personnel are to be involved in operations that transgress national borders."

"I'm a little confused here, Colonel. If you can't use U.S. military personnel, why are you buying me dinner?"

"Your government has been sporting enough to allow me to select an officer from the ranks of the U.S. military to assist in the formation of my strike force, codenamed Trident. Since all the technology and equipment will be from the U.S. inventory, it just makes sense to have the involvement of U.S. military personnel initially to get things going. Of course, they will have to be detached from the U.S. military temporarily while they participate in Operation Neptune, at the end of which, they may return to their positions in the U.S. military with all the promotions, pay upgrades, etc., like they were never gone. I'd like to offer you the job as strike force commander."

"I see..." Buck said slowly, possibilities and questions tumbling through his head.

The waitress arrived with their salads, giving Buck a moment to formulate a response.

"Will the strike team leader have any say in the number or configuration of Strike Force?"

"Yes and no. The U.S. government has set strict limits on the total number of personnel to be covered by the Letter of Marque and Reprisal at twelve. Secretary-General McLaughlin has set requirements on the composition of the Strike Force. He is adamant that the strike force contains law enforcement professionals. Being able to call it a law enforcement action, to address the problem of neutralizing the pirate threat without being accused of running a death squad for the U.S. will give him the political cover he needs.

"Beyond that...yes, I'm open to input. As of this moment, nothing is set in stone; but, before I can share the program's plan with you, you need to decide if you want to come onboard. Then we can align the Strike Force to best meet its objectives."

The main course arrived shortly with their smiling waitress, and Buck started in on his medium rare prime rib, after a couple bites he reached his decision.

"If I come onboard, it will be with a couple of conditions. First, no Smurf helmets." He was referring to the pejorative nickname given to the U.N.'s blue helmeted peacekeepers known for doing nothing while violence occurred all around them. "Or for that matter, no U.N. blue anywhere on the combat uniforms; it makes far too easy a target."

"Done... with one exception: the SOC must be flagged as a U.N. vessel. But we can reduce the flag size and placement to make it less conspicuous. What else?"

"Second - I want to pick my second-in-command."

"Is there someone in particular you have in mind?"

"Yes. Lieutenant Steve Ramage. He's the SEAL I trust the most to watch my six if we're going to go off the beaten path with this project."

Steve had been Buck's roommate at Annapolis and they had been best friends ever since. Steve was the football team's fullback, where he earned the nickname "Rampage

Ramage" because of the intense pleasure he took in bringing the fight to their opponents, often choosing to run someone over when he could run around them.

"I'll see what I can do." Colonel Barrett said, secretly pleased at the thought of two SEAL officers leading Strike Force Trident. "At this point, I don't think this will be a problem. I'm sure it will make all parties in the U.S government more comfortable knowing that two of their most capable officers will be at the helm of this strike team."

"If my two conditions are acceptable, then I'm in." Buck was pleased with the idea of having his own command with his best friend watching his back. His desk riding days would soon be over.

"I'm pleased to have you aboard, Lieutenant Kohl," Colonel Barrett said while raising his glass in salute, which Lieutenant Kohl mirrored.

"How soon before I can expect to ship out?"

"Within in the week, I would expect. But you're not going very far. We'll be training out of the Little Creek Naval Base here in Norfolk."

"That makes sense, since the missions of Strike Force Trident and the SEALs have considerable overlap, not to mention the infrastructure to support men and machinery."

"This is all in the formative stage. While the wheels have been set in motion politically to make this happen, we have yet to be allocated a pencil or paper. But, I want you to focus on the training and preparing the men, and let me focus on getting whatever you need to make their training and mission happen."

The rest of the meal was spent on bringing Buck up to speed on the political aspects and on his basic action plan. The two spent the next two hours planning the next move before they had to break it up and head for the sack. It wasn't hard to see that life was going to get very compressed in the next several months.

******

When Buck got back to his Bachelor Officer's quarters, he reached for the phone to call Rampage at the Naval Amphibious Base Coronado in San Diego, California, where he was based with West Coast Command for Special Warfare. It was a three-hour time difference between the two locations so he was sure that he could catch Rampage before he got too carried away combing the beachside bars looking for applicants for the title of Mrs. Ramage. Rampage answered on the second ring.

"Steve, this is Buck."

"Howdy, beachcomber, how're things hangin'?"

"Great! Listen, I've got a new gig. I'm so jacked, I can hardly sit still."

"Oh yeah? Doing what, pray tell?"

"Hunting pirates for the U.N."

"Say what?!"

"The U.N. is giving me my own task force to hunt down pirates for the Secretary-General of the U.N. It's got the full support of the President and Congress, too."

"You lucky S.O.B!"

"There's room in the sandbox if you want to join me. I told them I wouldn't take the job unless you came along as my second-in-command."

"Does this mean I'll get to ride one of the U.N.'s black helicopters I've heard about, the ones that the Tri-Lateralist kooks say fly over our cities at night? I've always wanted to find out just what they're supposedly doing."

"Hell if I know. I don't think they really exist, but I'm sure we'll find out. You in?"

"Are dyslexics teaple poo? Of course, I'm in. When do we start?"

"Soon...real soon. I'll let you know when I learn more. I just wanted to make sure you're a go. I'll talk to you later this week as info comes in. I just wanted to give you a warning order so you could start clearing your decks for action."

"I'm on it, Buck."

"Alright, I'll let you get back to your normally programmed evening of debauchery. I'll talk to you later."

"Adios, amigo."

18

The meeting with the President and the Congressional leadership turned out to be rather anti-climatic. Congress had wanted to keep a fairly low profile on everything until the program proved to be a success or a failure.

Since this was primarily Congress's show, they met in a larger conference room in the Capitol Building. The rich mahogany paneled walls gave a somber setting for the proceedings; the tones were hushed. Two copies of the Letter of Marque were passed to all eight of the House party leaders, each signing in their designated spot, all under the observation of President Tillman, who was asked to sign as a witness. When the signing ceremony was done, one letter was presented by U.S. Representative Tony Castillas to Secretary-General McLaughlin, who took the document and then gave a brief speech on the new era of international cooperation that they were embarking upon. When the brief ceremony was over, Cyrus Templeton, who was present for the conclusion of his efforts, asked if there was anything that the Secretary-General needed immediately to get started. Secretary-General McLaughlin gave him the names of the two Navy SEALs that Colonel Barrett had requested and imparted the necessity of having the two officers. The other thing that he requested was any assistance that they might be able to offer in smoothing the way with the U.S. military while they were getting started.

"I think that we have that well in hand," Cyrus told McLaughlin with a twinkle in his eye. "We've scheduled a meeting at the conclusion of this ceremony with all the military branches to impress upon them the seriousness of the value and success that we place upon Operation Neptune. You should have no problems."

After shaking hands with all the participants, Secretary-General McLaughlin exited with President Tillman, followed by the congressional members to a podium on the capitol steps where all gathered to give a brief statement to the press. After this, the President and the Secretary-General went to their respective motorcades while the congressional leaders were heading in en-masse for a meeting with the leadership of the armed forces.

They returned to the same conference room, passing many of the heads of the military branches and their entourage of aides waiting in the hall outside. It was all polite smiles and deferential treatment as they all filed in and took seats around the conference table where staffers had placed name placards designating the seats for the attendees. The eight congressional leaders sat on one side, the military leaders on the other. Chief of Staff for the Army General Wayne Blochette anchored the line of military brass, sitting in the rightmost chair. Next to him was the Air Force's Chief of Staff, General Tyler Armien; next was Admiral Joseph Tittinger, the Navy's Chief of Operations; at the end of the table was General Antonio Salazado, Commandant of the Marine Corps. Their aide de camps hovered near the back wall, standing like courtesans, waiting for a flick of the wrist of their leader to summons them forth.

Gen. Blochette didn't wait to let the politician build up a head of silver-tongued steam, before diving in. "What's the meaning of summoning all us at the last minute to come before you? May I remind you, that none of you exist in our chain of command. I'm sure you're also aware that we're at war conditions and have personnel in combat in three theatres of action?" He blasted the congressmen in front of him with a scathing look. "Do you know how inviting a target it is to have all the congressional and the military leadership in the same room?"

By agreement, the congressional leaders had agreed to let Speaker of the House Owen Dorsett and Tom Blackwood, Senate Majority Leader, co-chair the meeting. Dorsett started in as soon as everyone settled in.

"Thank you, gentleman, for accommodating this meeting on such short notice."

His non-reply was met with polite smiles and nods backed by frosted stares.

"The reason for the short notice was to add an extra layer of security to this affair; both personal safety," he paused and nodded to General Blochette by way of an answer, "and to ensure that the content of this meeting remained secure.

"You may not be aware that Congress, and Congress alone, retains certain rights to military action beyond the War Powers Act. The U.S. Constitution gives the ability to Congress to issue Letters of Marque and Reprisals, which are essentially licenses to commit acts of war by third parties with the blessing of the U.S. Government. And, I'm sure you're aware that just prior to this meeting, we," he paused to wave his arm around to acknowledge the other members of Congress seated, "issued a Letter of Marque and Reprisal to United Nations Secretary-General Andrew McLaughlin. This was done so with the participation, blessing and full support of President Tillman. The U.N.'s mission, code name Neptune, is to hunt down and capture pirates wherever they are operating on the seas of the world."

Tom Blackwood seamlessly picked up the narrative, "With the participation of the President, we've pledged to Andrew McLaughlin the full support of all the military branches of the U.S. Government. Your offices will be receiving memos and orders to that effect from the President to each of the Secretaries of your service through the Secretary of Defense's office."

Admiral Tittinger could no longer restrain himself, blurting out, "If you don't mind my asking, Senator Blackwood, if these orders are coming down the chain of command, then why in the hell have we disrupted our important duties to be told about routine affairs?"

Despite their best efforts not to acknowledge Admiral Tittinger's question to what they were all thinking, one or two of the generals could not stop slight nods of agreement.

"That's a great question, and it takes us right to the heart of the matter. Gentlemen, I know you take great pride and professionalism in carrying out orders given to you by the chain of command, even orders you may not agree with. However, like every organization, there are varying levels of enthusiasm for orders coming from above, especially, if one particular service or another feels that the Letter of Marque we have issued might infringe upon a mission traditionally undertaken by them. We are here to impress upon you that any such institutional sabotage will be viewed very dimly by Congress. 'So what?' the lower echelons might say, 'We don't answer to Congress.' Yes, this is true. But Congress still appropriates funds for your weapons systems, research and development, and pet projects. Should you desire to continue to enjoy the relationship you have with Congress, as expressed by your current funding levels, then it would be in your best interest to ensure throughout your ranks that when code name Operation Neptune is invoked; complete, unequivocal assistance is rendered immediately to the U.N.'s Strike Force; without subterfuge, withholding or reservation.

"If Operation Neptune fails, we," he said sweeping his hand around the room, "will bear the brunt of this failed effort. And, I can assure you, that if we feel that we were sandbagged in anyway at anytime by the armed forces, or if Neptune's Strike Force informs us of any lack of support, your service can count on doing without that new artillery system, carrier group, fighter wing or new brigade of rapid deployment forces that you claim is necessary. Do I make myself clear? I hope so, because I speak for *ALL* of Congress."

Back to Owen Dorsett, who tried a little softer sell: "Look, Operation Neptune is a small operation and will not disrupt greater military proceedings to any large degree. At worst, it will be a minor inconvenience to different commands from time to time. We would certainly be grateful for your complete cooperation."

The room was silent while the chiefs digested the carrot or stick offered from men they did not answer to nor much respect.

General Armien, the most politically adept of the group, suavely answered, "I think all of us can see that Letters of Marque and Reprisals, as a new tool in the anti-terrorist tool box, are well worth exploring, and you'll receive the utmost in cooperation from the military branches. If there are any questions, we will be happy to submit them through the Secretaries of our branches to the President for clarification. While this may be a new endeavor for Congress, we ask for a certain amount of patience while we integrate this new form of military action into our force structure. Now, is there anything else that we can assist you gentlemen with today?"

Again, silence as the congressmen looked to each other. "Oh, yes, one last thing," Cyrus Templeton spoke up while producing a sheet of paper from a satchel before him. "We'd like for you to immediately detach these two Navy SEALs from duty so that they can assume command of Operation Neptune's Strike Force Trident. They have a lot to do and as of today, the clock is ticking." He slid the paper towards Admiral Tittinger.

The Admiral quickly glanced at it, and tersely said, "I'll have my aide arrange this immediately."

This immediate compliance seemed to set the congressman at ease. They had clearly been anticipating dissension from the military leaders.

"If that is all, gentleman," General Armien said "we will take our leave." The service leaders in unison pushed their chairs back and showed their backs to the still seated congressmen as they headed for the door. Once outside, the service chiefs formed a tight little knot, their aides clustered behind several paces, as they made their way to their waiting cars, conversing in low tones.

"The way I see it, this little escapade will impact the Navy the most and probably some of the Air Force," General Blochette was saying. "Is that the way you see it, Antonio?"

"That's about the measure of it."

"That's easy for you guys to say," Admiral Tittinger said. "Neptune's mission is a maritime interdiction. That has always been the Navy's mission. The President didn't even ask for any scenarios or assessments before he turned the mission over to the U.N. And now they want me to bend over and grab my ankles to take it in the backside while they raid my personnel and disrupt my command."

"If I'm not mistaken, Joe, isn't that what the Navy is famous for?" General Salazado deadpanned. "I mean, bending over and taking in the backside?"

"Spoken like a true jarhead, Antonio," Admiral Tittinger retorted, as the others tried to hold back their chortles.

"All joking aside, this could get ugly," stated General Blanchette, who had been quiet until this point. "We don't really know what has been promised to these U.N. jokers. What if they've been promised some of our new weapons from Research and Development? What if they disrupt our research and development programs to adapt our weapons to fit their own program? They could set us back months or years if they do. Congress had better not rake us over the coals for budget overruns. If they do, all bets are off. Their little experiment can die a slow and agonizing death as far as I'm concerned."

There was a pause in their whispered conversation as each leader sobered to these new implications.

"We best keep in touch on this as it progresses," suggested General Armien. The others all murmured agreement and moved to the doorway of the waiting cars and the little knot of the nation's military leaders went their separate ways, their aides dispersing and catching up to their bosses now that it was safe to approach.

As Admiral Tittinger settled into the backseat of his car, his aide, Commander Keshaun Johnson entered from the other side. As soon as the doors shut, he started to vent, "I'll be goddamned if I let those spineless bastard politicians screw with my Navy on my watch. They're already setting us up to take the blame when their half-assed little adventure fails. What in the hell were they thinking when they partnered with the U.N.? Now there's some warrior ethos. Those blue helmeted pussies know how to say 'run away' in every language on the planet. I give this little misadventure six months, eight months tops, before the wheels come off." The admiral harrumphed and crossed his arms across his chest, letting his mind run free with anger.

"Keshaun," he said handing him the piece of paper given to him by Cyrus Templeton, "I want you to take care of this immediately. They want us to detach these two SEAL officers temporarily so they can command the U.N.'s little travesty."

"Yessir," Commander Johnson answered.

"But, Keshaun," he paused as he tracked his thoughts, "I want their records of discharge to read the cause of discharge was medical...psychiatric. They were mentally unstable and no longer fit for command due to inappropriate decisions and behavior. That ought to give us enough cover when the press starts to sniff around after this shit-pie starts to swirl around the toilet."

19

"Where do you think the Secretary-General's office is, Steve?" Buck asked while surveying the site from the corner of 1st Avenue and 42nd Street where the cabbie had dropped them off in midtown Manhattan. They studied the U.N. campus which consisted of several buildings for several moments.

"Well, there is a rule of thumb that I like to use: when looking for the Big Dog, look in the biggest building," Rampage said, pointing at the towering building next to the river. "It works for me every time."

"My thoughts, exactly."

"Trust me; I'm very psychic about these things."

It took them the better part of forty-five minutes to find the right entrance and then sign in through the guest entrance to get their visitors badges. After a lengthy elevator ride, their escort deposited them in the outer holding pen of an office complex where they checked with the receptionist before settling into the waiting lounge's chairs.

The room had four-foot plain wood paneling around the room in a light, natural wood tone that was broken in regular intervals by small gaps, giving the room a postmodern feel that was echoed throughout the building.

"You know, this looks familiar…" Steve said while looking around, "all that's missing is the whir of dental drills and the muted screams of patients."

"Behave, Rampage," Buck said in a mock scold.

Just then Colonel Barrett appeared beside the receptionist desk and strode across the waiting room, extending his hand to Buck. "Welcome aboard, Lieutenant Kohl," he boomed.

"It's a pleasure to finally be here, sir," Buck said rising. "Allow me to introduce you to Lieutenant Steve Ramage," he said turning to ex-roommate.

"Of course, I recognize you from the photo in your file. A pleasure also to have you on board Lieutenant Ramage," Colonel Barrett stated as he pumped Rampage's hand. "If you'll follow me back, I will get one of the office assistants to start shepherding you through the induction process." With that, he turned on his heels and headed back in the direction from which he appeared. They followed the Colonel until he arrived at a door, where he entered several numbers on a keypad beside the door, followed by an audible click as the door's lock was disengaged. "One of the new features that I've had to fight the bureaucrats here tooth and nail about," he said, pushing the door open and holding it for Buck and Rampage.

"A culture clash. The U.N. has no concept of operational security, especially when men's lives are on the line. They saw no need to lock and secure our operations area and offices. 'Who would want to go through your desk and see what you're doing?' they asked. Everything they do here is out in the open, except for the backroom deals. I tried to explain to them that there might be plenty of criminals out there that would pay plenty to know what we are up to and who we were after. They finally caved when I explained to them that we would need to get sensitive data from U.S. Intelligence and other intelligence services in order to do our jobs, which wouldn't happen unless it was held in a secure area."

As Buck passed the threshold, he glanced at the silver placard that looked like it had just been freshly placed there. It read: COLONEL DAVID BARRETT, PROJECT NEPTUNE DIRECTOR. A large anteroom with waiting chairs and a large secretary's desk configured in a "C" with ample bookshelves on two sides was located in one corner. Several doors for other smaller offices lined one side of the anteroom opposite the secretary's desk and waiting chairs in front of the secretary. The room was paneled in the same light wood paneling that Steve had so admired in the other waiting room. As Steve walked pass the doors, he glanced at the silver placards beside the doors and was surprised to see his and Steve's names on a couple of them with the titles "Strike Force Commander" and "Asst. Strike Force Commander" under them. He smiled at placard, starting to see the culture clash the Colonel had referred to thinking *Only a bureaucrat would call Rampage an 'Assistant' rather than what the military calls the 2IC,* mused Buck

"Gloria," the Colonel called to a middle-aged woman sitting behind the secretary's desk, "I'd like to introduce you to Lieutenants Brandt Kohl and Steve Ramage. Gentlemen, Gloria Steinmetz." The woman stood and crossed to shake their hands. She wore a tasteful white dress in gauzy, breathable fabric that came to just above her knees and high-heeled shoes highlighted her still shapely legs. Her ginger hair perfectly framed her face. A matching scarf and coordinated with her shoes completed her ensemble. While still a highly attractive woman, Buck was sure that fifteen years earlier she had been an absolute stunning beauty.

"It's so nice to meet you both," she said flashing a magnetic smile.

"Likewise," Buck answered amiably.

"The pleasure is all mine," Rampage said, flashing his most devastating smile, usually reserved for applicants vying for the title of 'Mrs. Ramage,' An inveterate flirt, Steve couldn't help himself from responding to her very feminine presence, despite the enormous diamond ring on her wedding ring finger.

"Gloria is my assistant, but if you need anything, please speak with her. She has access to the office's administrative pool. If she can't help you, she will get someone who will. Now, if you would, Gloria, would you please get the personnel people up here and get started on in-processing the lieutenants. We will be in my office until they get here."

"I've already notified them and they are on their way."

"Good. Gentlemen please, if you would?" The Colonel offered, stretching his arm in the direction of his office's door behind Gloria's desk. They stepped in the direction indicated and waited until a buzzer sounded, indicating that Gloria had unlocked the door for them. As they stepped into his spacious office, they noted a small conference table at one end, a desk at the other, and a small bar with glass built into the wall. Along with a generous assortment of liquors, they were also greeted by a stunning view overlooking the East River and Long Island beyond. "Please, sit down," Colonel Barrett said as he indicated two seats in front of his desk.

"Time is short, gentleman, so let's get started," the Colonel Barrett said as he settled in behind his desk. "We have two main tasks that are the most pressing at this moment. First we need to staff the rest of Operation Neptune. That will be my responsibility. Second, a training regimen must be developed based upon the mission of the task force. I've written an initial draft, which is on both of your desks. My background, as an SAS operative did not include substantial maritime operations training. Yours, as SEALs does, so I want you to perfect the training program. I trust that Lieutenant Kohl has already briefed you, Lieutenant Ramage, on the particulars of Operation Neptune?"

"Yessir."

"Good. We'll have more time later today to go more in-depth. Your first priority is to fill out all the necessary paperwork needed by the U.N. staff to get you started as employees. Gloria will be in charge of that. At 1630, we have a meeting with the Secretary-General in his office. He wants to meet the men whose leadership decisions he will be responsible for."

From a speaker on the desk, Gloria's voice piped in, "Colonel Barrett, Personnel is here for Lieutenants Kohl and Ramage."

"Thank you, Gloria," the Colonel said while fingering a button on the speaker.

"Alright, gentlemen, you have your directives. We will meet again here no later than 1620 hours to see the Secretary-General."

Buck and Rampage got up from their chairs and exited the office to find Gloria in the anteroom with two people wearing Personnel Department badges. After introductions were made all around, they were lead to their respective offices and given a stack of paperwork to fill out, including job applications.

The next four hours were spent filling out the myriad of forms needed by the different departments of the U.N. This bewildering array of paperwork was all new to the Navy SEALs, who had never held jobs in the private sector. Complicating it all was the fact that neither one knew just yet where they would be calling home.

"Don't worry about that now," Gloria told them, as they headed out for a quick lunch, "I'll put in a Change of Address Form for you when we get that all figured out."

Over a plate of Thai food, Rampage asked Buck, "So what did you put in the Job Application Form part that asked for qualifications?"

"Well, I made up some mumbo-jumbo about security training and anti-terrorist training."

"Me, too. I was tempted to put down expert sniper with confirmed head shots at eight hundred meters and leading successful black ops authorized by the President of the United States but figured that wouldn't get me any bonus points. So I just turned on my creative writing juices and laid in some major mo-gas. What a pile of crap! We're trained killers. What are we doing filling out job applications?"

Steve had noticed that several patrons in the crowded restaurant had discreetly turned to look at them worriedly, having heard his last outburst. He just smiled back at them, which made them even more nervous.

"Every big organization runs on paperwork.' Buck replied, "The Navy taught both of us that."

"Yeah, I know. But, I kinda hoped that since they knew our skill sets and hired us precisely because of them that we would be able to skip that sort of crap."

"No such luck."

20

Upon arriving back from lunch, Gloria informed them that they were late for their mandatory Cultural Sensitivity Training class. Their reaction was less than enthusiastic. She didn't notice them grimace and roll their eyes when she told them it was the first of several they would need to take.

During the class, Buck eyed Rampage with growing concern. He looked as if he was going to have an aneurysm. His eyes bulged; he couldn't sit still, and he was continuing to exhale loudly. Finally, Buck leaned over and whispered, "Hold it together, buddy. We don't want to get fired on our first day."

"What," he whispered back exasperatedly, "are we doing here? Am I supposed to understand someone's culture before I kill 'em? I'm supposed to know that it's impolite in their culture to touch their head with my hand but it's okay to aerate their brain with a bullet? What crap is this? I'm supposed to worry about their feelings while I put my crosshairs on their heart and pull the trigger? Or how about, 'Gee, I wonder if this killer's Islamic family is going to be really upset because the supersonic round that just ripped through his chest sucked his heart and lungs out the exit wound so they won't be able to bury him whole?'"

'Rampage had a rather large point,' Buck thought. *'They were trained to break things and kill people. How did that jive*

with Cultural Sensitivity Training?'

At this point, they were starting to get nasty looks from other people in the class who were eager to suck up this swill to make a good impression on their first day of work and were annoyed by the distraction of their whispering. Buck decided to hold his comments for latter.

After the class, the students piled into the halls and elevators to return to their offices. Buck and Rampage loaded onto the elevator with a bunch of other students and waited stoically for the others to disembark. When the door shut behind the last remaining students, Rampage turned to Buck, his eyes blazing.

"Christ, Buck! I think I'm going to need therapy after hearing that pile of psycho-babble, new-age, touchy-feely horse shit. Gloria said that we'll get more training later. I can't take another class. Just shoot me now."

"Awww, it sounds like someone is getting in touch with his inner-grump today," Buck snarked at his friends displeasure.

"No, I'm serious. I won't go to another class. They can't make me. I don't need to have my head screwed with."

"The only therapy you're going to need can be found in the bottom of a beer bottle and in the arms of some of these beautiful New York women."

"Oh, so you are alive," Rampage commented. "You've noticed the fairer sex of the local inhabitants; that's good. I was beginning to wonder if you were ever going to come around."

"Noticed...yes. But I wouldn't say I've come around," he replied, reminded once again of his wife and daughter. "But listen, I think you're looking at this all wrong. It's all about marketing. And we're in the marketing capital of America. Think of it this way: we come here, take some classes, learn about new and interesting people, and then we go out and hunt them down."

"Gee...when you put it that way, it sounds pretty good." The sarcasm dripped from Rampage's words.

The elevator door opened onto their floor and they made their way back to their offices. They took a few minutes to inventory their respective offices and put together a shopping list for Gloria of things they were going to need. Then it was time to meet the Secretary-General.

They met the Colonel in the outer office and fell in behind, single file, as they followed him up the stairs by the elevator. "The Secretary-General's Office is on the top floor," was all that he offered as an explanation over his shoulder as he ran up the steps two at a time, forcing Buck and Rampage to press just to keep up with him. In short order, they arrived at the Secretary-General's palatial offices, where the Secretary-General's lead assistant, a stunning tall and willowy woman with beautiful vibrant medium-brown skin recognized the Colonel and waved him in. "He's expecting you."

The Colonel did not break stride as he headed for the beautiful eight foot solid French doors, made of the same light natural wood that decorated the rest of the building. Secretary-General of the United Nations, Andrew McLaughlin, looked up from his desk where he had been writing as they entered. "Colonel, thank you for coming," he called as he arose from behind his desk. "I take it that these are the two young warriors that you told me about that are going run Trident's Strike Force for us."

"Yessir. I'd like to introduce you to Lieutenant Brandt Kohl."

Brandt stepped forward to shake the Secretary's hand, saying "An honor to meet you, sir."

"Thank you for stepping into the breach to help us, help

the world, with such a dangerous task. The honor is truly mine, Brandt," said Andrew, ever the politician.

"Please, my friends call me Buck."

"Alright, Buck."

"And this is Lieutenant Steve Ramage," the Colonel continued.

"A pleasure, Steve."

"Yessir," Steve replied formally.

"Please, sit down," Andrew indicated to the seats behind him. "Our arrangement with President Tillman has had you temporarily separated from the U.S. Navy. Of course, you may return to your rank and station anytime that you wish. But, for appearance's sake, you work for me. Technically, you're civilians, so the use of rank will no longer be necessary. I know you've worked hard to obtain your rank, but I'm sure you'll get used to it. We are a non military organization, the use of ranks would tend to confuse and even anger some of the member nations."

"Yessir," Buck and Steve answered in unison.

"We're a bit more informal here and it would help if you called me Andrew, Mr. McLaughlin, or Mr. Secretary-General, whichever you're comfortable with. Now," he said drawing in a breath and redirecting his thoughts, "I asked David to bring you up to my office so that I could impress upon you my thoughts of where and how Operation Neptune needs to be focused. The cooperation between the U.N. and the U.S. government in a groundbreaking law enforcement action is a historical event. I must tell you that military personnel were not my first choice. I would have preferred law enforcement personnel for the Trident's Strike Force. But David convinced me that a combination of law enforcement and military personnel would be the mix necessary to get optimal results in the shortest amount of time with the least amount of casualties. David and I have worked together for a while, and I have come to respect his judgment in these matters. I just want to make clear that this is a law enforcement action. Your main objective is to bring criminals to justice through the American court system authorized by the American Congress. Protect yourselves and your men at all times and shoot only when you have to. I realize that it may not always be possible to confront armed criminals and get them to lay down their arms peacefully, but I expect you to try. Any death incurred by Operation Neptune will be my responsibility and I'm answerable to the member nations and their press corp. I need to be sure that men that I trust are out there on the frontlines of this project doing everything they can to bring suspects in alive."

"Both Steve and I," Buck responded, "have had experience working abroad with law enforcement agencies to bring in criminals too difficult for normal police forces to handle, we understand the difficulties associated with that type of activity. We'll make it a priority to bring prisoners in alive when possible. But to speak frankly sir, it is my understanding that the people we're being tasked with apprehending are wanted because they are prone to violence and are heavily armed. If they weren't, anybody could have rolled them up. So a lot of my men could get killed if they are worrying about something other than taking down the perpetrators in front of them. I know that this may sound odd to you, but the most efficient way to minimize all casualties is to use overwhelming force to stupefy and subdue them before they have time to reach for a weapon. It's the operating principle of law enforcement agencies the world over. And it should be ours, too."

"Yes…all the same arguments that David has made to

me. It's not my area of expertise, but I trust that you'll use your best judgment when the time comes. Well, gentlemen, I just wanted to take a few minutes to let you now know where I stood. If you have any questions, I know you will take it up with Colonel Barrett."

Colonel Barrett took the dismissal, stood, and headed for the door; Buck and Steve followed after saying their good-byes.

Back at the office, Buck and Steve took a few minutes to organize their activities for the next day. Gloria promised that they would have computers tomorrow with the appropriate security software to start accessing the internet. It was going to take another day for the proper security clearances to be processed for the U.S. military and intelligence networks sent through Tobias Sterns at the White House.

"Looks like we're in a holding pattern here for the moment," Buck observed, frustrated.

"Yeah, kinda looks like it. Why don't we call it a day and hit the town tonight?" Rampage agreed. "It might be the only chance we get for a while."

They had no idea how prophetic his words were going to be.

21

A month later...

Colonel Barrett waited a minute for his computer hook up with Little Creek NAB to go through so that he could brief Buck and Steve on the Trident Strike Force personnel that would be arriving shortly. While he waited for the test bars on the computer screen on his desk to change to show the faces of Buck and Steve out in Chesapeake Bay, he had steepled his fingers against his chin as he contemplated the one last position he had yet to fill in his roster of twelve. The person he had in mind was going to need the intervention of the Secretary-General himself to obtain. He would be giving the same briefing to Andrew later today that he was about to give Buck and Steve. At that time, he would have to ask for the Secretary-General's help. But it had to be done delicately, given the circumstances.

The color bars on the screen changed to a pip in the center, which then exploded to a full screen showing Buck and Steve sitting shoulder-to-shoulder in a nondescript military office in Little Creek. "Are we on? Colonel, we can see you, can you see us?" Buck asked as he intently looked into the camera's lens.

"Yes, quite well, thank you. Now, let's get started, shall we? Right-o then. I have seven recruits heading your way; they should arrive in the next several days, but I thought you'd like to know who I've collected for you. Please note that their personnel records are en route to you and you should have them by tomorrow to study further. All will need temporary housing until they can obtain housing on their own.

"I'll start first with crew for the Mark V.1 Special Operations Craft. The boat commander will be Tadhg Ramsden, Lieutenant, British Royal Navy, Commander of an Archer Class patrol boat, the *HMS Smiter*. He is the second son of the Marques of Windum and therefore, will not receive his father's title. So, he did what countless other sons of royalty have done throughout time, take a commission in Her Majesty's Navy.

"Second in command will be Grels Persson, Ensign, Royal Swedish Navy. He has been serving on one of their CB 90 Patrol Boats.

"The last member of the Mk. V.1 SOC crew will be Lenz Synder, Chief Petty Officer, German Navy. He'll serve as the boat's engineer.

"Now, for the strike team: Harold Brisbane, Sergeant, British Army SAS; Cooper Randall, Sergeant, Australian Army SAS, and Datan Ben-Moshe, Sergeant, Israeli Defense Force, Sayeret MATKAL. All are among the best Special Forces operators in their countries.

"And lastly, Hubert Arceneaux, Special Agent, French National Police, Directorate of Territorial Surveillance - DST. He was assigned to one of the nine SWAT Teams in their Central Directorate of Public Security – DCSP -- before transferring two years ago. And," Colonel Barrett paused, "you will find this interesting, Buck - he is also a Savate national champion."

"What's Savate?" Steve asked Buck on the video screen.

"It's the French national sport of kick boxing. Originated with sailors out of Marseille; to pass the time on long voyages, they hung bags of rice or what not from the sail's spars and practiced striking and kicking them as they and the decks swayed in the ocean waves. Later, they incorporated the use of canes and sticks as weapons. Very lethal leg strikers. One of the legendary Savate fighters went to an open martial arts tournament in Asia. He was up against a kung-fu master who broke both his arms early in the bout. Rather than withdraw, this Savate champion stayed in the fight using only his legs. Kicked the crap out of the kung-fu master and won the bout by knockout."

Steve gave a low whistle of appreciation. "Man, that is one tough hombre. You think that this Arceneaux will be as tough?"

"From what I've seen of Savate champions that I've competed against in tournaments, you can count on it."

"Yep, he'll do, all-righty..." Steve bobbed his head in happy agreement.

The Colonel corralled the conversation and continued with his briefing. "I have also recruited an intelligence officer, who is also French. Major Phillipe La Barré of the General Directorate for External Security-DGSE, their external intelligence agency. He's the liaison officer between his agency to the DRM - Directorate of Military Intelligence, which coordinates intelligence between the military and civilian anti-terrorism agencies. In my opinion, Major La Barré is going to be a major asset to Operation Neptune."

"Why so?" asked Buck.

"As much as it pains my British heritage to say, the French are the best in the world at the intelligence game. All the French Resistance experience in World War II gave them a head start in the Cold War and they never looked back. That, plus the French have technology and commercial deals with countries that the British and

Americans boycott or embargo, and therefore, have access to societies not easily penetrable by the CIA or MI-6. Major La Barré's posting at the DRM has given him access to both the civilian and military intelligence they generate as well as being in position to exploit contacts of French agencies with other nations' intelligence services. Chances are that Major La Barré knows somebody that knows somebody we are interested in."

"Since the cornerstone to special operations is good intelligence, and the bullets will be flying on my end, it's good to know that we have the best intelligence available." Buck said purposefully leaving it at that. He knew that most plans that went to hell in a hand basket at first contact usually did so because intelligence was blind to a few critical facts. Even the best intelligence was about what happened yesterday. Then there were the totally random elements of life that could throw a monkey wrench into the best laid plans from out of nowhere.

The only other person not yet accounted for was their Information Technology Specialist, as the Colonel referred to the position. Buck just called it "The Hacker." "Do we have an E.T.A. on the computer hacker yet, Colonel?" Buck asked.

"I'll know more in the next day or two. Filling that slot is turning out to be devilishly more difficult than I originally thought. I have a target acquired, but it may be difficult to get him extracted from his current... uuhhm, position."

"I know you'll come through, Colonel."

"It's my specialty. Now, if you will excuse me, I need to go get Secretary-General McLaughlin updated on our progress. Good day," he said as he switched off the link. Of course, he knew full well what he meant by 'current position' was more like 'sitting in a Japanese prison cell' for computer crimes that listed longer than his arm.

According to the FBI's cyber-crime division, Yoshi Kazahiro was responsible for dozens of hacks into American corporation. What led to Yoshi's down fall was when he made the jump from hacking into corporate servers to attempting to hack the U.S. Air Force's communication network that controlled military satellites. He thought it would be a nice prank to retarget a few satellites onto at couple of generals to see how they liked being spied upon. Now, he was sitting in a holding cell of the Siatama Prefecture Police awaiting military transport to the U.S.

Well, it's time to get moving, David thought, *time to see if the Americans are going to be good to their word.* He gathered up his presentation materials and headed off to brief the Secretary-General. The briefing went well and, although Andrew made David work extra hard to justify the request of Yoshi Kazahiro, in the end he agreed to forward the request to Tobias Sterns at the White House. David could only imagine the ire that this would stir up with the Air Force's brass.

The next day, Sterns got back with permission to go speak to Kazahiro in Japan, but there were conditions, which was why David found himself two days later seated in an interrogation room in the Siatama Prefecture Police Center. Several minutes later, a cuffed and manacled prisoner wearing a prison jumpsuit of bright yellow shuffled in escorted by a black and white uniformed policeman that roughly shoved Yoshi Kazahiro into the seat.

David observed Yoshi for several minutes as Kazahiro tried his best to look indifferent to his surroundings or plight. His spiky yellow-white dyed hair, pierced ears laced with at least eight rings that David could count, seemed at odds with his quiet manner and inquisitive eyes. Just behind his veiled eyes, there was still a sense of fear. Fear was good. Fear could be manipulated.

"You must be a dangerous man," David started sardonically, conveying that he considered Kazahiro anything but dangerous. "From what I've read in your files, it seems to me that all we would have to do is cut off your fingers and be done with you, like pulling the tiger's teeth. There would be nothing left other than one sad pussycat."

"That's not what America does!" Kazahiro retorted. "I will be given an attorney, a fair trial and will be presumed to be innocent until proven guilty, which I won't. But even if they find me guilty, American laws prevent cruel punishment. They cannot cut off my fingers." Kazahiro was doing his best to sound like his superior understanding of American law would act as a shield against the fools, like David, they had sent to ferry him back to the United States.

"You're probably right about cutting off your fingers, since espionage only has two remedies: death or life imprisonment. But you are sadly mistaken on the rest of it. What you say is true, if you're an American citizen being tried in the U.S. criminal courts. But you boy-o, you're a foreign agent, a saboteur committing espionage. You'll never see the inside of a U.S. court. No, boy-o, you're bound for a military tribunal. And I can tell you, you try that 'presumed innocent until proven guilty' crap and you will find yourself having lots of painful accidents anytime one of the guards is around. You think that all those U.S. Military Police guarding prisoners at Abu Ghraib were just making naked pyramids of prisoners or letting dogs growl dangerously close to their man-hoods, do you? That's called 'containment' in the military. That's all the public knows about because pictures got out on the

Internet that the military could not retrieve. So they just copped a plea to what the public already knew about and offered up some little squadies to feed to the press. You know that the military is allowed to water board foreign detainees. And you certainly qualify as one. Do you think that you can stand up to water boarding day after day? Nearly being drowned several times a day? The bravest terrorist cries like a baby after just a day or two and tells the Americans everything they want to know. *Everything*.

"They are going to want to know what information you took from their satellites and who you gave it to. They are going to want to know everything about you, what your fantasies are, who you dream about, where you shop, when you quit wetting the bed... They will pry every little bit of humanity out of you before they are satisfied. If they damage you in the process, make you fear your own shadow, or unhinge your mind, well, so be it. They won't care. And anybody who does care about you will never get close enough to you to stop it." David paused to let that mental assault sink in. Of course, most of what he had said was untrue, but he was counting on the fact that Yoshi did not know that. It was standard prisoner interrogation technique: destabilize the subject by removing all items of familiarity and disrupting routines, including mental constructs, like beliefs in the process of law, to induce discomfort and decrease their ability to concentrate. It was an orchestrated attack on Maslow's hierarchical needs.

The little flicker of fear that David glimpsed behind Yoshi's indifferent posture had now been fanned by the picture that David had painted into a full-blown inferno of fear. "Who are you?" Yoshi asked, raw fear now just barely being contained below the surface.

"A man... but, more importantly for you, a man who

can change your present trajectory towards life behind prison walls in a foreign country, to one that might be more suited to your tastes."

Yoshi was highly suspicious, but the fear wrestling for control of mind would not let it go. "And just what kind of man might that be," Yoshi asked, "who can do all that?"

"My name is David Barrett; Colonel David Barrett, retired British Special Air Services. I work for U.N. Secretary-General Andrew McLaughlin. I am putting together a special project for Secretary-General McLaughlin, and I find myself in need of the services of a man like you."

"You do not work for the Americans? You are not here to take me to America?"

"Well, yes and no. All you need to know for now is that if you can impress me, I can have you released to my custody. If you continue to impress me, this nasty business about hacking into the American defense network could be forgotten. But, I'm a hard man to impress. And the second I quit being impressed by your efforts, you go right back to the Americans to finish what they've started. Do you understand your options? Remember, in the military justice system of the United States, there is no statute of limitations on sabotage or espionage."

"And just what would I be doing for you, Colonel?"

"I will need you to pull data from various data banks. Usually it will be given freely, but there may be times when some creativity will be necessary to obtain what is needed."

"And in return for this 'creativity,' what exactly will I get?"

"A nearly normal existence. You'll go to work every day, have your own place, get a paycheck."

"You said 'nearly normal existence.' What is the catch?

There must be something you are not telling me? There is no way the Americans are going to just let me go."

"True, the Americans insist on having you electronically monitored. You will have to wear an electronic ankle bracelet to let them know where you are at all times. And should you be tempted to try to tamper with or deactivate your ankle bracelet, there will be dire consequences, the least of which will be the termination of your employment for me. The Americans insisted that the ankle bracelet have countermeasures to immobilize you should there be any attempt to remove or disable it."

"What do you mean?"

"I don't know. They wouldn't tell me. They just said 'dire consequences' -- that's all I know."

Yoshi was silent while he tried to make sense of this new opportunity and ponder his possible future with a sinister ankle bracelet.

"Well, Mr. Kazahiro, you have a lot to think about. I will stop by tomorrow morning on my way out of town to get your answer." With that, he nodded to the guard that had been standing impassively the whole time, as he stood up. The guard opened the door, leaving Yoshi to ponder his future in the wake of David's cryptic offer of the future.

******

Good to his word, Colonel Barrett returned to the jail the next morning. After Yoshi settled into his seat, David began. "I hope you slept well on your decision. So, what will it be: yes or no?"

"I'll come to work for you on one condition..."

David stood smoothly without saying a word and turned for the door.

"Hey...don't you want to know what the condition is?"

Yoshi sputtered to David's back as Yoshi's escort reached to open the door for David. David took two strides and stopped in the open doorway before he pivoted to look at Yoshi.

"Wrong answer boy-o. It was a yes or no question, and you are in no position to make any demands. Have a nice life in prison, Yoshi." David turned and removed himself from the doorway, the door closing behind him.

"Wait, wait, please! The answer is yes. YES!"

Good, thought Colonel Barrett as he sauntered down the hallway to exit the building, *better to let him stew on the errors of his ways. It's better to start our relationship by instilling a little discipline in the ranks by firmly communicating who's in charge.* David would have Yoshi retrieved from Japan in a few days. In that time, he was sure that Yoshi would have utterly convinced himself that he lost his one and only chance to escape from his predicament. This would insure a much more compliant and grateful Yoshi Kazahiro when he showed up at U.N. Headquarters a few days hence.

22

Six months later...

The soldier dressed in the Buck Rogers uniform stepped up to the door and raised an odd looking gun at the doorknob. A small antenna rose from his small back pack and cords were routed up the center of his back to his helmet and to the weapon in his hands festooned with various sights and optics. He quickly sighted through the weapon's optics as he brought it to his shoulder, settled a green laser dot on his target, and pulled the trigger. The black AA-12 automatic assault shotgun emitted a roar as the slug of powdered metal from the door-breech round ejected out of the muzzle, delivering all of its kinetic energy into the door's locking mechanism and door jam. Both assemblies were blown to pieces before dispersing in a cloud of shimmering dust. The door was now free to swing on its hinges. The soldier moved smoothly to the side wall of the door handle, turning his back to the entrance before delivering a short powerful kick backwards to the lower half of the door. As the door flew open, the shooter continued his momentum to clear the entrance for the first of the entry team. As the remains of the door swung clear, the next man in line, standing to the hinge side, tossed in a flash-bang grenade. Two seconds later, a bolt of bright light and a thunderclap of sound erupted from the room. The headphones covering the assault team's ears not only magnified sound to make their hearing supersensitive, but it also automatically muted any noise in the decibel range that would be uncomfortable to the wearer, letting in only enough sound to register with the wearer and its direction.

Smoothly, the four-man team standing to the sides of the door slid into the room. The first man in carried a Kriss's .45 automatic submachine gun with a revolutionary design that eliminated recoil which was aimed at the centerline of the doorway as he entered, swinging his gun in an arc to the right. Finding no immediate targets, he moved to the right and followed the right hand wall into the room. The next man behind him flowed into the doorway, flipping his Kriss up to his shoulder from where he had been pointing it at the floor. He swung his weapon in an arc from center to left as he followed the left-hand wall of the room. The third man pressed into the room taking a right center search of room through his weapon's sights.

Suddenly, a figure appeared in the doorway and moved into the sector to the left of the third man who had just entered. In a few thousandths of a second, his Kriss's sights passed over center-mass of the pop up cardboard target, and he squeezed off two shots. Large holes a half-inch across appeared in the chest section of the "Bandito" target, as the team had started calling this particular type of cardboard target, even though this silhouette was of a man wearing a jallabeebs and kaffiyyet. Probably because he had two ammunition bandoleers strapped across his chest making a big X like some old western movie Mexican bandito.

Buck made a mental note from his perch on the catwalk above the room in the Kill House to remind Harold to utilize one shot on each target. Having been mortally wounded, the cardboard target flopped to the floor as the fourth man entered the room and immediately turned his back to the others to watch the doorway he had just entered. This was the breecher, who had busted open the door. He swung his AA-12 over his back and switched to his Kriss as the other had streamed into the room. The team cleared their sectors and formed up at the doorway into the next room where the target had appeared. Since the door was already opened, the breecher moved to his accustomed door-handle side and continued to give rear sector protection. The others quickly assembled and the lead man tossed in another flash-bang grenade from his tactical vest. Again, bright light sparked in the dimly lit indoor assault practice center accompanied by the thunderclap of overwhelming sound. As Strike Team Trident flowed into the next room, shots from an automatic weapon roared, and they were instantaneously met with the single shots from their Krisses. For this exercise, Buck had placed Steve on the catwalk above the next room with an AK-47 loaded with blanks with instructions to cut loose the instant he saw someone in the door. He was hoping that the added noise of Steve's gun would add another layer of confusion to an already chaotic environment. The disciplined reports of the Krisses instantaneously told Buck the team had found the terrorist cut outs and hostage dummies, and were dispatching the black hats. Three seconds later, all firing ceased. Buck walked along the catwalk to the other room to join Steve above the scene.

"How'd they do?" He asked as soon as he was close enough to Steve.

As Steve started to give his answer, they could hear the team below starting to check the hostages and then the tangoes' silhouettes for damage and injury. "Not bad for the second week of practicing with live ammunition," he replied. The Kill House's walls were lined with vertical strips of corded rubber compressed together to capture bullets fired in the room. "Single shots, center mass, with no misses. Time to get on target was acceptable this time, but will get better with each evolution. They're getting good."

Buck looked down at the team assembled below awaiting their next instructions. Buck decided to lighten the moment. "What's the matter, Harold? Aren't you getting enough beauty rest at night?" Buck asked ruefully. It had become common knowledge that the bachelors from England and Australia, Harold and Cooper, had been having a grand time chasing the single women of Norfolk, who found them to be new and exotic. It had also become common knowledge that the flashy smile and breezy attitude of Cooper was an instant hit with the ladies and that Harold was having to work three times as hard to stay competitive. "Are our American women proving to be too much for you?"

This comment was greeted with hoots from the other men, except Hubert, or Hu-Bear as the team had started calling him. He tended to be a little more reserved due to his married status. That and he considered Cooper and Harold to be novices when it came to the amorous pursuit of women, at which the French male was more talented, naturally.

"No problem with the women, sir. I have that 'squared away,' " Harold replied.

"Squared away?" Buck asked, "Where'd you learn that phrase? You been hanging out with Marines or something?"

"A few, yes."

"Watch out for the Marines," Steve warned the strike team, "they will get you drunk and steal your money."

"Well that explains a few things."

Buck turned his head to yell down to the strike team below, "Very good, guys. Let's do it again. And Harold, stay sharp, only one shot per target."

"Right, sir. I'll work on it. It's just the bloody SAS has conditioned me for years for double taps with nine millimeter. It's going to take a little bit longer to bugger out me trigger finger," he said holding up his right hand index finger and curling it a few times.

"Are you giving me some of that British SASs?" he asked, smiling at his double entendre. "Because it sounded like you were SASsing me."

"Oh, no, sir!" said an embarrassed and contrite soldier.

Rampage picked up on Buck's theme, "You're so damned cynical of anything not found in the British SAS manual..." He paused for a moment, thinking to himself, "Gentlemen, I think we have a new winner in the nickname contest. Henceforth, for your cynicism about things not S.A.S., I dub thee 'SAS-sy'." With that pronouncement, he made motions like he was knighting a kneeling knight.

"I like it!" hooted Coop, ganging up on his friend.

"Perfecte!" horned in Hu-bear.

Datan Ben-Moshe just smiled at the notion.

'Alright then," Buck called out, "let's take it from the top again, shall we?"

After three rotations the team was operating smoothly. Buck then changed the order of entry, changing their assignment also. He wanted every man to be able to perform every job without hesitation or instruction.

After two more hours of drilling, Buck was satisfied enough to call it quits and send them off to the showers. But before they departed, he reminded them that they would be practicing live boat launches and recoveries tomorrow. The following day they would practice ship assault boardings from the CRRC on a Coast Guard cutter that had been volunteered for practice during the day. After dark, they would be suited up in their scuba to practice submerged mission launches at sea, swim submerged to vessel in the Little Creek NAB harbor basin, and board her in the dark.

Strike Team Trident was coming together quickly. However, they had yet to receive and train with their own boat, the Mk. V.1 SOC. Tadhg was up in Maine right now with his crew, shaking down their boat. With luck and no major problems encountered, the boat and crew would be at Little Creek NAB by the end of the week. Their task was to ensure that the boat's propulsion, communications and navigation systems were complete and functional, making it seaworthy. They would use the five-hundred-plus-mile run from Maine to Little Creek to give the weapons systems a test run to identify any corrections needed. Identifying these problems now would also allow the maintenance crew of Naval Special Warfare Group Four to familiarize themselves with the U.N.'s boat and the special equipment it possessed. This was all designed to give them an opportunity to fix any problems that might be encountered before going operational.

Colonel Barrett informed him recently, that in keeping with the Roman nomenclature used in naming Project Neptune, the Mk.V.1 SOC was to be named the MV *Agrippa*, after Marcus Vipsanius Agrippa, the general who defeated Mark Anthony and Cleopatra VII's navy at the Battle of Actium, Greece, in 31 B.C. Evidently, Secretary-General McLaughlin liked the analogy that the faster, more maneuverable liburnians of Agrippa's fleet exemplified the strategy in which they were going to use their one vessel navy. Buck guessed these things were important when you only had one boat. However, at the Naval Academy, Buck had studied this battle and knew the outcome had more to do with the fact that Mark Anthony's quinqueremes galleys lost the battle because of a massive outbreak of malaria that had left his ships undermanned and hard to maneuver. Buck wasn't so sure that he could always count on nature to similarly handicap his opponents. He was also a little uneasy about naming his fighting platform after a general who won a push-over sea battle that was decided long before he showed up by a bunch of mosquitoes. And besides, naming a naval war vessel after an army general, like Agrippa, hit a dry spot in his throat every time he tried to swallow it. But, it was what his boss wanted.

Colonel Barrett was an Army man. So Buck understood that the he was not familiar with naval traditions, or more accurately, naval superstitions about the naming of vessels. Sailors felt more comfortable with vessels named after leaders or places with winning records and demonstrated fighting spirit. "Agrippa" was edging dangerously close to neither. True, Agrippa won several more battles to raise Octavia into the seat of Roman Caesar. But again, his victories had more to do with Mark Anthony's army deserting on the eve of battle rather than Agrippa's tactical or strategic brilliance. Still, Agrippa was lucky as all hell. Maybe that would be enough and rub off on his boat.

Buck made his way back to the office space that he shared with Steve for his daily progress update with Colonel Barrett. Today's call turned out to be a little different. After getting Colonel Barrett updated on the team's training, he was about to start their normal discussion on the training exercise regime when the Colonel interrupted, "Buck, we have received some intelligence on the pirates that killed Senator Templeton's nephew in the Red Sea early this year." Just then, Rampage walked into the room. Buck waved him over to his desk, motioning for him to be quiet, before reaching down and put the phone on speaker.

"Steve just walked in, Colonel and I wanted him to hear what you were saying, so I've got you on speaker."

"Alright…as I was saying, Major La Barré has developed some intelligence on the pirates that killed Senator Templeton's nephew. His name is Khalil, last name unknown. He was a small time crook that has developed a lucrative niche pirating vessels on their way to the Suez Canal off the coast of Sudan. It seems with each job he pulls, his boasts have grown bolder. He has used his ill-gotten gains and inculcated himself in a little fishing village called Hayiva in the Sudan. He's also captured a new prize since his attack on the ocean liner that he killed Ken Hamilton on. He now has a small coastal jump freighter. His new *modus operandi* is to launch small, fast boats from his freighter to pursue and subdue larger boats with RPG and automatic weapons fire. The pirates board and stop the ships and then the freighter comes alongside where they force the crew of the captured ship to off-load their cargo onto the jump freighter.

"According to Major La Barré, it would have been a lot more difficult to find who killed Ken Hamilton if they had not gotten so big and bold in their attacks, given the very limited number of intelligence contacts in that part of the Sudan. Had they stayed small time, we might never have known who did this.

"Now that we know the who and where, how much longer until you are ready to go?"

"I need at least three weeks more before we will be ready," Buck replied. "We don't even have Strike Force

Trident's Mk V.1 SOC, the *Agrippa*, yet. As you know, it's still in Maine right now with Tadhg and his crew doing sea trials and acceptance. Three weeks is assuming that there aren't any major problems. If there are, it will take longer. It's just too hard to call with any precision without having my hands on the craft yet. The last thing that we want to do is rush this part of the operations. If we rush into action with our main battle craft not yet fully tested, we could get ourselves into a world of hurt packing up and shipping it half a globe away from our support technicians when it's not ready. I don't want our first mission to be a disaster. Think Eagle One in Iran when President Carter made a half-assed attempt to rescue American hostages from the U.S. Embassy. That failed because they rushed the operation and no one thought about the effects of sand on helicopter operations. It was a cluster from the git-go.

"This job is risky enough without compounding risk by going into battle with an untested, unproven weapons system like our version of the Mk. V.1 SOC. And I'm just looking at it from strictly an operational standpoint. If it goes badly because we rushed it, you have a better understanding than I do about the political ramifications of failure or casualties."

"We may not have the luxury of time, Buck," The Colonel countered with an air of fatalism. "We both know that in intelligence and covert ops, everything is in a constant state of flux. We know where our target is now, but that can change in the blink of an eye. We have to strike when we know enough variables to make a cohesive plan. To study the situation *ad nauseum* would shrink our windows of opportunity. It's a delicate balance between blundering into a situation or taking a calculated risk. Having said that, I think we can only hold off for so long –

maybe a couple of weeks, at most. Plan on making a strike and organize your training schedule accordingly."

"Beg your pardon, Colonel," Steve interjected. "But how exactly do we train for a strike when we don't know if we will be executing a ship-on-ship engagement, a ship assault or a land assault?"

"Good question, Steve," David replied with a sigh, "one for which I do not have an answer at this moment. Major La Barré and I will continue to develop intelligence about this Khalil. As we learn more, I'll be putting together a strike plan based on available assets in the area of operation. A lot will depend on how we'll we get your boat to the battle scene and what assets the Americans can put in place for us. In the meantime, the best thing for you to do is get the *Agrippa* and Strike Force Trident working as smoothly together as time will allow. Any further questions?"

When there were none, "Good," said Colonel Barrett. "I will keep you appraised as we put together the strike plan to help guide your preparations and allow you to smooth out the wrinkles as we go. Until tomorrow...out." And then there was an audible click as the line was disconnected.

Buck pushed back from the desk and turned to Rampage behind him. "It looks like we're going to have to push our training schedule to the limit. We are going to have to train and test nonstop until we are told to go. I want you to go over to the Spec Warfare Group Four maintenance depot and talk to the commanding officer. Let him know what's coming his way. I'll contact Tadhg and let him know he need to step up his testing and hightail it back here."

"Orders are orders, Buck. But this isn't making me feel all warm and fuzzy. I hope we can get the *Agrippa* ship-shape enough to complete the mission."

"And not get ourselves killed doing it." Buck finished the thought for him. "I know, Rampage, I hope so, too."

23

The *Agrippa* arrived in the small hours of Friday morning and moored at the maintenance dock of Special Warfare Group Four. The commanding officer of the boat repair division had his techs waiting. They immediately inspected the propulsion and power plants for any unusual wear after the long shakedown cruise from the boatyard in Maine. Most of the power plant and propulsion were either similar or identical to the standard Mk. V SOCs the SEALs operated, so, all in all, the boat needed very little. There were a few glitches with one of the radios and the backup radar scope which were replaced and couple of seals that also needed to be replaced.

Excited, Buck rolled up to the dock at 0700 hours for his first look at his fleet's lone thoroughbred. The U.N.'s flag hung from the stern flagpole and he was surprised to see a cluster of SEALs, maintenance workers and SWCC crew members from other boats gathered dockside in front of the *Agrippa*. As he approached the cluster, he heard a lot of admiring hoots and excited discoveries as crewmen noted some of the many improvements they had made to the boat. He started to muscle his way through the crowd to the midship gangplank. His crew was expected dockside at 0800 hour to start loading the ammo and supplies stacked on the dock near the front of the boat. It was his crew's responsibility to refill the fuel and water tanks, and stock their own supplies. For the most part, the people dockside ignored him, enthralled with the glistening, new war boat.

Buck made it two steps up the plank when he heard a familiar voice from the throng call out his name. He turned to see Lieutenant Commander Tucker Risley, the Executive Officer of Special Warfare Group Four standing in the front row smiling at him. The Lieutenant Commander had been a SOC skipper back when he was commanding his own Mk. 1.

"Jeez, Buck! I know your mission is to take down pirates, but holy cow! You're loaded for bear with this baby. It looks like you could take on a small armada."

"The price of going into the lion's den with no back-up. Just being a good Boy Scout and being prepared."

"Why don't you give me a tour of your new ride?" he asked.

Buck hung his head and thought about it for a moment, then he looked back at Tucker, "Hell, why not? I haven't even seen her myself, yet, either. We'll check her out together. Come on aboard."

Tucker eagerly elbowed his way through the crowd, following Buck up the ramp. At the top, Buck paused and yelled at the deckhouse, "Tadhg, coming aboard." After waiting a few seconds for Tadhg to appear, he took a tentative step onto the deck followed by Tucker. Just then, Tadhg appeared in his Royal Navy dress blue uniform.

"Good morning, Tadhg! I've come to inspect your new command."

"Good morning, Buck!" Tadhg called back with as much enthusiasm. He was obviously very proud of his new boat, but he was working hard at acting nonchalant.

"This is a friend of mine, Lieutenant Commander Tucker Risley. Have you met before?" Buck offered by way of introduction as Tadhg nodded at his guest.

"Yes, we've met before on several occasions."

"Oh good!" Buck replied, "I've asked him to join me for my first inspection of the *Agrippa*. I figured the best way to answer all the questions from the lookie-loos on the dock was to take one of their own, show him around, and then feed him back to the pack."

"Good idea."

Tucker wasted no time firing off his first question.

"I could see, standing from the dock that the boat's hull is made out of something different than our Mk V.1. What is it?"

"Well, the hull is made out of identical materials as your Makos."

"The hull is made of the same number of layers of carbon fiber, a foam core and an outer layer of Kevlar." Mako was the nickname the Navy crews had started calling their new Mk V.1 SOC variant because the newly re-designed raked bow gave the boat a more sinister look and because of the way the new hull form sliced through the water. "But because our boats only have to carry six members of our Strike team and two CRRC instead of the sixteen SEALs and four CRRCs that your boats carry, we used the weight savings to put on lightweight armor plating on the hull sides and deckhouse. We use the same armor system that went into the U.S. Marine's new Expeditionary Fighting Vehicle. This armor is strong enough to defeat shaped charged rounds and calibers up to 25mm. We're about the same weight, fully loaded with armor, as your Mako.

"Of course we modified the hull to improve performance. We added three rows of serrations in the planing section of hull. These saw-tooths create low pressure zones in the water that pull air in through simple ducting from the deck and release it through a series of holes on the back of the serrations. The result is the hull rides on a curtain of bubbles that significantly reduces water surface tension and drag adding ten to twelve knots to our top end speed and less fuel consumption at intermediate speeds.

"We also added an L-shaped aluminum brackets at the vertical juncture of the side walls and the hull's planing surface. These act like the turning skags on a hydroplane racer reducing lateral drift when turning. On the upper third of the speed register, it helps decrease turning radiuses by thirty-eight percent.

"If you'll step this way, I'll show you the new weapons stations on the back deck." Tadhg walked over to the weapons station set close to the end of the wheelhouse on the side away from the dock and pulled a cover off the station.

"Whoa, that is some seriously nasty firepower!" Tucker exclaimed, ignoring the oohs and aahs from the gallery on the dock as he admired the weapons sitting atop the chest-high swivel mount.

"This is one of four identical gun stations mounted on the rear deck, just like yours. But unlike yours, which mount either a M2 .50 caliber BFG or Mk. 19 40mm grenade launcher, we mount both on every station. We have a standard M2 .50 cal., but mounted next to it is the new M307 25mm grenade launcher. Although this grenade launcher is smaller in diameter, it has a higher rate fire of around three hundred rounds per minute versus the Mk. 19's forty sustained rounds per minute. In addition, the M307 has the ability for the operator to set the grenades to detonate on contact or at a predetermined distance. This way, if combatants are hiding behind a wall or ship's gunwale, the gunner can fire a grenade over the wall or blast an opening and set follow-on rounds to explode as it passes over the enemy positions. Or, it can be sent through a window to take out targets hiding to the sides. The launcher uses a laser to determine the range and then it counts the number of rotations of spin imparted by the barrel's grooves to determine distance. The gunner can adjust detonation in one-yard increments, plus or minus. These mounts also have a bore sight feature that allows both weapons to be fired simultaneously at targets up to two hundred yards. After that, the trajectories diverge too far to put both munitions accurately on target.

"In between the two weapons is the sighting system," Tadhg said resting his hand on a small box with a piece of glass mounted on top that raked back towards the gunner at a forty-five degree angle. "This is like a fighter plane's Heads-Up Display. The gunner looks through the glass and the corrected weapon's pipper is projected up from the box and appears to float in his line of sight.   The system uses the M307's range finding laser and corrects for projectile drop depending on the weapon selected. Our Strike team is equipped with the Land Warrior System, which is tied into the targeting system. Each member of the strike team wears a transponder that identifies his position to the gunner. This allows for closer fire support. Or the strike team member can use a laser designator, like a pointer to show the gunner where to lay down fire. And this down below," he said pointing to a metal box, "is the gyroscopic stabilizing system. When the trigger is pulled, it engages the stabilizers to hold the gun steady on target. The gunner can make minor changes, but the guns won't swing wildly if the boat has to perform hard maneuvers during firing. The whole system is designed to limit the possibility of friendly fire casualties while reducing collateral damage and deaths."

Tucker whistled appreciatively. "What about these?" He said toeing one of the ten-foot long tubes that were positioned under the cable railing system on the back deck between each of the weapons mounts on either side.

"Oh those are a little surprise we cooked up out of bits and pieces of concept weapons from various labs. It's an EMP Torpedo. Rather than have an exploding warhead, it is designed to stop pirates from using captives as shields and running a hijacked ship into a safe harbor where there are more civilians. It does this by setting off a small EMP pulse when it passes under a ship. The EMP will disable any integrated circuits in the propulsion plant and fry any computer navigation equipment and communications."

Buck jumped into the conversation, "It is the U.N.'s policy that the best option is to not let pirates take their prize and captives into built-up urban ports where, if we have to fight them, there's a much greater chance of collateral damage and civilian death or injury. When we can, and especially if there are hostages involved, we want to take them on, *mano a mano*, on the open seas where we have the advantage. By disabling communications and propulsion, we isolate them and control the environment, giving us every advantage in negotiations or action."

Now it was Tadhg's turn to pick up the explanation.

"Of course, this weapon system will be useless against any older vessels where the valves and systems are run manually. But pirates are going after the newer, 'richer' vessels because that's where the money is. One of the axioms of pirating is that 'The fattest pirate has the fastest ship,' meaning it's hard to eat if your boat is too slow to catch your prey. Since the newer, faster vessels tend to be reliant upon silicon chip technology to improve performance, they're vulnerable to EMP attack. Moving on...

"This," Tadhg said, pointing to a locker set on the back wall of the wheelhouse with a waist-high padded, almost-circular stanchion that connected to the deck by three poles, "is the FIM-92 Stinger handheld anti-air missile launching station. The missiles are in that locker," he said pointing to one against the back wall. "The operator can slip into this station and lean against the rails to stabilize himself for firing."

"As you can see, one of the major departures from the standard Mk. V is the deckhouse structure. Whereas the models you use have a semi-enclosed structure around the bridge with open back to the deck that can be covered by a pole and canvass assembly, ours is one armored, fully-inclosed structure. The wheelhouse contours are sloped to be non-reflective to radar and any vertical surfaces, like the door, are covered in RAM, Radar Absorbent Material, and the edges are irregular to diffuse radar energy." He walked into the door at the rear of the deckhouse and held the door open for Buck and Tucker. As they entered, they saw that the door's edges were flush and nearly perfectly set into the wall to make a seamless bulkhead, like an F-22's compartment doors and canopy.

When everyone was inside the spacious room, Tadhg resumed his tour. "This is the strike team ready room where the mission gear is stored and where they ride when not working on deck or manning the weapons stations." The walls of the room had weapons and ammo lockers along front wall and equipment and supplies in lockers along the back wall. There were several computer stations and a small table for briefing. The men had gear lockers on the other side of the rear door where their body armor, Land Warrior gear, and combat harnesses were stowed during transit. A large plasma screen was fixed to the forward bulkhead to facilitate briefing data presentation and show any number of communications or feeds from the various systems on board. But what really caught Tucker's eye were the eight reclining chairs, each set on a thick pole arranged in the center of the space, facing the forward bulkhead.

"What kinda chaise are these?" he said walking over and rubbing his hand along the top edge of one of the chairs.

"They're reclined thirty degrees, like the seat in an F-16 Fighting Falcon. Because it could take hours of transit time before we are on station, our strike team members can relax before going into battle. As you well know, these boats slam up and down, even in light seas. The new Mako's design helps reduce the slamming, or vertical climb in tech speak, but it doesn't eliminate it. A strike team member sitting in a regular chair would expend tremendous amounts of energy just maintaining their upright position. Every time the boat hits bottom, he has to flex his muscle in his chest, arms, neck and stomach to decelerate his body and internal organs. It's like doing sit-ups for hours. Sure, our Mako can deliver the strike team on location, but what good is it if they're exhausted. The good engineers at Lockheed Martin did a lot of design research into seat configurations that allowed fighter pilots to pull continuous nine-G turns in the F-16, so we just borrowed the concept for our seats. You can ride in these seats all day and feel refreshed and relaxed. They even have flip up sea rails to hold you in, in case you want to sleep while we travel instead of using the seat harnesses.

"In addition, the mounting base of each chair has a shock absorber system of electronically controlled magnets that act on the iron particles suspended in oils in the column. You just set the digital control to your body weight," he demonstrated by punching in numbers on a keypad with a digital LCD screen on the side of the chair, "and the system will digitally control and optimize the shock absorbing characteristics.

"I tried it on the run down here from the boatyard," he said leaning in conspiratorially. "Had to test all the boat systems, you know. Slept like a baby. The best sleep I've ever had."

"Wow! Better not let our SEALs see these things, or there'll be no stopping their whining," Tucker said, winking at Buck, "You know what sissies SEALs can be."

"Let me show you the cockpit," Tadhg said as he disappeared through the door in the forward bulkhead. Tucker followed and Buck was right behind him. Buck was looking down to ensure his foot cleared the knee-knocker threshold when he ran into Tucker's back, who had stopped in the doorway.

"Jumping GEE-hos-e-phat!! Is this the bridge of the Starship *Enterprise*, or what?!" was all Tucker could say.

"Move over, Tucker, and let me in. I wanna see, too," Buck said as he gently shoved his friend to get him moving.

Buck slid into the doorway and was astounded by what he saw, even though he had helped design the boat.

There were three chairs just like in the strike team room, but these had curved control panels that rotated out of the way to enter the seat. Each control panel had various knobs and switches, plus two flat-screen monitors. The seats on the right and left had arm rests with joysticks on the right plumaged with an assortment of buttons, switches and coolie hat controllers mounted on it. The left armrests had what appeared to be a throttle levers on it similarly adorned with switches, buttons and hat controllers.

Tadhg had already planted himself in the right-hand seat, pulled up his control panel and was lowering the left armrest into place. "Yes, I guess it would appear a bit hi-tech after training in your boats," Tadhg said in typical British understatement.

"That's putting it mildly," Tucker responded, the awe evident in his voice.

"Well, as you can see, we have the same sort of seat as the ready room except I have rudder control on the right armrest with a computer mouse next to it, throttle, and trim control on the left. The computer screens are all touch-screen and can be configured to present any combination of data, controls, weapons systems, navigation or communication that the boat has. This," he said tapping his arm rest, "is the skipper's chair; the one on the other side is for the navigator/weapons systems officer's and the middle chair is for Buck when he is on the bridge or the engineer, who can monitor the power plants from his chair. The ship's propulsion system is all automated, which lets us run with just a three-man crew instead of the normal complement of five. We use the same 2285 HP MTU 12V396 TE94 diesel engines and KaMeWa K50S water-jets that are in your Mk. Vs, but with one little difference. That's this little red button here," he said, pointing to the red button under his thumb on the throttle control T-bar on the left armrest. "This is for the...what did you call it Buck? The kicker..."

"Kick-a-poo juice," Buck answered, smiling.

"The what?" Tucker was confused by their inside joke.

"It's for an emergency engine boost system we borrowed from truck hot-rodders," Buck continued. "When you press that button, two armor-protected five gallon propane tanks inject propane into the engines intake manifold. We get an instant twenty percent increase in power. Great for high speed get a ways or when you really need a hole shot to get out of bad situation."

"You guys have way too much candy, here," Tucker said with mock disapproval.

"But wait, there's more," Buck said, really enjoying the honest envy of his friend. "Tadhg, if you'll continue..."

"Yessir. As you've probably already seen, this boat comes equipped with a Bushmaster 25mm auto cannon in a small, remote turret on the foredeck. This is the newest model that is duel feed. It has two different feed routes so that the weapons officer can select between HE and AP munitions. You've probably also seen the GAU-134D mini gun and .50 cal. BFM in the turret built on to the roof of the deckhouse. Just like our aft mounted weapons station, these weapons are tied into an optical system that gives us infrared and low light visibility targeting. Those weapons systems are tied into the computer consoles. All the weapons officer has to do is to move his screen cursor with his mouse in fire mode and the weapon's fire follows the track. So he can center the cursor on a target for a short burst and the computer fire control will continue to track that target no matter what maneuvers the *Agrippa* takes, or he can move the cursor around to hose down an area.

"But what you may not have seen in the upper turret is the coil gun. We had to have the entire deckhouse structure reinforced to take the recoil."

"A coil gun? What's that? I've never heard of that," Tucker said, again befuddled by all the advanced technology.

"Like you said," Buck fixed his friend with a benign grin, "is this the starship *Enterprise*'s bridge or what?" A coil gun is the smaller cousin of a rail gun." Buck looked at Tucker who still had a blank look on his face denoting that he still was not following. "A Coil Gun and its bigger cousin, the Rail Gun, are hyper-velocity kinetic weapons. It shoots round aerodynamic ferrous iron projectile called a 'Pig', propelled by computer controlled pulsing magnets. It pretty much atomizes everything it hits including air. It scoots through the air so fast that the metal pig would melt if it didn't have a ceramic nose cone and coating. With the coil gun, we can go toe to toe with an older class destroyer or a newer frigate. We can even shoot down incoming sea-skimming missiles or jet aircraft because the trajectory is so flat and instantaneous.

"The only drawback is its rate of fire; the system requires its own generator and a bank of huge capacitors that have to be charged for every shot. All that extra gear is in the engine room."

"What is its rate of fire?" Tucker asked

"It takes forty-five seconds for each charge if we're hitting it with all the *Agrippa's* electricity generators. Normal charge is a minute and a half. The problem is heat. If you hit the capacitors with a lot of amps, they'll heat up quickly if you quick charge them. If you do that too many times without letting the capacitors cool down though, you'll melt them down.

"How many quick charges can it take without melting?"

"Theoretically? Five." Buck answered. "But it's never been done. This is hot out of the weapons laboratories; and you know how that works. They play it safe and mathematically calculate the breaking point. They never test something until it breaks because they don't want to admit any limitations or liabilities. They leave that kind of testing to the military."

"Well, how long can it stay charged before you have to fire it? I mean, it's not like a shell you put in a cannon that can stay cocked forever, is it?"

"That's another limitation of the system; you can only hold the charge for about ten minutes. The engineers who designed it had a hi-tech term for this problem: leakage. The high volume capacitors are short-term storage devices designed more for instantaneous dumps of their contents rather than long term storage. After ten minutes, they start to leak amps, and that creates…"

"Let me guess," Tucker jumped in, "heat."

"You guessed it. The longer you wait, the hotter they get and the less charge they hold, degrading the weapon's effectiveness. Not to mention that little melt down thing we just talked about."

"So why have it, Buck? If it's so limited, why mess with it at all?" Tucker asked, considering all the negatives he had just been told.

"Because it's a deal breaker, Tucker. With that weapon, we can stand and fight with anything short of a cruiser. At least long enough for us for us to use the *Agrippa's* speed, maneuverability and kick-a-poo juice to break and run. Not too shabby for an eighty-two foot vessel."

"Yeah, not bad for a craft originally designed for low and medium patrol threat environments and SEAL taxi service," Tucker had to agree.

Tadhg continued the tour for Tucker into the rest of the boat's spaces. Buck let them go on ahead. He wanted a few minutes' time on the bridge to get a feel for her. He also realized that he was now thinking of the *Agrippa* as a 'she'.

His reverie was broken as he heard Tadhg returning, his voice approaching, explaining a technical detail to Tucker "…with the air-gel insulation in the engine room, it completely masks our heat signature from thermally targeted weapons. And the material adds almost zero weight to the boat. The insulation weight for the entire engine room was less than five pounds." He finished as they arrived at the bridge.

"With the *Agrippa's* low profile, her stealth design properties of the boat and the radar absorbent material covering the boat, it would be extremely difficult for a radar guided weapons system to get a lock on us. We would force an opponent into bore sight shooting to target us. And with our speed and maneuverability, the *Agrippa* is a very, very hard target to hit. We even have sensors on the hull to let us know if we're being painted by laser designators. If we are, we go 'old school' and lay down a smokescreen. It's hard to paint something you can't see.

"All these upgrades have made this a stout, nimble, hard hitting fighting ship. So much so, that the manufacturer has designated this as a different class of patrol boat; they're calling it the Mk. V.2, Destrier Class patrol boat; after the battle horses used by medieval knights. But we just call it the Super Mako."

"Buck, this is one hellacious fighting boat you've got here," Tucker nearly shouted, his enthusiasm brimming. "When I heard that you were going to work for the U.N., I thought that you had lost your mind working for those, those..." he searched for the right word, "those politicians," he finally concluded. He spat out the word 'politician' with enough pejorative venom dripping off of it to let Buck know what he really thought. "But now it seems you were smarter than the rest of us..." his voice trailed off, his eyes fixed on something on the bulkhead. "What's that? Is that what I think it is?" he said nearly shouting, his finger stabbing the air in front of him.

Buck followed his gaze, although he already had a good idea of what Tucker was so excited about. *Yep,* Buck thought, *just what I thought.*

"Oh that," Buck started lamely, "that was a little something I had the yard add at the last minute."

"Those are fish finders!" Tucker was still stabbing his finger at them. Sure enough, there were three black framed screens of commercial fish finders, low powered sonar used by fishermen to spot fish.

"No, those are swimmer recover alert devices," Buck started to counter. "We can't use our regular sonar to locate swimmers in underwater operations because the acoustic sound footprint may attract the wrong kind of attention, and besides, the signal strength of the acoustic ping could injure a diver in the water if he was too near."

Buck watched Tucker to see if he was going to buy this story completely. It was true, he had originally wanted them to be used in diver recovery, but a millisecond later he also realized that the devices also had other uses. Like for instance, if he just happened to be in some exotic locale, he could vary the diet for the crew with some fresh fish, if circumstances weren't too pressing.

Buck could not hold his grin in any longer, and slowly it leaked to his face.

"I knew it! I knew it!" Tucker exclaimed, "You're a fishing fool. You've got the world's only state of the art, high speed, heavily armed, armored fishing yacht. Thaaat's jussst beautiful. Flippin' beautiful." His friend shook his head and headed for the door, mumbling.

Buck watched him go and could still hear him mumbling as the door closed behind him.

"How is she, Tadhg? Is she ready to go?" he asked now that it was just the two of them.

"Other than the things that you already know about, she's ready."

"No, I'm asking you how she feels to you as her skipper. Is she ready to fight yet? Just because everything is working it doesn't mean she's ready to go into harm's way."

"You're right. And no, we're not ready to fight yet. I'm still getting used to all the new technology, as are Grels and Lenz. We are still thinking our way through the operations, rather than reacting and executing. That will only come with time and repetition."

"I'm not sure how much time I can give you. That's one of the reasons I came down early this morning; I wanted to get you up to speed on some developments. Major La Barré has a line on the pirates that killed Senator Templeton's nephew, Ken Hamilton. The Colonel wants to strike while we know where they are."

"How much time are we talking about, Buck?"

"Two, maybe, three weeks, tops."

"That's not much time, Buck. You know that it takes time to really shake down a vessel and crew. Not every fault is immediately apparent. The *Agrippa* needs to be worked and worked hard before we will truly know that everything is as it should be."

"I agree. That's why the strike force will be training around the clock until we get the order to go. All we can do is to try our hardest to be prepared when it's time to go and know that there is always something that will go awry. When it does, we'll just improvise.

"Yessir."

"Now, how about showing me the rest of her?"

24

"We ready to get this puppy on the road?" Rampage shouted across the warehouse as he strode through the roll-up industrial door that served as Buck's garage door.

"Still waiting for the rest of the crew to show up," Buck yelled back from the porch of his two story craftsmen styled house built into the west wall of the warehouse that he called home. He started down the steps and cut across his 'front lawn', a large remnant of carpet that had been placed in front of his house. Scattered around the 'lawn' were couches, recliners and chairs all aimed at the big screen that anchored one end of the carpet. Beyond the big screen lay a stack of lumber that was the object, in part, of today's activities. It was this pile of lumber Buck was headed for.

Just as Rampage joined Buck at the lumber, another voice floated across the room, "Oy, mates! Let's get crackin'!" Cooper Randall and Harold Brisbane strolled through the door. As usual, a broad smile stretched across the effervescent Australian's face while his partner in crime, Harold Brisbane, maintained his typical British reserve.

"The sooner we get this done, the sooner we can get about the proper business of tipping a pint," chimed in Harold.

"Good call, mate." Coop congratulated his partner on his brilliant deductive reasoning as they wended their way through the machinery of Buck's automotive bay section of the warehouse. A red Porsche was up on the two post lift. "How's the red rocket coming?" he yelled at Buck.

"Coming along, coming along...I figure I'll have it done in another day or two. Just some minor finishing touches to the exhaust system and it'll be ready for a test spin."

"I want a ride in it when you do," Coop demanded, coming to a halt in front of Buck and Rampage.

"Me, too," demanded Sassy.

"Considering all the work you've done around here, putting the house together, it's the least I can do," answered Buck. "Maybe you guys can work as my pit crew when I take it racing?"

"Would this involve the consumption of aqueous, wheat-based alcoholic beverages in any manner?" inquired Sassy as they gathered with Buck and Rampage at a stack of lumber.

"Sure, yah, after the races usually; sometimes champagne when we grace the winner's circle. Why, is that important to you?" Buck asked in mock seriousness, knowing full well his two sergeants' thirst and their endless search for their last beer.

Just then, their banter was interrupted by the sound of more arrivals through the door. The sound of a little girl's giggle and squeal made the men's heads turn to the entrance. All they could see were the upper torsos of Hubert, his wife Sabine, and Datan, but they could tell that they were clucking after their two little girls. This was confirmed an instant later.

"Giselle, Bernadette!" Sabine scolded, "Stay away from those machines. You'll get your dresses dirty." Buck watched as Sabine stooped to grab one of the girls, while Hubert made a grab for the other. Datan stood slightly behind with a bemused, knowing smile on his face. With their daughters corralled, the party started to cross the warehouse. Hu-Bear was attempting to chastise the daughter in his arms, but it was plain that the French warrior's heart was not into it.

The French family and the Israeli soldier made their way across until the oldest girl, Giselle, in her mother's arms, spied Buck. "Uncle Buck!" She cried, flinging out her arms in the universal child's language that says 'hold me.'

"Hi, sweetie!" Buck called, stepping forward to scoop the girl out of her mother's arms. "How's my little cabbage? Have you been behaving your mother like I've told you?" Buck asked, all smiles.

"Yes," she replied in blue, wide-eyed seriousness that only a five year old could manage. Buck had embraced the Frenchman's family as a surrogate to his own. Hubert, over whispered pillow talk, had told his wife of Buck's misfortune, so she was glad to see the American's adoption of her daughters, sharing them without reservation.

"Good, because your Uncle Buck would be very sad if you were not being a good girl." Then he flashed Sabine a smile, his eyes giving her a warm welcome to his home. "I'm glad you all could make it."

"It ez my pleasure," the petite, stylish blond said. "You know, of course, my daughters adore you. When Giselle heard we were coming to see you, she put on her best dress for you."

"I did not, mommy," the little girl contradicted from Buck's arms.

Buck smiled as he handed the girl back to her mother before scooping the youngest daughter from her dad's arms. "And how about you, Bernadette? Did you put on your best dress for Uncle Buck?"

"Yes," she said, wrapping her arms around his neck and laying her head on his shoulder.

Turning to the slightly balding, sandy haired Hu-Bear and the dark eyed, intense Datan, Buck informed them, "We're still waiting for the Navy to show up."

As if on cue, another group of people appeared in the doorway, announcing their presence with a shout of "Ahoy! Permission to come aboard?"

Buck handed Bernadette back to her father before waving in the crew of the *Agrippa* through the door. Tadhg Ramsden led his crew through door followed by Lenz Snyder and his wife, Greta. Grels Persson was still a bit of an enigma to Buck. Always precise and thorough, the quiet Swede had not shown much of his personality beyond their professional dealings during training operations. Perhaps he just needed more time to open up, Buck thought as he watched them approach. And that's what today's activities were supposed to encourage. The team had been training relentlessly for weeks now, and Buck sensed he needed to change the tempo and shift gears lest he dull the razor's edge of performance they had worked up to.

Lenz on the other hand, was everything he seemed to be. The big, rough handed former German farm boy was more comfortable with machines than he was with people. Nearing the end of his naval career, he was ingrained with the distance between the enlisted ranks and the officer corp. The close camaraderie and informality of rank that Special Forces units bred and encouraged was something that the Chief Petty Officer was having difficulty adopting, and seeing his unease at being in the home of a superior officer was obvious.

His wife, Greta, was altogether a different matter. Nothing much fazed the German country girl. Without much commotion or notice, really, she had adopted the entire strike force as her extended family and tended to see them all, including Buck, as long lost sons. She ministered to their needs, showing up when someone was injured in training to ensure that medicine was taken, sleep was procured, and doctor's orders were obeyed. Usually she left with an armful of laundry needing mending, and only after she had cleaned the apartment and straightened out the kitchen. She did this regardless of the person's rank.

All in all, Buck was really amazed at how all the different personalities, cultures, ages and lifestyles had melded into a superbly performing team. The American leadership provided an open forum, the Australian and British soldiers brought comic relief and the energy of the youth; Datan the philosopher kept everything in perspective for everyone. Hubert and his family kept everyone grounded in reality. Lenz and his wife ministered to their needs, mechanical and otherwise. Tadhg's role as a self-effacing commander kept any rivalry from developing between the soldiers and the marine contingent. It was only a matter of time before Grels stopped worrying about being perfect and found his place, and Lenz would find his own comfort zone eventually and relax, he was sure.

Everyone was now gathered in the vicinity of the stack of the lumber beyond the wood working section of the warehouse.

"Can I have your attention, everyone?!" Buck yelled over their heads as he jumped up on the pile of timbers. "Thank you everyone for coming today. I thought it would be a good idea to change up the pace of our training with little diversion, so I decided to introduce you all to two great American traditions.

"It is an American tradition for neighbors to come together for a barn raising. We aren't exactly raising a barn today, but this indoor gun range will fit the purpose since this is all about being neighborly and helping with a heavy project and getting together with family."

"What's the other tradition?" called out Coop.

"I'm glad you asked," a broad smiled creased Buck's face, "the other American custom we will explore today is our tradition of mixing guns and alcohol."

The Australian busted out laughing and hooting. The Europeans on the other hand, were far more tempered in their response. Buck's little joke served only to reinforce their continental view that all Americans were closet cowboys.

Buck saw their discomfort and smiled inwardly as he continued. "For today's festivities, I have brewed a keg of bitters for you, Harold; Lenz and whoever else, I've brewed a fine, crisp ale. In the third tap I brewed a root beer for the non-drinkers," he said with a nod at Datan.

"Now, who has any carpentry skills?"

Cooper, Rampage and Grels raised their hands.

"Good, you three with will be with me; we'll build the shooting shack. The rest of you go with Lenz. I'm putting him in charge of building the backstop." He gesticulated to a mound of tires and sand a hundred yards away towards the end of the warehouse. "First, I want to meet with Lenz and his crew. Ladies, if you will adjourn to the house-- as usual feel free to use anything you want. My home is your home. Okay?"

The women nodded and shuffled off with the children in tow.

Buck met briefly with Lenz and his crew explaining how the downrange backstop was to go together before turning them loose. When he was finished, they shuffled off into the distance and started to organize themselves for their tasks.

Then he turned to his crew and introduced a sketch he had made of the structure they were going to build, pointing out its key features. Then he assigned specific tasks after which he took a few minutes to collect all the tools they would need. In the distance, he could see Lenz already had his crew erecting columns of cabled-together used tires in preparation for them to be filled with sand.

About noon, the women brought out a delicious and hardy potato soup with sandwiches. After a forty-five minute repast, they started again.

By mid afternoon, the barriers were complete and Lenz's crew joined Buck in finishing the shooting house. An hour later, they all stood back and admired their handy work.

The indoor shooting range consisted of a hundred yard line for rifles and a twenty-five yard range for handguns. The shooting house was constructed of heavy railroad ties stacked so they could absorb any accidental discharges so the walls and roof of the warehouse were safe. Firing slits in the front wall allowed firing only in the direction of the backstops. A heavy wood projection in front of the firing slits also prevented shooters from shooting over the backstops by limiting the elevation of bullet trajectory. Shooters had to shoot through large plastic fifty-five gallon drums laid on their sides with openings cut in the top and bottom set on X frames in front of the slits. These acted as suppressors, capturing the expanding gases from the guns. It wasn't perfect, but they would reduce the sounds released to a manageable level. What little sound escaped would be blocked by the heavy walls of the warehouse. No one outside would be the wiser of the indoor range, which was exactly what Buck wanted since he wasn't sure what the local zoning laws might be on private indoor shooting ranges.

"It's about time we put our handiwork to the test. Why don't you guys grab some cold beers off the taps? I'll be right back with some guns we can shoot with." Buck said as he disappeared inside the house with Rampage. Moments later, they returned with several gun cases and boxes of ammo.

"Alright," Buck said, slapping a thirty round magazine into a CAR-15 and pulling back the charging handle to chamber a round, "Who wants to go first?" Buck saw Brisbane and Cooper both start to reach for the gun.

"Well," Buck cut them off, "I think that we ought to let Lenz go first. He is the eldest," he said thrusting the weapon at Lenz.

"No, let someone else go first," Lenz said, holding up his hands to fend off the offering. "I'm not a soldier," he continued in his German-accented English. "I fix machines, not shoot guns. I would probably miss the target."

"That's the whole idea, mate," chimed in Harold Brisbane. "By you going first, you'll make the rest of us look good. Besides, you do man a weapons station on the back of the *Agrippa* when the strike team is not on board, so don't give me that malarkey."

"Yes, but not like that gun," he gestured to the CAR-15 being offered. "The *Agrippa* has special electronics and sights, I just put the dot on the target and pull the trigger; I don't have to do any calculations."

"Oh, that makes me feel safe," Brisbane said smiling sarcastically. "I'll remember that next time we call for covering fire from the *Agrippa*."

"Here, I will help you," Hubert said, stepping forward. "Together we'll show these two that anybody can learn to shoot as good as them."

"I'll help, too," said Datan. "Shooting is more about relaxing than anything else. I'm sure that you can do that."

"Alright then," the elderly German said after looking into the Jewish and French warriors face. Grels, who had been standing off to the side, relaxed a little, happy that the mechanic would be the focus of warriors' exhortations.

Just as Lenz settled into a fire position, Buck felt his phone vibrate, followed by a special ring tone telling him he had an incoming text message from Operation Neptune's headquarters in New York. The ring tone was echoed by similar sounds emanating from the cell phones of the other members of the strike force.

Buck pulled his cell phone from his pocket, flipped it open, and pushed a few buttons to display the message: "REPORT IMMEDIATELY TO BASE. PREP M/V *AGRIPPA* FOR TRANSPORT AND STRIKE FORCE FOR IMMEDIATE DEPLOYMENT. CALL SECURE ONCE ARRIVED ON BASE. BARRETT."

Buck flipped his cell phone closed and looked up to see the rest of the team doing likewise. He also glanced at their wives, too, who had just joined them from the house. They were all too familiar with such phone calls and knew instantly without being told what the phone call meant. Worried glances were exchanged between Lenz and Greta, Hubert and Sabine.

Sabine broke the silence. "Come Giselle and Bernadette," she said holding out her hands to her two daughters, "Papa has to go to work now." Sensing the change of mood in the adults, the girls skittered up to their mom, placing their hands in hers without a fuss.

And Buck wondered, as he watched everyone gather up their things in silence, what fears he would be feeling at this moment if his wife and daughter were alive today.

25

Buck saw Major La Barré, who had flown in just prior to Strike Force Trident's departure walk through the door to the hanger. Buck had been so busy with the loading and transport of the *Agrippa* on the U.S. Air Force's C-5, that he had had little time to spend with their intelligence officer on mission planning. Since Major La Barré had first learned the whereabouts of the pirate Khalil, Phillipe had been sending a steady stream of intelligence, allowing Buck to formulate a tactical plan to pick where and how to deal with the pirate. He knew that they would have some twenty hours of travel time -- transiting the Atlantic and then the Mediterranean with several fuel stops in the mix-- to catch up on the latest intelligence and make any needed adjustments to the plan.

The Navy had dispatched a team of support personnel eight hours earlier on a C-130 out of Norfolk International Airport. Since the C-130 was almost half as fast as the C-5, it needed a head start to ensure that the support team's arrival corresponded with Strike Force Trident's. This left Buck free to focus on mission preparation rather than the logistics of their unloading.

Shortly after the C-5 went wheels up and had climbed to cruising altitude, Buck undid his lap belt and made his way between pallets tied to the plane's floor to where Philippe was ensconced on a canvas fold down seat with laptop computers to either side of him. Buck picked up a laptop and plopped down beside the French major. "Any new developments that I need to know about?"

"Aside from the fact that Khalil's patterns continue to be erratic and unpredictable, I suppose not," replied the Frenchman.

"Is he still returning to the same dock and house every time he leaves?"

"Oui, nothing ez changed."

"It's a crappy business that we are in, Philippe. We try to eliminate variables and build contingency plans for those things that we can't predict. I'm satisfied with the assault plan, it will let us pick where, when, and how we will engage."

"I am not sure I follow you, Buck. How can you say that you are picking the time of engagement when we know not when the pirate will be home?"

"Simple. It's irrelevant what day we make our move. We have the support of a British Frigate in the area. We will just hang about and live off the frigate until the satellite views show us that Khalil is returning home. What is important is at what point in time on any given day we make our assault. We've been studying his patterns for several weeks now. Like any lazy criminal, he enjoys sleeping in his own bed at night, preferably after a night of revelry, with a woman, a boy, a goat, it makes no difference. It's important to him to get his beauty sleep, so he sleeps in. In this regard, he is predictable, which we will use to our advantage. We only have to know when he is in residence. When we know that, we will land Strike Team Trident ashore and strike an hour before dawn when everyone is exhausted and deeply asleep."

"You Americans are so full of colorful expressions: 'beauty sleep.' It is almost French-like how you speak. I will have to remember that one."

"Sure, Philippe, enjoy it. I have lots of extra sayings; I'll never know that one is gone," Buck said straight faced as a look of confusion spread over Philippe's face at Buck's tongue-in-cheek remark that only seemed to bring confusion to the Frenchman. It was one of the few drawbacks to the magnificent team that Colonel Barrett had put together. Everyone spoke English and could communicate with precision and fluency. However, he had learned that fluency and comprehension were two different things. He could make the members of Strike Force Trident understand exactly what he wanted done, but he could not always make them understand his attempts at humor. "You know," Buck said, changing direction, as he watched his little joke crash and burn to the floor in front of the two of them, " the only thing that I'm dissatisfied with about this mission's orders is the stipulation that we must identify ourselves and give the pirates an opportunity to surrender before we do anything. That gives away our most important tactical advantage: the element of surprise. I know what they're trying to do with this directive. They are trying to cover their political butts and not look like the bad guys. I've argued 'til I'm blue in the face that this tactic will *cost* more lives than it saves. The best way to save lives is to move in with overwhelming speed and violence to control your targets before they have time to rouse themselves or organize a defense."

"I share your concerns, Buck. But this order comes from the Secretary-General, himself. Look at the bright side, if there is one. All the action will be captured by the gun cameras of your suits and the *Agrippa*. If things go wrong, as you and I suspect, it will all get caught on video."

"Geez, Philippe! I'm not looking to say 'I told you so'. My ass is going to out there on the firing line with bullets flying my direction if it goes bad. I just don't want myself or any of my team to get hurt or killed because we have politicians dictating tactical procedures in a live-fire zone."

Philippe looked calmly at the young warrior, who was now slightly agitated. "You miss my point, Buck. This mission is a lost cause. The order has come down, and we both know that we will obey the desires of our superiors. But, by proving their errors this time, you may be able to prevent the mistake from happening again, and save lives in the future. They will see that telling a person who knows how to do their job that they know not what they are doing is a risky, dangerous proposition. Nothing is so convincing as to see one's mistakes on a video screen for everyone to dissect. Warriors know the value of a post-attack debriefing to learn where or how they can improve; but to a politician, it is like holding their feet to flames. This mission will show our handlers that it is better to leave such matters to the professionals, thereby saving lives in the future."

Buck could see why the major excelled at intelligence; he was already three moves ahead of Buck's focus. "Yeah, I guess you're right when you look at it that way. Well, let me know if anything important develops," Buck said as he took his leave of Philippe, handing him back his laptop.

As Buck approached the other side of the cargo space, he could see most of Strike Team Trident sacked out on any surface that could offer a few hours of relative comfort and sleep until the plane's first fuel stop. Bodies were draped across fold-down seats, the floor, and pallets, using anything from jackets to backpacks as pillows. Soldiers of every stripe learned to get sleep any time an opportunity presented itself, because one never knew when the next opportunity to sleep would come. The only thing that did not differ was that all the sleeping warriors, from different countries and cultures, slept with one hand on their personal weapon. Some things of the warrior ethos just transcend cultural differences.

"Everything copacetic with our French spy?"

Rampage, still awake, called over the roar of the plane's turbojets out as Buck approached.

"Yah. No change," Buck said as he slumped into the canvas jump seat next to Rampage, tilting his helmet over his eyes and folding his arms across his chest. "I'll check with him in a couple hours before we land in Bur Sadan and give the team a final briefing," he mumbled from under the helmet covering his face. "Time to get some shut eye. Let me know if anything happens."

"Aye, aye, Buck."

As Buck drifted off to a light sleep, he was glad to have Rampage along on this trip. Yeah, he was a bit of a joker and free spirit, but when the bullets started to fly, there was no cooler head to be found in the heat of combat than Rampage. He felt a sense of comfort that Rampage would be watching his six if this went bad, which Buck's little inner voice was whispering it would. The feelings of comfort and dread wrestled with each other until Buck slipped into an uneasy rest.

26

The trip aboard the cargo jet and subsequent landings for fuel had left Buck's senses dulled. The continuous roar of the plane's jet engines for hours had worn all the members of Strike Force Trident to a nub of lethargy. Yet, with the trip winding down and the action phase approaching, energy was what was now demanded. Buck willed himself into action, rising to go check in with Major La Barré to see if there was any significant intel change. Buck checked in with the cockpit over a headset before he made his way around the cargo hold of the jet to find Philippe's position relatively unchanged. With one laptop on the seat beside him and the one in his lap that he was scrutinizing, the Frenchman looked unchanged and unfazed by the hours in the air.

"Any changes that I need to know about before I give the team their final briefing?" Bucked asked as he approached.

Buck's voice seemed to startle the intelligence office out of his concentration. Looking up, it took him a few moments to find the source of the voice addressing him in the dimly lit plane interior. "The situation is unchanged. The Americans flew a satellite over about an hour and fifteen minutes ago. The pirate's ship was not at dock in the marina and it was not identified in the immediate vicinity. So we are in a watch-and-wait pattern until the target returns. Other birds," he said referring to spy satellites, "and ground sources monitoring radio activity report there have been no calls of distress from boats or ships within thirty miles of their home port that might give us an idea of what they are up to or where they are. So we will just have to wait until they return."

"How about the weather?"

"Beautiful and clear. Meteorological reports show a high-pressure zone over the center of the Red Sea; sunny and hot, with afternoon clouds forming over the Red Sea for the next four days. Just what you would expect in this part of the world, no?"

"Thanks, Philippe." Buck did an about-face and headed back to his assault team arrayed in various positions of repose on the other side of the plane.

"Rampage," Buck called out, "round up the strike force for a final briefing." By "strike force" he meant both the members of Strike Team Trident and the crew of the *Agrippa* which combined comprised Strike Force Trident of Project Neptune.

"Aye, aye, Buck."

Moments later, everyone was gathered around. Shouting over the engine's roar, Buck briefed everyone on the status of their target and the weather in the operation zone. They went over their plan of assault again before Buck asked if there were any final questions.

Brisbane piped up, "Any possibility that the part of the plan where we announce our presence and order them to surrender over a loud speaker could change, sir?"

Like most Special Forces operators around the world, the good sergeant was feeling exposed by giving up one of their most basic operating principles: stealth and surprise. With surprise gone, the strike team would shift from being the side dictating the action to the one that was reactionary, the former being preferred in small unit operations. Harold was just giving voice to what all of the strike team was thinking.

"No," replied Buck evenly, "that aspect of the plan remains unchanged and is one of the absolutes of the mission." He could see in all their eyes, they were hoping for a last minute change of heart to this flaw in the plan. Buck did not like it either, but those were his orders. "Alright then, we should be starting our descent into Bur Sudan shortly. You know what to do. That's all." On cue, the whine of the engines lessened and the nose of the plane angled down as it started its descent.

The pilot put the plane on the ground twelve minutes later in a smooth touch-down that was followed by a very bumpy taxi before the plane came to a rest and the engines were shut down. As they gathered themselves, the rear cargo doors on the big transport cracked open to the whir of the hydraulic motors. Blinding light flooded the cargo bay, making everyone shield their eyes while they adjusted. This was followed by a rolling wave of heat as the cool air of the stratosphere that the plane had been traveling in minutes ago was exchanged for the dusty inferno of the desert's climes. As their eyes adjusted, they could see the advance team personnel waiting beyond the plane's doors to start the unloading process.

An hour later, the *Agrippa* was cast off and the advance team waved goodbye from the harbor's dock; their work having been completed, they now looked forward to catching some sleep in the hotel the Navy had booked for them. After a shower and some sleep, they'd be ready to sample some of the exotic experiences of the Middle East while they waited for the *Agrippa* to return from its mission and the reverse process of loading the boat for its return trip would begin.

The *Agrippa* headed southeast across the Red Sea to

rendezvous with the British Frigate, *HMS Winscott*, which was on station twenty miles south of the pirate's port, where they would wait for the pirates to return and then set their assault into motion.

Everybody onboard the *Agrippa* started to rid himself of the jitteriness induced by prolonged travel. It felt good for them to be doing what they had trained for in a familiar environment. First, the team removed two Combat Rubber Raiding Craft from the on-deck storage lockers and inflated them. Next, they equipped the boats with an armor system that could be deployed to protect the boat and its occupants with a turn of a valve on a regular SCUBA air tank secured in the bottom of the boat. The lightweight armor panels would be lifted into position by air bladders or flipped over the side to expose the hi-tech armor plates that could stop the largest of small caliber rounds yet was light enough to float. Some of the armor, called Dynema, was even used to provide ballistic protection on the *Agrippa*. Next, the strike team members set about preparing their personal gear, weapons, and Land Warrior components for the upcoming action.

The sea conditions in the Red Sea were mild, with gently rolling three-foot swells which allowed the *Agrippa* to cruise at a very comfortable pace of twenty-three knots. They had over two hundred fifty plus miles to cover before they could offload their extra fuel and supplies on the frigate and clear their decks for action. But in the Red Sea, one could never tell what might happen. The Middle East was not known for its stability or its civility, even in one of the world's greatest maritime thoroughfares in the sea lanes leading to the Suez Canal.

However, the thirteen-hour run southeast proved uneventful. The *Agrippa's* crew took shifts navigating the boat, while the others got a chance to sleep in one of the extra transport chairs in the strike team room. After seeing to it that their fighting gear, weapons, and electronic systems were ready, Buck and the strike team members were able to get a restful sleep in their transport chairs.

They arrived at the frigate's coordinates in the dark of the night and Buck decided that the transfer of fuel bladders would be best accomplished during daylight hours. The frigate's captain agreed. So the *Agrippa* took station about a mile off of the frigate's stern and followed her as she made a lazy oval of twenty miles on each half. The *Agrippa* followed the larger British vessel because of her low silhouette, low radar observation design and RAM material; it made seeing her in anything other than the best visual conditions difficult if not downright impossible. The frigate crew had other things to worry about rather than trying to keep tabs on something as slippery as Strike Force Trident's strike craft and not run it down.

While the strike team was getting its shut-eye, Lenz slipped in to catch a few winks at which point everyone became aware of his thunderous snoring. Everyone endured it for three hours until his turn came up for a wheel watch. For three blessed hours the strike team room was a haven for the weary until he slipped back in after his shift steering the Agrippa. His return to the strike team's ready room was announced shortly by a return of the man's obnoxious nocturnal mating call which roused everyone awake in the predawn hour of the morning.

"Just as well," a bleary-eyed Buck thought. The sun's first rays could be seen starting to lighten the eastern horizon. Time to get the strike team up and organized for the day's activities. Rampage, suffering from the same perturbations and hearing Buck's rustling, arose, too. First, they went to their lockers where they grabbed their latrine kit bags and headed down to the boat's wardroom where the head was located. The *Agrippa* had not been built for long term patrols and carried no desalinization equipment or water beyond what they carried in their tanks. Buck and Rampage were only able to take towel baths to conserve water and wipe yesterday's grime from their faces and bodies before shaving. The rest of the strike team had military background and were use to such privations, except for Hubert. His experience had all been in law enforcement where, after a sweaty day of training, there was always a hot shower waiting, but he seemed to be taking the new working conditions in stride. *'Funny,'* Buck thought looking in the mirror, *'of all the things to worry about that could go wrong on this mission, I'm worrying about how the impact of no showers will affect the combat effectiveness of the strike force.'*

Another quick splash of cold water on their faces to finish off their morning routine before a final inspection in the mirror: improved, but only marginally. Weariness and fatigue seeped through their visage.

"Alright, Rampage," Buck started, "let's get the men up and get some chow in them. After that, we will rendezvous with the frigate and transfer the extra fuel bladders. Then I want each man to fully load up in mission gear and assemble on the back deck for live weapons fire practice. Have them find anything on the boat that will float to use as targets that we can shoot full of holes. Then have each man go through Stinger missile deployment before cleaning their weapons.

"That should be enough to get their systems kick started and in cycle. Nothing like a little live fire to get the cobwebs cleaned from one's system. I'm going to go to the bridge and get the boat crew going and check in with Major La Barré."

"You got it," Rampage replied and turned to climb the steeps that led to the deck above where the rest of the crew was still sleeping in the Strike team ready room.

"Alright, gentlemen, time to rise and shine," Rampage announced loudly and forcefully as he flipped on the lights.

The men rustled, arose, stretched and yawned.

"Crikey, mates!" Cooper said as he stretched, "I had the worst dream about an out of tune German diesel that was trying to run me over."

"That was no bloody diesel, it was Lenz," Harold answered. "The man snores louder than the engines he dotes on, kept me up half the night."

Rampage interrupted, "Hu-Bear, after you get cleaned up, go to the galley and cook up some breakfast for us."

"Why moi? What have I done to deserve this privilege?" Hubert asked.

"Well, you're French," answered Rampage, somewhat puzzled by the obviousness that was lost on the Frenchman.

"*Oui.*"

"That automatically makes you the best cook on this boat."

"Oui, this is true." The Frenchmen breathed on his nails before buffing them on his shirt, his braggadocio act designed to nettle the others.

"You're a real figjam, Arceneaux," the Australian said, rising to the bait.

"What is a 'figjam'?" Datan asked joining the conversation.

"It's Australian for someone who thinks highly of themselves. It stands for 'Fuck I'm Good, Just Ask Me.'"

"That about bloody well covers it," quipped Harold, joining the repartee.

"Let me share a little wisdom with those of you who do not come from a naval background or are unfamiliar with our traditions," Rampage said while raising his finger in front of his face, affecting the air of a wise sage. "Rule number one is: do not mess with the cook, unless you like eating cockroach and sawdust sandwiches."

"Man's got a point," Buck heard the English sergeant say as he exited the ready room into the bridge. As he slipped onto the bridge, Buck found Tadhg and Grels already at their stations conversing in low tones as they discussed the fuel bladder transfer coming up. He eased into the middle chair and waited until they finished their discussion.

"Alright then, I will conn us in a shallow, low speed approach on the starboard side under the stern deck crane of the frigate and hold station there. You will monitor the off-loading via closed-circuit TV on your monitor. If at any point you do not like what you are seeing or someone on the back deck yells 'BREAKAWAY, BREAKAWAY, BREAKAWAY' on the boat's comm net, I will commence breakaway on the third word. We will inform the strike team members working the deck with Lenz to seek safety if they hear these words. Any questions?" There was a pause of silence.

"Please call the Officer of the Deck of the frigate and inform them of our plans. Coordinate a time with them."

Grels fired off a brisk Swedish-accented "Aye, aye," before turning to his computer screen, touching various points with a stylus and then talking slowly into the boom mic in front of his mouth, calling the frigate.

"Good morning, Buck," Tadhg said without acknowledging that Buck had been watching him for several minutes or taking his eyes off his console as he made several adjustments to the boat's systems. "We have winds out of the southwest at eight knots, seas are relatively calm. The meteorological report is unchanged for the next twenty-four hours; however, after that, a low pressure front can be expected to bring rain and winds fifteen to twenty miles per hour. Grels is coordinating a fuel transfer time with the *Winscott* now. The boat is running smooth and normal, all systems within operating parameters and no mechanical casualties reported."

"Very good, Mister Ramsden," and after a pause, he added, "I see you were excited to get an early start on the day, too."

"Yes, sir. Too many things left to accomplish today. Couldn't sleep past zero four thirty. You?"

"The same," he said failing to add his thoughts on Lenz's sleeping habits. "Rampage will be in shortly to coordinate today's activities with the crew. Carry on."

"Yes, sir."

The rest of the day went by without a hitch. The fuel bladder offloading to the frigate went smoothly, as did the planned strike team exercises that concluded a little after noon. With the men cleaning their weapons, Buck was summoned to the ready room comm station by an urgent request from Grels over the ship's communications circuit on the boom mic/earpiece that everyone wore while onboard. "Buck, you have an urgent communications from Maj. La Barré."

"Roger."

Buck went into the ready room and plugged into the communications set. "Kohl, here."

"Lieutenant, Major La Barré. We have satellite confirmation that our target is approaching the harbor. ETA is two hours. It would be a safe bet that they will be harboring at the strike location tonight. It looks like your show is a go for this evening."

"Confirmed, we have tentative go for this evening. Keep me apprised of any changes. I'll want the latest intel on how many bodies disembark from the ship and where they all went. I'll want that two hours before we push off at 0300 local."

"*Oui*. Out."

"Kohl, out."

Buck took a moment to calm the butterflies in his stomach before he replaced the receiver in its cradle. Some of the men who weren't cleaning their weapons or repacking their gear filtered in nonchalantly. All were busy at appearing to be busy and look as though they had not been eavesdropping on Buck's conversation.

Buck turned to Rampage who had also materialized in the room. "We're a probable go on our mission for this evening," Buck said loud enough for the rest of the team to hear. "You know what that means?"

"Yes, I do. I'll prepare the back deck immediately."

"Roger. I will go consult the instruments in the bridge and then join you shortly."

"Aye, aye."

The rest of the Strike team exchanged glances with each other, unsure of what Buck and Rampage were talking about.

Buck slid into the bridge and proceeded to the forward bulkhead where he flipped on the power switches of three electronic boxes. Three little LCD screens jumped to life, displaying a kaleidoscope of colors in V's and dots on the screen. Buck studied them intently, fiddling with adjustments on the devices. Tadhg and Grels watched silently. Buck turned and addressed Tadhg, "We have a probable go for this evening, so we're going to kill a little time by loitering. Keep this heading and throttle back to seven knots. Grels, keep an eye on these instruments and let me know on the ship's comm circuit if you see any large blips appear on the screens. I'll be on the back deck if you need me."

Buck strode with purpose as he left the bridge through the ready room, where the remaining members watched him out of the corner of their eyes, trying to figure out what was going on. As Buck stepped out on to the back deck, he saw that Rampage had already changed into a colorful Hawaiian shirt they favored for their favorite pastime and had already unfolded one of the flimsy plastic and aluminum folding chairs. The second chair was in his hands which he unfolded and placed next to the other chair at the top of the boat launching ramp between the two CRRC that had been assembled for the evening's mission. Rampage reached into a boat locker where a pair of fishing poles were nestled and produced another colorful shirt that he tossed to Buck who donned it. Rampage finished his set up with a flurry as he produced a small plastic tackle box and a bait bucket, which he placed between the two chairs.

"It looks like they're running two to eight meters deep."

"Yep," Rampage replied, "just about where you'd expect them, just under the thermal break boundary between the top heated layer and colder deep water." He finished his sentence as Buck seated himself in the closest chair. "May I offer you a cigar? Cuban."

"Where'd you get Cuban cigars?"

"I've learned," Rampage said as he handed a large tapered cigar to Buck and then began preparing the end of his own before lighting it, "that this job has certain perks. Last time I was at the New York U.N. Headquarters, I just happened to run into this guy who worked at the Cuban U.N. Consulate..."

"Oh yeah? Where was this exactly?" a hint of sarcasm

starting to creep into his voice.

"Oh...at the Cuban Consulate."

"Well, shazaam! Who would have thought..." the sarcasm was dripping now from Buck's voice.

"Any-who, the conversation came around to cigars, and this guy offers to get me some handmade Cuban cigars. How could I refuse?"

"Exactly! Was this before or after you offered him money?"

"After, of course. That's the way it works in Cuba. I was just observing local customs. Weren't you paying attention in the cultural diversity classes we went to?"

Both men were puffing now to get their stogies lit after bringing a match to the ends. Billowing clouds of aromatic smoke were whisked astern from the *Agrippa's* minimal headway, the slight breeze helping to keep them lit.

"Now, let's get to some serious fishing," Buck said, stuffing his cigar in his jaw and standing to cast his baited leader.

"Aye, aye, Skipper." Steve said doing the same.

Both men then settled into their chairs, lapsing into silence, enjoying the moment.

******

"Blimey, mates! You've got to see this. The C.O.'s gone daft," Harold said watching the two strike force leaders through a window looking out on the back deck. "The two of them are out back fishing like they're on bloody holiday."

"Let me see, Sassy," Cooper said, elbowing Harold out of the way and peering through the window for himself. "Crickey, all they need is a couple of coldies to make the picture complete."

"I told you, Coop," replied Harold.

Harold felt a sharp elbow to his ribs and knew it was Arceneaux wanting to take a look. "Careful Hu-Bear, no need to get violent," he said yielding his position at the window to the Frenchman. The team had seen Hu-Bear's Savate workouts and his ability to delivery devastating kicks and strikes; they gave the Frenchman plenty of room when he started to land blows.

"What iz a 'coldiez'?" he asked, as he peered out the window to see what everybody was gawking at.

"Beers, mate, beers," Harold answered for Randall.

"You would think that Messieurs Buck and Rampage would be more focused right before a mission; especially their first," the Frenchman observed dryly.

"That is exactly what they are doing," sounded a reply from back in the room. All heads turned towards Datan Ben-Moshe, who had been quietly cleaning and assembling his sidearm at a table near the door.

"How's that, Rabbi?" Coop asked.

"Men deal with coming battle in different ways. Some find comfort in doing repetitive, mindless activities; like cleaning their weapons," he said, waving the pistol in his hands, "to fill the hours before entering into combat. Others sleep, so as to minimize the amount of time they have to face their inner demons. Still others, like Buck and Rampage, choose to pursue a pastime of pleasure so as to intensify their desire to live. Whatever path one chooses, each warrior must appear on the battlefield ready to meet his creator. If he has not prepared his soul, then he will not leave the battlefield standing. If Buck and Rampage choose to find god in the pursuit of fish compelled to impale themselves upon their hooks, so be it. And I'm much happier for it, because that means their heads and souls are clear, and their decisions in battle that could mean my life or death will be as good as the situation will permit and not be clouded by business left undone."

The room was silent for a moment as each internalized Ben-Moshe's observation, before the reverie was broken. "Well...let's go see what's biting..." Coop challenged the others as he pulled open the door to the back deck.

27

The quarter moon washed its weak reflection upon the waters of the Red Sea as two rubber boats, barely noticeable to the unaided human eye, made their way through the surf at the peak of high tide. The high tide ensured that they could slip over the reef system and avoid any unknown underwater obstacles like shifting sandbars with only the slightest of worries. The time, three thirty a.m. local, had been chosen not for the high tide peak, a fortunate coincidence, but because that was when the human bio-rhythm pulled the hardest on a human body for sleep. The lack of light did not hinder the three men in each boat. Clad in black military fatigues, laden with strange backpacks, gear and night-vision goggles, they sped towards the beach in front of them. The light intensifying night vision goggles, or NVGs, worn by each man made the whole approach to the beach appear as detailed as the early morning sun in the green-on-green tones of the imagers two inches in front of their eyes. One man, at the throttle of each boat, steered from a crouched sitting position, while the other two riders lay stomach first astride the port and starboard pontoons of the inflatable. One rider focused his attention on a small GPS device that he kept in front of his NVGs, making sure the boat proceeded to the way points that had been entered in hours before, giving corrective hand signals to the man at the throttle when needed. The other rider's sole job was to scan the seas and beach for any sign that their approach had been spotted or raised an alarm ashore.

Even though each man had computer and voice communications, habits born of experience had taught them that stealth was an advantage not given away until necessary. So they communicated using only hand signals until the men landed on the beach.

Their caution, while warranted, was unnecessary. No one ashore had the slightest inkling that an assault from the sea would ever occur to their little town. The pirates, the target of tonight's mission, had slumped asleep in whatever positions they were in when their alcohol levels exceeded their bodies' ability to deal with it or the debauchery they were endeavoring in no longer stimulated their pleasure centers enough to warrant continued wakefulness. Although Muslims, who foreswore the imbibing of alcohol, the men strewn about the various rooms of the two story building in an alcohol-induced stupor were not good Muslims in any sense.

The rubber craft rode though the five-foot surf and landed four hundred meters north of the two story house that served as the pirate's shore base. As the boats' noses were carried up the sandy, cream white beach by the momentum the little twenty-five horse motor imparted to the small craft, the throttle man flipped the outboard's propeller out of the water to protect it from being damaged. Simultaneously, the two riders slid from the positions astride the pontoons and used the dying impetus of the craft to sling them in front of the boat into crouches, weapons shouldered, scanning for targets. Each man was tethered to the boat to prevent the surf from pulling it back out to sea.

In a well-oiled and rehearsed ballet, the throttle man

exited the boat and grabbed the rope railing on top of the boat's rubber hull, and all three simultaneously and silently hauled the boat up the slight forty-meter, incline of the beach. They carried the boat until they reached the lee of the sand berm that marked the storm surge high surf mark where they stashed the boats, concealing them from the land side. The men assembled into a small huddle while a quick head count was taken. When every man was accounted for, the leader gave a quick hand signal, dispersing the black clad warriors to execute their part in the planned assault. The men separated into two maneuvering units and moved out noiselessly in two directions: two men, led by Rampage, moved inland while the group lead by Buck continued to move down the beach in the shadow of the storm surge berm. Each maneuvering unit was carrying identical loads of equipment. The plan was to ring the house with the six men and create cross-fires for the different weapons each was carrying.

Each man was so intent upon his surroundings that they had totally forgotten that their progress was being monitored by their unseen boat offshore they had launched from a half hour earlier, the infrared beacons each man wore to mark his position easily made them visible to the *Agrippa*'s sophisticated electronics.

They were also being monitored from space. President Tillman had insisted on watching his little experiment's first foray into anti-pirating action for himself. He had tasked one of the nameless, initialed agencies that controlled a constellation of 'weather satellites' with infrared capabilities to be over the target coordination at the designated time. Yoshi had tied the comm links of the strike team and the Agrippa into the video feed so that the President could also hear what was happening, but could not talk directly to the strike team members; another stipulation of Buck's: no armchair quarterbacking. Had it not been for the real bullets in the pirates' guns to keep them focused on the task before them, the six men might have been unnerved that their stealth was just an illusion; their mission, a little drama, was being enacted for judgment by men almost half a world away.

Five thousand miles away, in the White House, President Tillman, along with Clayton Biggs, Tobias Sterns and Colonel Barrett watched the proceedings from a basement communications room. Senator Templeton and Congressmen Castillas had also been invited due to their special involvement and interest in bringing about tonight's event. Yet the mood in the room lacked any sign of a party. It was filled more with apprehension than anticipation. Senator Templeton was not his normal larger-than-life self tonight. He sat quietly off to the side; his white knuckled, clenched fists lay in his lap, an indicator of the emotional turmoil beneath his calm demeanor, as the hunt for the killers of his sister's son scrolled forward on the monitor.

"Are you sure that your boys are ready?" President Tillman asked Colonel Barrett.

"If they're not, Mr. President, then some of them are probably going to get shot to hell tonight."

"Hardly a ringing endorsement, Colonel."

"If you're not confident," Clayton cut in, "then let's call this off before anyone gets hurt." And then added under his breath, "And before we have a mess to clean up."

"I'm confident that I have in the field some of the finest, most well-trained special operators in the world, Mr. Biggs. I am confident that if the mission can be done, these are the men to do it."

"What do you mean 'if the mission can be done'?" This time it was Tobias Sterns asking the question.

"What I mean," replied Colonel Barrett, "is that there were parameters placed upon this mission that were outside the normal protocols and means with which a mission of this nature would typically be carried out. Namely, the Secretary-General's insistence that the pirates be given a chance to surrender before the strike team takes any direct action, thereby, compromising any advantages of stealth and surprise; these advantages can mean the difference between the mission's failure and success, and those brave men's lives.

"You're asking me for absolutes; absolutes that I can't give you. Once they light the lights, announce their presence, the situation will become very fluid. There is a very good chance that some of them will get shot to hell despite their training and preparation."

The room turned quiet leaving each man and his thought as they watch the action unfold.

******

Buck led the first maneuvering element along the sand berm, while Rampage led the second element inland a hundred meters before turning south. The plan called for each element to drop a man off at each corner of the house as they moved parallel to it, with Buck and Rampage taking up positions opposite the front and back of building. This would provide overlapping fields of fire for each man, plus it would give the corner men assistance in covering two of their fields of fire. Each group had forty-five minutes to cover the four hundred meters to the house and get into position. The corner men were to place remotely-activated, battery-powered floodlights on the midpoint of each wall of the building and then move to a position of cover, fortifying it with whatever time was left until the assault started. Steve and Rampage carried remotely activated speakers which they would place on opposite sides of the building. When the time came, they would activate the speakers that contained pre-recorded Arabic phrases instructing the pirates to surrender and what to do.

As Buck's group approached the target house that sat just on the other side of the sand berm, he called a halt. Crawling, he ascended to the crest of the berm where he could study the building. It was nothing more than a glorified two-story mud hut that sat on a gentle slope with a view of the sea. Overlooking the berm, the building took advantage of the sea breezes for cooling. The house appeared to be no different from many other buildings of the village, measuring no more than forty-five by thirty feet. There were no signs of fortification; they weren't expecting company.

One of the advantages of working in the Middle East was that Arabs considered dogs to be unclean animals, so they were fewer in number than most other parts of the world. This house did not appear to have one guarding it.

After studying the building for several minutes, Buck determined that there was no activity and it was safe to proceed. He crawled back down the berm and joined the two men waiting below. He hand signaled to Bear and Sassy to follow him. Seventy-five meters later, he stopped and signaled to Bear that it was his drop off point. Bear slithered up the berm's slope with his M-249 5.56 mm SAW cradled in his arms, backpack containing the remote light he was to place and his Barrett Arms REC 7 chambered in 6.8 mm strapped to his back as he disappeared over the berm's lip.

Another fifty meters later, it was Buck's turn to slip over the berm. He gave a brief wave to Sassy, who was carrying the IAR, or Infantry Assault Rifle chambered in 6.8mm. It had a selector that could make the weapon fire from a closed bolt to keep debris out of the chamber or fire from an open bolt position to help keep the barrel cool for sustained firing like a machine gun. He was also packing a CQX 12 combat shotgun tonight. Before slipping over the top, he paused to confirm that there was nobody that might spot his movement and give away his position before he scrambled over the top. On the other side, he slithered to the base and waited for any sign that his presence had been detected before moving towards the house, looking for a good spot to place his loudspeaker. He found one fifty feet from the front of the building where the shore vegetation petered out into the hard packed clay of the coastal alluvial plain. He stabbed the speaker's metal spikes into the ground, adjusted the aim of the speaker and moved back into the vegetation. He looked for another spot, far away from the speaker, to set up his hide for the next phase of the mission. It also had the benefit of creating the illusion that there were more attackers than there were by giving the pirates in the building one more point of distraction to focus their attention upon.

After he settled into his hide, Buck announced his readiness on the open communication channel of the strike team. "One is up," he whispered into the boom mic in front of his chin.

The others quickly followed.

"Two is up," Brisbane to his left.

"Three is up," Bear to his right.

A quick look on his Land Warrior video screen monocle showed that the others were still getting into position. Ten minutes later, Buck heard the other elements report in:

"Four is up." Rampage was in position.

"Five is up." Datan on the southern back corner was ready. He had the other M-249 SAW and was on the opposite corner of the house of Bear's SAW.

"Six is up," came Coop's signal that he was ready.

Buck checked his watch. They still had nine minutes to wait until the balloon went up on this mission. It was a very, very long nine minutes.

Finally, the second hand on his watch counted down the last seconds and swept past the twelve on the dial face. He whispered into his mic, "Switching lights on now." He thumbed a button on a remote fob that had grown sweaty in his hand over the last nine minutes.

Suddenly, the night was cast aside as powerful floodlights lit up the house the strike team had set-up, the intense light blinded Buck initially. His eyes hurting, he was forced to squint and alternate opening eyes until the pain ended and his eyes adjusted to the new level of light.

"Northeast light on," came the report over the earphones in his helmet, followed quickly by identical reports on the other lights.

Buck thought he would wait until his eyes had adjusted to the new lighting before triggering the first message on the remote speaker, figuring that if his eyes were adjusted, so were the rest of the team's.

28

Khalil was awoken by the crash of door to his room being thrown open. He cracked one eye open to see the outline of a man centered in the doorway being illuminated by a strange bright light.

"Khalil, wake up!" Salah's familiar voice shouted, "The U. N. has surrounded us with soldiers!"

Khalil's alcohol sodden mind was slow to grasp his surroundings, the meaning of Salah's statement, or the half naked teenage girl passed out across his chest that the local warlord had given him as a bonus to Khalil's required tribute from his haul.

"This is the United Nation's Anti-Piracy Unit. You are surrounded. Come out of the building with your hands in the air, and no one will be harmed..." a loud metallic voice called.

"Khalil, wake up! Tell us what to do!" Salah implored again from the doorway.

Khalil could now hear the other members of his crew being roused and the clink of their weapons as they armed themselves. Finally, enough information penetrated his sluggish brain and he threw off the teenage girl, staggering to his feet as he searched the room for his AK-47. "My gun! Where's my gun?" he demanded of Salah. Salah rushed into the room and rooted through clothes, overturned cushions and a tray of food that had been knocked to the floor before he found his leader's gun and slapped it into his chest.

Khalil staggered to the window of the second story room where Salah had found him. He looked outside, but all he could see was the intense light illuminating the building, blinding him to anything beyond. Again the loud electronic voice was repeating its message:

"...out of the building with your hands in the air and..."

Khalil staggered to the adjacent window only to be greeted by another blinding light whose beams filled the room's ceiling with harsh blue tinged shadows. Khalil's mind was struggling to understand what was happening outside. But the one thing he was sure of was that whoever was out there wanted a fight. "The U.N.? We have nothing to fear, Salah. The U.N. is a toothless old goat! Tell the men to shoot out the lights with their RPGs and then join me on the roof where I can get a better look at who is out there."

Salah disappeared out of the doorway as Khalil staggered towards it. As he entered the hallway of the upper floor, he heard Salah shouting his commands downstairs. Khalil staggered to the end of the hallway, turning right into a small room. There, in the corner, was a spindly wooden ladder with rungs lashed to the poles that led to the roof. He staggered to it, nearly falling over backwards as he swung his AK-47 over his shoulder in order to climb the ladder. At the top, he threw aside the board that had covered the roof opening. He had trouble getting his wobbly legs to make the transition to the roof, settling to half roll, half flop his way onto the roof. He lay there a few moments before crawling to the two-foot knee wall that enclosed the roof area. He propped his back against the wall, craning his head over the edge just in time to see the first salvo of RPG rounds erupt from the windows below, their bright orange tails following them all the way to detonation.

******

Buck saw three RPGs erupt almost simultaneously from the windows on his side of the building. His first reaction was to bury his head in the sand. His second was to shout into his comm link "RPGs! Everybody get low."

The men stationed on the corners -- Bear, Coop, Sassy and Rabbi-- were in relatively good locations since the men launching rockets were shooting for the lights. But Buck and Rampage were located on the long sides of the building. The RPGs were being fired in the blind; one of them could get lucky and accidentally find either one of them.

"Suppressive fire! Get suppressive fire on those RPGs!" Buck ordered Strike Team Trident. Immediately he heard the team's two SAWs cut loose with long bursts, watching through his gun's sights as the 5.56 millimeter bullets stitched from window to window across the front of the building. At the same time, he flipped the selector switch to full auto and cut loose with his own REC 7. After he emptied a full thirty round clip into the building's windows, he ejected the clip and slapped home a new one, the bolt of the weapon slamming forward, chambering a fresh round. He quickly laid aside his REC 7, switching to his Multiple Grenade Launcher with its six Mercury rounds. Not wanting to expose himself any more than he already was in this fire fight, Buck rolled to his side to unfold the stock, then rolled back to his stomach, shouldering the weapon in one fluid motion.

The noise of the firefight was deafening. The Land Warrior's headset was filtering out most of the roar from Hubert's SAW to his right, the blasts of Brisbane's CQX-12 shotgun in full auto to his left and the detonations of the RPG rounds coming from the house. Buck could feel the concussion of the ordinance being transmitted through the earth on which he lay, pummeling his skin and his internal organs.

Quickly sighting the grenade launcher, Buck squeezed off all six Mercury rounds at the building. As he sighted through the launcher's optics, he was only vaguely aware that the building was beginning to dissolve in a cloud of dust as hundreds of angry hornets of lead attacked the hardened clay walls of the structure as he searched for targets.

After he emptied the launcher, he peered into the cloud of dust encasing the building and saw no signs of return fire or further RPG launches. "Cease fire! Cease fire! Cease fire!" he yelled into the team's comm. link. He need not yell because the comm link was tuned to carry his voice at conversational levels.

As silence descended on the scene and the dust started to lift, his first thought was to see if anyone was injured. "Count off. One good." As he flicked open the launcher, dumped the spent casings beside him and started to load six new rounds, the replies started to come back in.

"Two good."

"Three good," and other voices answered until all strike team members reported in with no injuries.

The light placed earlier on his side of the building now lay on its side, knocked over by the RPG rounds but still giving partial illumination. As the dust started to lift, Buck saw that his grenades had punched six two-foot wide holes in the building, and its exterior was scored by hundreds of rounds blasted at it in the last seconds, but it was still intact.

"Rampage, what's it look like on your side?"

"Lots of holes. No targets. Can't spot any downed bad guys. The place is built like a bunker."

"Well, they got a taste of what we can dish out. Maybe they've had enough. I'm going to try the remote speaker and give them another chance to surrender." Buck thumbed the remote control for the speaker, but nothing happened. He mashed his thumb down again.

Nothing.

He unclipped the remote control from its location on the chest of his battle harness and shook it before thumbing it again.

Nothing. The speakers must have been damaged in the firefight.

"Rampage, I've got no remote control here. Try yours."

"Roger." After a delayed pause and no announcement, Rampage's voice came back. "I've got nothing, Buck. The speakers must have gotten shot out. What do you want to do now?"

29

Salah's head popped out of the roof's opening as the interlude in the fight settled over them. He craned his neck until it settled upon Khalil, hunkered down behind the knee wall. Seeing his leader trying to peer over the wall's lip, he scrambled the rest of the way up the ladder and onto the roof where he scuttled over.

"What do you want to do, Khalil?" Salah shouted, his ears still ringing from the cacophony of the fight that he had just endured in closed quarters.

"They have stopped firing. They are probably thinking what a mistake it was to start this fight and are probably retreating right now. I want to teach them a lesson. Tell the men to shoot on my order with everything: RPGs, guns, stones if they have to."

"That won't be necessary. There are plenty of guns and ammunition available below. Three men were killed in the last exchange and two were wounded, but they can still shoot. The dead men's guns and ammunition were being distributed when I climbed up here."

"Good. Now go and tell them to fight like demons when I give the word."

Salah crawled back to the hole in the ceiling and yelled Khalil's orders through it to the men below and then awaited Khalil's command.

Khalil raised his head above the wall's lip. The dust of the battle was lifting, yet he could see nothing of the area surrounding the building, despite the sun's first rays beginning to creep over the sea's eastern horizon. Seeing nothing only convinced him that his own bravado had been correct. And, if he was correct, shooting up the hillside would only waste ammunition, of which he could always steal more. "Now, Salah. Now!" he yelled at the prone form over the opening. The dark form repeated the order in shouts into the hole below. A few seconds later, gunfire and RPGs erupted from every window and some of the holes blasted in the walls, engulfing the hillside.

******

Five thousand miles away, men in the White House's basement watched their monitor as the RPG rocket fire and the gunfire turned the building they had been observing from nearly overhead into some kind of bizarre Chinese fireworks display.

"I don't think they want to play nicely," Tobias Stern observed dryly.

"What is your team going to do now, Colonel?" the President asked the concern in his voice obvious.

"I'm sure that Lieutenant Kohl has the situation in hand," Colonel Barrett replied as calmly as if they were discussing room paint color schemes.

President Tillman turned back to watch the large wall monitor with the overhead view of the battle, in part to follow the action and in part to hide the cloud of doubt on his face that Colonel Barrett's dubious assertion had evoked.

******

"Well, I guess that settles that question," Buck answered Steve's question, planting his face in the dirt as the building and surroundings erupted in a new round of fire. "It looks like they want to play rough. It's time to reach for a bigger hammer."

"Roger that," Rampage concurred from the other side of the building.

"Lieutenant Ramsden, come in, please."

"You rang, Strike Force Trident leader?" came Ramsden's immediate, dry reply.

"Listen, Tadhg, we're up against a tougher nut here than we can crack. I need you to make a gun pass on the target to soften it up. I want you to hit it hard, but leave the town intact. You copy?"

"Roger. Were on station one click out, commencing gun run now. We are thirty seconds out. I suggest you get tucked in very low. Over."

"You know," came Rampage's voice over Buck's headset, "this reminds me of what my old pappy used to tell me about handling mules."

"Oh, yeah? How's that, Steve?" Buck bit.

"He told me that the first thing to do when you meet a mule is to grab a two-by-four, calmly walk up to the mule and smack it upside the head as hard as you can."

"What for?!"

"To get its attention. I think that we're about to get the attention of those mules in the house."

"My dad used to tell me the same thing," they heard Coop chime in.

"Just remember to keep your heads down."

"I hear that," Steve answered for everyone.

******

On the bridge, Tadhg's left hand was already shoving the throttles on his twin turbo charged diesels to full throttle, as he brought the *Agrippa's* nose around and lined up for a pass on the target. The boat's stern hunched in the water as the power of the diesels surged through the massive propulsion pumps, launching it out of the hole like a high-octane dragster.

"Lentz," Tadhg called on the boat's communication channel, "man Gun Station Three for a port side gun pass, south to north: fire at will when you're in range. Remember, we have friendlies on the ground, so be damned sure of your target selection."

"Aye, aye, Captain."

"Grels, take the center turret mount. Once I get her lined up and on autopilot, I'll take the twenty-five millimeter. Copy?

"Roger."

"And Grels,"

"Yes, sir?"

"You heard Buck-- keep the collateral damage to a minimum."

"Yes, sir."

Tadhg just about had the *Agrippa* set up on a shallow closing line that would loop the *Agrippa* within two hundred yards of the shore. Using a stylus to draw on the computer's screen, he penciled in the course line he wanted the boat to follow, then toggled a switch to activate the autopilot. Once the autopilot engaged and took control of the boat, Tadhg quickly converted his terminal to weapons station configuration; a small window in the upper right corner continued to show vital ship functions. Overhead, Tadhg heard servomotors swinging the gun turret as Grels brought the weapons in the turret to bear on the target.

Tadhg was still lining up the twenty-five millimeter on his computer console when the fifty caliber BFG in the upper turret cut loose, followed almost immediately by Lentz's fifty on the back deck. Two angry lines of green-white tracers converged on the dark shore; four thumb-sized metal jacketed lead slugs between every tracer were being delivered at five hundred rounds per minute.

Two seconds later, Tadhg had the pip on his weapon's display centered on the pirate's house, the gyro stabilization of the weapon compensating as the Super Mako sliced and bounced through the waves. Satisfied, he flipped the selector lever for high explosive rounds and squeezed the trigger. The firing of the chain gun added a rhythmic base note to the two hammering fifties.

The first rounds from the boat slammed into the house, unnoticed by the occupants , whose attention was focused on ducking into an open window or wall opening long enough to spray a prolonged burst wildly at the outside. The heavy fifty-caliber slugs punched through the mud walls like it was tissue, their high velocity turning the mud and stone amalgamation of the wall into high speed projectiles which amplified the slugs' effect when it met the flesh of the gunmen inside. The first two criminals to die were literally cut in half and never even knew they were under fire.

******

Salah had barely been able to crawl back to where Khalil lay curled in the fetal position next to the wall. The impact of the big caliber slugs and the cannon's explosive shells ripping into the structure bounced him uncontrollably across the rooftop, like sand on the skin of a drumhead being beaten by a three-year-old. When he finally made it to Khalil, he screamed at the top of his lungs "Khalil, make them stop. Surrender! Make them stop!"

His words had no effect on Khalil -- either he could not hear, or he was too petrified with terror to uncurl from his position. It made little difference. He had nothing white to wave anyhow.

******

The *Agrippa* had now moved into closer range. Grels flipped a switch on his console and added the GAU 134D Gatling gun's weight to the weapons pass. A loud ripping sound and a six foot tongue of flame spewed from the gun as fifty thirty-caliber bullets a second arched across the water in the predawn glow to bury themselves into the target. The boat was almost abeam of the house now, and all guns were shooting nearly broadside. Both Tadhg and Grels started to walk their pipper across the targeting screen side to side using their styluses. The boat was now well into bore sight range of Lentz's M-307 twenty-five millimeter grenade launcher and its explosive shell, which he added as a staccato punctuation to the mix of the boat's weapons output.

Buck unburied his face from the sand long enough to peek in the direction of the house. The sight that met his eyes was one he imagined to be equal to the utter vengeance and the wrath of God. The building was engulfed in a plume of dust. Inside the cloud, dozens of red and white explosions occurred every second, rocking the ground as they seemed to devour the building. He lay in utter awe as the building disintegrated before his eyes. Dumbfounded, he found himself thinking that nothing inside the building could survive such a maelstrom. He was right. Seconds later, the building collapsed into a heap of rubble.

******

Salah and Khalil felt the building fall away beneath them. Over the continuous roar of gunfire, detonations and sounds of the building's collapse, a high pitched scream floated over the din. It was unclear whether it came from one or both of the pirates on the roof.

******

Back in the basement communications room of the White House, the gathered men watched the metal firestorm consume the building, its disintegration, and finally, its collapse. The infrared view the satellite had been providing had not been hampered by the dust cloud that enveloped the small building as it was being torn apart by gunfire, and now as it lay in a jumble of debris, it was clear that no one could have survived in building. The men were stunned into silence at the swiftness and ferocity with which the house and its occupants had been dispatched.

Except one man.

Senator Templeton slowly arose from his chair, unclenched his fist and nodded to the room, "Well, it looks like they won't be cutting off anybody's head in the near future." He paused just long enough to look President Tillman in the eye before finishing, "Now, if you'll excuse me, gentlemen. I have a call to make to my sister." He turned silently and stately walked out the door.

30

Buck watched the building before him collapse into dust and rubble and thought, "*What a waste.*" Unsure whether he had thought it or uttered it aloud, he quickly switched mental gears and focused on his duty as Trident's Strike Force Leader. "Cease fire! Cease fire! Cease fire!" he called to the *Agrippa*.

Tadhg had seen the building's collapse, figured the irregular form of the building's rubble was more likely to ricochet incoming rounds and that further fire was unlikely to add anything useful to the situation. He was already commanding his crew to stand down as Buck's call came over the radio.

Buck called again for a head count of the strike team members to see if anyone was injured. All reported in positively before Buck issued new orders.

"Everyone hold your position and monitor the house."

Buck looked at the eastern sky and estimated that it would be another forty-five to fifty minutes before they could safely inspect the rubble for survivors. "We will wait until we have better light before we look for survivors. Out."

"Copy" was echoed five times as the order was acknowledged.

******

"I've got a survivor." The call came from Sgt Brisbane on the seaward side of the house. "Lieutenant Kohl, you'd better take a look at this."

Buck ran around the rubble pile that used to be the land base of the pirates until he came to Harold standing over a small pile of debris. As he approached, he could see a set of legs sticking out from under a large chunk of the building that had been tossed out as the building fell in upon itself. He stepped over the legs, rounding the hunk to where Brisbane stood over a torso. The large piece of wall had crushed the man, almost dividing him into two pieces. He was in obvious great pain, waving his arms weakly, a trail of dried blood ran from the corner of his mouth. Unable to scream, he was only able to whisper a stream of Arabic in bursts that seemed to take all of the body's remaining energy to project.

"I was afraid to move the boulder," Sassy offered his dry synopsis as one of the team's medics, "it's probably the only thing keeping the poor bloke alive. His back is broken. Most of the internal organs are crushed, the rest are pushed up against his diaphragm. The boulder has probably pinched off the blood supply to the crushed and torn arteries across his midsection."

Buck eyed the weakly flailing man, taking in the situation. "Yeah, you're probably right. The second we pull it off, he'll start to hemorrhage, probably bleed out in thirty seconds. If we leave him, he is sure to die, we could shoot him full of morphine to ease his pain but given his condition that would probably kill him too...six of one half a dozen of the other..." Buck fell silent.

"Well, what do you want to do?" Sassy probed.

"Let's shoot him full of morphine before we pull the chunk off. That's the best we can do for him. But before we do that, I want to find out who he is," Buck determined. Toggling a water-proof rocker switch on his chest, he opened his comm link. "Rabbi, I need you at my position to translate. Rampage, I need you, too."

He heard two clicks in his earpiece from each strike force member acknowledging his order.

Moments later, two soldiers appeared from opposite directions. The first to arrive was Rampage followed moments later by Rabbi.

"What's up, Buck?" Rampage asked

"I wanted you to hear any intel we might get from this…" Buck pause to wave at the disjointed body next to him, "suspect."

"Roger, that."

"Rabbi, see if you can get this man's name and any information about who was in the house," Buck ordered.

Rabbi swiftly knelt to whisper into the pinned man's ear then put his ear to his mouth to catch the barely audible reply. After repeating the process several times, Rabbi stood to report to Buck and Rampage.

"He says his name is Khalil. No last name. All he kept saying was 'Please, please don't let me die. I can reward you. I have money, I'll give you anything you want, just don't let me die.' He just kept repeating it. I couldn't get anything else from him."

"Alright, if that's all there is…give him morphine, then Flexi-cuff his hands and feet so he doesn't do anything crazy when we pull that block off him."

Sergeant Brisbane knelt down and jabbed two ampoules of morphine into the man's shoulder then proceeded with the restraints. By the time he'd finished, the morphine had taken full effect so the soldiers gathered and gripped the chunk of rubble.

"On Three. One, two, three," someone counted and the men grunted and lifted the stone before tossing it to the side. They all turned to see the once pinned man writhing in agony that cut through the morphine. Unintelligible words formed on his mouth but got no farther. His writhing quickly subsided as the life drained from him until he was still. The men looked on, serving to bear witness to the man's passing.

At that moment another call came over the comm link: "I've got another live one over here..."

Buck turned to see Rampage wiping a thin layer of dirt and small clumps of clay from a prone form not six feet from where the nearly severed man lay.

"He's out cold. Big gash on his head, but there doesn't appear to be any external wounds."

"Flexi-cuff him," Buck ordered.

"Alright, then," Buck said to the man kneeling beside the still form next to him, "Sassy, let's go take a look at the one Rampage found. Hopefully, he will survive so that at least we'll have one live one to take back to stand trial for their crimes."

31

The return trip went smoother than the outbound leg, probably because there were no tensions of an upcoming mission to constrict the thoughts of the members of Strike Force Trident. The prisoner they had found in the rubble had suffered a severe concussion, but he was expected to survive to stand trial. The French frigate had stabilized the prisoner well enough for transport and a helicopter had been dispatched from a U.S. destroyer in the Red Sea to retrieve the prisoner for transfer to the States for trial.

It was Buck's understanding that the U.S. Congress, under whose Letter of Marque and Reprisal he was operating, was deadlocked on how to try the pirate. Democrats in Congress wanted to try him in the U.S. Criminal Justice System and give him Constitutional protection. Recent U.S. Supreme Court rulings on unlawful combatants captured on the battlefields in Afghanistan seemed to indicate there may be grounds for credence to this point of view.

The Republicans wanted to try him in a Military Tribunal. There also were legal precedents for this action. Terrorists captured by various means and detained at the U.S. base at Guantanamo Bay Naval Base, Cuba, had already been through this process.

The rub was that these precedents were applicable to unlawful combatants captured on battlefields at a time when the President was operating under authorization of the War Powers Act granted by Congress. The question to be answered was where did this prisoner lay on the legal landscape?

To Buck it was clear. This criminal had robbed and murdered people on the high seas. His prisoner was an Egyptian national, captured in Sudan, by the U.N. on behalf of the United States of America for crimes committed on the high seas against American citizens, where there was no controlling authority. Clear as mud. It seemed to Buck that the only natural impediments to justice were laws.

It was clear that this problem was beyond his expertise. His mission was to bag them or (toe) tag the bad guys. Of that, he was confident that he could meet those expectations. He was on his way to New York with Rampage to debrief his mission to Sudan with Colonel Barrett and Secretary-General McLaughlin. They had arrived back in the United States forty-eight hours earlier, which allowed them to get a solid block of sleep after unloading the *Agrippa* and their equipment before catching a flight to the U. N.'s headquarters

After arriving in New York's JFK Airport, Buck grabbed a local newspaper to see what had been happening in the world since he had stuck his head in the sands of his mission to Sudan nearly a week earlier. Hailing a cab at the curb, Buck tucked the paper under his arm and opened the door for Rampage as a yellow and black checked Ford moved forward from the taxi stand. Both men were feeling the lingering effects of extended travel across the globe and the let-down from a high stress mission. Both seemed content to let the soothing silence and irregular thumps and clattering of the interstate on the taxi's suspension massage their still stiff muscles.

Buck used the time to peruse the tabloid that New

Yorkers called a newspaper while Rampage just stared out the window. Just as the taxi left the interstate to navigate the bump and grind of surface street traffic, the first bit of trouble appeared on their horizon.

"Huh-oh. Get a load of this, Rampage," Buck said, agitatedly shaking the newspaper at its centerfold, before quartering the paper so that he could read with one hand 'U.N. Botches Raid.' Dateline: Cairo, Egypt. Confirmed reports of a failed raid by U.N. troops on the known headquarters of a local pirate gang destroyed one building and killed nineteen people. Reports of those killed included women and children from the village. Details of the pre-dawn battle are limited. U.N. spokesman, Tibor el-Hibiji, offered no comments, saying only 'The U.N. is looking into the matter,' when asked to deny the claims. The Sudanese government, when contacted about the incident, also stated that it is currently gathering facts 'concerning the alleged incident.'"

Steve, who had been reading over Buck's shoulder, tried to find the bright spot in the story. "At least it's below the fold. On the third page..."

"We haven't even debriefed and the press is already mangling the facts," Buck fired back, the fatigue slowing his ability to clamp down on his anger.

"It is what it is," Rampage offered back serenely. "We don't know how many people were killed in that building. We had neither the time, tools, nor manpower to sift through the rubble of that building. For all we know, there *could* have been women and children in that building. We only asked La Barré to tell us how many disembarked from the ship and where they went. There was no way to tell how many were in the house already or who may have joined them in the hours after our intel was formed. I believe they call that the fog of war."

"I can see it now: Secretary-General McLaughlin will get cold feet, blame us for this supposed mess, and cancel the program."

"Listen, Buck. You're a good leader and a helluva field officer. You did nothing wrong but follow the cockamamie orders you were given to the best of your ability. If the Secretary-General can't take a little spilled milk, well screw 'em. Maybe he should get out of the anti-piracy business and quit wasting our time and putting our lives at risk."

"You're right. It's just that I had high hopes for Project Neptune. I felt we could do some real good in the world," Buck said lapsing into silence until they arrived at the U.N. headquarters.

The trip through building security and the procession to Project Neptune's offices seemed like a long walk to the gallows for Buck. He had the irrepressible feeling that despite his best efforts, the program was now doomed, only awaiting the cinch of the executioner's thirteen looped noose.

When he entered the Project's main office, Gloria Stienmetz, jumped out from behind her desk, charging them both.

"There you are! Colonel Barrett wanted to see you the second you came in."

She now had maneuvered behind them, grabbing them both by the biceps and steered them towards Colonel Barrett's door like a determined sheep dog herding its flock, only in a well tailored dress and cashmere sweater.

The alacrity with which he and Rampage had been beset upon only served to deepen Buck's sense of foreboding.

Gloria bustled them through Colonel Barrett's door with barely a knock, to find Colonel Barrett standing behind his desk, facing the large window that looked over the east river, his hands clasped behind his back in a military 'at ease' stance.

"Colonel," Gloria announced, releasing her grip on them, "Lieutenants Kohl and Ramage are here."

Barrett turned to face his two subordinates. "Sit down, gentlemen, please. Would you like anything to drink?"

Buck vacillated between requesting hemlock or nothing. He finally went with, "Nothing sir, I'm fine."

"I'm fine, too, sir," Rampage echoed.

"Thank you, Gloria. That will be all, for now."

Gloria backed out of the door, shutting it as she exited.

"How are you feeling this morning? Have you worked all the kinks out from the travel yet? I'm afraid I just don't travel as well as I did when I was in Her Majesty's service. Always found that a good run seemed to work the kinks out satisfactorily. But all this paperwork seems to keep me from exercising," he said gesturing to his spotless desk. "Besides, where do you run in a city like this? Take a taxi to Central Park? There just seems to be something disingenuous about taking a taxi to go for a run in the country."

"Ahh… well, I can see your point, sir. A good run would be most welcome right now," Buck agreed.

"The Secretary-General would like to see us and we have an appointment with him in a few minutes."

"Sir," Buck started, "I just wanted to say that I take full responsibility for the Sudan mission. Any shortcomings in the performance of Strike Force Trident are mine and mine alone."

"That's very nice, Lieutenant, but what the bloody hell are you talking about?"

"Sir, it's all in the paper -- the press is calling it a 'botched' mission, saying we killed women and children. I just assumed, given the negative blow back, that

Secretary-General McLaughlin would want to make major changes to the program or cancel it."

Colonel Barrett fixed Buck with a paternal smile, "So that's it, is it? You assume that the Secretary-General believes everything the press reports? Let me assure you, the Secretary-General is firmly behind this program and the results it produced. I watched the mission tapes with him. He was quite irritated that the pirates refused to surrender, causing you to destroy their building. It is true that there were several teenage girls that the pirates held as sex slaves taken from the local warlord. But just so we're clear, the Secretary-General feels that it was the pirates that put those girls' lives in danger and ultimately killed them, not you, Lieutenant."

Buck felt a weight lifted from his shoulders.

"The Secretary-General stands firmly behind this program. He knows there will be opposition to his decision to take active combat actions against pirates. It's the way of politics -- there will always be opponents that will want to sabotage you at every turn. And the press are their useful idiots."

"But sir, what about the Sudanese government's inquiry into the mission? Won't that be a problem?"

"I can assure you that the mission was taken with their full knowledge, permission and blessing. The warlord in that area was gettin' too big for his britches. The Sudanese felt that a raid against some non-Sudanese National pirates would be a good objective lesson for him. From what I understand, the warlord is the one crying shame and releasing the story of women and children killed. Could not make the Sudanese happier; to them, the more the warlord cries, the more they know their little message is being taken to heart."

"Then the Secretary-General is not going to make any

changes to Project Neptune?"

"Not in the least wee bit. He wants to thank you personally for your efforts on the last mission. It'd be my guess, watching the ordinance go off on the mission tapes kind of drove it home for him that this was not make-believe and that people, his people, could get killed."

"Wow, I guess I had that all figured wrong," Buck said to himself introspectively.

"Don't be too hard on yourself, Buck." Colonel Barrett said as he came around the desk and put a hand on Buck's shoulder. "I know that, as a warrior, it's hard to trust politicians. After I retired from the Service, I went through a similar transition of sorts when I came to this job. I know that you've not spent too much time with the Secretary-General. But, I can tell you, he is a different kind of politician. He's made of pretty stern stuffing; he's not one to cut and run. As you get to know him, you'll learn that it's difficult as hell to get his word on something -- he's not the type you can corner easily. But when he gives you his word, it's good as gold."

Colonel Barrett glanced at his watch. "It's time to go see SEC-GEN McLaughlin. Gentlemen..." gesturing towards the door, indicating that now would be a good time for Buck and Rampage to un-ass themselves from their chairs.

On the way to the SEC-GEN'S office, they continued their conversation. "Secretary-General McLaughlin has been fully updated on the debriefing you gave me while flying back from the Red Sea. I believe that there are a few questions that he wanted to ask you himself."

"Do you know about what, sir?"

"Knowing the man's humility, I have an idea. But not enough of one to proffer a guess."

"Colonel?" Rampage broke his silence.

"Yes, Steve."

"The paper said that the death count was nineteen. Do we know if that is an accurate number?"

"No, we don't. That part of the coastal region is effectively controlled by local warlords. The Sudanese government has no way of safely confirming the count, even if it had an interest in doing so."

"So the claim of eight more deaths than the dozen pirates that we know entered the building could be totally bogus?"

"That would be my guess. These warlord types are always aggrandizing. They think that an inflated victim count is the way to get sympathy, status, or free relief from the world community. But the truth of the matter is that they slaughter far more of their own for no reason other than because they can. It's something you get used to working at the U.N. It's a way of shifting focus from their heinous acts. I don't put much stock in such claims. Neither does the SEC-GEN.

"Besides, eight additional deaths," Colonel Barrett continued, "seems a little out of line. We knew that there were a dozen pirates that left the boat and entered the house. That would mean that nearly two-thirds of them had their own concubines, an unlikely proportion. Even more unlikely that they were family men and had brought their families from Egypt while they ransacked and pillaged. Until it is proven otherwise, all that we know for sure is that twelve pirates entered that building and eleven of them died."

"What about the prisoner, Salah?" Rampage tried once more to make sure that his conscience could be clear. "What does he say?"

"Right now, he is saying anything that he thinks that we want to hear. Initially he said that only members of his crew were in the building. Then he changed it to 'there might have been two or three local girls there.' When the report of nineteen deaths first emerged a couple of days ago, we asked him if there were six other locals in the building. He said yes. So who knows?

"By the way, he confirmed that the man you found nearly severed in two was the pirate leader, a man named Khalil. Salah and he were on the roof during the firefight trying to direct their fire."

Buck let out a little "tssk" at this news. He had no idea that the tactical situation had been that out of control. That meant that turning on their lights and broadcasting their surrender terms over the loud speaker had allowed a numerically superior opposition enough time to organize a defense from a strong position, and to get command and control elements in spotter positions. If it had not been for the firepower of the *Agrippa*, used when it was, it was very likely that the strike team would have been badly mauled. Buck vowed that he would never have that happen again. He would refuse to lead a mission that put them at such a disadvantage.

They had arrived at the top floor and the Secretary-General's office, finishing the last of their conversation in the waiting lobby. Shortly one of the secretaries disconnected herself from the phone and approached the waiting party. "If you will follow me, Secretary-General McLaughlin is ready to receive you."

Colonel Barrett, Buck, and Rampage followed the secretary through the outer office and through a double set of doors leading to the Secretary-General's office suite. "Gentlemen! Welcome," a booming Australian greeting belted them as soon as they entered, "please, have a seat." It took a moment for Buck to find the location of the voice in the palatial office. Secretary-General McLaughlin was organizing documents at a credenza along a wall, his greeting tossed over his shoulder.

When finished, he strode up to Buck with hand extended. "Lieutenant Kohl, fine work in the Red Sea. I'm glad to see that you accomplished your mission unscathed." He pumped Buck's hand a couple times and turned to Rampage.

"Lieutenant Ramage. Congratulations. Well done," he said with another quick pump of the hand.

As everyone settled into their chairs, Andrew McLaughlin started in without preamble. "I'm sure that Colonel Barrett has told you that I have reviewed the mission tapes with him and view the loss of life as regrettable, but unavoidable given the reactions of the pirates. I believe that they were given every opportunity to surrender. Colonel Barrett has walked me through the tapes pointing out that you were outnumbered and in open positions, giving you no option other than to call upon the *Agrippa* for assistance."

"Yessir," Buck acknowledged.

"I just have one question for you and Steve: Is there anything that could have been done differently to produce a better outcome?"

Buck hesitated for a moment before deciding to go for it. "Yessir, there is."

Andrew could tell that the young lieutenant had something to say but was holding back. "Go ahead, Lieutenant Kohl, you may speak freely. The goal here is to improve as we proceed."

"Yessir." Buck stalled as he tried to figure out how to tell the superior in front of him that his screwed up rules of engagement came perilously close to getting him and his team killed. His mind was screaming the obvious, but he understood that tact was a better option with the still unknown quantity of the Secretary-General.

"Sir, I believe the rules of engagement for this mission led considerably to the outcome. Information gained from interrogation of the prisoner we took indicates that the tactical situation was far worse than even I knew at the time of the assault."

"What do you mean?"

"Sir, according to the prisoner, he and their leader had positioned themselves on the roof and were directing the fire of the occupants inside."

"Yes, I've been kept appraised of his interrogation."

"Well sir, that means that the opposing forces to Strike Team Trident had enough time to organize their defenses against our attack, time they got by us turning on the lights and making repeated announcements to surrender. These men were heavily armed and determined. They were numerically superior and fixed in a good defensive position. You saw the defense they put up on the video. There was no way that the strike team could have dug them out of that position. It would have taken six times that number of people to dig them out of that building in a frontal assault. We aren't built for that.

"The Letter of Marque limits Operation Neptune to twelve members, which leaves six slots for ground pounders. Given those parameters and our mission objectives, Strike Team Trident has been built for speed, stealth and surprise, not for frontal assaults more suited for larger, more heavily armed forces. The rules of engagement did not let us use our assets in the best way. It's like using a scalpel to crack nuts, instead of a hammer. Sooner or later, the scalpel is going to get broken. We were fortunate this time that the target was within effective distance of the *Agrippa's* guns. Otherwise, Strike Team Trident would surely have had its butt kicked between its shoulder blades.

"I believe that rules of engagement contributed to the unnecessary loss of life on this mission. If the strike team had been allowed to perform a tactical breach entry, there would have been a better chance of taking more prisoners."

"I see," said Andrew, steepling his fingers in front of his chin and leaning back in his chair. "And what would you suggest we learn from this first effort?"

"Sir, I suggest that you let us use the experience, talent, and skills for which we were hired. Tell us what you need to have done and let us figure out the best way to get the results you need."

"Are you suggesting that I quit micro-managing you, Lieutenant?"

"No, sir. I am merely suggesting that perhaps the more efficient way to get the results you seek may be to set the objectives and then let the strike force you have assembled work unencumbered using their expertise to get the best results possible."

"That still sounds like you're telling me to quit meddling." A tense silence filled the room. "But, the problem is, that I could not agree more with you." The tension departed as quickly as it brewed. "I am left with the unshakable lesson that my interfering with military matters, with which I have no expertise, may have contributed greatly to those deaths," he concluded, speaking more to himself than those in the room.

Snapping forward, placing his palms on the desk, Andrew broke out of his internal examination. "It would be a waste if we," he paused, "I... did not learn from this first outing. In that vein, I have a new assignment for you.

"As you recall, Dr. Cadburess and the original crew of the U.N. research vessel *Constellation* were killed or taken, except for one person, by pirates off the Caribbean coast of

Mexico. The *Constellation* has been refitted and is putting back to sea to continue the research of the original crew. Their research is deemed vital to the world. We've not been able as of yet to develop any information about the pirates who struck the ship so there is a chance that the new crew of the *Constellation* may be heading into jeopardy. I want Strike Force Trident to keep an eye on them and make sure nothing happens to them."

"I've read the reports of that attack. Something has always bothered me," Buck confided. "The lone survivor said that the pirates killed one of the crew indiscriminately before looking for Dr. Cadburess. Why did the pirates single out Dr. Cadburess by name first and kill him? According to the witness, the doctor was first separated and then stabbed, which triggered a killing frenzy by the pirates."

"I too have been puzzled by those events," Colonel Barrett injected.

"What kind of research," Rampage put it directly, "were they doing that was so important that a pirate would know the lead researcher's name and want to kill him?"

"Oil exploration," answered Andrew.

"I wonder what is so exotic about looking for oil that marked the crew for death," Buck continued the thread of thought.

"To a pirate, probably nothing more than being in charge of a large boat, richly bedecked with expensive equipment," Colonel Barrett pointed out.

"Yeah, but to call him out by name?" Buck persisted.

Andrew McLaughlin steered the conversation in another direction from the speculation. "A mystery we may never know the answer to. Now, Lieutenant Kohl, I want you to take Strike Force Trident to catch up with Dr. Melrony aboard the *Constellation* in Cozumel, Mexico. Your mission is to protect the U.N.'s vessel and hunt for pirates. You'll need to coordinate with the ship's research schedule."

"I've already got Yoshi and Major La Barré working out the last details of transportation right now. They will start the egress oh-eight hundred tomorrow morning," Colonel Barrett informed Buck and Steve.

"Who else knows about this deployment?" Buck asked.

"What do you mean?" asked a surprised Andrew McLaughlin.

"What he means," stepped in Rampage, "is that it was awful fishy that the pirates knew the name of your lead scientist. That means that he had to have had inside information. Knowing a captain's name is not difficult to obtain; he has to register with harbor masters and other government officials when he enters port. But a lead scientist? That could mean someone was talking to the pirates from inside the U.N."

"We don't know that for sure," Andrew countered.

"Still," Colonel Barrett said jumping into the fray, "it is reasonable to assume that someone who knew about the *Constellation* was giving the pirates information. It makes operational sense, given that possibility, to keep the information about Strike Force Trident's deployment limited to only those who need to know."

"I have to tell Dr. Espenoza, the head of the Mineral Resource Research Division. He is Dr. Melrony's supervisor. I've already shared with him that I intended to deploy Strike Force Trident for protection."

"Does he know when we are to be deployed?" Buck pressed.

"No. I told him I needed to confer with you before I would know when you could deploy. He is aware that I am meeting with you today to discuss the details, and he expects to get that information shortly after we adjourn."

Colonel Barrett could see that Buck and Steve were starting a slow boil at the news that their deployments were being broadcast throughout the U.N. Covert operators like Strike Force Trident were used to having their whereabouts kept as closely guarded secrets; their lives depended on such secrecy. The knowledge that information about their activities was being passed, probably by memo, to some mid-level bureaucrat would scare the living daylights out of any covert warrior worth his salt. He didn't blame Buck and Rampage for their anger; they might as well have posted Strike Force Trident's travel agenda on the cafeteria bulletin board. Still, he had to act fast to avert Buck or Rampage from saying something regrettable to the Secretary-General.

"This is not good. Release of this sort of information is a major breach of security. Secrecy is how we stay alive in this business," the Colonel gently chided the Secretary-General. "But, I think we can make it work for us in this situation, though. You have given Dr. Espenoza no information yet on Project Neptune deployments, correct?"

"As I said," the Secretary-General said sheepishly, chagrined at unknowingly putting their lives in danger, "I was to tell him the arrangements after this meeting."

Colonel Barrett put his chin on his chest, his gaze looking inward. "Good. Tell him that Strike Force Neptune will need ten days to refit and replenish. Plus, they need three days' travel time to get on scene, so he can expect them in thirteen days' time."

"Colonel, we've already completed our refit and replenishment cycle. We can deploy to Cozumel in twenty-four hours," Rampage volunteered.

"Yes, I know that, but I don't want anyone else to be privy to that kind of information. Mr. Secretary-General,

do you know when the *Constellation* was to sail from
Cozumel?"

"In three days. I was led to believe that it would only
take a few days for the *Agrippa* to be ready. So I gave Dr.
Espenoza an approximate idea so he could plan his ship's
research schedule."

"Tell Dr. Espenoza to go ahead and have the
Constellation sail in three days as planned." Colonel Barrett
directed, "Tell him that Strike Force Trident will be
delayed and will catch up with the *Constellation* after
thirteen days." He looked up Buck and Rampage, "That
ought to set-up things right. Buck, I want you to deploy
Strike Force Trident immediately. You should be able to
launch out of Cozumel in thirty-six hours. Make contact
quietly with Dr. Melrony in port before the *Constellation*
sails. I want you to leave Cozumel's port as soon as you
can. Ship out a day early if you can -- that way no one will
be able to link you with the *Constellation*. Have the
Constellation load on your extra fuel and stores. If the word
is out that you're not expected until two weeks later, no
one will be looking for you in two days. If someone from
the U.N. was talking, then he'll be put to use sending out
disinformation," he finished, satisfied with his little
subterfuge.

Both Buck and Steve had looks of relief on their faces at
Colonel Barrett's remedy, which slowly gave way to sly
grins at his masterful reversal.

"Anything else then?" Colonel Barrett asked. "No? Then
I think we're done here."

"Alright then, good luck and God's speed," Andrew
said, rising from behind his desk in a fluid, polished move
of dismissal. In a jocular tone, he continued, "After the last
mission, hopefully a quiet cruise on the Mexican
Caribbean would be a welcome change."

"Yessir," Rampage and Buck answered in unison.

"David, would you mind staying a moment? I have some other business I wish to discuss."

"Certainly, Secretary-General. Buck, Steve, go on ahead. I'll catch up by phone later on. You've got a few hours before your plane leaves -- go see the sights of New York or do some shopping," he said waving them out the door.

******

As soon as they cleared the Secretary-General's office pool, Rampage could no longer repress his bachelor's good luck. "Join the Navy, see the world. Next stop: Cozumel."

"We probably won't be in port long enough for you to do any carousing. And if we are, I'm sure you'll be too busy," Buck countered.

"One can always hope. Besides, I work fast. I won't need much time to pack in my carousing."

"Now, Steve," Buck started, a sternness settling into his voice, "I know that this sounds like a milk run, babysitting some scientist, running around the Caribbean, Cozumel, and all. But I want you to start getting your head into the game, here. I need you to start focusing on the important details of the mission. The Super Mako isn't really set up for long cruises, so we are really going to need to be very precise on fuel and supplies."

Rampage looked askew at Buck's seriousness, not sure what was up with his friend.

"I need you to start by finding out what kind of bait, poles, lures, etc. we're going to need for an extended milk run and what fish are running," Buck said breaking into a huge grin, Steve laughing at being tricked.

Both men were still laughing as they re-entered the inner

offices of Project Neptune. Gloria heard them enter and turned to the noise with the cold look of a spider that feels the vibration of a fly in its web. She moved to intercept Rampage before he could enter his office and start the important work outlined moments before.

"Colonel Barrett tells me that your schedule is clear for the rest of the day and it's not 'til late afternoon that your flight leaves, so I booked you for the rest of your day in cultural sensitivity training. It's mandatory, and you have yet to get it done."

"My dear Gloria," Steve said suavely, grabbing both her hands and alternately kissed the knuckles of both hands, "I could not possibly bear to go to cultural sensitivity training right now."

Unused to such physical contact in the austere professional environment she worked, Gloria turned several shades of red at having her knuckles kissed by such a large, handsome man.

"I'm much too fragile now to explore the beauty between cultures. You see, the life and death mission I just returned from has sapped my inner defenses. I need several more days," He paused again to kiss her knuckles, "before my vulnerability will be lessened enough to so that I can absorb the beauty of differences without having an emotional collapse." He had been maneuvering for the office's front door and now was standing in front of it. "I must go now," Steve said with his best hang-dog expression and slipped out the door, leaving Gloria flustered and swooning.

Buck, who watched the scene, shaking his head at the performance, slid into his office still chortling to himself. "The boy's got talent," he was saying to himself as his cell phone started ringing. It was Rampage.

"Hello."

"Did she buy it?"

"She was still standing in front of the door, kinda swaying to herself, last I saw. Nice touch with the 'vulnerability': a stroke of genius. Solid nines across the board on the performance...the Polish judge gave you a ten."

"Well, what can I say? I was feeling inspired. Listen, I'll find an empty office to do the work I was going to do in mine. Meet you in the lobby in an hour?"

"Roger."

32

Demetrio Salterez was sitting in the same bar in Cozumel, at the same table as the last time he had done business with the man in the linen suit and no name. He had been surprised when their mutual acquaintance had told him the stranger wanted another meeting. He was told that there was a new problem that needed his special touch. The last problem had been very lucrative for Demetrio.

The ten thousand dollars he was paid last time had been a major bonus. He had not told his pirate crew of the contract to kill the scientist, and he kept the money for himself. His crew had been just as surprised as that of the captured ship when Demetrio had called out one of the passengers by name before killing him. But their surprise had soon been forgotten as the crew started to collect their lucrative haul. It had not mattered to them how their leader had come by the information that such a wealthy, unarmed prize ship would be at the place and time where they had lain in ambush.

The haul from that capture had allowed Demetrio to upgrade his operations. When he had ransacked the *Constellation*, there had been more, much more booty than he could load into his small boat. He had to leave so much equipment behind. Every day, Demetrio agonized over the equipment and plunder that he had been forced to leave because he had no capacity to carry it away. The food stores alone would have fed him like a king for a year.

Using a large portion of the proceeds from that prize before paying the crew, Demetrio had purchased a small coastal freighter. An old rusted tub, it was neither fast nor elegant, but it could haul tons of equipment and booty from the ships they plundered. So now, Demetrio's pirate operation was a two-boat affair. A fast chase boat loaded with men and weapons to subdue the target boat and the slower, larger freighter that would pull up alongside so that stores, equipment, and machinery could be off - loaded.

Demetrio's next professional goal was to buy himself a warehouse with its own pier. This way, he could start to warehouse his plunder and sell it on the black market when the market was at high tide. He had been quickly fencing off his spoils to third parties who made larger profits, selling it to less than reputable shipyards owners looking to pad their margins of profit. Now he was aiming to do the same. All he needed was a place to store his collection of spoils.

It was with this thought-- how he was going to spend his next round of profits from the stranger--when the lifeless, hard blue eyes walked through the bar's doors.

Demetrio waited until the man's scanning eyes met his before he gave any sign of recognition with a small nod. The man's tan linen suit had been replaced by a brown one, with a nondescript open-collar shirt. The one thing that had not changed was the man's cold stare.

"Greetings, my friend! We meet again," Demetrio called, forcing jocularity as the man pulled out the chair opposite and sat down. "I knew that you would need my services again. Demetrio gets things done, makes his customers happy to come back for more."

The blue-eyed man said nothing, only staring; nothing in his demeanor acknowledged Demetrio's greeting. Demetrio grew uncomfortable under the man's gaze. He suddenly remembered why he disliked the man. But he liked his money, so he made another attempt to open a conversation. "Very clean last time, *sí*? No witnesses."

"Yes, quite," the man finally spoke. "I have a new chore for you. Just like last time. I want you to intercept the *Constellation* again. She sails in two days, same destination as before."

"The same ship? She's come back?" Demetrio's eyes glazed over briefly as he marveled at his good luck. A second bite at the same equipment-rich ship that he had thought about every day since his misfortune of having too small a boat the first time he hit her. And she must have been refitted, meaning all the equipment would be new. Now for sure he could afford a warehouse. But his natural wariness snapped in, as he considered the ramifications of plundering the same ship again.

"You want me to hit the same ship again? This is very bad," he lied. "They undoubtedly will have better defenses this time. Nobody is stupid enough to send out a ship unprotected twice. No, this cannot be done."

"I will pay you the usual fee. The ship has made arrangements for protection, but it has been delayed for many days, so the *Constellation* has decided to sail without it. She sails in two days. So, you see, there is no cause for concern."

"So you say. Even so, if this is true, the ship has surely increased its on-board defenses making it more difficult and dangerous to board. If you want me to capture the vessel again, I will need three times the price of the last contract. That is only reasonable."

"You will get the same fee for the same work, or you

will get nothing at all. Or, perhaps you would prefer the alternative, a knife buried to the hilt in your chest. I'll give you a few minutes to make up your mind."

"Who do you think you're threatening?! It is you who will not leave here alive," Demetrio blustered.

The calm of the stranger was unnerving. When he threatened the blond man, his only reaction was a slight narrowing of his eyes, which only served to underscore the threat the man exuded.

"Two seconds."

"Fine, fine, I'll do the job. But twice the pay."

"One second."

"Okay, okay. Just give me the money."

"Before I give you anything, you need to know what I want done."

"I got it already," Demetrio said hotly, "intercept the U.N. research vessel again when it sails in two days. I assume that I am free to do what I want with the boat and crew again?"

"Yes, but this time there is someone different on the boat that you must make sure dies. You must make sure you kill Dr. Melrony."

"We'll kill everybody," Demetrio tossed off.

"Say the name," a hard flint in his voice.

"Whose name?"

"Say it," the man hissed.

"Alright. Dr. Melrony. Satisfied? Can I have my money now?"

The hard-eyed man reached into his suit's breast pocket, pulled out an envelope and dropped it on the table. "I'll be satisfied when I read about the good doctor's disappearance."

Demetrio started to reach for the envelope then yanked his hand back as if scalded, suddenly remembering his business partner's mongoose-like strike with a knife last time. Thrusting his hands back into his lap, he chose to just stare, until the man got up without a word and turned towards the door.

Demetrio watched until he saw that the man was near the doors before he reached for the envelope. His hand was close to closing in when a knife flashed through the air, imbedding in the tabletop and piercing the web of his thumb. The searing pain caused him to yank his hand back instinctively. This only caused the razor sharp edge of the black switch blade's knife to neatly dissect the remaining thumb web. The wound started bleeding profusely. Demetrio wrapped it in his shirt before looking up to see the blue-eyed man standing at the door.

"That," he said in his quiet, menacing voice, "was for trying to negotiate."

The bar's doors opened, and Demetrio squinted against the bright daylight, catching a brief glimpse of the man's silhouette before he was gone.

Out in the bright daylight, the stranger took a moment to put on his sunglasses before he strode to his rental car. Before slipping into the leather seats of the Mercedes convertible, he withdrew a cell phone from his pant pocket, pressing a speed dial number on the way to his ear. On the third ring, the familiar voice of his client answered.

"Yes."

"It has been arranged."

"Good. Any problems this time?"

"None that I could not handle Mr. Minister. These peasant criminals are so predictable."

"When will your people make their attack?"

"Two days from now, shortly after the *Constellation* sails."

"Excellent."

"Yes," he said into the phone, but the other party was already gone.

33

The transportation of the *Agrippa* went much smoother this time out, arriving in less than twenty-eight hours. She was tied up at a nondescript pier at the far end of Cozumel's commercial waterfront. When he left, Rampage had been busy overseeing the last of the provisioning when Buck decided it was high time to make contact with Dr. Melrony aboard the *Constellation*. He had slipped below decks to change into civilian clothes before making his way across the deck to the pier. He no sooner emerged from the strike team room onto the deck when the catcalls started from the members of the strike force.

"Are we on a mission or a sightseeing tour, mate?" Coop called out.

"Blimey, boss. Why didn't you tell me to bring my shorts? I've got a lovely pair of lime green Bermudas I've been holding back for the right occasion," said Sassy, hauling a heavy ammo box up the gangway.

"Great knees," Lenz commented dryly from where he was working on one of the rear deck gun mounts.

"Who dresses you?" Bear called, looking at the rumpled shorts and nondescript olive green polo shirt as he came up the gangway with a box of fresh food that had just been delivered dockside.

Rabbi just looked on, smiling from where he was unloading a box into a deck locker.

It was all in good fun, and Buck was glad to take their

ribbing if it meant that unit cohesion had finally reached a satisfactory level of comfort and the men were in good spirits.

At the bottom of the gangway he found Rampage excitedly inventorying the bait that had arrived. "It looks like it's all here," he informed Buck as he departed.

Buck had asked the deliveryman of the bait, who was going in the direction he needed, to wait and give him a lift to the pier where the *Constellation* was birthed. When he arrived, the dock was a hive of sweating workers ferrying bags, boxes, and pallets of materials to the cranes that were lifting their loads to the ship's deck. He found the gangway and made his way to the top, where he was engaged by one of the ship's officers standing in a white tropical uniform, a clipboard clutched in one hand.

"Can I help you?" the officer asked.

Buck had decided that his best cover for entering the ship would be something vague dashed with a liberal dose of the truth. "Hi, I'm Bill Thorton, with the American Consulate," he said thrusting out his hand. "I'm here to see Dr. Melrony."

"Nice to meet you. You'll find Dr. Melrony on the back deck," he said waving his pen in that general direction before raising his clipboard to log the visitor's arrival.

Buck made his way towards the stern of the boat until he paused at the top of a steel stair that led to the aft deck. Surveying the deck, Buck was able to sort the ship's crew, distinguished by their youth and the sweaty work they were doing unloading the cranes' deposits and the scientists, mostly older men, who seemed to be doing the supervising. Their main function appeared to be to point and give directions. He had not received any information about Dr. Melrony or a photo to identify him. No problem, he had figured, he'd just ask someone to point him out.

Close to the ship's super structure stood a young woman dressed in a tank top, oversized shorts with lots of cargo pockets, hiking boots like the kind favored by graduate students, a floppy boonie hat jammed on her head with white zinc-oxide ointment slathered over her nose, and holding a clipboard. Obviously a graduate student or intern, she was the perfect person to ask. As he approached, he noticed the tanned skin was heavily freckled on her shoulders, with a light smattering on her visible delicate features.

"Hey, Mel. Boxes one-one-two-seven-J, K, M and ... B," one of the older men yelled across the deck to her as he peered at a pallet just deposited.

"Got it. Thank you," she yelled back, making checkmarks as she found them on the list.

"Excuse me," Buck said sidling up next to her, peering out onto the deck, "but can you..."

"Mel!" Another man shouted from out on the deck. "Boxes two-three-three-seven E, F, G and J."

"Got it."

"...tell me which one of those gentlemen is Dr. Melrony?" he finished in between their shouts.

"Ah, that would be me," said the voice at his shoulder.

Surprised, Buck turned to examine the person next to him. Slightly embarrassed, he stammered, "I'm sorry, I just thought that one of them..." he vaguely waved at the deck, hoping his animation would help pass as an explanation. "You're Dr. Melrony?"

"Yes, I get that all the time," she said matter-of-factly. "I'm almost used to it... *almost*." The last word accompanied by just the slightest flaring of her nostrils. "What is it that I can do for you?" she said with brevity in a clipped Irish accent that belied the irritation she was feeling towards Buck.

"My name is Buck Kohl, I'm in charge of your security detail, Strike Force Trident, sent by U.N. Secretary-General McLaughlin. I need to talk to you."

A look of confusion came over her face, "I thought that you weren't supposed to be here for another eleven days?"

"A security precaution…the bogus arrival information. Is there someplace we can talk?"

"Sure. Just a moment, please," she said before she yelled to one of the elderly scientists examining crates. "Phil, can you take over for me for a while?"

As one of the scientists took the clipboard from her, Buck was already headed back up to the top of the stairs for their private conversation. She caught up with him a moment later.

"Listen, I want to apologize again," Buck started. "Not a good way to start an assignment," he said thrusting out his hand. "Let's start over, my name is Buck Kohl. I'm here to protect you and your crew."

"Apology accepted," she said, her delicate hand accepting his. "Doctor Lila Melrony, head of this research excursion."

For the first time, Buck was able to see her face beyond the freckles and ointment. She had large, brilliant green eyes, slight creases in the corners due to her life outdoors, which only served to highlight her long lashes. Under the nose slather, he could see that she had a straight petite nose with a slight upturn at the end that was framed by the large, high apples of her cheeks. A dainty, handsome chin anchored her face, perfectly balanced by her full lips. The tanned face that Buck could now see was framed by tufts of red hair that had escaped from under the boonie hat. The flame of her hair seemed to set off the brilliance of her white smile that she was now beaming at him.

"My orders were to make contact with you once we arrived. Unfortunately, the only contact information they gave me was Dr. Melrony. I should have figured it out by the guys calling you 'Mel'."

"Well, that's all good and well," she said in her Irish lilt, "but I'm still a bit confused. Why did they not tell me that you were here?"

"As I said, a security measure. There were some concerns about Dr. Cadburess's death, and it was felt a prudent measure not to announce our presence, even to you, until you were about to depart."

"Ah, yes, poor Dr. Cadburess." A cloud of sadness drifted across her face and then passed before she continued. "It is my understanding that you will be hovering about while we do our work."

Buck smiled at her choice of words. "Yes, we will be in the vicinity, but you won't be able to see us."

"What, will you be invisible, like little leprechauns?" she said, flashing him another brilliant smile.

"Something like that," he said flushing just ever so slightly. "If you see anything suspicious, anything out of place, anything that gives you concern, ask the captain to tune to this frequency," he said, thrusting a piece of paper at her, "and say the code word 'Blister.' We will be there in seven minutes or less."

"You'll be that close, and we won't be able to see you?" A look of doubt crossed her face.

"Like I said, you won't be able to see us...visually or otherwise."

She raised her eyebrows, pursing her lips slightly as she digested this information.

"But we will from time to time need to rendezvous with you to refresh our supplies." He quickly outlined that fuel and water bladders would be delivered shortly dockside and Strike Force Trident's need for replenishment at sea. "Long term sea patrols are better suited for larger, longer range cruising ships than us, but well, we're all that the U.N. has."

"That seems like it will encumber our deck space, possibly compromising our research. Certainly, we hadn't planned on time for an at-sea-replenishment of another ship. This will impact our schedule too much. I'm sorry, but I just cannot allow this much delay."

"The alternative could be worse. Just ask Dr. Cadburess to see what he thinks. Oh wait, you can't...."

Scowling, Dr. Melrony acquiesced, "All right then. Is there anything else?"

"No, just carry on with your research. Pretend we're not there. We'll pick you up as you leave the harbor and shadow you. Just don't tell anybody else on board about your escort until you're outside the harbor."

"What about Captain..."

"Including the Captain," he cut her off.

"He'll need to know about the bladders."

"He still believes that we are joining him in eleven days. The bladders will be no problem to the cover story. Any other questions?"

Dr. Melrony shook her head.

"Well, good sailing. With any luck, this will all just be a quiet cruise for both of us."

With that, Buck took his leave, retracing his steps back to the dock, where he hailed a taxi.

34

"Keep us just below the horizon, as we discussed, Tadhg," Buck directed as they picked up the *Constellation* as it emerged from the harbor.

"Very good, Buck."

"You know, if anything is going to happen, I think the greatest likelihood will be in the next twenty-four hours. I've examined the reports of when the *Constellation* was found adrift last time. When they found her, it was three days after she left port, forty miles out to sea. I've studied the lone survivor's statement, the meteorological data, and the tide and current charts. I think the *Constellation* was attacked somewhere around twenty miles after she left port. At, say, seven knots an hour... that puts the attack in the first three hours."

"Makes sense to me, Buck. The pirates stay close to the port, so maybe they have someone scouting potential targets in there and pick them off as they come out. Twenty miles would be about right too-- far enough out that nobody could respond to a call for help in time but close enough to Cozumel to sell what they steal while enjoying the benefits of the city."

"*Ja*, that's the way I see it, too." Grels added. "If I were a pirate, that's the way I'd do it. The further out you get, the more difficult an intercept is. Unless, of course, a protracted chase can be executed without calls for help from the Mexican authorities or someone else in the area.

Since the Mexicans have very little coastal presence in law enforcement or military, the further away from major ports, the less likely you are to get help. It all comes back to a quick pounce shortly after coming out of port."

"What's the radar solution look like?"

"Relatively light," supplied Grels. "Approximately thirty contacts."

"Anything suspicious along the *Constellation's* predicted path?"

"Impossible to tell, Buck. We have contacts traveling in all directions, some stationary, several doing circles. Lots of fishing vessels and coastal traffic."

"I guess we'll just have to wait it out then. I'm sure the *Constellation* will call us if they see something that makes them nervous."

******

Three hours into the trip, and Dr. Lila Melrony was beginning to feel that they were out of the danger zone. She had stayed on the bridge for the initial transit of the waters outside Cozumel, in case there was an attack. But as minutes stretched into hours, her fears lessened, so much so that she decided that she would go to her cabin to review the geological data of the search area, the Chicxulub Crater, on the northwestern corner of Mexico's Yucatán Peninsula, when her cabin's intercom started to buzz. Lifting the hand set to her ear, she heard the first mate's voice before she could even say a word. "Dr. Melrony, could you please come to the bridge?"

"I'll be right there."

Dr. Melrony arrived on the bridge to find every available pair of binoculars on the starboard wing trained on the rear of the boat. The viewers' concentration was so intense that her presence went unnoted until she asked what was going on.

"Here, take a look," the Captain handed her his pair of binoculars.

She could easily see the small, open outboard-powered boat filled with men riding up their wake three hundred yards behind them without the binoculars. In the sharp relief of the glasses' optics, she could see the boat had eight men, all clinging to the gunwales as the little boat pounded in the wake's waves and the ocean's swell. Obviously, the little boat was running at full throttle to catch up to them. "Who are they? Any idea?"

"Could be pirates. Could be locals trying to sell their catch or fruit to us. I can't tell. It's a little odd to have that many men in a boat this far out, but I can't see any weapons or anything to suggest a threat. So I'm just going to wait to see what happens. I don't want to call our security just yet. Not until I know a little more."

******

The little boat had swerved to the starboard side to clear the wake and was now in the *Constellation's* rear quarter, gaining rapidly to pull even with the bridge.

Demetrio, who had grown more sophisticated in his pirating methods, eyed the big blue ship, gauging the distance. Satisfied, he yelled, to his second-in-command, "Now, Emilio! Show them the fish!"

******

From the starboard bridge deck, Dr. Melrony and the captain watched, a man in the bow of the small boat stood, braced by those behind him and held up a rope with several large fish strung on it, smiling broadly. This little subterfuge always allowed them to get in close for good, clean first shots.

"Just fishermen trying the sell us some fish," the captain said from beneath his binoculars, a sigh of relief evident in his voice. Both the captain and Dr. Melrony removed the binoculars from their eyes, satisfied to identify the boat as a non-threat.

Dr. Melrony moved to go back into the bridge while the captain moved to the platform's outside railing to wave them off.

The boat had pulled even with the bridge and was starting to edge forward. The captain gave a series of waves, arms crossed over his head to signal they were not interested, when suddenly three or four men in the boat bent down, then straightened up to settle rocket launchers on their shoulders. Before he could even yell a warning, three rockets fired, white smoke trails erupting from the red orange flames at the grenade's tails as the warheads accelerated straight for him.

Two warheads impacted directly on the starboard side of the bridge aft of the wing's door. The third glanced off the front of the bridge before detonating.

Dr. Melrony was three steps into the bridge when a sudden wave of heat and overpressure punched into her, violently thrusting her forward. A shower of glass projectiles that had been the bridge's forward windows on the starboard side slashed her right shoulder, arm and cheek before she was slammed into the starboard navigational console.

Stunned and bleeding, Lila did not know how long she lay smashed against the console. Slowly her senses, one-by-one started to register with her brain. The first was pain, from all over. Her back and kidneys screamed shooting bolts of pain that clogged her brain's capacity to process anything else. Ever so slowly, these started to recede enough that she could start to feel the other parts of her body. Her left shoulder was on fire where she had collided with the console. She could feel a warm wetness trickling down her right arm and tasted copper saltiness in her mouth.

Slowly she roused herself, turning to look for the captain. The door to the starboard wing had been torn from the doorway and hung dangling from the bottom hinge, one corner dug in the deck. Through the opening she could see the mangled grating and rails of what had once been the wing. Through the white gray smoke that was filling the bridge, she could make out three bodies that had been the lookout's, first mates and the captains lying twisted at grotesque angles, red stains and splotches staining their white uniforms.

Overcoming the pain, she forced herself to her feet, her legs seemingly undamaged by the blast. A klaxon roared on the bridge, threatening to drive all remaining thoughts from her head. She stumbled and staggered on the canted deck, the ship in a hard right turn, to the radio console which she found covered in glass but relatively intact from the blasts. After a moment's concentration, she remembered the frequency for the U.N. Security Force in the area, dialed it in before mashing down the talk button on the microphone.

"Blister! Blister! Blister!" she shouted before succumbing to the pain and slumping to the floor.

35

"Blister! Blister! Blister!" blared over the speaker on the bridge of the *Agrippa*. Buck, Tadhg and Grels had been passing the time on the bridge with small talk and ribbing one another that the emergency code word took them by surprise. Everyone froze for a heartbeat before Buck started issuing orders: "Battle stations! Tadhg, flank speed! Set intercept course for the *Constellation*!"

A klaxon started blaring on the *Agrippa*, Tadhg had to let the crew get to their reclined chairs and strapped in for a high speed run before he could throttle up the Super Mako; otherwise, the high speeds and sudden maneuvers may hurt the crew or throw some one overboard. In a compromise move he brought the nose of the Super Mako around to the *Constellation's* position and slowly started to throttle up. Within seconds, the members of Strike Force Trident started to check in from their assigned chairs. When all were accounted for, Tadhg slammed the throttles full forward. "Tally ho!" he breathed into the boom mic. The turbos on the diesels howled and the Super Mako shot out of the hole hitting sixty knots in just seconds while still accelerating.

Buck had been monitoring the ship's comm circuit from his seat as the ship prepared for battle, now he grabbed a microphone tuned to the *Constellation*. "This is the MV *Agrippa* calling the *Constellation*. MV *Agrippa* calling RV *Constellation*, please state your emergency. Over."

Silence.

"This is U.N. MV *Agrippa* calling RV *Constellation*, please state your emergency. Over."

Again silence.

"Mister Ramsden, weapons status?"

"Forward mount on line," Grels answered for him. "Estimate four minutes to range of the twenty-five millimeter. Center mount: fifty cal and minigun online. No Targets identified."

"Very good. We don't know what we might run into when we get on station...Grels, charge the coil gun. I want all weapons systems available."

"Aye, Aye, boss. One minute thirty seconds until charge complete," he said rapidly tapping the screen before him.

******

After the grenades exploded on the bridge, the *Constellation* was thrown into a hard right turn into its attacker. The sudden change of course and close proximity forced Demetrio's man steering the boat to veer away hard into a right turn to escape from being rammed and crushed by the bigger boat. The abrupt turn cause one of Demetrio's crew who was standing at the inside rail firing an RPG, to be thrown over the boat's side.

"You jackass," Demetrio screamed at the man steering the outboard, "Circle around. Pick up that man in the water!"

The steersman complied, bringing the boat in a tight circle as the *Constellation* passed, easing up on the man in the water. Unfortunately the man who had fallen overboard was not a good swimmer. Precious minutes were lost as the semi-floundering man dog-paddled the last few feet to the boat before the crew could lay hands on him, dragging the gasping man slowly over the gunwale.

Demetrio glanced at the *Constellation*, which had straightened from its turn and increased speed. This only infuriated Demetrio more. "Hurry up! Hurry up! The ship is trying to make a run for it!"

******

"MV *Agrippa*, MV *Agrippa*, this is Research Vessel *Constellation* calling MV *Agrippa*. Over."

Buck jumped at the handset, ecstatic that the *Constellation* was making contact. He mashed down the communications button on the radio's microphone, "MV *Agrippa*. State your emergency. Over."

"I think we are under attack by pirates. Over."

Confused by the voice's lack of certainty, Buck sought to sort the situation out. "Who's speaking? Over."

"This is Seaman Stan Giacomo. Over."

"Where is your captain? Over."

"Dead. First Mate too. We have a total of three dead so far. Dr. Melrony is injured along with four, maybe five others. Heavy damage to the bridge. Over."

It had been a nice morning, clear skies with temperatures in the low eighties. A few cumulus clouds were starting to form. Now, around midday, the Super Mako was hammering across light swells in excess of sixty knots, both diesels at full throttle, screaming towards an unknown battle taking place just beyond their visual range. Buck was heading pell-mell into a battle space with little or no idea what was going on. And all he could get out of an excited and confused voice on the radio was cryptic answers.

"OK, just tell me everything you know. Over."

"Some fishermen came alongside trying to sell us some

fish, and then there were some explosions on the bridge. I was a couple decks below when the explosions happened. Rushed up to bridge to see what happened. When I got here all of the bridge crew were down and the ship was out of control. I've managed to get the ship straightened out and increased the speed. I heard you calling, but, hell I've had my hands so full I haven't had a chance to call anyone. Can you help? Over."

"Roger. We are three to four minutes out. We can see you. We are on your starboard aft quarter. What about the fishermen or pirates? Over."

"Hell if I know! I'm kind of busy here, you know."

All pretense of proper radio communication were gone now, the man's mounting anxiety and frustration at not knowing what was going on or being able to answer Buck's questions ratcheted up his fears.

Just then Grels piped up, "Target acquired! Small boat sitting dead in the water astern of the *Constellation*." He fiddled with some adjustments and his monitor closed in on a view of the small boat. "It looks like they are pulling something from the water…yes, they just pulled a man from the water. They are throttling up to pursue the *Constellation*!"

"Do you have a shot?"

"Negative, sir. Given the angles, the boat is too close in alignment to the *Constellation*. I can't guarantee that a twenty-five millimeter round will not just pass through the boat and bounce off the water into the *Constellation*. We're not yet in range of the smaller caliber guns."

"Okay. Tadhg, sheer off a few points to starboard to give us some angle on the target.

"Roger."

"Okay, Stan," Buck said into the microphone, "we have the pirates off your stern giving chase. Can you have your crew kick one of the fuel blabbers off the back of the deck? Over."

"Yes, but why?"

One thing Buck had learned as a naval officer was when and where to take charge. Now was one of the moments. "Because I said so! Double time it, like your life depends on it, because it does. Over."

"Yessir."

"What's your plan, Buck?" Tadhg asked.

"Grels, the fuel bladder will float," Buck explained to the two other men seated with him. "When the pirates get close to the bladder, I want you to take one shot at it. If we are lucky, we should be able to create a nice little diversion for the *Constellation*. Can you do that?"

"I think so, Boss."

"Which weapon system offers us our best shot?"

"We are six thousand yards, max range for the Bushmaster at a target that small. If we only have one shot, I think the coil gun is the best weapon for the job."

"I concur," seconded Tadhg.

"Alright then, prepare to take the shot. Gun's hot."

Grels made a few taps on his screen before the coil gun's targeting screen appeared on his monitor. Buck tied the terminal attached to his chair into Grels's chair so he could follow the action. He watched as Grels acquired the *Constellation*, then tightened the view to watch a dozen men from the *Constellation* pry, kick and shove one of the *Agrippa's* fuel bladders to the equipment launching and recovery ramp at the stern of the ship. In less than thirty seconds, the men had shoved the bladder down the ramp, where it rolled, gathering speed before plunging deep into the churning wake of the *Constellation's* propellers at full speed. The bladder disappeared from view.

"Stay with the bladder, Grels," Buck coached.

Grels widened the view so that he could more easily spot it when it came back to the surface. Ten seconds later, the black fuel bladder bobbed to the surface amidst the white froth and green water of the ship's prop wash.

Buck watched as Grels centered the crosshairs on the bladder then locked the gun's stabilizers on it. "Target locked up," Grels announced.

"Grels, widen the view. Let's see how close the pirates are."

The view on Buck's screen widened until the pirate's boat came into view. About three more seconds until they would draw abreast the bladder.

"Hold..." Buck directed, "hold...hold...FIRE!"

The Agrippa rocked as the ceramic coated iron "pig" left the coil gun's muzzle at close to eight thousand feet per second. An incredible ripping sound and boom accompanied the weapon's blast as the projectile was accelerated by magnetic contractions, causing it to super heat the air around the projectile's path. The "pig," covered the distance to the bladder in a little more than half a second.

The pig slammed into the bladder at Mach 5.5 vaporizing, compressing, and igniting its contents into a tremendous fireball as the low-order explosive yielded a red, roiling ball of flame wrapped in black, sooty smoke which gathered briefly before angrily forcing its way higher into the sky. The shockwave it created knocked several men to the deck on the back of the *Constellation* who had helped roll the bladder into the drink.

"Well done, Buck," Tadhg congratulated as he surveyed the scene of chaos and disruption that Buck's impromptu plan had wrought.

******

The optics of the *Agrippa's* systems were among the best in the world. Even so, at the range the coil gun had fired, it was difficult to judge distance between objects by eye on a monitor. This was a very lucky break for Demetrio. His boat, at detonation, was not passing the bladder as close as the screen portrayed. He had actually been a hundred yards to the side of the bladder. Having seen the bladder go into the water, he waved the man at the tiller well wide. Even so, the blast had swept two men overboard and nearly swamped the boat; portions of the boat's gunwale had disappeared, some of it embedding in the men.

Demetrio, not knowing where the shot had originated from or what other weapons the *Constellation* had, his crew depleted and injured, determined that today was not the day on which he was going to fulfill his contract to the blue-eyed man. He signaled the boat's driver to head back to their chase boat as fast as possible.

36

The fuel bladder blast rolled across the water and penetrated the confines of the *Agrippa's* bridge. The blast initially obscured Grels's sighting picture, but slowly the sea started to settle and the mist of the ocean subsided. Grels scanned furiously, looking for any debris of the pirate's boat. It was not until he pulled back the camera view that he found the boat leaving the scene at a slower rate than it had chased the *Constellation*. "Buck, I've found the pirate boat. Evidently, they survived the blast but it looks like the boat is damaged; it's going slower, too. It's hard to tell because they may have injured lying in the bottom of the boat, but there appear to be three fewer occupants in the boat now."

"Do you want to go after them, Buck?" Tadhg asked.

"No... our first priority is the *Constellation*. Proceed to her to see if we can render assistance." Then he added, "Grels, mark and track the pirate's boat on the radar. It doesn't look like they're going any place fast. We'll give assistance first, and then come back and deal with the bad guys."

"Okey-dokey, Buck." The slang sounded kind of strange to Buck, said in a Swedish accent. "I do not know how long we can track them, though. It's a small, low boat. Our radar mast is not that tall, so we will lose them in the radar's surface clutter of the swells the further away they get."

"Just give me the best you can, Grels."

Then into the microphone, "RV *Constellation*, this is MV *Agrippa*. Over."

"Go ahead, *Agrippa*. Over."

"Just wanted to let you know the bad guys are in full retreat. We'll be alongside in ninety seconds to render assistance. Over."

"Roger. We're on channel thirty-two CB for ship to ship. Give us a call when you are alongside. Over."

The *Agrippa* was still blasting ahead at close to seventy miles an hour, quickly covering the last two thousand yards.

"Tadhg, have the crew stand down from general quarters and have them prepare a boarding party to assist the *Constellation*."

"Aye, aye."

Grels started to take the ship's weapons systems offline. Buck grabbed his binoculars and started scanning the *Constellation's* bridge for damage. Smoke was still rolling out of the bridge in wispy fingers, but the only apparent external damage was two circular scorch marks on the side of the bridge. As they got closer, he could see the tangled grating and stairs that had once led to the bridge. The bridge door was also blown off its hinges. Finally, the full extent of the damage was revealed in the last two hundred yards as Tadhg started to slow the *Agrippa* and maneuver her alongside. Buck could see that over half of the bridge's windows had been blown out. Many panes had jagged chunks still hanging in parts of the frames.

The last thing I want is for the pirates to double back when we're occupied assisting the Constellation, Buck thought. "Have one of the deck weapons stations manned," Buck ordered.

"Aye," replied Tadhg. "Sergeant Cooper, man weapon

station two." He piped into the ships comm circuit.

"Weapons Station Two, manned and ready," came over the ship's comm circuit shortly.

Buck picked up the microphone attached to his chair and changed the frequency setting on his monitor to the CB Channel. "RV *Constellation*, this is the *Agrippa*, we are pulling up alongside your starboard now. How can we assist? You guys look like you took a beating."

A young, swarthy dark-haired sailor stuck his head out of the damaged door of the bridge, gave them a quick look over, followed by a two or three second's wait before there was a response. "Man, am I glad to see you guys," came back the response. "Yeah, they kicked the crap out of us, but I think the worst is over. Our doctor tells me that except for the men that died on the wing, most of the other injuries are minor: bruises, sprains, some minor lacerations. He's getting everyone fixed up now. Says he should have everyone patched up in the next half hour. Ship-wise, we're in pretty good shape, considering. Power plant and propulsion are okay. Steering and back-up navigation are intact. Only the starboard side communications, radar screen and controls were damaged in the blast, so we still have full control of the ship and can safely navigate. We put out emergency calls to the Mexican authorities, but they don't have anybody available to respond."

"No surprise there. What assistance do you need from us?"

A pause, "Nothing I can think of, really. I need to turn this ship around and go back to Cozumel for repairs and to see to our dead. Can you escort us to make sure the pirates don't come back to finish us off?" There was more than a little anxiety in the man's voice at this request.

"Yah, we can do that. But first, I want to try to hunt

them down. They can't hurt you if we find them first."

"I don't know… I'd feel more comfortable if you just escorted us first."

"Trust me, the best defense is a good offense. It's better this way. If we don't find them in the next four hours, we'll come back and escort you to town."

"Roger."

"If somebody else starts to bother you, just give us a call. We'll come running, all right?"

"Will do. Good luck. I hope you catch up to them. Out."

"MV *Agrippa*, Out."

"Grels, do you have a track on the pirates?"

"I did. Radar contact was intermittent until we finally lost them in the sea clutter."

"Okay. Give Tadhg a heading on the last known track. Tadhg, take us out at a fast cruise. Have the strike team buckle in so we can cover some sea quickly."

Both men acknowledged the orders. The *Agrippa* swung away from the *Constellation*, turning in the direction to intercept them. After brief orders were passed, giving the strike team time to secure the back deck and then themselves in their chairs, Tadhg throttled up the Super Mako to thirty-five knots.

Buck and Tadhg scanned the water with binoculars, while Grels did the same with the radar. After fifteen minutes, they had found nothing. "We're too far out from land. In their condition, there is no way they could have made it a third of the way to shore." Buck said in speculation. "We should have found them by now. There's no way they could just disappear."

"They were damaged," Tadhg joined the speculation. "Maybe they sunk."

"Still we should have seen men and debris in the water. So where are they? They couldn't have gone far."

"Buck, I think I have something," Grels said. "The plot that the pirates took after they called off their attack confused me at first. I thought that they would have headed for shore. Instead they headed slightly out to sea. I thought that they were doing that just to throw us off their scent. But, if I extend their radar track, it takes them roughly towards this ship here," he said while tapping the screen to indicate which radar contact he was looking at. "Judging by the radar return, it appears to be a small coastal freighter or a large fishing boat. Maybe they saw where they went."

"It's worth a shot. Tadhg, move us to intercept that contact." Yet again the *Agrippa* swung on a new course in search of the vanished pirates. Ten minutes later, the radar contact began to emerge from the gray horizon as a small coastal freighter. Buck and Tadhg glassed the boat to get a better view. It was a small, rusty freighter, with a tall stern wheelhouse, low cargo deck amid ship and large forecastle; two cargo crane masts, fore and aft. Their booms, the type where the end attached near the base and could raise or lower the tip from cables attached to the crane's masthead, were secured amid ship over the cargo deck. Using the targeting optics of the central turret's weapons system, Grels was able to get a clearer view of the ship.

"I think we found them," Grels said, peering intently at his screen.

Unable to see anything remarkable about the freighter through his binoculars, Buck inquired, "What makes you say that?"

"Here," he said as he duplicated the view on his screen to Buck's monitor. "Look low in the water behind the freighter. You can see a small boat, like the one our pirates were using, tied to the back. We won't know for sure until we get closer, though."

Buck studied the picture. Indeed a small boat did appear to be tied behind the ship. "Kick it up a couple of notches, will you, Tadhg?" The steady purr of the diesels increased in pitch as the throttles were hiked; the nose of the Super Mako rose a few more degrees as she sliced through the water like a true shark on a blood scent trail.

Two thousands yards out, Buck ordered the crew to general quarters. Strike Force Trident quickly manned their battle positions again, stating their readiness from their positions form the manned guns on the back deck. Tadhg quickly briefed everyone on the ship they were approaching via the comm link.

******

"Demetrio! Demetrio! An armed ship is approaching us from the north," Emilio yelled down the stairwell from the bridge. "Come quick!" Emelio had been left in charge of the bridge while Demetio had gone to the galley below to help patch up his crew.

Not that Demetrio actually cared for his men, far from it; he viewed them as expendable tools that he would use to get the job done. If one of them was killed, it was no loss. He could find another to take his place with no problem in the barrios of Cozumel. The promise of his fast buck was more than they could resist. In fact, a crewman's death could actually be a positive. If he died doing the job, it was just one less share to pay, which would default to Demetrio. The trick was to get them killed after the job's success was in hand. His main motive in patching up the crewmen who were hurt in the explosion was rooted strictly in his fear of the hard-eyed man that had paid him to kill Dr. Melrony. He believed the man's promise that failure would result in a visit that he would remember for eternity. His crew was already down two wounded and the two men lost overboard in the explosion that hadn't surfaced. Well, maybe that was a stretch. He had not stayed around long enough to find out if they had. In fact, he could not actually remember even looking for the lost pirates. His boat was still in contact with the *Constellation*, tracking its blip on his radar screen. He still had enough patched-up men to get the job done.

Demetrio's first salvo had seriously damaged the ship; he had seen the dead bodies and the smoke roiling out of the ship's shattered bridge windows. Yet, it still remained on its northward track, seemingly impervious to the damage he had inflicted upon it. His fallback plan had always been to damage the ship enough to force it back to port, where he could kill Dr. Melrony when she left the ship or sneak aboard at night and finish the job. It would be much easier to finish the job in one of Cozumel's shipyards than on the busy industrial docks, teeming with workers. He could not figure out why the ship had not turned around. All he did know was that he still had at least one person he had to kill, and possibly a ship to strip of its mechanical and electronic treasures.

Demetrio was still pondering the inexplicable actions of the *Constellation* when he heard Emilio's urgent shouts. He flew up the steep steps two at a time, arriving out of breath.

"There, two thousand yards out." Emilio was pointing ten points off the port bow with one hand, holding a pair of binoculars out to him.

Demetrio snatched them up and soon found the boat bearing down on him. The sharp pointed nose connected to a deep V hull looked ominous with the small cannon turret on the fore deck and a low bridge structure behind it with another turret packed with protruding gun barrels on top. It looked like a gray ocean racer with guns sprouting all over her.

"Fool!" her cursed Emilio, "why didn't you call me earlier?! It's almost on top of us. Weren't you paying attention to the radar?! You were asleep, weren't you? I'll cut off your ear if you were asleep at the wheel of my boat, you pile of pig shit!" he screamed while trying to count the oncoming ship's guns and take her measure.

"Captain, I was not asleep. I promise," Emilio pleaded, "The ship is not on the radar screen. Look for yourself. It still does not show up." he swept his arm towards the round, green glowing glass screen mounted to the bridge's forward wall.

Demetrio shoved Emilio aside and walked to the screen and took a quick look, then out the window at the approaching boat, then back to the screen. "You've got it adjusted wrong, you idiot!" He started fiddling with the radar's knobs, each time checking out the window to make sure where the approaching boat was. Nothing worked. The boat failed to appear no matter what he did. "The damn thing is broken. Broken! And at the worst possible time! Piece of shit!" He raised his fist to smash the radar...

"But it is not broken, Demetrio! Look... it is still showing other ships on the screens."

Demetrio froze his blow in its backswing and looked at the screen again... "Interesting," he muttered to himself. "A boat that does not show up on radar," he said, thinking out loud. "Who would have such a boat? Not the Mexican Navy. They can't even afford to buy old used ships from other countries or keep the ones they've got running. It must be the Americans. They're the only ones that have such ships. But what are they doing here?" He looked again at the approaching boat through the binoculars. "It's a small boat built for speed, not an ocean going vessel...must be short range...If it is American, then it has no authority in Mexican waters..." He paused, deep in thought.

Then Demetrio jumped and started shouting orders, "Emilio, quick, go cut loose the chase boat. Then tell the men to grab all the RPG launchers we've got. We're going to arrange a little surprise for the Americans."

37

"Ease up when we get close to that freighter, Tadhg. Bring us alongside at two hundred meters and pace the ship. We don't know for sure the pirates are on it," Buck ordered.

"But we just watched them cut loose the boat, and we know that was the boat that was chasing the *Constellation*," objected Grels.

"True," Buck countered, "but we don't know that the people on the boat are the same people on the ship. Or, for that matter that all the people on that ship were on the boat. The pirates could have had another boat out here and transferred to it to make their escape. The freighter could have come by and found the boat floating, salvaged it, thinking it was their lucky day. Maybe, they just got nervous seeing our bad mama-jama boat busting hard at them, with guns everywhere, and cut the boat loose just to avoid an argument with a bad *hombre*. Don't forget we're in Mexican waters, and that's how they do things down here. Or the worse case scenario, the pirates have captured the freighter to get away from us and are holding the crew captive or killed them. Either way, I want to know if this is hostage situation before I do anything else."

"How are you going to do that?" This time it was Tadhg.

"You," Buck said looking at Tadhg, who had swiveled his chair around to him, "are going to slide us up on their side where I can ask them some questions. If it looks or smells fishy, we'll send over a boarding party. If they have nothing to hide, they won't mind. If they protest, we'll force entry. That's all the probable cause I need."

"I see. I'll have Rampage get the crew started on rigging out the CRRCs for the boarding party." Tadhg turned back to face forward and uttered quiet commands into his boom mic.

Tadhg took the *Agrippa* on a heading for a port-to-port head on pass at four hundred yards before turning into the small freighter's stern for a closer inspection pass.

******

"Remember," Demetrio yelled down to his crew from the small stair landing next to the bridge, "don't fire until I tell you to. I want to lure them in for a sure kill shot before we tip our hand." The eight men ducking below the gunwales, four holding loaded RPG tubes and four men holding reload grenades, all acknowledged their leader's orders.

******

"All right Tadhg, bring us up alongside. Keep us at fifty meters. Grels, keep the twenty-five, fifty and the mini gun hot, but don't train them on the boat. I don't want to scare them -- there is the possibility they may not be our pirates. Also, tell Rampage to man the deck guns, but don't train them on the ship."

"Ja," Grels acknowledged, "I will track and lock with optics only."

Tadhg slowly eased the *Agrippa* along side the small freighter's port side and steadied up. Buck picked up the hand mic, adjusted a knob on his console to select for loud speaker, and hailed the ship. "This is the U.N. Vessel *Agrippa*. We are in pursuit of pirates that attacked another ship in the last hour. Please identify yourself, cargo and destination."

All eyes were focused on the small freighter, looking for the slightest threat. After a few moments a heavy set man with greasy, curly hair wearing stained pants and a T-shirt came out on the bridge's stair landing. In his hand was a piece of cloth, two foot square, that passed for white that he started to waive with one hand for several seconds. He then cupped a hand to his ear and leaned at the *Agrippa*, indicating that he had not heard what was said.

Buck repeated his call again over the speaker. The man again went though his pantomime that he could not hear and vigorously waved for the *Agrippa* to come closer.

"Tadhg, bring us in another twenty meters," Buck commanded.

******

"Careful...careful, she's coming closer," Demetrio cooed at the men hidden on the ship's deck, "We almost have them."

The boat had moved to within a thirty meters and now was pacing directly alongside, in perfect position to plug her full of RPG shots. Demetrio was already beginning to think that he might be able to take this vessel and plunder her armaments. This would more than make up for the botched attack on *Constellation* earlier. His greed was just beginning to make him flush and tingle, when the armed ship alongside started another announcement.

"This is the U.N..."

"Now!" screamed Demetrio to the men on deck.

******

"...Vessel *Agrippa*..." Buck froze in mid sentence as he saw the rail of the ship's cargo deck suddenly bristle with men aiming RPGs at them. "Ambush! Get us out of here!" he shouted.

Tadhg, seeing the same thing, had not waited for any commands. His left hand slammed the throttles forward at the same time his thumb sought the red button on the end of the throttle lever that would force feed propane boost into the cylinders while the turbos were spooling up. His thumb found the button and mashed down on it. Propane under pressure was released into the air induction of manifold feeding the twin twelve cylinders of the engine, mixing with the diesel and air. The engines rocketed with the sudden surge in power. However, the sudden surge of engine torque caused the water-jets to cavitate and the *Agrippa* lost traction for half a second.

While Tadhg's reflexes were quick, the pirate's RPGs were quicker, aided by momentary loss of the water-jets' thrust. Four rockets snaked across the separating water just as the water-jet's blast gained traction, launching the Super Mako forward, slamming all the boat's occupants against their seats or restraints. The sharp move caused one of the rockets to slide past the deckhouse structure's trailing edge, passing between the two forward gun mounts of the rear deck before sailing over the far rail. One of the rockets was an errant shot, the gunner too nervous to take proper aim. His shot sailed high over the Super Mako.

However, two rockets found their mark, impacting and exploding at the same time. One impacted and exploded against the rear deck's side directly over the engines. The other slammed into the deckhouse side of the strike team room. Grey smoke enveloped the back deck. The sudden acceleration and explosions caused a riot of momentum, knocking all the strike team members manning weapons stations to the deck. Stunned, their safety straps prevented them from being ejected over the side or rolling off the stern. Rampage was bent double over the railing of his AA station.

"Guns free! GUNS FREE!" Buck yelled into the comm circuit.

Grels's hand struggled under the sudden G-load, fumbling to find the button on his joy stick to release the weapons of the forward and mid turret.

Red lights and warning tones instantaneously lit up on the pilot's console screen and sounded from the bridge's speakers. Tadhg, having been thrown sideways in his seat by the impacts, took the Mako's rudder joystick in his grip with him, bending the *Agrippa* into a steep right hand turn towards the small freighter. Combined with the boat's sudden acceleration and snap roll, it started veering out of control in front of the freighter, which threatened to cut the *Agrippa* in half in a collision.

Grels's finger finally found the switch to release the guns, slaving them to the sights that still remained targeted on the freighter through all the boat's wild gyration, and squeezed the fire trigger with a death grip. It took both gun mounts seven tenths of a second to slew and align with the optics, before they discharged their first round.

Grels had targeted and locked the twenty-five millimeter's optics to the freighter's engine room as the *Agrippa* had approached. He had selected the gun to feed from the high explosives magazine thinking the freighters sides were so lightly skinned that armor piercing rounds would probably pass right through without much damage in case they got into some kind of row. He was right. The auto cannon started pumping high-explosive rounds into the freighter at two a second. The first round opened a three-foot hole in the side of the ship, where the following rounds entered, detonating in the interior amongst the ship's vital machinery and engine.

Grels had locked the fifty and the mini-gun centered amid ship, right where the RPG gunners had popped up. The sheet ripping like roar of the M-134D mini-gun was interspersed with the steady thumping of the Ma Deuce fifty-caliber belt-fed machine gun. From such close range, the red orange flame of the mini-gun seemed to almost reach out and lick the side of the freighter. And where it's hot breath brushed the freighter spark, smoke and flame erupted leaving a tightly stitched string of holes that danced upon the ship's side. The wild gyrations and acceleration of the Super Mako served to walk the fire across the ship as effectively as if Grels's were using his joystick to spray hot lead across the boat's deck and structure.

Sassy had managed to stagger back to his feet and get his mount back into the fight in bore sight mode pumping fifty caliber rounds and twenty-five milliliter grenades into the fray.

At fifty rounds a second, the mini-gun's thirty caliber bullets didn't just penetrate the thin metal walls the RPG gunners and loaders were hiding behind, they chewed them up. The sheer number of bullet strikes created so much heat that it ignited what little paint still covered the metal, turning the steel into perforated, twisted hunks that looked like some bizarre art sculpture. The men that had fired the RPGs from behind the steel sides disintegrated from pink clouds of mist into mounds of ground meat interspersed with bits of cloth.

The first twenty-five millimeter round exploded just under and behind the vessel's captain, who was standing at the bridge rail where he had stayed to watch his attack unfold. He was thrown over the land rail by sympathetic explosions deep within the ship, set off by the cannon's explosive rounds. These explosions also ripped the bottom of the freighter out and she began to take on water at an incredible rate.

As Tadhg regained control of the boat, he swung the Super Mako back to the left. In the intervening eight seconds of continuous fire, the forward mount had swung through its full range of traverse before hitting its stop. The mid mount, however, had unlimited traverse in a three hundred sixty degree circle about the boat. It continued to fire for another four seconds before Grels released his trigger finger, by now the target was obscured by flame, smoke and sea spray kicked up by stray bullets and explosions.

Buck, who had followed the action on his terminal through the video feed from Grels's gun cameras, saw the listing freighter ablaze and knew the ship was done for. He could still hear firing from the back deck. "Cease fire, cease fire," he directed into the comm circuit. The hammering stopped.

Tadhg had now slowed the boat down and put it into a tight left hand turn to circle back to the sinking freighter, careful not to approach at more than three hundred meters broadside so all guns could come to bear.

"All stations, check in," Buck commanded, dreading to know if there were casualties to report.

"Buck, this is Steve. Back deck has some minor blast damage, one of the CRRCs, was punctured by fragmentation from a RPG round we took in the starboard side, just below gun mount number two. Beyond that, everything else is operational."

"No casualties?" Buck asked unbelieving, having felt the impacts to the ship and knowing the men on the back deck had been totally exposed. "Not even at gun mount number two?"

"Lots of bumps and bruises...a few cuts. Datan, who was closest to the round that hit the deckhouse and he got knocked out. But he's fine, no signs of major concussion, although he's sure to have a headache later."

"What about Brisbane? He took a round just under his station. You sure he's not injured?"

"Naw, he's fine. Checked him myself. I'll tell you what, though, he sure didn't appreciate getting fired at with an RPG. It just pissed him off something fierce. He scrambled to his feet quicker than any of us and was laying into the pirates with curses and lead."

"Okay. We're going to go back to look for survivors. I want at least two men manning the guns at all times until I say so, in case they try any more of their white flag of surrender crap again."

"I hear you, Buck. Wilco."

Switching his attention back to inside the bridge, he said "Tadhg, damage report."

"Lenz reports no hull penetrations or water incursions. Engines running normally, steering and navigation are online. Communications are good. The RPGs tripped a couple of breakers, which I've already reset. We have over eight-five percent of our fuel load and we used less than a tenth of our propane boost. It looks like the Dyneema armor did its job, the boat is fully intact."

"Very good. How about you, Grels? What's the weapon's status?"

"All weapon systems functional. We have thirty-eight hundred rounds of thirty caliber left in the central turret magazine, enough for seventy-six seconds and a little over sixty percent of the magazine in the fifty. Forward turret still has a full complement of AP and ninety-three percent of HE available. Full complement of reserve ammunition in stores. Coil gun still has twenty three-rounds left, eleven in the magazine, a dozen in stores."

"Thank you, Mister Persson. Good work to both of you. Now, if you will, Tadhg, take us in to see if there are any survivors, please."

Tadhg deftly steered the *Agrippa* into the freighter. Ablaze, sinking by the stern, which was now almost fully submersed, the bow sticking up at a rakish seventy-five degree angle, the ship was barely visible under a cloud of black smoke.

"She won't float another minute," Tadhg offered his appraisal. There were no takers on the implied bet. There also was no sign of survivors on the sinking ship or in the flotsam field that had already started to accumulate around the ship.

They watched the bow slide beneath the waves and then the water roiled in a green-white oily eruption of bubbles before the ocean's surface glassed over, totally erasing the death of a ship a minute earlier.

"Take us out slowly, Mr. Ramsden, if you would. Secure all weapons stations. We have a research ship to escort back to Cozumel," Buck ordered.

Slowly, Tadhg started to pick his way out of the fenders, seat cushions, ropes, wooden deck planks, and hundreds of other items that were still bubbling up from the sunken ship. Tadhg had just cleared the field, backtracking along the freighter's original path. He was starting to throttle up and swing around to go back to the *Constellation* when the call came over the ship's comm circuit.

"Man in the water! Ninety degrees to port. Two

hundred meters."

Tadhg swiftly idled the diesel while everyone on the bridge grabbed glasses and started to scout the water in the direction indicated. "I see him! There!" Grels called, pointing so that everyone else could see him in case he lost sight of the man bobbing in the water. With the man's position fixed in the water, Tadhg sprinted the boat ahead and pulled up within thirty meters of the swimmer. Meanwhile, under Rampage's directions, the strike team had readied a life ring and grappling pike to help fish the man out of the water. Buck went to the back deck to supervise. When he got there, Rampage was just getting ready to throw the ring.

"Belay that, Rampage!" Buck shouted. "I recognize that guy. He was the guy who came out on the bridge and waved the white flag. I'm sure he's the pirates' leader. He doesn't look hurt, but I want to question him first."

"Wouldn't that work better if we pulled him out first?"

"Go with me on this, will ya? You speak Spanish don't you?"

"Yah. Can't survive in San Diego if you don't."

"Good, you can be my translator."

The man in the water had been feebly alternating between treading water and dog paddling, while Buck and Steve talked. He had seen that Steve was just about to throw the ring and then he saw him set it back on the deck. He released a torrent of Spanish that Buck could tell vacillated between pleas and curses.

But first, Buck turned to see who was closest behind him. "Cooper, go into the team room and bring me out one of the spare Land Warrior infrared beacons."

Buck and Steve settled on the boat's rail closest to the swimming man that had now come to within twenty-five yards. "Ask him his name," Buck directed.

Words were quickly exchanged in Spanish. "He says his name is Jose."

"Tell him he's lying. Tell him we've been watching him and that this isn't going to go well for him if he doesn't start telling us the truth."

As Steve translated, Cooper returned with a small green plastic device about the size of a hockey puck with a white cross-hatched, plastic dome on top and handed it to Buck. Buck held the device up in the air so the man in the water could see it. "Tell him this device emits a low frequency sound designed to attract sharks." Steve started translating again. As he did, Buck made a show of bringing his other hand up and flicking on a switch on the green puck. "Now, tell him I've turned it on." Again Steve translated. Before he finished, Buck let it roll from his fingers and drop into the water.

"Is that true, will the IR beacon really attract sharks?" Steve asked out of the corner of his mouth.

"No idea."

The man fired off another stream of Spanish.

"Well, it seems to be working. He now says his name is Demetrio. I won't bother with the rest, 'Don't let me die, I'll give you my sister, blah, blah, blah...'"

"Tell him he doesn't have much time now, the shark's will soon be arriving to dine. Ask him if he attacked the *Constellation* seven months ago."

A short exchange ensued, "He says no, today was the first time he ever laid eyes on the boat.

"He's lying again. The M.O. is the same as the first attack, RPGs fired at the bridge..."

"Make way...coming through." It was Brisbane. He pushed his way to rail and set down a bucket of bait fish intended for Buck and Steve's fishing. With a flourish he reached into the bucket and pulled out a foot long fish holding it high. With his other hand he produced a knife and gutted the fish letting the entrails hang out before dropping it the water. "If you're going to persuade the little bugger, you might as well do it bloody right, I always say," he said with a dark smile as he dropped a second fish. He did two more fish, being sure to throw them at the paddling man, bracketing him with fish.

"Now ask him again, did he attack the *Constellation* seven months ago?"

The man was now freely flowing with information. "He says yes, he attacked the *Constellation*."

"Ask him how he knew Dr. Cadburess's name and why he killed him first."

The man skipped a beat in his frantic dog-paddles, his face filled with confusion before he stammered a reply. Upon taking in the man's answer, Rampage, laughed to himself before translating. "He wants to know how we know about that. Seems he's under the impression that no one survived, and that were just making it up.

Another blast of Spanish passed between them. "He says a man paid him to board the *Constellation* with specific orders to kill Dr. Cadburess."

"Did he have orders to kill anybody today aboard the *Constellation*?"

Steve barked another question. Halfway through the answer, Steve started translating. "He says yes. The same man as last time paid him to kill Dr. Melrony, but he does not know the man's name. An intermediary contacts him when the man has a job for him."

"I want that man's name or he's not getting out of the water."

Steve interrupted the jabbering man to make the demand.

"He says he was never told his name, and he never

offers it, nor does he ask."

"Here," Brisbane offered, "this should loosen his tongue some more." He picked up the bait bucket and tossed the rest of its contents over the man in the water.

The man in the water shrieked and started jabbering like he was getting paid by the word. Steve could barely keep up. "He says he can give you the name of the man who acts as the go-between, but he doesn't know the name of the man who hired him. The only thing that he knows about the man is that he is white, has blonde hair, blue eyes, speaks flawless Spanish with a hint of a Portuguese accent, and he likes knives. He says that he killed Dr. Cadburess with his knife last time."

"Tell him he's not telling me anything useful."

Steve started to translate when he was interrupted. "Shark!" It was Arceneaux. The man in the water may not have spoken English, but he certainly understood what the sharp bark accompanied by excited pointing at something in the water near him meant. Buck had a hard time not smiling. There was nothing in the water and he knew it. Hubert was just ratcheting up the pressure on the man.

The man spun in the water looking for the fin that had been pointed at and started to plead, yabbering in a high pitched whine. Buck started to turn his back on the man. "Wait, Buck! He says the girl is still alive and that he can take us to her."

Buck whipped around. "What girl?!"

"He says from the *Constellation*, a young blonde girl. They did not kill her, but took her, selling her to somebody named Ernesto."

There was only one person on the *Constellation*'s roster that fit that description, Penny Hartwell. "Who is this Ernesto? Where is he? What did he do with her?"

The fun and games were now over, the rest of the strike team became deadly serious at the mention of a hostage somewhere out there beyond the water's edge. Brisbane, Cooper and Randall all started shouting "Shark!" and pointing in the water.

"He says that Ernesto is a pimp and runs a brothel thirty miles down the coast in Tiljara."

These words seemed to galvanize Buck. "Get that piece of crap out of the water. Steve, finish interrogating him as soon as he's been fished out. I want to know everything about this mysterious man, especially if he has hired others to kill Dr. Melrony. And I want all the intel he can give us on this Tiljara."

"I'm on it."

Next, Buck called Tadhg on his ship's circuit headset. "Lieutenant Ramsden? We have a change of plan. Contact the *Constellation*. Have them turn around now and tell them we will escort them back Cozumel. Also, tell them that Dr. Melrony will need to be transferred to the *Agrippa*. We will send a boat for her as soon as we rendezvous, so she needs to be packed and ready. After you get that done, have Grels patch me through to Colonel Barrett. We have a new mission: hostage rescue."

Coop and Sassy finished pulling Demetrio out of the water and flexi-cuffed him, handling the murderer and slave runner with asperity.

38

While Cooper and Harold were retrieving Dr. Melrony in the CRRC, Buck and Rampage held an impromptu meeting on the back deck.

"We are prepped and ready for the excursion into Tiljara," Rampage started his report. "Major La Barré says he will be unable to obtain any information on the target location other than old coastal geographic survey satellite photos. He's sending them now."

"Good. At least we'll have a rough layout of the terrain and town, so we won't be going in totally blind." Buck was thankful for that, at least. "I've briefed Colonel Barrett on our plan. He has green-lighted us to 'use whatever force and means we deem appropriate to effect the rescue of any *Constellation* survivor.' He will brief the Secretary-General to let him know of our incursion onto Mexican soil. The Colonel and I are counting on the normal time lag of diplomatic communications with the Mexican government. By the time they give their blessing, we should already be back aboard the Super Mako with the survivor if she's still there. If she was sold into slavery, I doubt the Mexican government will make much of a stink about it. I'm sure the disclosure of slavery of a foreign national in their country is one of those things they'll want to sweep under the carpet and keep as quiet as possible. If it turns out this was a wild goose chase, then the Secretary-General will have coverage for having notified them of our little look-see trip."

"I wasn't able to get much more out of the prisoner," Steve started his recap of his interrogation. "The only other thing that he could tell was the date of their last transaction and that he saw the man get into a rental Mercedes-Benz convertible. He also says that he met with the guy three days prior to the attack on the *Constellation*. He's says he doesn't know if there are any more contracts on Dr. Melrony -- his client never volunteered any information."

"How does he know it was a rental?"

"He saw the rental company's sticker in the window of the car."

"Well, it would be a safe assumption that once the man with the Portuguese accent learns that the *Constellation* survived the attack and that Dr. Melrony is alive, he will make another attempt to have Dr. Melrony killed." Buck reflected.

"Why not put it out that Dr. Melrony was killed in the attack? That way you could take the initiative; set the tone by being the aggressor. He wouldn't know that you're coming."

"This cat is a cautious character. He sets meetings through intermediaries, doesn't volunteer information to the hired help. He's trying to cover his tracks. It would be reasonable to assume that he is possessed of normal to high levels of paranoia. He's sure to have covered his tracks and has some sort of rear guard or trip wire to know when I start getting close. The last thing I want to do with a guy like this is to walk into his kill zone. No, I want him to come after me on my terms."

"So you're going to use Dr. Melrony as bait then?"

"I wouldn't quite put it that way, but yes, that's the general plan."

"Does she know that?"

"No. And she's not going to know. She just needs to know that she is being put into protective custody until we run down the people who want her killed." Switching direction, he said "The Mexican government may not have the most sophisticated tracking service on people entering and leaving the country, but you can count on business enterprises to keep better records. Get the information on the rental car to Yoshi and have him start tracking it down. Then have him correlate that to airline flights around the days that we know he was in Cozumel."

"Roger that. Here comes the CRRC."

The *Agrippa* was idling along at five knots, just enough to give it steerage. Another CRRC occupied the port side of the ramp, so the Combat Rubber Raiding Craft lined up to the starboard side fifty feet from the stern and gunned its twenty-five horse motor. The little craft rapidly gained speed and hit the stern of the *Agrippa* at full speed, sliding to the top of the inclined ramp that was the stern of the Super Mako. Just as the rubber boat ground to a halt at the top of the ramp, Brisbane jumped from the nose of the boat and lashed a bow line to cleat in the deck, securing the craft. He then went back to the boat to help their guest from the boat. First came a canvas suitcase that Harold placed at the top of the ramp before returning to offer his hand to the woman seated in the middle of the boat. The hand was offered and accepted as a courtesy. As Buck watched, Dr. Lila Melrony, floppy boonie hat and nose ointment ever present, lithely bounded out of the craft with the grace of an athlete. She made straight for Buck as soon as her feet hit the deck.

"What is the meaning of this?" She demanded, getting into his grill.

"I'd like you to meet Steve Ramage, Dr. Melrony. He's

my second-in-command of Strike Force Trident."

She had barged right past Rampage without so much as a glance, but now she turned a little sheepishly towards him. "I'm sorry. Hi," she said extending her hand, "I'm Dr. Melrony." Then turning back to Buck, "I'd like an answer, please. I'm the person responsible for this geological expedition and I have a damaged ship, and dead and wounded. And now you demand I leave my expedition without so much as a reason. I believe I'm due an explanation." Fire flashed in her green eyes.

"You're right. As you can tell from the scorched holes in the side of our boat, we caught up with the pirate marauders who attacked the *Constellation*. In the ensuing battle, we sunk the pirates' vessel. We fished a lone survivor, the pirate leader, out of the water and have him in custody. He told us in interrogation that he had been paid specifically to kill you. Since he couldn't tell me if there are others who might have been paid to kill you besides him, I thought it prudent to take you into our protection until we know more about the situation and can find out who wants you dead."

"Oh, my," Dr. Melrony said, shrinking back a step as the gravity of the situation hit her.

"He also told us that there may be a survivor from the first *Constellation* attack. We're on our way to investigate this lead as soon as the *Constellation* enters the harbor at Cozumel. If there is someone still out there trying to kill you, the *Constellation* would be too exposed in the harbor without our presence. Since you seem to be the target, the safest place for you right now is with us, on the *Agrippa*."

"You're right, of course," she said. "I just let my temper get the best of me. I'm sorry. I'm still shaken up a wee bit from the attack this morning. I guess it was easier to get angry at you than to think about the dead and how close I came to joining them."

Buck noticed for the first time two butterfly stitches in her hairline over her right eye, and the bloodstained tears in her right sleeve and shoulder. He decided not to say anything, knowing all about survivor's guilt and how it could twist your guts up into knots. "Steve, will help you get settled in for the trip back to Cozumel. It looks like you could use some rest."

"I don't possibly see how I could rest right now," she protested.

"You won't have a choice, believe me," he smiled at her. His smile returned by a smiling quizzical look.

"Steve, would you escort the doctor to the team room and program one of the chairs for her? See to it that she gets strapped in and is comfortable."

"Will do. This way, if you would, Doctor," Steve said sweeping his hand towards the door in a half bow.

Buck followed the doctor and Rampage into the team room, leaving them as he made his way to the bridge. As soon as he was seated in the third chair with his headset on, he fired off a question at Tadhg. "What's our status?"

"The *Constellation* is steaming at top speed. We'll make Cozumel in another hour and a half. From there, it is thirty miles to Tiljara. I figure we can make it in forty-five minutes at top speed for these sea conditions. We have about another five plus hours of daylight left, so you want to tell me your plan? Do you want to go in before sunset or under the cover of darkness?

"I want to get in and out as quickly as possible. Since we don't have a lot of time or information to study Tiljara, we need to go in during daylight. The clock starts running as soon as the *Constellation* pulls into Cozumel's harbor. As shot up as it is, its appearance is bound to start tongues wagging, especially once our presence in the area is known. The crew will talk sooner or later - they'll have to. The Mexican authorities will want an explanation. I have no way of knowing how or if there is a connection to the people holding our hostage and a spy in the harbor.

"We'll launch two CRRCs from offshore. You'll follow us in and give us covering fire on extraction if needed. The satellite photos that Major La Barré sent showed the target building is on the outskirts of the town, near the jungle. There will be no way for the *Agrippa* to give us covering fire if we get pinned down. We'll just have to fight our way back to the docks. Your job is to see that the docks stay open and no one messes with our CRRCs."

"It's getting late in the day; if you get caught up in the town for whatever reason, you might have to extract at night. Are you sure you don't want to wait until tomorrow? You'll have all the daylight you'll need, plus additional time to plan."

"Yah, Buck," Rampage's voice came from behind. He had slipped onto the bridge unnoticed. "Why don't we just go in tomorrow rather than rushing it today."

Buck turned. "How's Doctor Melrony? All settled in?"

"Sleeping like a baby. Couldn't keep her eyes open once I got her strapped into the chair -- adrenaline crash. Back to the question, Buck…why not wait?"

"Because…" Buck fixed first Tadhg and then Rampage with a steely-eyed stare. "You heard what the prisoner said: he sold her to a pimp named Ernesto. I will not let her stay a pimp's prisoner one more minute than she has to. *That* is why we are going in now," he said with finality.

"Rampage, after the strike team is done replacing the damaged CRRC, I want them to start prepping their Land Warrior suits for urban combat, full loads of grenades on each man, flares and NVGs. I want you and Bear to take an over-watch position on this mission. I want Bear on a

Barrett 82A1. In addition to your spotters duties I want you to pack a M249. I don't know what we might be getting into, so I want the heavy punch of the fifty-caliber and the fire power of your SAW available. Configure each maneuvering element in standard land assault gear: REC-7s, IARs, AA-12s and M-32s."

"Roger."

The next ninety minutes went by in a flurry for Strike Team Trident's impromptu rescue mission. Before Buck knew it, the *Constellation* was signaling its departure from the *Agrippa's* escort outside the mouth of Cozumel's harbor.

"All right, Tadhg, let's go to Tiljara. And don't spare the horses." Tadhg acknowledged the order, and after getting everyone settled into a chair, throttled up the big boat. The Super Mako slashed through the offshore swells, the Mexican jungle to the port a blur of endless green as the man-o-war flew to its target on a mission of mercy, or, judging by the look in Buck's eye, vengeance.

39

Two odd, black crafts appeared out of the horizon's gray haze, headed at the docks of Tiljara. The whine of their outboard motors at full throttle grew louder, the pitch growing higher as they drew nearer. At first, the motor's noise drew no attention from locals on or near the town's small rickety docks. The town's fisherman all used outboard engines to power their small fishing boats. But, it was unusual to hear engines being run flat out for so long. Soon, ears and eyes were cast seaward to find out who would so foolishly abusing their motors.

What they saw were two black rubber boats skipping along the sea's surface, headed for the cove's mouth. Both were weaving irregular paths as they beat towards the town's docks, odd humps atop each of the low slung sides of the boat. The locals' curiosity grew, but an alarm was never sounded collectively. Rather, each observer determined that the odd humps were men astride the inflated tubes - men with drawn guns. Only then did they individually scurry to find a safe place to hide.

So the town's docks were cleared of any possible interference before the CRRCs ever tied up. The boats were landed and tied to the docks in crisp, efficient motions. Six men, in full battle rigs emerged from the boats. Their vests were crossed with electronic connectors and grenades as they moved in pairs, flowing from one position of cover and support fire to the next like and oozing mist blown in from the sea. They quickly moved down the docks and entered the town of Tiljara, moving along building walls, pausing at corners and alleyways, until two men could sweep the upcoming street or alley, one high, one low, with the weapons. Their weapons rarely left their cheeks, their gun sights giving them their view of the little hamlet that was Tiljara.

The men moved so fast that the residents in the town's center were unaware of their presence until the men swept past them. When they did, the residents darted into the nearest door, disappearing behind whatever they could, seeking the furthest corner away from the street.

Two of the men peeled off and headed for the tallest building in the town, the Catholic church at the town's center. After a prolonged pause, the remaining men started to move again. They communicated with hand signals, their only sound the fall of boots on the packed earth with the occasional soft clatter of their equipment rubbing on cloth.

"Trident One, Over-watch One is in place. No activity to report. No targets. No sign of armed guards outside target building. Over."

Buck acknowledged Rampage's transmission by double clicking his transmit button while still on the move to his next cover position. The two maneuvering elements, Buck and Coop in Element One, Datan and Harold in Element Two, had moved through the town and paused at an intersection within view of the cantina Demetrio had described. It appeared to be a two-story clay building like many they had passed on their way across the town, with a high fence around the back that appeared to stop at the jungle's edge. Buck pulled out a small set of binoculars that he unfolded and held up to his eyes, observing the cantina. As he watched, a couple of local men in shorts, sandals and unbuttoned short sleeved shirts walked out of the front laughing and talking loudly, leaving in the opposite direction. After several more minutes with no further comings or goings, he had seen enough.

"Alright, listen up," Buck put out on the team's comm circuit. "It appears to be nothing more than what it is, but that doesn't mean that the patrons or proprietor aren't packing heat of some sort, so watch yourselves. We'll go in standard sweep formation, clear room by room until we find our survivor. Datan's number one, I'll be two, Cooper then Harold. Any suggestions?" There were none. "Let's move. We'll form up our queue before we breach. Go!"

The men sprung into action. Sprinting, they took four different paths before merging again at either side of the cantina's door. The men slid their backs against the wall as the waited for the signal from Buck to breach. Buck was just about to give the signal when the door opened and a slight Hispanic male in a tank top and a stained baseball hat appeared in the door.

Startled at the presence of armed men, the man froze. Buck yelled without hesitation. "GO!" Datan punched the man in the gut, knocking the wind from him and into next week, before he shoved the disabled man back into the room, sending him crashing to the floor. With the doorway clear, Datan blew past the downed man, sweeping his weapon from right to left across the room before moving to the left side wall. It was a small room with a bar at one end and six or seven tables in the rest of the room, three of which were occupied. One man was by himself, the other two tables had a pair of men. Datan continued to keep the room under the muzzle of his gun while shouting for the men to get on the floor. Buck blew in through the door immediately on Datan's heels and broke right along the wall where he covered the room in a crossfire with Datan.

The men just sat at their tables, mouths agape as Cooper and Herald rushed in shouting instructions to get face down on the floor. Cooper pushed the man that had opened the door flat and flexi-cuffed him quickly and duct taped his mouth, before moving to help Harold, who was doing the same to the other men sitting at the tables. Once they were secure and the man who had been behind the bar had joined the others face first, cuffed in the center of the floor, they proceeded to the door that had been opposite the one they entered. It turned out to be the kitchen. Two frightened women were found huddled in the back. These were cuffed and herded into the front room to join the growing collection. With the ground floor cleared, all eyes of the strike team focused on the staircase to the upper floor. The stairs were on the same wall as the door to the kitchen. Silently they queued to proceed up the stairs, keeping proper intervals. Stealthily, the team slipped up the stairs and found themselves in a long hallway with four doors on each side, some open, some just ajar. One element slipped into the rooms to check the occupants and to clear them while the other covered the hall. If the occupants weren't who they were looking for, they were cuffed and gagged before the team moved to the next room. Hopefully, somewhere in one of these rooms was a tall blonde girl from Texas.

40

"Penny Hartwell?" Buck asked from the door seeing a blonde woman lying on a stained mattress along the wall opposite the door.

Penny had not even looked at Buck in the doorway. Reflexively, she pulled down the flimsy nightgown to expose her breast and beckoned him to join her.

"Penny Hartwell?" he tried again.

This time her head snapped towards the figure that was slowly emerging from the doorway, back-lit by the hall's lights.

"Penny Hartwell?" Bucked asked again, lowering his weapon and sliding it on its strap to his back. "My name is Brandt Kohl. I'm with the United Nations. We're here to rescue you." He took off his helmet and smiled gently at her.

Suddenly, Penny realized where she was, how she was posed and worst of all how she must look to the man now kneeling beside her. A wave of shame flushed over her. She snatched up her shoulder strap, and curled away from him searching for the sheets of the bed to pull over her. As she did, other emotions started to break loose in her brain, tearing themselves from the pits into which she had buried them away while she had focused on survival.

"Here, let me help you with that," Brandt said, reaching to help her drape the sheet over her shoulders.

"Thank you, Brandt." Penny finally found her voice.

"Buck, if you like. Everybody calls me Buck. Only my mother calls me Brandt, and that's only at Thanksgiving," he said smiling. "Can you walk? Are you injured?"

"No, I'm fine. I can walk."

"Good, because it's time to go. We've got to move."

He helped her to her feet and watched her wrap the sheet around herself, trying to regain her dignity. Buck gently steered her to the door and into the hallway. Only when she turned towards the stairs did she become aware that there were other men similarly dressed standing guard outside her room. Buck re-donned his helmet before grasping her elbow and steering her towards the stairs.

She did not budge.

"Wait!" She said tearing her elbow from Buck's grip. She spun in her tracks, running into Sassy, who thought they were on the move and had closed ranks watching the team's rear. "I'm not going without Selena!" Penny started to push past Harold down the hall, calling in Spanish, "Selena! Selena! Come here sweetie, we're leaving!"

Buck caught up with Penny, grabbed her, spinning her to face him. "Ma'am, we need to go. This is not a stable situation. If we go now, before any shooting starts, maybe everyone gets to go home to their families tonight. So let's go!"

"I told you, I'm not going without Selena. If you'd quit arguing with me and help me, we'd be on our way out the door by now."

"Who's Selena?"

"My friend. She kept me alive in this hell hole." Just then, a petite, curvaceous Mexican beauty appeared at a doorway in Buck's view over Penny's shoulder. The presence of all the armed men in the hallway and Penny's heated argument with one of them had clearly frightened her, despite Penny's calls to come out. She stood there trembling, yet she held Buck's stare. Penny, seeing Buck staring over her shoulder, turned to see what it was. "Selena! There you are!" She rushed over to her friend and threw her arms around her shoulders. "I'm going home! And you're coming with me, like I promised."

"I do not know…" Selena replied, "These men are angry. They do not want me to come."

"Nonsense, honey, it's okay. I just needed to talk some sense to them. But we have to go now." Penny gently started to steer Selena toward the strike team crowding the hall, the newcomer's gait betrayed a heavy limp.

"Alright," Buck decided aloud, "she can come. Cooper, help her. I don't want her slowing us down on our egress. Brisbane, you're in charge of Ms. Hartwell, stay with her."

"Yessir," both answered.

"Great. Now, let's get this circus on the road. I'll take point, Datan take the rear. Let's move, people." The column of men and women started down, retracing their steps. Buck snaked the column through the tables on the cantina's main floor, past the patrons still lying on the floor until he was at the front door. He pried open the door just a crack, to see if any opposition to his presence had formed and was waiting outside to ambush the strike team. His observations were interrupted by shrieks to his rear.

"Bastard! BASTARD!" Penny had found Ernesto, her pimp and owner, trusted up on the floor and could not help herself. She was savagely kicking him in the ribs, the cuffs making it impossible for him to protect himself.

Harold was making a weak attempt to try and pull her off.

"Harold. Let her be," Buck said quietly on the comm channel. Harold stepped back, watching her go about her business in earnest now.

"You BASTARD!" Penny's rage had taken full flight, her brutal kicks finding their mark. Buck could hear a couple of the man's ribs break under Penny's relentless kicks. Penny, now started to stomp on the man's face, his head making sickening thuds as it bounced off the floor with each blow. Penny's fury started to abate as the man's head was transformed into a bloody pulp.

"OK, Harold," Buck said impassively, "that's enough stomp therapy. Grab Ms. Hartwell. We need to roll."

Harold stepped forward and gently took her elbow. She did not resist, but took one last, well-aimed stomp on the man's groin. A low moan escaped from what was left of the man's lips as Penny turned her back on her recent past to face the front door and her future.

"Over-watch One, Trident One. We're ready to start egress. Anything happening out there?" Buck whispered into his mic.

"All clear, Trident One. You're good to go."

The streets were clear as Buck led his column out the door and back to their waiting boats. The town had become a ghost town -- nary a soul was seen as they filed out on the town's docks.

As the boats headed out to sea and the town faded from sight, so too did Penny's iron will. At first, just a tear rolled down her cheek, pushed across her face by the winds of the motor moving the boat across the water and could easily have passed as the effect of a sharp wind in the eye. But the rolling tears were soon accompanied by a rhythmic rocking, her hands clutched across her chest, followed in progression by racking sobs and soulful moans muffled into Selena's shoulder that mingled with the sound of the outboard engine. The men in the boat were equally torn between the instinct to hold and comfort and the desire to give her space that had been denied to her for so long.

41

"Congratulations, Buck!" Colonel Barrett said, bounding up the lowering loading ramp, before it had even hit the ground. "Well done! Well done! You have made quite the haul on this trip: one pirate leader, saving a U.N. Scientist and..."

The rest of his sentence was cut off by screams of joy from the couple standing behind him as Penny stepped forward from the plane's interior. Both parties sprinted at each other, colliding in a melee of hugs, kisses, and tears.

"Need I say more?" Colonel Barrett concluded, watching the scene with a satisfied grin that could only come from the satisfaction of knowing that he had helped, if only in a small way.

Selena had drifted to the top of the plane's ramp to watch her friend's reunion with her family, a wistful smile on her face at the joy she was witnessing. Penny sensed her friend's presence and broke away from the huddle long enough to wave her friend to join her. Selena hobbled down the ramp and across the tarmac where she was enveloped, taken in as one of their own.

Dr. Melrony was walking down the plane's ramp, catching Buck's attention out of the corner of his eye. "Dr. Melrony!" Buck waved her over, "I want you to meet my boss. This is Colonel David Barrett, head of Project Neptune. Colonel, I would like to present to you Dr. Lila Melrony."

"Nice to meet you," both said while exchanging handshakes.

"I'm glad I caught both of you together," Colonel Barrett started. "I have instructions for both of you. Dr. Melrony, the Secretary-General and I both agree that it is much too dangerous for you to return to your home and regular activities. Therefore, you will be held in protective custody."

"No!" Dr. Melrony protested. "This isn't possible. What? Am I to give up my life, my work? For how long? I have work to do. I've got to get busy rescheduling another expedition. If you stop me from doing my research and that was the aim of the assassin, then he might as well have succeeded."

"It won't be much of a life if you're dead, now will it, Dr. Melrony? Someone is interested in killing U.N. scientists doing oil research. If we know one thing about this person or persons, it is that they are persistent. They have killed one already, along with the entire crew of the *Constellation* and now, seven months later, they've made another try with you. Listen to reason, Doctor. If the person who wants you dead was willing to kill the entire crew of a ship just for good measure, how safe do you think your friends and family will be around you if you return home? You will only just put their lives in danger."

Her heart wanted to continue protesting, but Dr. Melrony was a creature of reason, and unfortunately Colonel Barrett's argument was logical and persuasive. She acquiesced with silent acceptance.

"Good, we understand each other. Buck," Colonel Barrett said turning to face him, "Dr. Melrony is your responsibility. I want her with you twenty-four hours a day. I don't want you to let her out of your sight for a minute."

Now it was Buck's turn to protest "Where? How? I'm not set up for protective custody. Just where am I supposed to house her? Why not let the FBI or local police protect her? I've got a killer to catch."

"You're right. You do have a killer to catch. And you may not be successful without Dr. Melrony's help. But in the meantime, keep her in your protection because you've hit the nail precisely on the head: we can't give her to the FBI or local jurisdictions. The attempt on her life was made in Mexican waters. The FBI or local police have no jurisdiction on any crime that was committed outside the country. Even if they did, there is this little thing of her not even being a citizen of the United States of America. She is a citizen of the Republic of Ireland. And don't bother..." he said holding up his hand, "I've already checked with their Irish Embassy. They felt that her presence would bring undue safety concerns that they are not in a position to handle. As to where you should keep her, that's your decision. You have the full support of the United Nations to keep Dr. Melrony safe. I would highly recommend that you stay on familiar ground. I suggest you take her home with you."

"What?!" Both of them protested in unison.

"From what I've heard about your home, it sounds ideal for this assignment. Now, I would like both of you to go home now. Call me at oh-nine-hundred tomorrow morning, and I will brief you on the latest developments. That is all." With that he turned on his heels and walked to a waiting car.

A long drawn-out, awkward silence followed before Buck turned to Dr. Melrony. "If you'll give me a minute, I need to check with Rampage, let him know of this new 'development.' Excuse me," he said before disappearing into the breaking dawn of the tarmac, only to reappear a few minutes later. "Rampage is off to get us some transportation. He'll give us a ride to my place, and tomorrow morning fetch us in my truck that I left on base. This is him, here."

A Humvee pulled up, Rampage waving from the driver's seat. Both Dr. Melrony and Buck piled in with their gear and rode in silence for what turned out to be a frosty ride to Buck's home. Both Buck and Dr. Melrony were resentful of the intrusion on their personal lives, and Rampage was too tired to notice or care.

Rampage wound his way through downtown and then an industrial waterfront before he turned down a thirty-foot wide paved street between two warehouses. He stopped one third of the way down the causeway at a door in the side of a large gray cinder block warehouse next to a large rollup door also set in the side of the building.

"Why are we stopping here?" Dr. Melrony asked.

"Because, I live here. Welcome to your new home," Buck replied.

"I don't understand. You live in an alley way?"

Rampage snickered from behind the wheel. He had said much the same thing the first time Buck had shown him the place.

"Of course not, silly," Buck mocked her with a huge smile on his face. "I live inside," he gestured with his arms wide apart at the whole building. "What? You don't like my landscaping?"

Still thinking that she was having a joke played on her, she decided to go along. "No, it's a lovely home. I especially like how you've incorporated the Navy paint scheme of gray into the home. It gives it character. In a world of impersonal sameness, it's so nice to see an owner put his personality, his mark, into a home. I think it says some much about a person..." She watched in horror as

Buck started to pull his gear from the rear of the Humvee and deposit it on the pavement. "You're not serious, are you?"

"As a heart attack. Come on, let's go." He had now pulled her suitcases and set them in front of the door. Not sure what was going on, she complied, exiting from the vehicle. As soon as her door shut, Buck waved to Rampage. "See you tomorrow morning, Rampage." The throaty diesel engine rumbled louder and pulled away, leaving Buck and Dr. Melrony alone in the causeway. "Let's get our gear inside, shall we?" Buck stepped up to the keypad next to the door and entered a code before stepping to the door. He produced a key and unlocked the door, holding it wide open, exposing a dark cavern inside. Dr. Melrony stepped into the abyss with her suitcases in tow, their little wheels rumbling across the pavement before clunking over the door's threshold and the smooth concrete on the other side. Buck stepped in beside her, his gear hung over one shoulder, letting the door swing shut. She heard him fumbling along the wall as the wedge of narrowing light from the closing door illuminated the stygian darkness.

The light had almost vanished when she heard several light switches being flipped, coinciding with the snap of large light fixtures popping to life all over the building. At first the light was soft, but grew quickly to expose an amazing interior. She had expected warehouse stacks and rows of cartons and boxes. Instead, the interior was completely void of any of her preconceived notions of industrial decorations. The warehouse was mostly empty. Immediately to her right was a row of cars in various stages of disrepair and a flat twin pontoon-like boat canted at an angle. Beyond them was a cluster of large rolling toolboxes, welders, torches, lathes, mills and other machines for working steel she did not recognize. There was a two-post car lift amidst the machines, tables, and tools with a low slung red car atop it. At the closest end was a yellow two-story Craftsmen style home complete with front deck and all in the angular lines so evocative of the style. In front of the home was a large 'lawn' of carpet with sofas and reclining chairs all facing an immense big screen TV. Beyond the 'lawn' in the corner of warehouse, beside the house, appeared to be a fully stocked woodworking shop.

"This is marvelous!" she exclaimed, astonished to find a fully erected building within a building.

"Thank you. My wife and I always wanted a little Craftsman bungalow for our own," Buck said heading for the front door, Lila falling in close behind. "We just loved the simplicity, the emphasis on natural wood and craftsmanship. And besides," he said over his shoulder as he started towards his home, Dr. Melrony in tow, "the beauty of it is that it's built indoors. The climate stays constant and it never gets rained on so the paint never weathers and needs repainting; unless I want to change the colors. It's built on a concrete slab so I'll never have to worry about foundation issues like settling or termites. The roof will never leak. It's the perfect maintenance-free home. Plus," he said waving to the ceiling, "I control day and night with the flip of a switch. This is a good thing after running all night on maneuvers. I can come home, flip off the lights and get a good night's rest, even if it's blazing high noon outside. The walls are thick enough that it keeps out all the noise. There is enough thermal mass in the concrete floors and walls that the temperature hardly varies from summer to winter. It stays about fifty-five all year round, so heating the house costs just a few dollars a month." They had arrived at the stairs to the front door.

"Come on in, and let's get you settled," he said as he bounded up the stairs and blew through the unlocked front door.

Dr. Melrony pulled her suitcases up the steps and stepped into an amazing home. Hardwoods in bright varnish everywhere, a circular staircase in the front entrance, the furniture comfortable and tidy. Buck had disappeared into one of the hallways. Thirty seconds later, he returned and motioned her up the stairs, "You said you and your wife always wanted a home like this. Is she here? It would only be proper to meet the mistress of the home."

"My daughter and wife died a year and a half ago," he said flatly.

"I'm sorry, Buck."

"Thank you," he replied automatically.

From the second story landing, he led her down a hallway to a bedroom before showing her a spacious bath.

"I'm going to turn the lights outside off. Please feel free to make yourself at home. The phones have an intercom feature. You're at extension four. I'll be at extension one if you need anything. I don't have any real food in the house, so let's get some shut eye and maybe later on this evening, if you're up for it, we can go out for a bite to eat?"

"On one condition - please call me Lila."

"Fair enough, Lila. I'll see you in nine or so hours. Goodnight."

"Goodnight."

42

Buck arose refreshed seven hours later. Not wanting to disturb Lila, he showered, dressed, grabbed a phone and went out into the warehouse. Using limited lighting, he started working on the red car on the lift. He had been putting the finishing touches on the custom exhaust system before he had left for Mexico. It needed a couple gaskets before being bolted to the custom headers and a few muffler hangers before it would be ready to run. He was just attaching the last muffler hanger when the phone chirped to life on the tool box where he'd left it. It was Lila on the intercom.

"Hello."

"Good morning. Or should I say good evening? I saw some lights in the warehouse so I knew you were up. I just wanted to let you know that I'll be ready to get a bite to eat in an hour."

"Great. I know a great little Italian restaurant downtown. Love the food, but it comes with a price – jacket and tie required. That sound good to you? I hope you don't mind, but I haven't eaten there in a while. I haven't had anyone to go with."

"Sounds lovely to me. I'll meet you in the front entrance in an hour."

"You got it," he said and rang off.

Perfect, he thought. This gave him enough time to finish the car and get it on the ground. He was itching to take it for a test drive and tonight's dinner would give him the perfect opportunity. He quickly finished the last item and got the car off the lift to give it a test fire. The engine sparked on the first turn and rumbled sweetly. He shut it down, rushing to the house to change his clothes.

An hour later found Buck standing at his front door in a sports jacket, tie and jeans examining his watch for the fourth time in as many minutes. He was feeling a little nervous, and he wasn't quite sure why. The soft swish of cloth at the top of the steps caused him to glance up.

Buck was stunned to see the vision descending towards him. He had only seen Dr. Lila Melrony in some version of her standard field garb: hair tucked under a floppy, wrinkled hat, baggy shirt, long cargo shorts, and hiking boots, her nose usually lathered in zinc-oxide paste.

The delicate, curvy creature in the simple white peasant top and hugging denim skirt bore no resemblance to the woman he knew as Dr. Melrony. This creature had long beautiful auburn hair that was thrown over a shoulder, framing green eyes that were luminescent. Lips that he had never really noticed before popped from smooth bronzed skin, her legs were masterpieces in elegance in the simple open-toed sandals.

"Will this be appropriate?" she asked, reaching the bottom of the stairs, twirling for his inspection.

Buck was stunned into silence. The lilt of her Irish accent now seemed so musical; the twirl she made gave her a sweet grace. The freckles that he had noted earlier on her shoulders and cheeks now seemed like devices sprinkled on her features by the divine as an afterthought to insure that her beauty was real and not an illusion or mirage. Her injuries and bruises were barely noticeable through her beauty.

She took Buck's silence as a rejection of her efforts. "I've got one more dress I could put on if you'll give me moment."

"No...no, that won't be necessary. You look fine just the way you are. I mean the way you're dressed," he fumbled for the right words. "It's just that ...that I was expecting something different."

"My, that sounds ominous," Lila said, flashing a brilliant smile. "When you say you were expecting 'something different,' one would almost believe that you were expecting a troll or ogress. Have I been that bad to you?"

"No! No...it's just that you look completely different."

"Oh, you mean embracing my feminine side?"

"Exactly..."

"Well, that comes with the territory, so to speak. I've learned the hard way that in the realm of earth sciences, one's love of rocks isn't taken seriously if you sport any kind of sign of femininity. It's best to hide such things if you plan on being judged by your work, especially if you're going against convention or working in the tight confines of a research ship."

"Well, for whatever reasons, you look terrific. Shall we dine?" Buck said offering his arm.

"How could a lass say no to such an offer," she said, curtseying before taking the proffered arm.

Buck escorted her out the door, down the steps and out to the waiting car. When they arrived at the car, he opened the passenger door for Lila. She stood in the car's doorway, staring at her seat without moving. "Is there a problem?" he gently inquired.

"It's rather low. I'm not sure that I can get in with this dress."

Buck took a look at the seat and her dress, realizing the difficulty she was in. "I'm sorry, Lila. I forgot how low this car was to the ground." The seat bench before Lila was only twelve inches from the concrete floor. "Unfortunately, it is the only other car in my collection that is running at the moment and my truck was left on base. This is the only ride we have available. Here," he said coming from out behind the door. "I'll help you into the seat."

Buck grabbed her hands, interlocking their thumbs in a palm lock while maneuvering her into the seat. In the process his cheek brushed her neck, which sent an electrifying jolt of its own down one side of his body, intensified by her fragrance of perfume and lilac scent wafting from her hair as it brushed by his face.

"Thank you," she murmured, her smile heartfelt.

"My pleasure," Buck said shutting the door. His return smile was just as heartfelt at the sudden thrill of his brush-by encounter. Buck slid into the driver's seat, and waited until the door was fully open before he turned on the ignition, the engine rumbling to life again on the first turn. Carefully he backed into the night, making sure the garage door closed behind him, letting the car idle and come up to operation temperature. Satisfied all was ready, he shifted into first and started the car rolling.

"I don't recognize this car," Lila said, "What is it?"

"Ah, that is actually a difficult question to answer." Buck answered, pleased at being asked about the project he had been working on for the last couple months. "It's a little of this and a little of that. It started life as a nineteen-1973 Porsche 914. Now it's a modified Karman-Porsche-Volkswagon-Chevrolet-Kohl special."

"Oh, you mean like a Volkswagen 914?"

"I'm impressed. You know your stuff. I forgot that they were badged and sold by Volkswagen in Europe. In America, everyone thinks they're Porsches even though they were actually designed by Karman."

"But what was the rest of it? Porsche-Volkswagen-Karman – something –something…"

"Oh that – well, I've added later model Porsche suspension and brakes and dropped in a Chevrolet high-performance small-block V-8 putting out about four hundred horsepower. The car weighs next to nothing since it's a monocoque chassis, meaning it has no frame it's just all sheet metal welded together. Since it's so light and mid-engined, it can hang with any three hundred thousand dollar sports car you care to name," Buck said affectionately patting the dash, "at least hang close enough so that it comes down to driver skill. With a few tweaks to the aerodynamics, this car can do over two-hundred miles an hour. I was planning on racing it competitively later this year."

"That is quite a hodge-podge. I had brothers who fixed up cars. They were always recruiting me to come help them: come hold this, step on the brake pedal until I tell you to let go, that sort of thing."

The conversation continued on cars, brothers and Buck's race car until they arrived at the restaurant, Buck was pleasantly surprised that Lila knew her cars.

"Here we are," Buck pointed out.

Buck had pulled up to a cloth canopy over a door and put the car's parking brake on before exiting to help Lila out of the car. After parking, he met her inside before being seated. Somewhere, after the antipasto salad, Buck proposed the question that had been bothering him. "You know, Lila, what I can't get is why you and Dr. Cadburess were specifically targeted for death. What could be so important about two geologists looking for oil? People do that all over the world. The only thing that I can think of is that's tied to both of you is where you wanted to search, the Chicxulub Crater. Maybe someone doesn't want you digging around there."

"That isn't exactly true."

"What do you mean?"

"While our exploration goal was to look for oil, Dr. Cadburess' and my research had more to do with what was in the oil and where it came from rather than if there were large enough quantities present for commercial exploitation."

"I'm still lost."

"Are you familiar with the Abiogenic Origin of Oil Theory?"

"No, never heard of it."

"This was Dr. Cadburess's area of expertise. He was one of the world's leading experts and proponents of the theory. I came to do my Ph.D. under him and stayed on after I graduated to head up his laboratory. Have you ever heard the phrase 'it's all the same dinosaur' when people talk about oil?"

"You mean like dinosaurs were turned into oil? Yeah, I've even seen cartoon commercials from oil companies depicting dinosaurs turning into oil."

"Those of us that are proponents of the Abiogenic Origin theory believe that is a fanciful and wrong proposition. In order to understand the fallacy of the currently accepted origin of oil, one only has to have a rudimentary understanding of tectonics, the shifting of the earth's crust plates.

"In a simplified version of the currently accepted theory of oil production in the earth, dinosaurs lived long ago. They end up in the ground when they die. Over time, under pressure and heat, their remains are converted to crude oil, which we find in deposits in the earth's crust."

"So far, so good," Buck acknowledged.

"Right, then. The study of tectonic plates holds there are

different plates of crust floating around on a sea of lava, bumping into one another. Where they meet, something called sublimation can occur where one plate rides up on the other, forcing the other plate to go under. This process is responsible for creating mountain ranges and earthquakes as the plates slide past one another. The bottom plate is forced into the earth's bowels, presumably to be subsumed and claimed by the lava again. The friction is so great that it forces up the other plate along the edge of collision into mountain ranges.

"We know that all organic material, that which contains carbon in its molecular structure, is contained in the uppermost strata of the crust- the thin layer of mulch where trees, plants, animals and even the dinosaurs decayed only averages twenty meters worldwide, thinner or nonexistent in some places, thicker in others. Doesn't matter. Pick the thickest spot of the organic layer and use that as the basis of your argument. However thick you argue the organic layer is, it is still an incredibly thin layer compared to the crust's thickness, which is measured in miles.

"Now picture these tectonic plates colliding together, hitting each other with such incredible force, forces we cannot even imagine or measure. Now, with all this brute force and friction, we are supposed to believe that this thin layer of organic material miraculously isn't scraped off by the weight of the top plate. This thin layer of organic material somehow manages to slide in under the tectonic plates whose friction is creating mountains. Then this thin layer that has miraculously been forced under another tectonic plate through heat and pressure is converted to crude oil before being subsumed by lava, which then flows through the earth in some sort of unidentified river, oil-ifer, or whatever to collect in vast bodies that we then tap and extract."

"It does sound kind of fantastic when you put it that way," Buck admitted.

"Wait, it gets better. The same theory tells us the pressure is so great between tectonic plates that it squeezes these organic molecules, along with some heat, into chains of hydrogen and carbon atoms to make crude oil. This same pressure that is incapable of scraping off the organic layer, now somehow has the power to initiate chemical reactions. This is very selective force, indeed.

"This is the currently accepted theory of where oil comes from. I personally think it is akin to thinking babies come from storks."

"Okay, then, what's your theory?"

"I support the Abiogenic Origin of Oil Theory, because it doesn't rely on so many improbable preconditions. The Abiogenic Origin of Oil holds that we do not know everything about what goes on in the earth's crust or below, a true statement if ever there was one. The theory states that it is far more likely, given the abundance of carbon and hydrogen in the composition of the earth, that there is some process in the earth's mantle or just below that is manufacturing petroleum all the time. This petroleum then seeps to the earth's surface all over the world all the time. This would account for the widespread and natural occurrence of petroleum in every ecosystem of the world. This seeping oil collects under geological formations that are impermeable, like salt domes or captured in shale or sand formations created by other naturally occurring ongoing processes, where we tap and extract it.

"We don't know whether this manufacturing process is evenly distributed around the world or happens only in certain spots, all the time or periodically."

"Alright, that has a certain logic to it, but how does the Chicxulub Crater fit into all this?"

"The Abiogenic Origin of Oil Theory has been around since the fifties. At that time, some scientists tried to prove the theory by drilling for oil in Sweden. They theorized that the best place to get a look at what might be going on under the crust was to look at places where the earth's crust had been shattered, like meteor or asteroid impact craters. The idea was, if petroleum production occurred everywhere, then there should be more oil in an impact crater due to the fractured organization of the strata. Essentially, impact craters are points in the earth that have been uncorked as far as oil production was concerned. So they picked a large meteor crater in Sweden and started drilling.

"After months of drilling the team found absolutely nothing and the theory fell into disrepute and was nearly forgotten.

"But, as earth sciences have progressed since then and the Dinosaur Theory seems less likely, the Abiogenic Theory has inversely gained credence and converts. The rub of the matter comes down to one thing, though. Molecular analysis of crude oil the world over shows biological markers that could only come from biomass – DNA and cellular components like proteins. That is how the whole dinosaur theory came about. They started with the biological markers and reverse engineered the theory to meet the results.

"The Abiogenic Theory has yet to explain this one very important, crucial piece of data. One of the things we are finding is aerobic and anaerobic microbes at depths not previously thought possible. Scientists recently found a species of bacteria five thousand feet below the surface that drew its energy for metabolic activity from the naturally occurring radioactive decay present in rock formation. So who knows, we may eventually find a microbe present and reproducing at the depths we extract oil from that can account for the biological markers.

"But the original plan for research in the 50's had merit. So first, Dr. Cadburess, and now I, were surveying impact sites, like Chicxulub to determine if there are larger amounts of petroleum present. If the sub-crust process occurs randomly, then we just might get lucky and find an impact sight that is leaking oil. Then test wells could be driven to get a better understanding of what is going on under the earth's crust and hopefully, to get untainted samples that should allow us to test for biological markers."

The main course arrived, "So how would any of this threaten anybody?" Buck continued the conversation, intrigued.

"If oil was found to be a renewable source, it would change the world's economy overnight. Greenies would lose their leverage in government policy. Oil, which has been demonized by the Green Movement, would now be a natural process of the earth, which is supposed to be released into the environment. We already find petroleum naturally occurring in all ecosystems. We also know that there are naturally occurring microbial agents that eat the petroleum in every ecosystem, which, by their presence, demonstrates that oil has been a long term, naturally occurring part of the ecosystem. The by-products of this natural microbial food cycle are identical to the emissions of automobiles. If it were found that auto emissions are exactly what nature will do with oil seepages, then it would drastically alter the auto industry.

"The balance of power would shift in the global economy. The middle east Arab-doms would no longer control the largest 'reserves' since the concept of reserves, which connotes limited amounts, would no longer apply. Government policies on oil drilling would be drastically altered if they knew oil was a renewable resource and that car emission byproducts were inevitable by natural processes. OPEC would lose its grip on the control of oil production if it were found that oil could and would appear in any of its neighbors at any point in time.

"Whole industries and global treaties would collapse. The Kyoto treaty would be debased and the economies it spawned would no longer be empowered. The Carbon Credit and Global Warming industries would vanish, putting this research at odds with ex-U.S. politicians selling carbon credits, the Nobel Peace Prize Committee and the U.S. Academy Awards Committee, not to mention the Green Party of Europe.

"That is why this research was so important to the U.N. and why they are sponsoring the work of Dr. Cadburess. It could make oil ubiquitous and available to every person in the world if the Abiogenic Theory of Oil were to become the accepted scientific model."

Buck whistled softly, "That is some enemies list. Let me see, OPEC and all its crazy despots, and the entire lunatic fringe of the Green Movement - fringe and Green Movement being oxymoronic - ex-U.S. politicians making millions in the carbon credit industry, the whole Global Warming industry; any one of thousands of groups with the motive and means to pay a pirate ten thousand dollars to have you killed."

"I hadn't really thought of it that way. I've just focused on how my work might help millions, perhaps billions, of people."

They were interrupted momentarily by the waitress clearing their now empty plates and over the rest of the evening's small talk, he was digesting not only his meal, but also the implications of Lila's work.

43

The next morning, Rampage showed up as promised at seven thirty in Buck's truck. A quick drive to the base was followed by a long security clearance process to get Lila into the secure area where Buck and Rampage's offices were located. Buck had gone ahead, while Lila walked through the processing and by ten had caught up with him in the office. Buck set up Lila on a computer and phone, while he and Rampage weeded through the latest intelligence updates on pirate activities they were tracking around the world

After they had cleared their desks and minds to their immediate business, he, Rampage and Lila turned around their chairs to face the middle. Rampage started, "I've checked with Major La Barré, and without further identifying features to our mystery man who ordered the hits on Lila, Dr. Cadburess and the *Constellation*, he says he won't be able to get anything probative. He says there have been no whispers or rumors circulating about any contract killings in Mexico of foreign nationals. Essentially, he's got bupkis. Nada. Nothing."

"Let's check in with Yoshi, maybe he's turned up something," Buck suggested.

"Let me set up the video feed." Rampage turned to his compute, and two minutes later, the face of a slightly wild haired Asian man, wearing square wire rim glasses, appeared on the screen.

"Hi, Yoshi. Buck here, with Steve and Dr. Melrony, who I don't think you've met. Have you made any progress on the rental car information we sent you two days ago?"

"There are two rental car agencies in Cozumel," Yoshi started, "that rent Mercedes-Benz in the color and model you identified. In the time frames that you gave me, both had cars out. I came up with four names based on the credit cards used to rent the cars. I cross checked the names and no name shows up on both occasions. I cross checked all the names against airline manifests for three days before and after the dates of rentals. Two of them checked out, a plastic surgeon from Sioux City, Iowa, and a real estate developer from Boise, Idaho.

"Two names, however, have been problematic. The first name is Juan Gonzales, and the second is Jose Riveras. The problem is these are extremely common names. Airline flights show several of each that could have rented the car."

"What about driver's licenses?" Buck asked. "Most rental car companies take photo copies of licenses, just to make sure people can actually drive. Especially if you are renting out a Mercedes-Benz, I bet."

"One moment, while I check," Yoshi said as a pause followed accompanied by the click-clack of fingers flying across a keyboard. "Both Gonzales and Riveras rented from the same company, so I'm opening a socket to their server ...I have it now. This is interesting... I'm posting data to your screen now." Soshi's face shrunk to a small box in the upper left-hand corner, replaced by two pictures of driver's licenses side by side. One was of Juan Gonzales of Columbia and the other was of José Riveras of Venezuela. Both had the same picture of a blue-eyed man with blond hair.

"Well, well, well... what have we got here?" Steve

wondered aloud, examining the pictures. "He didn't even bother to change the picture for his fake license, whichever one it is." He pushed a button on his computer to print the driver's licenses.

"Both are fake." Buck broke in.

"How can you tell?"

"You already spotted it. He used the same picture on both. That means he had them made at the same time, probably from a stock picture. Most drivers' licenses require you to stand for a photo each time. He probably has fake cover IDs made by the bushel. Uses them once and destroys them. I'm sure if we follow the credit card purchase, it will eventually lead to a dead end post office box where the card was prepaid from an anonymous money order or cash."

"So where does that leave us?" asked Lila. "Are you saying that now that we have a face, it won't get us anywhere?"

"Not necessarily. It actually tells us a lot. But first, Yoshi, can you send a copy of this driver's license picture to the U.S. authorities holding the prisoner we captured in Mexico and have them confirm that this is the guy that hired him."

"It's on its way now," Yoshi replied.

"Now, back to your question, Lila," Buck redirected. "We now know that we're dealing with a pro, someone that has the means and ability to create cover IDs. We also know that he is vain and needs his comforts. He met the prisoner both times in a suit...in the tropics. He rented a Mercedes. Not the kind of 'I want to stay invisible while I'm in town to hire contract killers' car kind of guy. There is no way this kind of cat would be a coach class flier. Thing is, flying first class would draw even more attention to him. Nothing says `look at me' quite like a first class seat, then making the rest of the flight file past while you sip a Bloody Mary. He may be vain, but it would be suicidal to have so many witnesses establish your whereabouts. He's smart enough to cover his tracks with false IDs and leads at a rental car company but then prominently displays himself on flights in and out of the country? That just doesn't jive. When you go about hiring a contract killer, the last thing you want to do is make yourself memorable to so many. Even if this guy did fly in coach, which I doubt, he almost invariably flew to an intermediary airport, deplaned, switched IDs, and then boarded a flight to Cozumel.

"Well how else could he have gotten to Cozumel?" Rampage asked rhetorically. "It's an island, right? There are only two modes of travel: fly in or boat in. He had to get there one way or the other," Rampage insisted.

"I highly doubt that he boated-in," Buck continued his extemporaneous calculations. "Boats move too slowly for his kind of business. Anything small enough not to draw attention to himself would be too slow or limited range for him, in case he needed a fast get-away. Any boat big enough to make a fast get-away out of Mexican territory and make it to another country would draw too much attention."

"You have eliminated flying in and now boating-in. Just exactly how did he get there then?" Lila asked with a little exasperation in her voice.

"Not completely. Yoshi, check all the private flights into Cozumel in our time window. I'm betting our mystery man has his own transportation."

"I'm checking now..." Yoshi's voice came from the computer's speakers, his face now expanded to fit the screen, "There were fourteen flights in our time window. Twelve of them are listed as corporate charters. Two were individuals, one was an American movie producer, the other a Fleet Street financier. No two match from the target time windows."

"If he was skilled and cautious enough to minimize his exposure on each visit by changing his ID, he probably also covered himself with bogus flight plans and listed identities. It would be an easy matter to file a flight plan stating your point of origin was one South American country and then altering your flight once you're airborne. All you would have to do is come in from the general direction stated in your filed flight plan and no one would think twice. I doubt the flight manifests and passports will match our two drivers' licenses."

"Correct, Buck," Yoshi said, scrutinizing data on his screen.

"So we're back to the beginning, bup-kiss," Lila grumbled.

"I'm betting that our man is a creature of habit," Buck began, prepared to make a point. "He did it twice by renting from the same car agency. Transportation between countries is a tricky business. Finding a charter company that will fly into a country is easy. Finding one that will falsify flight plans and passenger manifests and keep quiet about it is a much rarer beast. Yoshi, see if there are any matches between our two time windows on the same airline charter services?"

There was a sense of an impending break in their pursuit that hung in the room. Steve and Lila felt that Buck's logic was dead on track. So it was with an audible sigh of disbelief when Yoshi had an answer. "I'm sorry, Buck, no match."

"Check the plane numbers filed on the flight plans, Soshi. Falsifying paperwork is one thing, but repainting an aircraft every time it is used is something different. I'm betting that our Mr. Gonzales/Riveras's precautions to cover his tracks can only go so far."

"You're right, Buck!" Yoshi shouted from the screen. "I have a match on plane tail numbers. You want me to start researching the charter companies?"

"No!" Buck shouted, knowing how fast Yoshi's fingers could fly across the keyboard. "No. Anybody this cautious has surely set up the fake air charter companies to waste our time. He probably has trip wires set up so he's alerted to anyone who starts asking questions giving him time to bolt. I don't want to spook him. Inquiries into a false identity probably only used once would tell our target we are in pursuit. Government inquires are broader, less specific. I want you to start checking government registrations for this aircraft. This would be less likely to tip him off. Also call the FAA, Homeland Security and FBI with the tail number. If this plane attempts to land in the U.S., we'd like to talk to the pilot. The pirate we captured said that he spoke with a very faint Portuguese accent. That suggests Brazil or Portugal. Start there. My gut tells me that this guy is from Brazil. It has a large expatriate population from Europe where blue-eyed blondes are common, which would make him a perfect middleman to hire killers for someone who did not want to get their hands dirty. If Brazil or Portugal doesn't pan out, start working the other South American countries."

"I can do," Yoshi replied in broken English. "It will take time to check the different databases. I'll get back to you as soon as I find something on the plane, even if I have to check the manufacturer's database."

Lila's cell phone started to ring and she withdrew, sliding her chair back a few feet, to answer it.

"If you do, do it quietly."

"They won't even know I was there."

"Perfect. Thanks for your help, Yoshi," said Rampage.

"Hey, no problem," Yoshi said in his best imitation of a New York accent; an imitation that was definitely a work in progress. The screen cleared of Yoshi's face.

"Good job on the counter-intelligence reasoning," Rampage offered his friend. "I'll bet you were the teacher's pet in counter-intelligence school during SEAL training. Did you sit in the front row; do all the extra credit assignments?"

"Actually, it was the decoder ring that I got in a box of cereal last week that really turned it around for me," retorted Buck.

Buck and Rampage looked at each other, about to continue their conversation when they became aware of sudden gasps emanating from Lila. They turned to see her rigid and drawn, her knuckles white from gripping the phone hard.

"Has his family been notified?" she was saying into the phone. "What do the policía say? Do they have a suspect?" She listened to the response. "Please see to it that his body is returned to the family posthaste as soon as it's available, will you Sihg?" There was another pause before she said her goodbyes and hung up the phone.

"That was Dr. Kummat. I left him in charge of the expedition when I transferred to your boat off the Mexican coast. He called to tell me that one of the crew went missing yesterday. He turned up this morning dead, his body found in an alley between some warehouses in the dock district. The police have no suspects, and are treating this as a run-of-the-mill robbery gone bad. White Anglo in the wrong place at the wrong time. But I don't believe it. Sihg tells me that he was beaten excessively; all his fingers were broken and he had burn marks on him. That doesn't sound like a robbery. It sounds like he was tortured."

"Tortured to find out if you were on the boat, and if not, where you'd gone would be my bet." Rampage said gravely. "In the graft-run waterfront, it won't take long for whoever was asking questions of the dead crewman to figure out that you left with us and are now in the United States. Fortunately, with all the restrictions put in place by U.S. Homeland Security, getting into the United States right now is pretty tough to do in case he's thinking of coming here to finish the job."

"I wouldn't count on it. Whoever this guy is," Buck said waving at the picture of the driver's license, "he doesn't seem to have any problems penetrating borders. I'm sure he's well versed at getting into this country. Despite Homeland Security, it isn't all that difficult to get into the country if you have the right connections."

44

"There appears to be a problem that I thought you should be aware of, Mr. Minister," the man seated at the stern of his yacht said into the cordless phone. His sunglasses reflecting the midday glare off the marina's water, the man was anything but relaxed at this moment. He raised himself to a sitting position, swung his feet to the teak deck and reached for his iced drink on the built-in deck table of the boat, taking a sip before continuing. "My man in Cozumel reports that the *Constellation* returned to port two days ago. He was able to question one of the crew, who told him that Dr. Melrony had transferred to a U.N. ship shortly after they foiled an attack on the research vessel. In checking with his sources, he reports a military boat matching the description the *Constellation* crewman gave was removed from the water later that same night and flown out in military transports. A woman matching Dr. Melrony's description was seen moving with the transported boat's crew. It seems that Dr. Melrony has survived the attempt on her life."

"That is indeed bad news for you. You have been compensated well for the job that I expected to be done by now," said the voice on the other end of the connection. "The problem I see is what to do about a contractor who has taken my money and botched the job. You see, I keep people around that solve my problems, not create them for me." Although his tone was conversational, the threat in his words was unmistakable. "The man I work for has a very simple rule of governance: remove anything that gets in your way. I find that this is an excellent model to follow. Do you want to rethink your previous statement, perhaps?"

"I understand completely," the blue-eyed man responded. "The little deviation in the plan will receive all my personal attention. I simply thought it prudent to keep you apprised of all pertinent developments. I can see now that was an error in my judgment. Do you desire to be notified when the job is complete?"

"That won't be necessary. Because if I don't read about the poor doctor's demise in the next week, I will simply conclude that your personal attention was not enough. Regrettably, this will force me to re-evaluate your usefulness to me."

"That won't be necessary. I'm sure that this business will be concluded shortly to your satisfaction."

"Of that, I'm certain." The phone line went dead.

Dolph took another sip of his drink, trying to bring order to the cascade of thoughts flashing through his mind, his blue eyes on the horizon but not seeing. When he had them sufficiently corralled, he called to his assistant, "Klaus, call the hangar. I'm going abroad for a few days."

45

As an arms dealer, Dolph had developed business relationships in all sorts of places, high and low. This allowed him to reach into the highest strata of the illegal drug business community, which in turn made him more valuable to the upper crust of polite society due to his notorious reputation; it gave him an edgy appeal. His pedigree and contacts allowed him to facilitate deals for drugs, guns and murder-for-hire, among other things. It was for this reason that he was landing in one of Miami's lesser airports tonight. The jet landed and taxied to the Immigration ramp. After checking in, the plane taxied to a private ramp where a rented Mercedes was waiting. Dolph tossed his bag in the trunk before getting behind the wheel. He had made this drive several times before, and twenty-five minutes later, he was at the gate of a large estate belonging to Jorge Guitarez, the Medellin cartel's top distributor in America.

Pulling up to the front door, he exited the car, handed his keys to one of the armed men who had appeared, and raised his hands to allow the search of his person, a prerequisite for admission to the home of a cartel member. Once he was patted down, the front door was opened from inside and he was bowed inside by a servant. Inside Jorge's number two man greeted him and then showed Dolph into the boss's study and bid him to take a seat.

"Señor von Buhl, what a rare honor it is to have one of

our association's top suppliers come to visit," a voice boomed moments later as a salt-and-peppe-haired Hispanic man in a collared, open necked shirt swept in and offered his hand to Dolph.

"Thank you, Jorge, for seeing me on such short notice. I apologize for intruding on your privacy," he said, taking a cigar from the offered box Jorge had picked up from a nearby table.

"So tell me, what brings you so urgently to America?" Jorge produced matches, offering one to Dolph before striking his own, carefully lighting the end of the cigar.

Dolph did the same before answering, "I have an urgent matter which I need your assistance with. There is a woman staying in Norfolk, Virginia, that needs to have a fatal accident. My friends in the Brazilian government tell me that she is the guest of a new experimental U.N. force working against global piracy based out of Little Creek Naval Amphibious Base in Norfolk, Virginia."

"Ah, that is too bad. A naval base is a hard nut to crack. I could certainly smuggle a kilo or two of product on or off the base, but it is another thing to get onto a military base, kill someone and then return, especially someone that is being watched that closely."

"She is only staying on the base during the day. At night, my informants tell me she is kept under guard by members of the unit off base. We have not yet been able to tell where she is being kept. All we have is a name and the description of the truck, including the license, of the unit's leader. I was hoping that you could place men to watch the gates and follow him. They should be able to learn everything they need from him."

"Much better! This I can arrange. One question: is this a quiet accident or does it matter?"

"Actually, it does. I would like this to be as loud and

messy as you can make it. The more public, the better. "

"Ha!" Jorge gloated, hitting the desk with his hand. "Even better. So we are to send a message then?"

Dolph pondered this for a moment before answering. "A message? Yes...of a sort."

Jorge picked up a phone, summoning his number-two man. When he entered, Jorge rapidly rattled off instructions, sending four men to the airport for a trip to Virginia. When he finished, Dolph handed a manila envelope to the man, who took it without looking inside handing it straight to his second-in-command.

"My men will be in Virginia by tonight. In the meantime, I insist that you stay a day or two while your 'matter' is taken care of." Jorge may have been a street thug that had risen to power through violence, but he was also a shrewd operator with a Latino's pride. He wanted to show off his abilities to Dolph, who usually did business directly with Columbia. He knew that a few days' face time with such a well connected person could only prove to be beneficial in the future.

On the other hand, Dolph's instincts told him to put as much distance between this operation and himself as quickly as possible, but Dolph knew that refusing would be a foolish move on his part and insulting his host. "I would like that very much. I will re-arrange my schedule so that I might stay a day or two and enjoy the pleasure of your lovely home," he said, forcing a smile that was belied by his cold blue eyes.

"Excellent. Brandy?"

46

Jorge's second-in-command hit the speed dial from the front seat of the big, rented BMW sedan and waited for his boss to pick up, which he did after the second ring.

"We followed the man to a warehouse on the waterfront in the industrial part of town. We've looked, but the building is a fortress, and we don't have the necessary tools to break in. What would you like us to do?"

"You know what needs to be done," Jorge answered. "Extract the information from the man so that you can kill the woman. I'll leave it up to you how to get it done, just as long as it is very public and messy so that those meddlers from the U.N. get the message."

******

Buck slid the Porsche into first gear and eased it out into the sunshine when the roll-up door had lifted far enough to allow it to exit.

"So where exactly are you taking me again?" Lila asked for at least the third time.

"I told you, a little spot I learned about years ago. It's where I go when I want to get away from it all. I used to bring my wife and daughter there when we felt like we needed some alone time," he added softly after a moment's hesitation.

"Are you in need of some alone time now?"

"Yeah, I was feeling the need. How about you?"

"I must say, I thought it a brilliant idea when you proposed it. And truly, I'm honored that you would share this place with me." She reached out and touched his arm holding the steering wheel.

Her touch gave Buck a warm glow where it had briefly rested. The rest of the trip was spent in small talk over little things of major consequence interspersed with laughter until Buck finally pulled off onto a private road to a lakeside resort. A mile and a half later, a beautiful vista opened in the Virginian countryside's canopy to reveal a resort nestled on the shore of lake. A sign proclaiming "Welcome to THOMPSON'S Resort" hung from chains on a post in front of the building.

******

"Perfect," the leader of the cartel execution squad said to his companion. "our luck is strong, having the woman and the man in the same place. This road goes nowhere. This way we can take care of both at the same time. They must go back out the same way to get back to the highway. This is much too secluded a place to kill them if we are to make it messy. We will wait until they leave, pick them up on the highway, sandwich them between the two cars and then gun them down on the public road with many of spectators. This is turning out to be much easier than I thought.

******

"So, this is it. What do you think?"

"It's quite lovely, Buck. What exactly did you have in mind?"

"Relaxation...mostly."

"Uh-huh."

"Haven't you ever been on a picnic before?"

"If you mean, eating food in a beautiful natural setting? The answer is yes, every day I spend in the field."

"Good point. Hadn't thought about that one...alright, let me rephrase the question. Have you ever spent the day with me, eating fried chicken, potato salad, wine, crackers, fruit and cheese while doing nothing more strenuous than breathing and relaxing?" Buck had gotten out of the car and was retrieving a blanket and picnic basket from the trunk.

"Now that you put it that way," Lila smiled brilliantly at him as she stood, getting out of the car, "No, I haven't. From your description, it sounds like I might be terribly under-qualified for such work."

"Oh, I'm thinking you'll be a quick study. Shall we?" Buck offered his arm.

"Why, thank you," Lila said taking it.

"See, you're getting the hang of it already."

They found a shady tree with a view of the lake under which to spread their blanket upon the grass. Before long, the blanket was bedecked with a bottle of opened wine, cheese, plates, napkins and food, artfully spread in one corner of the blanket.

Lila, in another simple blouse, her hair loosely knotted in a ponytail by a black scrunchie, looked every bit as stunning as she did the night they had gone out for dinner. She kicked her shoes off and sat on her knees. She offered her hand to Buck. "Are you going to join me or just stand there all day?" she teased.

While Buck got settled, Lila busied herself pouring wine for the both of them. "Generally," she started, offering him a glass, "the first thing that I would do in a setting like this would be to start looking at the rocks. Then I would go down to the lake's shore and see what the sedimentation could tell me. Plus, the flat lake would afford me a view of the surrounding topography. But today," she paused to sigh, "I think I'll put my work aside."

"Are you sure? For all we know, this lake could have been made by an impact."

For a half second, Buck could see Lila's eyes refocus as she started to evaluate Buck's proposition, then just as abruptly, they softened. "Nice try, U.N. Man."

"I'm hungry. I didn't eat this morning in anticipation of the fine cuisine I knew would be available this afternoon. How about you? You ready for something to eat?"

Lila looked deep into Buck's eyes. "I'm extremely hungry."

Buck hesitated a moment, confused by Lila's flirtation before he shook it off and started dishing up food. After the chicken and potato salad were consumed and put away, they lounged on the blanket.

"There, now you have officially experienced an American picnic, replete with fried chicken and potato salad."

"What did you have in mind for your next act?" Lila asked playfully.

"Well, I thought I would read to you."

"That sounds lovely. What have you got?"

Buck fished in the picnic basket and pulled out three books. He took the topmost, a skinny bound book and held it up. "Do you like poetry?"

"Oh, the classic seduction scene? Read poetry to me while plying me with wine, cheese and fruit in an idyllic setting? Does that have a high success ratio for you? Only problem, I'm not much taken with poetry. What else have you got?" A beautiful smile spread across her face as she snatched away the other two books from Buck's hands.

"As a matter of fact, yes; the poetry usually is a lock."

"Too bad. I'm afraid you're going to have to work for this one. Here, try this one," she said handing him back a book.

Buck was surprised. This was his personal book that he had planned on reading if the opportunity presented itself. It was an action adventure story of survival set in Southeastern Alaska where men and killer whales battled a giant shark. He looked up at Lila with a surprised look on his face.

"An occupational hazard, I'm afraid. Working in remote locations, often for months, you get bored and start swapping books with other researchers, all of whom are usually men. Ever try swapping a romance novel with six men? I can assure you there are no takers. Even if one was so inclined, the harassment he would take from the others would prevent such a scurrilous act. Over time, I've rather grown fond of the genre."

"I don't know," Buck said flipping to the last page, "it's a pretty thick book. I doubt we'll do more then put a small dent in it today."

"I was hoping to stick around for the finish," Lila said, stretching out on the blanket next to Buck, her leg touching his.

"Your wish is my command." Buck lay down beside Lila, propped his head up and started into the book. The book, *TOOTH*, had a ferocious beginning, finding the main character catapulted into blue Alaskan skies by some unknown force then jumped back in time detailing the death of the last megalodon on earth at the hands of killer whales. Halfway through the chapter, they switched. By this time, the wine, food, relaxation and the pleasure of being read to, lulled Lila to sleep despite her deep interest in the story. Buck heard her deep, rhythmic breathing and stopped reading, just content to have such a beautiful woman sleep in his company. Buck was unsure how long he watched her sleep before this sweet interlude was shattered by the jarring ring of his cell phone on the other side of Lila. Her eyes snapped open, taking a moment to register her surroundings before focusing on Buck.

"I'm sorry my phone woke you. You were sleeping so peacefully." He rolled over, reaching for the cell phone on the other side of Lila. Doing so brought him face to face with her, his lips just inches away from hers. He hung there for what seemed an eternity, their eyes locked, cell phone forgotten. Slowly, he bent down until their lips met. The warm moistness of her lips blended with his hunger for her touch. His universe collapsed to nothing else than the union of their lips and the brush of his nose against her cheek in the embrace. He breathed in her fragrance, intensified by the touch of her lips. Slowly, he felt her arms encircle him from below. A sudden surge of powerful emotions swept through him, bringing the jarring phone back to his reality. He slowly disengaged, until he was inches away again. He was torn by an overpowering hunger to lose himself in her embrace again and in the surge of emotions her touch had evoked. The phone kept ringing.

"If I don't answer it, it will just keep on ringing," he murmured, his eyes never leaving hers while he found the phone and brought it to his ear.

"Kohl, here."

"Buck! Where are you?!" It was Rampage.

"I'm up at Thompson's Resort in ..."

Rampage cut him off, "Listen to me! Yoshi just got contacted by the FAA. We put out the tail number of our mystery man's jet to all airports to be on the look-out if it landed in America. Nobody bothered to look if it was already here. It's been on the ground in Miami for two days now. We just found out about it now. Every time that jet shows up, somebody gets killed. You've got to come in, now!"

Buck snapped to full alertness. "I'm leaving now. I'll call you from the car once we're rolling and update my position," he snapped the phone shut. "We have to go, now," he said firmly to Lila, popping up from his position over her.

"Why? I was rather looking forward to finishing that last thought." Lila was clearly confused at the switch from romance to business.

Buck, now standing over her, reached his hand down and pulled her to a standing position. "We need to go, now," he repeated again firmly.

"Oh, alright then. I'll get the blanket folded and you…"

"Leave it," he commanded, dragging her off the blanket. "We're leaving now."

"Buck, what's going on? You're starting to scare me," Lila said, now walking rapidly beside Buck towards the car.

"The plane of our mystery assassin just turned up at a Miami airport. Through an oversight, we're finding out about it two days late."

Lila, now more than a little frightened, slipped her hand into Buck's as they walked rapidly towards the car. Buck felt naked. He had left his gun in the car, thinking that it might spoil the romantic mood he was hoping to create. Now, as he was walking what seemed to be an interminable distance to the car, he felt a pang of regret that he had let romance outweigh his caution this one time.

Finally they reached the car. Buck hopped over the

Porsche's door without opening it and slid down into the seat, inserting the key into the ignition. The engine fired up with a roar, Buck not caring to finesse the machine at the moment. Lila slid into her seat and shut the door.

"Buckle up. Use the five-point harness," he instructed as he buckled in.

Due to the Porsche's enhanced performance, Buck had replaced the original two-point lap belts with both a three-point restraint for everyday driving and a five-point harness for road racing. Lila fumbled with the five-point harness, having never worn one. Buck reached over and helped her with hers before putting on his.

He handed his cell phone to Lila while he made the final connections on the harness and put the car into reverse, backing out quickly and turning the car's nose towards the exit. He revved the engine and let the clutch out sharply, spinning the wheels in the loose gravel. He'd worry about the paint damage when he got home.

47

Buck turned from the resort's road onto the highway, retracing his route home. As he eased through the car's gears and got up to the speed limit of fifty-five, he turned to Lila.

"Call Rampage. He's in my speed dial -- just press and hold the number two. Tell him we're southbound on Highway 258, just a mile or two south of Isle of Wight in Isle of Wight County. If anything happens, we'll give him a call. Also, tell him to have Homeland Security impound the jet and detain the pilot in connection with a terrorist plot."

"Alright."

Buck listened to Lila make the call and pass on the information to Rampage. Satisfied, he turned his full attention to driving. In his rearview mirror, he noted that a black late-model 7- Series BMW sedan had appeared and was gaining on him slowly. He'd carefully looked both ways before turning on the highway and had not seen a car in either direction, so he wasn't sure from where this car had appeared. But he had been preoccupied talking to Lila the last couple of minutes; he could have very easily missed the car.

Buck came over a small rise, to find that another, BMW, identical to the one behind him had just pulled onto the highway and was accelerating slowly. His warrior's subconscious antenna started vibrating at this coincidence as pondered what the odds of two identical BMWs appearing out of nowhere at the same time to sandwich him. *"No way in hell that's a coincidence,"* he concluded as he relaxed his grip on the wheel in preparation to what he thought might happen next.

The road was divided by a double yellow line, so Buck could not pass and was forced to slow down. The other BMW had now caught up and was riding his back bumper, acting impatient to get around the slower cars.

"Is your harness tight?" He asked Lila, watching the rear car in his mirror.

"Yes."

"Tighten it some more. I think things are about to get interesting." As he finished his sentence, the car to the rear moved into the oncoming traffic lane in a lazy attempt to pass, despite the double yellow lines' prohibition. Buck watched the car swing wide in his review mirrors as it slowly moved alongside him. When it entered his blind spot to his left rear quarter, he did a head check to see what the car was doing. Just as his head turned he saw the muzzle of a gun coming out of the window.

Instantly he jammed on the brakes. If there was one thing Buck's car did better than accelerate, it was braking and cornering.

The low- profile wide tires on all corners nearly locked. Since the 914 was a true mid-engine sports car, unlike its Porsche brethren, it was perfectly balanced fifty-fifty front and rear, so all four corners bit into the pavement. The Porsche launched backwards just as a burst of gunfire ripped into where the car had been milliseconds earlier. Lila screamed at the sudden roar so close.

The black cars, taken by surprise, reacted slowly to their disappeared target. Buck saw their lights flash red and the tails of the big black cars' rear up as the drivers jammed on the brakes.

In a blink, Buck went through his options. Unlike most cars, the Porsche's gas tank was in the front, best to keep that away from gunfire. The Porsche's engine was right behind him by three to four inches and covered all but the top of his head. It could protect him from rearward fire. The assailant's cars were now in front of him, cutting him off from safety and help. They had automatic weapons, he had only his pistol. His only chance was to run away from them and trust that his red rocket could step it up to a level he knew the euro-sedans could not sustain. His best chance was to have the assailants chase him so that he could force them into a driving error and use his superior performance as a weapon.

The Porsche screeched to a stop in an unbelievably short distance, slamming both Buck and Lila hard against their five-point harnesses. As the deceleration G's abated and he fell back into his seat, he shoved the stick shift into reverse and accelerated backward, with a short blip on the gas pedal. Again, he was thrown against the front of the harness as the engine's four hundred thirty-eight foot/pounds of torque launched the lightweight car backwards. Buck slipped his hand down to the parking brake on his left hip, stabbed the clutch and simultaneously turned to the right while yanking the parking brake up; his thumb was on the release to prevent the brake from locking. The Porsche spun in a skid on its center of axis in a one hundred-eighty degree pivot.

As Buck saw the landscape in the windshield flash from green foliage to black pavement with blue skies above, he turned into the skid and dumped the brake, disrupting the spin. The car settled, pointing nearly straight down the road. He jammed the stick shift into first, pounded the gas and dropped the clutch. The tremendous power of the engine was more than the lightweight car could transmit to the pavement. The rear wheels just spun in place, a roiling cloud of white smoke belching from the wheel wells. "*Just as well,*" he thought as he smoked the tires, "*need to get the tires hot and sticky, anyway.*" Buck eased off the throttle just enough for the wheels to find traction. When the tires did bite, the acceleration slammed them back into the seat as his car launched down the road they had just traveled.

Quickly he ran through the gears, and in a little over ten seconds, he was a quarter of mile down the road, the car easily accelerating in third gear through a hundred twenty miles per hour with three grand left on the tachometer and another gear yet. Buck could see in the rearview mirror that the Beamers were just getting turned around on the narrow country road. He took his foot off the gas pedal and let the car's engine wind down, the compression of the motor acting like a brake.

"What are you doing, Buck?" squeaked Lila's voice, high pitched from fear. "We've got to get away! Go! GO!"

"Lila, give me the phone," Buck ordered in a controlled tone.

Lila gave him a bewildered look before handing him the phone that she had managed to hold onto through all the wild gyrations of the moments before.

Buck punched Rampage's speed dial button and jammed the phone to his ear. Steve answered on the second ring.

"Rampage here…"

"Steve," Buck cut him off, "trouble here. I've got two black BMW 7s on my six. They have automatic weapons. I'm cut off. I'm heading northeast towards the coast on 258. I'll try to lose them and circle back on Highway 10. Send help now. Gotta go, partner, time to get busy." He snapped the phone shut and handed it back to Lila, then downshifted to second, keeping his RPMs high.

She had turned to look out the rear window and saw that the black cars were almost on top of them. "Buck! What're you doing?!" She nearly screamed in his ear.

"It's hard to play Cat-and-Mouse without the Mouse," Buck said calmly.

He let the black cars come flying up on him until it looked like they would ram him and then punched the throttle. When impact appeared imminent, the red car rocketed ahead, always just feet from the sedan's bumper. This time, Buck accelerated more slowly through second and third, allowing the big sedans to stay with him, their engines being pushed to their limit.

The road was narrow and twisting. Buck kept the speed up to around ninety, knowing that at these speeds, it would be impossible for the shooter in the passenger seat to get off a shot. The big cars were drifting heavily through the corners making the drivers over-control and their suspensions work to their limits, jerking the passengers around. Buck remembered a small town ahead and he was afraid of injuring bystanders as they came barreling through, so Buck started a series of slow-downs and speed-ups to bleed off some velocity until he could get through the town. The last thing he wanted to do was to dump angry killers with automatic weapons in a small town. Cresting a small rise, the town came into view four hundred meters ahead. And he saw his worst thought realized. An old pick-up truck was pulling into his lane, blocking it. He was on top of the truck in seconds, at the last instant swung into the oncoming lane, passing the truck before it even knew he was there.

Startled by a red car darting around him, the driver of the truck jerked his wheel to the right onto the soft dirt shoulder. The truck's wheels caught in a rut and the driver overcorrected, wildly launching the pickup back on to the road in front of the oncoming pursuit.

Buck wasn't sure how the Beamer drivers missed the truck, but they did. One swerved to the right and the other to the left. A cloud of dust erupted where the one had swerved right onto the dirt shoulder. *"Good,"* Buck thought watching in his review mirror, *"with any luck, someone will call the local constable to report what just happened."* The thought of help gave him comfort for a half second before he visualized some lone constable confronting killers with automatic weapons and being cut down. *Probably not such a good idea, after all.*

With that last image in his head and the town behind him, it was time for him to take the gloves off and quit playing nicely. He quickly throttled up his racer and opened a small lead.

The BMWs responded, their engines straining to make up the distance. Buck came upon a tight blind left corner and downshifted to second. Using the whole road, he set up wide right and kept his foot into the throttle until the last instance, going deep into the corner before braking allowing the Porsche's superior braking to stretch his lead. He eased up on the throttle while at the same time slid his gas foot to cover the brake pedal. Adding a touch of brake, he expertly shifted the car's weight onto the outside wheels of the turn. Picking his line, he cut across both lanes to nick the pavement's edge just after the apex of the turn. As the turn deepened, Lila and he were pushed against the right sides of their harnesses, pulling almost a single lateral G. The Porsche took the corner thirty miles an hour faster than the European sedans could, opening up more margin between them.

Halfway through the turn, Buck dumped the brake and

replaced it with more throttle, accelerating hard out of the corner, adding another fifty meters to his lead. The drivers behind him now had to know that Buck was playing with them; he was outclassing them on every turn and straight away. Buck almost started to laugh. *They had probably acquired the big sports sedans thinking they would have the advantage against their target,* he thought. *Ennnn-wrong! Boy, did they pick the wrong hombre to mess with today. Time to turn the tables on these assholes.*

Up ahead Buck saw the setup he had been looking for: a long straightaway ending with a sharp bender left with guardrails. Buck eased off on the throttle, letting the lead car catch up to him.

"Buuucckk! What are you doing?" Lila had remained quiet during most of the high speed chase, now she came to life as she turned to see the big black cars barreling down on them again.

"I'm letting them catch up, of course. So they can start shooting at us."

"Why?! This isn't some game!"

"I'm about to teach them a lesson. Keep your head down."

Buck eased on throttle in third gear until he was doing around sixty. He watched the car behind him intently in his rearview mirror. The big sedan's hood stood just barely below his rearview mirror so Buck could look right into their front seat. He watched as the passenger undid his seat belt, picked up the short barrelled version of an AK-47 that Buck had seen earlier, and rolled down his window. He also noted the driver was slipping his seat belt off, probably hoping to get a few shots off with a handgun he briefly brandished while cocking the weapon. He watched as the gunman half crawled out, half stood sideways on the front seat, preparing to start shooting.

Once he was out of the window, Buck knew he wouldn't want to get back in until he had riddled the Porsche with bullets. In fact, he was counting on it. Slowly Buck sped up to sixty-five. He also knew that the short-barreled AK-47 had a nasty tendency to climb right on anything more than a single shot. His plan was to slowly up the speed, and jink left every time the shooter got lined up and let the hard maneuvering and gun work against the shooter while keeping him pinned in the window. They were up to seventy now as the shooter swung the gun's barrel onto his car. Buck waited, waited, and then stabbed the steering wheel left, juking the car hard left before bringing it back center again.

The targa top was off, so the thunderous burst of fire was deafening. The shots went wide of his car and the shooter was unable to track his weapon on the Porsche, the barrel hitting the BMW's A-pillar. The driver instinctively tried to match his moves, and the shooter whip-sawed in the window, struggling to keep his balance and bring the gun to bear again.

Buck could hear the V-8 behind him slowly spooling up. *Had to be approaching eighty now*, he figured. The shooter, with an eighty mile an hour wind in his eyes, would have an even tougher time now trying to line up a shot. But still, it only took one lucky shot, Buck reminded himself.

Buck took his eyes off the rearview mirror to glance down the highway, he was still six or seven seconds away from his turn-in at the corner. He glanced again in the rearview mirror just in time to see the shooter line up again. He stabbed the wheel left again before bringing it back to center. This time he saw the pulses of light from the gun's muzzle to accompany its roar as another burst passed over his car. Bullets chewed up the pavement in front of where his car had been, accompanied by sparks and flashes as the bullets either ricocheted or burrowed into the pavement.

Again, the shooter widely thrashed to maintain his balance in his precarious perch as the driver tried to stay right behind his car.

They were doing ninety now, Buck only had a second or two before it was time to turn. He forced his eyes away from the rearview mirror, his last glimpse was of the shooter was lining up for a third burst, the big sedan stuck to his rear. Buck moved to the right hand side of the road, making it easier for the shooter to kill Lila and him, but necessary for his plan.

Buck held the car right, waiting for the bullets to start ripping into his car and his flesh. The corner seemed to come in slow motion.

Finally, he could wait no longer, he was out of pavement. He pitched the Porsche hard to the left, cutting both lanes. A millisecond after the car started to move left, he heard the gun's report, and watched as two bullets stitched his front hood, starting center right and moving to the car's front corner, smashing into the pop-up headlight assembly.

Buck again expertly loaded the right side wheels and shifted the momentum to the outside wheels of the turn. This time the wheels started to squeal as the tire's contact patches were taken to the brink of their traction co-efficient.

His attention split, Buck had been late entering the corner and held a bad line. The Porsche swung wide through the turn, drifting to the far edge of the pavement. Buck had to come off the gas to hold the car in the corner. He came within a foot and a half of the guard rail before he was able to corral his race machine and bring her in line. The bad line had cost him momentum coming out of the corner, coasting out before applying power again.

The black BMW had not been nearly as fortunate. The driver, preoccupied with getting the kill, had followed Buck's race machine hard into the corner. The big sports sedan had way too much momentum and too little traction to change its direction. Its tires squealed in protest as the driver tried to force the big sedan into the corner before losing total adhesion to the road's surface and slamming into the guardrail. At ninety miles an hour, the nose of the car slammed into the guardrail first, whip-sawing the rear into an even more brutal impact.

The gunner, already partly outside the car was launched in an arc over the embankment rail before his back wrapped around a tree. The sickening snap of his spine was masked by the grinding, tearing shrieks of tortured steel as the carcass of the BMW was folded and the guardrail posts snapped, acting like a rubber band, stretching and deforming to absorb the car's impact. The metal rail stretched as it absorbed the kinetic energy being imparted to it, but it wasn't designed for ninety mile an hour impacts. With one last high-pitched squeal, the metal rail shrieked before it came apart. The black sedan passed through and started to tumble in a sideways roll down the embankment, disintegrating as centrifugal force threw off car parts.

The second car saw that the lead car was going in too hot and its driver backed off, braking to negotiate the corner. He was able to dart through the corner while the lead car tumbled down the embankment.

Buck still had a considerable lead, as he watched the second car clear the accident scene and accelerate after him. He had cut the number of pursuers in half, but they still had a job to do; that was to kill the woman beside him. He watched in his rearview mirror as the new driver started stalking him.

Buck seriously considered just running. It would be easy to open a lead and keep putting distance between him and his pursuers until he reached safety. But he figured all that would accomplish would be to let the killers escape so they could pick another day and place of their choosing to execute an attack. Maybe next time he wouldn't be so lucky as this time where he had the advantage of the better car. But that was based on the supposition that the men in these two cars were the only attackers. For all Buck knew, there could be more killers out there and the pursuing car's job was to herd him into a larger, prepared trap. His training was to attack into an ambush.

Cat-and-mouse had worked so far, so he saw no reason to change his strategy. Buck backed off the throttle, letting the new player catch up and roll the dice. The second sedan bore down on his sports car. He downshifted to second and held steady, waiting for the other car to get close. Just as the car started to close the last twenty feet, he floored the gas pedal. The tachometer surged past five grand as the fuel injectors awoke all its four hundred twenty seven horses of the V-8. The Porsche squirted ahead easily on the straight-away.

But the new driver had been coy. He had saved a little power in reserve while running down the Porsche, not flooring it until the last second. That little burst of speed caught Buck by surprise. His engine was redlining at seven thousand RPMs and even though he had initially gotten ahead, the BMW had lunged and looked to ram his rear end. Buck needed the next gear to escape but had no time to clutch a gearshift, so with engine howling he was forced to jam the stick up into third in a speed shift. If he blew it, either the car behind would ram him, or he would destroy the transmission and they would become sitting ducks. He threw his shoulder into it, jamming the stick shift up and right. The synchromesh gears clunked into contact in the transmission but did not shatter under the tremendous load. The little red car gave a small lurch forward, just enough that the BMW's bumper just missed ramming the car's rear fender and accelerated away.

With the gas still floored and in a taller gear, the Porsche again started to open a lead. Buck had been caught in the wrong gear, and it had almost cost him their lives. The Porsche's curb weight was just under two thousand pounds; the German sedan was nearly twice that. At the speeds they were traveling, even the slightest bump from such a heavy car was sure to knock his racer out of control.

The big sedan backed off while it chased Buck through a few curves before another straight away opened up before the speeding cars. The driver of the big sedan seemed to be in no hurry now, trying only to keep in contact with his car. This worried Buck. Did it mean that the assailants had help coming? Was he driving into a trap? He knew something that Buck did not, and was obviously up to something.

So they merrily drove along down a three-quarter mile long straight-away, at a mere ninety miles an hour. Buck was content to let the car follow him while he led it on a chase. The James River, where it met the Atlantic Ocean at Hampton Roads, would soon be coming into sight and he would turn south and east, leading the chase back towards the population centers and help. At the end of the straight-away was a sharp right-hand turn with another guardrail. He decelerated heavily, pitching them against the front of the restraint harnesses. By now, Lila knew what was coming and was holding fiercely to her door's handle to control the effect of the G-forces the car was placing on her. Buck smoothly eased off the brake a little at the turn-in point while moving his foot to cover the gas to add some throttle. The car had just started to shift its weight to the outside wheels when he saw a flash in his review mirror.

In an instant, he knew they were about to die.

Buck now saw the trap the other driver had laid for him. Buck had set up for the corner expecting that the other car would want to follow him. In a millisecond he realized the other driver had no desire to negotiate the corner. Instead he had floored his engine while Buck had been braking and closed the gap, aiming for where Buck would be putting the Porsche, just in front of the apex of the turn. He was going to use the big car's weight and ram him at full speed. And he knew exactly where Buck had to be to make the turn, which made him a sitting duck. In an instant he understood that the other driver had calculated that they might survive if he used his car's weight and airbags as weapons. The other driver had timed the impact to neatly T-Bone his racecar in the side as he went through the turn with the big sedan's forward momentum.

Reflexively, Buck dumped the brake and floored it. The engine's howling from the high revs turned into a scream as he went full throttle in the front half of the turn- in. The red rocket jumped forward in an incredible burst of speed.

He waited to feel the crushing impact that was sure to come. Lila screamed, seeing the big car barreling down on her with only the little car's thin door for protection. But, the rocket racer performed magnificently, the burst of speed just enough for the Porsche to escape past the point of impact before the BMW got there. The black sedan missed their car by the width of a finger.

Buck, preoccupied, had lost his line and was a way high

in the corner due to his burst of speed. His right front tire hit a small divot in the road's shoulder at the instant the big sedan was brushing by the rear fender. The slight bump was enough to shift the car's weight changing the tire's contact patch ever so slightly. Simultaneously, all four tires lost their traction.

The Porsche flew two car widths sideways before it landed cat-like on all four feet, made contact with the pavement and instantly tracked down the road.

Almost simultaneously, the black sedan crashed through the guardrail. The back end of the sedan flipped over the guardrail absorbing the impact of the nose, initiating a nose-tail cartwheel. The car did one and a half rotations before hitting a stout tree, crumpling into a wadded ball of steel and plastic. The car's vital fluids spilled out to puddle and mix with the occupants' on the ground.

Despite Buck's driving skills and the superior engineering of his racing machine, it could not overcome the fact that it was out of pavement. Its lateral impetus now carried it off the pavement and onto the narrow margin in front of the last few feet of the guardrail. Luck was with them this time. The tires bit into the hard packed dirt just enough for the car to travel forward, missing the guardrail's end by centimeters. As the car slid across the far shoulder, Buck wrestled to bring it back under control. Amidst the billowing cloud of dust, the car straightened and shot out toward the paved road.

Buck tried to brake and steer at the same time, and the car wig-wagged on the pavement before he lost control again. The sports car spun about the stick shift lever, like a top, as it went in a straight line down the road. No longer in control of its actions, all he could do was grip the steering wheel and hold on for dear life, his feet jammed on the clutch and brake. The world whirled by, the revolutions slowing until with a final lurch it came to a stop seventy five meters later, facing the corner that had nearly killed them.

Slowly, Buck came to his senses and looked over at Lila. She was frozen, her face drawn white, knuckles bleached of any blood in a death grip on the door armrest.

"Lila!" Buck called. "Are you alright? Lila!"

Not breathing, she slowly turned to Buck. Finally, he saw her suck in a deep breath and relax just a little bit. "Are you okay?"

All she could do was shake her head. Then she started to tremble. Her trembles turned into uncontrollable shakes as tears starting to well in her eyes.

The engine was still ticking over and seemed to be intact, so Buck slipped it into first and drove the car to the side of the road before stopping and parking the car. He undid his harness before reaching over to undo hers. He slid over next to Lila, holding her while she cried on his shoulder, for how long, he was not sure. But eventually the racking sobs and tremors subsided for her to breathe normally again. When she did, he silently redid her harness before returning to his and started to head back to Norfolk, a large, greasy pall of smoke emerging from the tops of the trees in his review mirror.

48

"The jet took off before Homeland Security could detain it," Colonel Barrett informed Buck, Rampage, and Lila, who was sipping a cup of hot cocoa. The three were sitting around a computer screen back in Strike Force Trident's office at Little Creek. Colonel Barrett continued, "But we were able to track it back to an outlying airport in San Paolo, Brazil, where it landed about an hour ago. Yoshi finally tracked down the plane's registration to a small charter service there: a one-man operation owned by a man named Victor Negro. The information on him has been emailed to you.

"The Virginia State Police already have identified one of the men who tried to kill Dr. Melrony earlier today. He was a foot soldier in the Medellin cartel in Miami. I suspect that the other three bodies will have similar histories."

"Well, that fits perfectly with our mystery man hiring middle men to do his dirty work." Rampage affirmed. "What about the information he gave Customs in Miami?"

"Same as the IDs -- same photo, different name. This time it was Manuel Pojertas. Guaranteed to be an alias," Colonel Barrett answered.

"So where does that leave us? Where do we go from here?" Lila asked from behind her mug of cocoa.

"We follow the plane," Buck stated. "We go to Brazil and we convince the pilot to come back here for questioning."

"I presume you have a plan to make that happen," the Colonel deadpanned from the computer screen.

"Absolutely."

"Pray, tell..." Rampage challenged.

"Easy. We fly to San Paolo and hire the pilot and his plane to fly us back to Miami. When he gets here, we detain him and convince him it's in his best interest to give up the identity of his client. After all, he did enter the United States on false papers."

"And when you say 'we,' by that you mean you and I?"

"Soy-tainly," Buck responded in his best imitation of Curly of the Three Stooges.

"Why not just go down to Brazil and interrogate him there?" Lila asked. "Wouldn't that be quicker?"

"Yes, it would," Buck responded. "But we have no resources to draw upon in Brazil. We would have no way of controlling Mr. Negro after we spoke to him other then kidnap him. And that could get messy quickly. We have no crime in Brazil to charge him with and nothing to involve the local authorities. Who's to say that he doesn't have connections with the local police for that matter? Hell, for that matter, our mystery man could have someone on the payroll at police headquarters, who would be alerted as soon as we brought the pilot in to the police. No, the only safe bet is to lure him to our turf where we can control him."

"Excellent," the Colonel remarked. "I'll have you booked on the next available flight out of Norfolk, then. Gentlemen, I suggest you go home and pack; you're going to Brazil. What do you intend to do with Dr. Melrony while you're gone?"

"We've got two options," Rampage picked up the narrative. "Since an attempt on Dr. Melrony's life has now been made on American soil, the FBI is now involved. Because the assassins were hired by a foreign national in Miami, and they traveled over state lines to conduct their crimes, the FBI has agreed to take Dr. Melrony into protective custody. Or we can set her up in the Female Bachelor Officers Quarter here on base. The NCIS agent assigned to Little Creek has agreed to take custody of her in our absence. It's her choice." Buck and Rampage turned, looking expectantly at Lila.

"Think I would rather stay here on base, since I already have some measure of familiarity with it. Plus, it just feels a whole lot safer with all these military people around."

"Then it's settled," concluded Colonel Barrett.

"One more thing, Colonel," Buck interjected. "While Rampage and I retrieve the plane's pilot, I would like to have Lieutenant Ramsden prep and load the *Agrippa* and have it ready for immediate deployment when we return. We're hot on the trail of our mystery man; any unnecessary delays may allow him to slip through our fingers. We know that he's well connected enough to have multiple fake IDs and access to travel. In all likelihood, we're probably going to have to go snatch him from some foreign soil, most likely Brazil. My bet is that he's still in the San Paolo area. I'd like to have the Strike Force ready to roll as soon as we have target information."

"Agreed. I'll get started on making the proper arrangements. Keep me appraised, I want regular progress reports," the Colonel's finished and a second later, the screen went blank.

"Okay, champ," Rampage said turning to Buck, "tell me about your plan to bring back the pilot to America with us.

As he did, Rampage started laughing.

49

The long plane flight and requirements of commercial flight had not allowed Buck the needed rest to recover from the affects of the adrenaline rush from the car chase of the day before, so he lurked in the corner, concentrating on not frightening the hotel's patrons with his bedraggled appearance while Rampage checked them into their San Paolo hotel. Rampage appeared after an interval, thrusting a key into his hand.

"We're in the Ambassador Suite, Room 1258. Now come, my personal zombie...follow me, and I'll have room service send up a nice plate of steaming human entrails for you to gorge on."

"Want brainnnssss," Buck moaned before concluding, "I look that bad, huh?"

"The man at the check-in desk wanted to know if you needed the hotel's physician to come to the room to assist you." They stepped onto the elevator, pushing the button for their floor. "I just told him that you'd partied all night with models before flying; the caviar must not have agreed with you."

"I did? What'd the models look like?"

"Oh, I don't know...if you've seen one hand-model, you've pretty much have seen them all..."

"Well, at least they had a nice touch."

"Oh, witty, very witty..." Rampage retorted

The lift arrived at their floor and opened the door.

"Oh, I don't know, most hand-models have faces made for radio," Rampage continued, getting in the last jibe.

Arriving at their suite, they had to swipe the card in the door lock three times before the green light went on and a faint click acknowledged the door was finally open. Carrying his bags toward one of the bedrooms, Buck shouted over his shoulder, "Wake me in a few hours. I'm going to get snore-izontal," before he disappeared behind one of the doors.

Buck awoke dressed, face down on a bed in a dark room. It was nighttime, a heavy rapping at the door accompanied by Rampage's voice rustled Buck closer to consciousness.

"Time to get up, my precious. I have a nice plate of steaming victuals for you. And if you're nice, I'll even throw in some stimulating company."

Buck roused himself from his bed, staggered to the door and emerged, blinking into the central suite. Rampage was sitting over a plate of food at a small dining table in the main suite, fork busily shuttling between the plate and his mouth. Upon seeing Buck stumble forth, he stopped long enough to wave an invitation with his fork at the silver-domed plate across from him. Buck lumbered to the table, plopping down in the indicated seat. They ate quietly for several minutes before Rampage broke the silence.

"You were so exhausted that I took the liberty of going to the U.N. Mission to pick up our supplies." He pointed to a slim briefcase sitting by a sofa a few feet away. By supplies, Rampage meant money. In order to entice the pilot to fly strangers on such short notice, they were going to have to flash a considerable amount of cash to convince him it was worth his while.

Buck nodded at the briefcase, then looked back at Rampage. "I thought that you said you'd throw in some stimulating company, too?"

"Thought that you'd find this," Rampage took Buck's free hand and slapped a stainless steel pistol into it, "stimulating company."

It was a stainless steel .45 Smith and Wesson SW99. He ejected the clip; it was full, before pulling the slide back to see if a round was chambered. It was empty. Replacing the magazine, he slapped it home with his palm before chambering a round and de-cocked the hammer. He put the pistol in the small of his back and pulled his shirt over it.

"That certainly is stimulating," Buck concluded. After getting caught in the open in yesterday's car chase, he had been feeling naked without a weapon, especially now that they were in the hot pursuit of their mystery man in his own backyard.

"I also hired a taxi," Rampage continued, "to take me out to the airport where the jet last landed. It's still there. I was able to ask around and get the phone number of the charter service that runs the jet. All we have to do is call him in the morning and set a meeting."

"Good work, Rampage. One last thing: call the front desk and let them know that we'll need a limousine all day tomorrow."

"You got it."

"Now, if you'll excuse me, I need to get some proper sleep. I want to be able to shoot straight in the morning."

"Okay... I'll take first watch...then" Rampage said, in an exaggerated sarcastic voice, since he was the only one left. Then he turned serious, "I'll come get you in four hours." With all that cash in the room, it was only prudent to keep someone awake with a gun at all times.

"See you in a while..." Buck said, heading back into the bedroom he had used earlier.

In the morning, after ordering in breakfast, a shower, shave, and a fresh change of clothes for each, Rampage made the call. The charter service answered on the third ring. He quickly explained their need and set a travel time for that afternoon.

Curious, Buck asked "What did you tell them?"

"Just that you had been recalled home due to urgent family business."

The late afternoon departure gave them enough time to go out, and buy an expensive designer suit for Buck and have it tailored before their meeting. It would not do for them to show up looking to spend several tens of the thousands of dollars on an airplane charter when it looked like he could only afford to shop at Macy's. To that end, Rampage slipped the hotel's concierge a wad of bills to arrange for some curvaceous arm candy to escort them in their limo ride to the airport.

They arrived back at the hotel and checked out before re-entering their limo, which had been filled with the requested arm candy. When they got into the limo's two opposing seats, the two beautiful girls immediately started to snuggle up to both Buck and Rampage, provocatively throwing their legs over knees, rubbing against and perching their heads on the men's shoulders. The car pulled out into traffic as Rampage looked in the limo's bar, finding an iced bottle of champagne. He handed glasses to the two women before opening the bubbly and filling their glasses.

"This is killing me," Rampage grumbled, "maybe we can ride around a little while before we go to the airport. These lovely escorts are much too fine to be wasted on such a short trip, especially since they've already been paid for the whole day."

"You already know the answer to that one."

"Yeah, I know. Mission first. Where were these ladies last night when I could have done something about it?"

"Haven't a clue, but it wouldn't have been a bad idea. It would have helped build the legend of a spoiled American playboy being called home by daddy."

"Oh, I thought about it. But it just wouldn't be a proper conquest if all you have to do is slip the concierge a wad of bills."

"Spoken like a true gentlemen."

Rampage started to speak to the girls in Portuguese, which he wasn't all that fluent in. But enough communicated to let them know that the show was needed at the airport, when they got out. Both women removed themselves from the men, smoothing their skirts back into place and started jabbering, ignoring the men as if they weren't even there, causing Rampage to roll his eyes at Buck.

Fortunately, the ride was mercifully short, lasting only twenty-five minutes. As they drew close to the airport, the two women went into their act again, like the seasoned pros that Buck suspected they were. The limo driver rolled up to a non-descript building on the flight line next to a large hangar and honked his horn. Through the open doors of the hanger, Buck could see the twin-engine executive jet sitting just inside. As they pulled up, playing his role as confidant to a spoiled, rich playboy, Rampage exited first and came around to open Buck's door, offering his hand to the closest beauty, followed by Buck in an expensive designer suit and polo shirt. While Buck was helping the second escort extricate herself, the limo driver extracted three bags from the limo's boot. The limo driver deposited their luggage at the plane's steps. The women made a big show, kissing and squeezing Buck until he was able to shepherd them back into the car. All the while,

Rampage did his best to contain himself and ignore the attention that his friend was getting.

When the two women were loaded back into the car, the driver drove off as Buck waved to the beauties, whose names he had never learned, but whose kisses still smoldered on his cheeks and lips.

The pilot had emerged, catching the tail end of the production from the plane's steps. Rampage had proceeded to the steps and was handing up the first piece of luggage to the pilot, when Buck turned back to the plane.

"Wait!" he commanded Rampage. "How much are you paying this guy?"

"What?" Rampage was taken off guard. "We're paying him twenty-two thousand reals, a little over twelve thousand dollars, U.S."

"Tell him that's too much. If he had wanted twenty-two thousand reals, he should have been loading our luggage for us, not making us do it ourselves."

Rampage hid his face from the pilot for a moment and gave Buck a 'what the Hell are you doing look.' Buck just responded by gesturing for him to get on with it. "Go on. Tell him."

Rampage put down the bag and started to speak to the pilot, who became animated as Rampage translated. The two argued back and forth a couple of passes before Rampage turned to Buck. "He says that we had a deal and the agreed upon price was twenty-two thousand reals."

"That was before we started doing his work. Tell him I will pay him twenty thousand reals now."

When Rampage relayed the new price to the pilot, he did not need Rampage to translate the pilot's no. The pilot made a counter offer, which Rampage repeated.

"He apologizes for the laxity in his service and offers to

take off five hundred reals."

"No. The price is twenty thousand."

The pilot shook his head 'no' when he heard the terms had not changed.

"Come, Steve. We are leaving then." Buck turned his back before he could see the look of confusion on Rampage's face and started to march out of the hangar. Rampage looked at the pilot, shrugged his shoulder, then picked up the rest of the luggage to follow Buck. He had gone three steps when the pilot shouted at them.

"Wait, Buck. He says that he will do the job for twenty-one thousand reals. Buck stopped and turned to face the plane. "If he is so lazy that he can't pick up our luggage, how do we know he's not too lazy to do the proper maintenance on this jet? How do we know that it will even make it to Miami or that he even knows how to get there?"

Rampage smiled to himself; now he knew where Buck was going with this. He turned to the pilot and translated. After listening to the pilot, Rampage relayed the information. "He says that he personally flew this jet back from Miami just three days ago. He assures us that he and the jet can make the flight."

"Alright, then tell him that I'll pay him twenty one thousand reals, half when we're wheels up and half when we deplane in Miami. And tell him if for any reason he has to divert, he won't get the rest of the money."

Rampage told the pilot the new terms to which he readily agreed. He ran down the steps before Rampage could move and scooped up their luggage, hustling up the steps before disappearing into the plane's doorway.

With the pilot inside, Rampage turned to Buck. "You had me going there for a minute. I had no idea what you were trying to do."

"Sorry, Rampage. I had to do it that way. The surprise

on your face had to be real. The pilot undoubtedly speaks English; he'd have to understand flight controllers if he's flying into the United States. I couldn't take a chance on him hearing anything we might be discussing on the side."

"How'd you know that he wouldn't get the luggage?"

"I didn't. Not that it would have mattered. I would have found something wrong to renegotiate the deal and walk out on the guy. Stressing him was the only way we could reliably find out if he was our guy. If we asked too many questions up front, he was liable to get suspicious. But he's definitely our guy."

"Okay, but once you found out that he had just flown from Miami, why did you make a counter offer, instead of just accepting what was on the table?"

"Just playing the part...now, let's get going."

The engines started to spool up and they buckled into the leather seats. In a matter of moments, the plane was taxiing out of the hangar and onto the runway. The jet gathered speed quickly as the pilot pointed the plane down the runway before lifting off and climbing quickly to cruising altitude. Buck opened the metal briefcase that he had carried from the hotel and counted out the agreed upon price from the stacks of currency.

"Here," he said, handing a wad of cash to Rampage. "Give this to the pilot. And get an ETA."

From the briefcase, Buck extracted a satellite phone and waited for Rampage's ETA before dialing Colonel Barrett's number to update him.

******

Nine hours later, they descended into the Florida morning and settled on to the runway. The pilot taxied the plane to the Customs tarmac before shutting down the engine followed by the wheels getting chalked. The pilot was so busy flipping switches and shutting down the rest of the plane's systems that he did not notice the swarm of men emerging from the doors of the Customs Office wearing blue windbreakers with an assortment of yellow block letters reading FBI, HLS, and CUSTOMS stenciled on their backs and left chest. It was not until the touch of cold steel of Buck's .45 made contact with his head in front of his right ear, accompanied by the sound of a gun being cocked, did he stiffen and become aware of what was happening.

"Now before we open the door to let the others come in and play, I believe that you have some money of mine," a voice whispered in his ear.

50

"We have a target." Buck reported. "His name is Dolph von Buhl."

"You've only been on the ground for two hours. That's excellent work in such a short time," Colonel Barrett congratulated.

"It was not my doing, Colonel. The FBI guys interrogating him really knew what they were doing. They cuffed him and threw a black bag over his head before tossing him in the back of a van. They drove him around the airport runway and taxiways a few times so he'd be nice and disoriented before they taped him to a chair in an empty, pitch black hanger. The guy wasn't part of von Buhl's operations other than as a winged taxi service. Von Buhl would call in a destination and cover ID, and he would file the paperwork. The pilot wasn't a hardened criminal; he cracked right away, especially after the FBI told him they would confiscate his plane as part of a suspected drug trafficking ring if he didn't cooperate. After that, he was a fountain of information.

"Evidently, von Buhl sometimes flew with a male assistant. According to the pilot, he lives on a yacht in the Rio de Janeiro harbor basin at the Sao Padrina Yacht Club. He doesn't know much more beyond that, says he only knows this because he's heard von Buhl talk about it to his assistant. He says the name of the boat is *Geäch Tete*."

"Strange name for a boat in Brazil," Colonel Barrett

observed.

"I agree. It shows that he still aligns himself with his Germanic heritage rather than his Brazilian. Who knows, it might be useful information to the interrogators when we get him back to the U.S. I want to have the *Agrippa* flown to Santos. Once it's offloaded, Strike Force Trident can make its way north to Rio to rendezvous with me and Rampage.

"How are you planning on getting there?"

"Well, we have this nice executive jet just sitting here; we'll just hire a pilot to fly us back to Rio. That way, I figure that we can have eyes on von Buhl's boat for at least a day or two before the strike team arrives. That should give us plenty of time to devise a snatch plan. Whatever the obstacles are to snatching von Buhl, I'm sure that we can overcome them. My concern is ex-filtrating him. Our actions may sound an alarm. We don't know anything about von Buhl's resources or contacts. It would increase our vulnerability and mission's difficulty if we try to air transport him out. Our best bet is to escape to the sea. But beyond the twelve mile limit, what do we do with a prisoner off the coast of Brazil?"

"I believe that I can help with that," Colonel Barrett responded. "When you told me that you might need the *Agrippa* ready to go to Brazil, I started making some calls. I called Tobias Sterns at the White House to check on the availability of U.S. ships off the eastern coast of South America. The U.S. Navy has two ships, a Ticonderoga Class cruiser and an Arleigh Burke Class destroyer operating in the immediate area. The cruiser *Charlestown* is off the coast of Suriname and the Destroyer *Hadley* is off the coast of Brazil; either can be repositioned to support your operation. In addition, I have made a call to the Brazilian Navy to schedule the *Agrippa* for a familiarization cruise to facilitate future training operations with their navy. This will give us the cover needed to get into Santos and cruise about their coast."

"Excellent. Let's leave the cruiser where it is and use the destroyer for prisoner transfer. If we do this quietly, the Brazilian authorities will never know what we are up to."

"We'll just let the U.S. and its attorneys sort it out after we have von Buhl in custody."

"In the meantime, Colonel, could you have the Rio UN Mission pick up a few more supplies for me?"

"Sure, what do you need?"

"Oh not too much," Buck said with a gleam in his eye. "Just some fishing gear...of a sort. "

51

When they arrived in Rio de Janeiro, they rented a car from a vendor who specialized in much older, well used cars for much less reals that blended into the surroundings. A quick stop at the U.N.'s mission yielded a couple of large zippered bags of the requested supplies before they set off for the harbor yacht club.

The Sao Padrina Yacht Club was hidden from view by a six-foot concrete block wall that ran the length of the street to the edge of the property before turning to disappear into the water. The gated entrance was bracketed by expansive flowers beds and artfully arranged shrubbery. A uniformed guard prevented unwanted solicitation by the locals or from thieves while a barbed wire fenced breakwater prevented intrusion from the land. Buck and Rampage found a spot on one end of the wall along the street that allowed them to look into the yacht club.

Using binoculars from the supply bag, they glassed the yacht club's slips until they located the *Geäch Tete* which required a move to the opposite end of the club's fence. Tied to the end of one of the central docks, she was one of the largest boats in the basin, her name written in gold and black lettering across the stern. Made of fiberglass, the eighty-five foot boat's upper deck molded seamlessly into a swept glass bridge with a spacious cockpit behind it on the fourth deck. Small oval tinted-glass ports broke up the smooth lines of the ship along its sides; large skylight glass panels were set in the foredeck. The open deck at the end of the second level featured contoured seats and tables, ending with a set of steps on either side that led down steps to a small weather deck at the water line at the stern, where a speedboat was tied.

Rampage took the first watch while Buck fished out a laptop computer from one of the bags. Using the special sending unit and crypto gear brought with them, Buck was quickly able to secure satellite communications with Project Neptune's NYC offices.

"Yoshi says that the *Agrippa* is still three hours out of Santos, plus unloading time. Figure five hours to get her in the water and supplied. Another ten hours to transit the two hundred fifty miles from Santos to here... I figure they'll be here sometime midmorning tomorrow." He fell silent as he started to peruse the file.

"Our target is 5'10", 185 lbs, has blue eyes...but listen to this," Buck said. "our Mister von Buhl is a very slimy customer. His main business appears to be arms dealing, specializing in supplying the drug cartels. Occasionally he serves as a conduit for communist states in brokering deals with several South American countries, including Venezuela, Peru, and Argentina. It also says here that he's known to have links to the business community in both Sao Paulo and Rio, having brokered several deals between Brazilian financiers and wealthy German expatriates. His family bio looks like he would be the poster child for the Manson family. His paternal grandfather, a Nazi SS Officer of notable disrepute, moved the family to Brazil at the end of World War II.

"The file is sketchy on his earlier years. Went to good private schools, didn't really stand out in anything. After graduation, he just disappeared off the screen until about ten years later as a major power broker and arms dealer.

The file also notes that the man suspected of killing his uncle was kidnapped shortly after he dropped out of sight and was returned to his family in pieces, slowly, after the ransom was paid. The parts were delivered over three weeks. The coroner said that the parts were cut from a live person each time one arrived. Von Buhl was suspected, but never charged.

"It also says that he's known to travel with an assistant and an occasional bodyguard."

From behind a set of binoculars, Rampage commented, "That would explain the Medellin shooters that came after you. Clearly this guy has access to them. Now we know what he was doing in Miami -- the Medellin cartel has a strong presence there." Rampage fell silent as he continued to watch the boat. "Wait a second. I think our target just stepped out onto the aft deck."

Buck pulled another pair of binoculars out of one of the bags and put it to his eyes. The person was talking on the phone; after watching the figure on the boat's rear deck for fifteen seconds, he confirmed, "That's our man. And it looks like he's got company, too."

Another, slighter, man, with dark hair and delicate features, appeared on the rear deck briefly, taking instruction from von Buhl before leaving.

"I would guess that was the assistant," Rampage offered. "Not much to look at as a bodyguard, unless he spits poison or ray bolts come out his rear."

"That would make him a 'crack shot' wouldn't it?"

"Oh...good one. That was a real knee slapper..." Rampage said rolling his eyes.

"What's this?" Buck asked rhetorically, "It looks like we have another player." A third man had stepped out on to the deck. "Let's see if we can play 'What's My Line.' Please sign in, mystery guest... Arlene Francis you're first."

"Is it bigger, that bread box?"

"His neck is. So that would make him hired muscle."

"My guess, too."

They watched the boat for the rest of the day and didn't see any more persons other than the three they spotted. At three in the morning, Buck decided that it was time to take a swim and reconnoiter the boat. Two hours later, he returned.

"No booby traps or trip wire alerts on the boat, but there are trip wire devices on the deck, so we'll have to infiltrate from the water."

"Good. That settles that part of the plan," Rampage responded. "Oh, by the way, after staring at the boat all night I got curious about the name and sent it to Yoshi. 'Geäch Tete' is German for 'outlaw'."

"So, our bad guy fancies himself an outlaw," Buck eyed the boat before replying, "Well, That makes us the posse."

52

Buck and Rampage spent the rest of the day reviewing the schematics of the boat that Yoshi had sent them and refining the plan. In the afternoon, they were able to make radio contact with the *Agrippa* and coordinated the strike team's activities with their snatch plan. Tadhg was holding the boat twelve miles offshore until it was time to do a run in. Rio de Janeiro sat inside a large bay, occupying the western third; much like San Francisco in America. The *Agrippa* would have to travel another ten miles once inside the bay's mouth to reach the yacht club. It was an easy sprint for *Agrippa*, but the problem was there were millions of eyes that could watch her pass; all the more reason to plan their snatch for the wee morning hours when most people would be sleeping. It would take at least forty-five minutes to reach international waters and deliver their charge to the waiting destroyer once they had their target on board. That was a lot of distance to cover, an eternity for something to go wrong.

An hour after the lights went out, Buck and Rampage slipped into their wetsuits and slipped down to the water carrying their swim gear and small waterproof belt packs. Once they were chest deep in the water, they paused to put on their belt packs, mask and fins before pushing out into the water. Both started out in easy, powerful strokes learned in the waters off San Diego, California, in BUD/s training, the SEAL crucible designed to weed out the unworthy.

Circling the breakwater to the marina, they reached the small platform over the boat's stern, where a speedboat drifted on a short lead, and pulled themselves slowly out of the water to stand on the platform. Unzipping their waterproof belt packs, each produced a Taser, capable of delivering sixty thousands volts.

Stealthily, they ascended the stairs on their respective sides. At the top of the stairs, half-doors to the deck swung out towards them; Buck slipped a hand over the rail, unlatching his first. The door swung open silently, and from his crouching position at the top of the stairs, he had an unobstructed line to the main salon door that opened onto the deck. In a crouched run, he covered the distance across the deck, kneeling to a stop in front of the glass door of the salon. Curtains covered the door, so Buck couldn't see in. Afraid that his silhouette might be backlit against the curtains from the faint lights of the yacht club's docks, he worked fast. Snapping his pack around, he extracted a small canvas satchel. By feel, he found his lock-pick tools and quickly started to massage the door's tumblers with the pick and lever until he felt the door's lock give. Rotating the handle completely to disengage the latch with one hand, he slid his tools back into his pack, and motioned for Rampage to join him. Scurrying across the deck, Rampage stopped on a knee next to Buck. Simultaneously, both produced and donned night vision goggles. On a hand signal, Buck threw open the door, getting out of the way so that Rampage would be the first one in. In a low crouch, Rampage dashed into the room, disappearing to the left before Buck did the same, heading to the right.

No alarm had sounded.

They proceeded to clear the boat, deck by deck, in the

areas that they didn't expect to find anybody. On the bridge, Buck found the keys in the ignition, which he pulled out partway before snapping off the rest of the key to disable the engines.

Two of the four decks had now been cleared; it was time to start clearing the living quarters. They snuck back down to the salon deck and descended to the lower deck. The first room was empty. The second proved otherwise.

Kneeling on either side of the door, Buck, who was closest to the handle, quietly slid the door open. From inside, their electronically enhanced hearing was greeted by the soft puffs and gurgles of a man sleeping. Rampage advanced slowly into the room, tracking the sound of the snoring until he could make out the form of a man lying in a bunk mounted to the wall through his NVG. He advanced until he was less than a meter and half away and pulled the trigger of his Taser. The pop of the nitrogen canister as it expelled the two electrical leads sounded like a thunderclap in the small confines of the room. The startled man didn't have time to react before the leads embedded high in his chest and discharged their high voltage into his body. For the next thirty seconds, the only sounds were soft grunts from the man as he tried to fight the pain and paralysis and the soft clicking emitted by the gun.

After a tortuous half-minute, the man and the gun's voltage were spent, Buck and Rampage moved in to finish the job. The man turned out to be the security guard they had observed. As he lay paralyzed in his bed, Buck and Rampage extracted plastic zip ties and a small roll of duct tape from their packs. Buck peeled a strip of tape from the roll and slapped it over the man's mouth; all the while the whites of his eyes shone wide in the dark from terror. Roughly, they rolled him to lay face down while they hogtied him. In less than ten seconds, they were back out in the main passage. Rampage paused to remove the spent cartridge for his Taser and reload with a fresh one. The rest of the rooms on this deck proved to be empty which was concerning. *'Did we miss something on the swim in?'* Buck wondered. *'Where is the assistant? He was supposed to be on this deck."* A faint thread of doubt started to creep into his mind, in a mission that so far had gone without a hitch.

Ascending to the salon deck again, they started with the first door on the left, which proved to be an empty office. The second door they tried was across the hall from the office. According to the schematics they had studied, it should have also been a living quarters, presumably a guestroom. It was, but it proved to be empty also. *'Crap! Where is that assistant?'* All that was left now was the Master's Quarters, and the assistant was still unaccounted for.

Buck was sure that Rampage was feeling his concern too, but neither could give voice to it. At the last door at the end of the hall, they paused one more time before gathering themselves. At the nod of his head, Buck swung open the door. Rampage went first through the door and moved left, while Buck went right.

Inside was a large bed flanked by two nightstands and the light of one was still on. Von Buhl and the assistant were in bed, both sitting bolt upright at the sudden intrusion into their sanctum. Neither Buck nor Rampage could shoot due to the way the men were holding the bed covers in front of them

Instantly, von Buhl recognized the weapons they were holding what they meant to do with them. He leapt over his assistant to the floor, pulling the remaining man out of bed by his hair. Von Buhl, using the other man as a shield, grabbed a black handled switch blade from the nightstand and put the blade point to his assistant's neck.

He shouted something in Portuguese, which Buck didn't understand, but his meaning was clear. The assistant, unable to move with the knife to his throat, whimpered loudly. Von Buhl whispered something in his ear in German and the man visibly relaxed. Kohl, who was fluent in German, only heard "...I won't hurt you."

Although the room was spacious for a boat, there wasn't enough space for both Rampage and Buck to maneuver the men into the corner. It was a Mexican standoff. Buck quickly ran through his options. He could shoot the hostage with the Taser. Anybody touching the hostage could get the full effect of the voltage and he could disable both men with one shot. However, the high voltage was just as likely to convulse either man, resulting in the knife being thrust into the hostage's neck. Buck had to find a way to separate them.

He had just cast his eyes away to examine the room for options when von Buhl made the decision for him. Seeing Buck look away, he took the knife from the man's throat and savagely thrust it up under his assistant's back, just below the rib cage into the man's liver. The look of confusion, pain and incomprehension froze on the man's face as von Buhl shoved him at Rampage while leaping on the bed, making a break for the door.

Simultaneously, Rampage caught the assistant, lowering his Taser, while Buck squeezed the trigger of his weapon. Instead of the whoosh of the nitrogen cartridges discharging, there was nothing as the semi-naked von Buhl charged him from on top of the bed. He squeezed the trigger again with the same result. The waterproof belt pack he had transported the weapon in had leaked slightly and fouled the reload cartridge.

Von Buhl leapt from the bed, knife raised high, swinging in a vicious arc towards Buck's neck or chest. From years of training and tournaments, Buck's acted without thought. He caught von Buhl's wrist that held the knife with a crossing block and pivoted, pulling down on his arm and twisting into a bow, redirecting the man's leaping momentum into the dresser bureau behind him. Von Buhl crashed uncontrolled, back first, into the big chest of drawers at a cocked angle and slid to the floor. The blow caused the knife to fly from his hands as he tried to right himself. Buck maneuvered to place himself between the door and von Buhl. Behind von Buhl, Buck could see Rampage beside the bed trying to save the stabbed assistant's life.

Von Buhl staggered to his feet and settled into a fighter's crouch, appraising Buck with fiery eyes. Buck, unfazed, took a loose boxer's stance, elbows low to protect his body, fists guarding his head. Seeing this, a crooked smile crossed von Buhl's face.

Von Buhl made the first move, hopping on the balls of his feet to snap off two quick jabs. Buck was glancingly struck, there was no room to retreat, only deflect the blows aimed at him. If he yielded ground, the doorway would be open to escape. So, Buck stood his ground and ducked both punches enough to take the sting from the blows. Buck was playing for time, time for Rampage to finish his care of the downed man and help him subdue von Buhl or Taser him.

Realizing Buck's dilemma, Von Buhl's crooked grin stretched into a lopsided smile, now believing that it was only a matter of time until the black suited man yielded the meter between him and the door.

Von Buhl danced in to throw another series of left jabs at Buck's head setting him up for combinations of rights and lefts. Standing flat footed, Buck ducked and weaved evading von Buhl's punches.

While boxing for the Naval Academy, Buck had been known for his heavy hands. Not that they were slow; to the contrary, his quickness was astounding and he packed one hell of a punch. Buck stepped into the man's attack and delivered two jabs that snapped back von Buhl's head, followed by a powerful right that landed flush on von Buhl's jaw, staggering him back a half meter before he was able to right himself.

Before Buck could take advantage, von Buhl changed tactics. He fired a high haymaker right, looking to clip Buck's ear and forcing him to duck under the punch. As soon as Buck reacted to the punch, von Buhl swooped low and lunged at his hips. Buck's weight was already in motion downward, which von Buhl used against him, grabbing his upper thighs before he could fully sprawl away. For a moment it was a stand-off; von Buhl had only enough leverage to immobilize him, and Buck had no leverage to throw his opponent or break his grip.

Von Buhl gave a series of shrugs, with each improving his position until he was able to lift Buck and throw him to the bed. Buck grabbed hold of the other man, making sure that he went down with his opponent. Together, they hit the bed, bounced, and slammed to the floor on the opposite side of Rampage. Rolling, each man looked for an opening. Buck was able to deliver two powerful elbows to von Buhl's temple, which opened up a cut in his eyebrow.

In the cramped quarters there were was no room to maneuver for throws or stand-up striking, so Buck had been looking to take the fight to the ground, his preferred style, when von Buhl had obliged him with his charge. When the grapple ended, von Buhl was on top in a kneeling position between Buck's scissor locked legs prepared to rain down blows on Buck's upturned face.

Von Buhl reared back and dropped a heavy punch into Buck's face. Buck moved his head and arched his hips trying to disrupt von Buhl's aim. He was only partially successful; the blow instead of hitting fully, glanced off his cheek and thudded into the floor. Buck attempted to grab von Buhl's wrist, but missed as it retracted for another strike. Von Buhl feinted one way and then another, hoping to get Buck to commit himself before striking. Buck remained motionless, a snake coiled, waiting to strike.

Von Buhl lunged as he attempted to smash Buck's head into the floor with another powerful blow. Like the first, it was partially deflected. This time Buck was able to grab von Buhl's right wrist. In a blur, he whipped his legs from von Buhl's waist and wrapped one of them around his head, isolating the arm between his legs as he wrenched the wrist around to full lock. With his legs, he slammed von Buhl's face into the carpet of his million-dollar yacht. At the same time he arched his hips up and pulled back on the contorted arm, imparting tremendous torque and leverage against a joint that was never built to take what Buck was doing to it. At the same instant von Buhl's face slammed into the floor his humerus was torn from its socket with a muted thud as ligaments snapped and bone sheered.

Momentarily stunned by the face plant in the floor, it took a moment for the agony of the mangled limb to register in von Buhl's mind. When it did, all he could do was to sharply suck in a lungful of air in preparation of a scream.

When Buck felt the arm tear away from the man's shoulder, he gave it one more vicious tug; after all, the man had paid people to attempt to kill him on two occasions, before letting go. With incredible speed, he scrambled onto von Buhl's back, wrapped his right arm around the stunned man's neck and locked a choking grip with his other arm behind the man's neck for leverage. He yanked the man's head back, settling into a kneeling position while squeezing, crushing the gun dealer's throat.

The scream he had been preparing remained locked in his chest as Buck's hold cut off his wind pipe and pressed harder closing his carotid arteries. Von Buhl struggled feebly against the constricting arm around his neck with his remaining arm, but his efforts quickly diminished.

Just before the struggles subsided completely, Buck relaxed his hold just enough for von Buhl to gasp a breath. Buck moved his mouth next to the man's ear whispering, "I bet that hurts, Dolph, doesn't it?" He paused knowing that his chokehold prevented a response. "Here's the way this is going to go. Pay attention, your future hangs on the decisions you make in the next two minutes. Oops, did I say hang?" Buck clamped down on his hold, cutting off the man's air again. "My bad," he released his hold again as the man gasped for air again. "I promise I'm not going to kill you. My boss would be *very* upset with me if I delivered you as a corpse. But here's the deal: I need you to tell me a few things before we get on with the rest of your life. You know, this hold you're in is more about cutting the blood flow to your brain by restricting the carotid arteries than choking the living shit out of you. All I have to do is squeeze the sides of your neck and you'll start to get lightheaded, followed by gray out before you become unconscious. Here, let me show you..." Buck tightened his grip. Immediately, von Buhl started slapping at Buck's arm around his neck with his still functional arm.

"See?" Buck relaxed his grip slightly; von Buhl went limp as blood rushed back to his brain. "The problem is every time I do that, it kills brain cells. Cutting off the blood flow to your brain is such an inexact science. If we have to go several rounds to get the answers I'm looking for, it's very likely you are going to suffer brain damage. My only obligation is to deliver you as un-bruised as possible. My boss doesn't much care whether your mind is intact or not. With luck, you'll be so brain damaged that you won't know that you're drooling all over yourself. So, shall we give it a try?

"Are you ready? Good. Now, for your first question: Why did you pay to have Dr. Cadburess, Dr. Melrony and the crew of *Constellation* killed?" He released his grip slightly so von Buhl could talk.

"I dont' know who those people are," he muttered.

"Dolph, are you comfortable? I know sitting here like this I'm starting to cramp. Hold that thought while I stretch." Buck slammed his knee into von Buhl's injured shoulder socket, which made him spasm in pain. "All right, Dolph, you were going to say something; you were going to tell me why you paid a pirate to kill all those people.

It took a few moments for von Buhl's pain spasms to subside before he responded.

"I was paid to arrange their deaths."

"Who hired you?"

"I can't tell you. He will kill me after he kills you."

"Not the kind of cooperation I was looking for...night, night, Dolph."

Buck tightened his grip. Von Buhl struggled feebly until he went limp. Buck loosened his hold, allowing the man to revive.

Buck could tell from the twitches and jerks as von Buhl was gathering his senses and re-assembling his understanding of what was happening to him. "Did you have a nice nap? Dolph? Can you hear me or have I gone and killed the part of your brain responsible for comprehending speech?"

Von Buhl tried to shake his head in acknowledgement. "Let's try this again. Who paid you to kill Dr. Cadburess?"

"Miguel Torres."

"Who's he?"

"He is the Oil Minister of Venezuela."

"See that wasn't so difficult, was it."

He removed his arm from around the man's neck. Von Buhl rolled to the ground gasping. Buck pushed him face down, put a knee in his back and extracted wire ties from his fanny pack. He pulled the good arm behind his back, cuffed it then did the same to the mangled arm, which sent von Buhl into a paroxysm of pain.

When he finished, he looked up to see Rampage standing over him, his hands red, blood making his suit look shiny and wet.

"How long you been standing there?"

"Long enough to watch you rip that arm off. I've heard the threat 'I'll rip your arms off and beat you over the head with them' before, but I always thought that was metaphorical..."

"You know, you could have jumped in anytime to help."

"What, and miss the free show?"

"I could've been getting my ass kicked while you were lollygagging with the wounded guy."

Rampage snorted like Buck had said something really hilarious. "I knew you had it under control. The guy that can kick your ass hasn't been born yet. And if that ever happens, I'd buy tickets to see that fight."

"How's the other guy?"

"Didn't make it. Bled out."

Buck didn't respond as he got up. "Help me get him to

his feet, will you? Let's put him and the security guard in the salon while we signal the CRRCs."

Amongst gasps of pain, they lifted the injured von Buhl to his feet and Rampage started to steer him to the door. "What do you want to do with the assistant?"

"Just leave him. He's more useful to us if he stays," Buck replied.

They laid von Buhl on the couch in the salon while Rampage retrieved the security guard, who was roughly pushed down next to his boss on the couch. Buck kept watch while Rampage went to the deck with his flashlight. He pointed it towards the opening and flashed a series of light signals. Almost immediately, in the distance, Buck could hear a couple of outboard motors throttle up, closing rapidly. Within less than a minute, Coop and Sassy pulled up to the stern in two small rubber boats. While Rampage helped tie them up to the stern, Buck got the prisoners to their feet and herded them to the deck and down the steps to the waiting CRRCs. They loaded the security guard in one boat then Buck started to load von Buhl into the other.

"Hold it a second," Buck ordered as von Buhl stepped to the edge of the platform.

"Sassy, give me one of your socks."

Caught off guard, Sassy could only reply, "What?"

"Quick, give me one of your socks," Buck repeated impatiently, motioning with his hand.

Confused, Sassy complied.

Looking into von Buhl's eyes, sock in hand, he ordered "Open up." When he did not comply, Buck simply asked, "How's that arm hanging, Dolph? Hold that thought. I feel another cramp coming on."

Dolph responded, dolefully opening his mouth. Buck stuffed the soiled sock in his mouth, before slapping tape over his mouth. "Alright, load him in."

Cradling his damaged arm, von Buhl awkwardly attempted to step into the boat but slipped and crashed to the CRRC's bottom on his injured arm. The piercing scream that tried to escape his lips was muffled by the sock, escaping as only a low moan, before he passed out.

Rampage looked at Buck, "Good call on the sock. How'd you know?"

"Lucky guess. Stay here, I've got one more thing to do," and he leapt up the steps, disappearing back through the boat's salon to the stairs. A few moments later he emerged and quickly clambered into the boat while urgently whispering, "Let's go, let's go."

The boats pulled away agonizingly slowly, keeping their outboard motors throttled down to reduce their noise signature, and the danger of alerting the yacht club to their exit. Once outside the yacht club's entrance, they opened up the throttles and skimmed along at twenty-five miles an hour. Shortly they found the Super Mako cruising where they had left it and ran their CRRC's up the stern ramp. As soon as von Buhl and his bodyguard were transferred and secured, Tadhg kicked up the throttles and pointed the *Agrippa* for the harbor entrance ten miles away. Buck was still on the back deck when a large flash of light caught his eye from the direction they had come. He turned to see a large fireball mushrooming from the direction of the yacht club, the boom of the explosion muffled over the Mako's twin diesels and wind whistling over the deck.

Rampage joined him, watching the fireball claw its way into the night before burning itself out. "Nice... how'd you set it up?"

"I just opened the value to a propane tank in the engine room and ran. It was only a matter of time before something electrical turned on and ignited it."

"Now, I know why you wanted to leave the body of the attendant. An exploding ship with three souls onboard would look kind of suspicious if they found no bodies."

"Exactly. They'll figure the other two bodies were blown to smithereens and the crabs in the yacht club basin are being well feed. By the time they figure it out, if they ever do, we'll be long gone."

Buck hesitated for one last look before turning back to Rampage, "Come on, we need to update Colonel Barrett."

On the bridge, Buck slipped into the open middle-seat, donning a headset while Rampage put his on, leaning up against the bridge's bulkhead. Colonel Barrett was expecting their call.

"Give me a sit rep," he commanded as soon as Buck was online.

Buck outlined the execution of the snatch, concluding with the destruction of the yacht. "We're about twenty minutes out from the *Hadley*. We cleared the harbor's mouth about five minutes ago and she knows we're inbound."

"Good work, lads."

"Sir, there's one more thing. While we were in the presence of von Buhl, he volunteered the name of the man that hired him."

"Volunteered, you say? Did he now? Go on."

"He claims the Venezuelan oil minister, Miguel Torres, hired him to assassinate the *Constellation's* scientists."

"What is your confidence level in the veracity of his claim?"

"Sir, I have a high level of confidence in this information."

"How so? Explain."

"Well, he seemed really eager to share the information

with us. He was very cooperative."

"Uh-huh. Well, we'll check into. I'll see if we can find some corroborating evidence once we get him back here for questioning. If what von Buhl says is true, then we may well have business in Venezuela. In the meantime, once you drop off your passengers, I want you to start making your way north. Rendezvous with the American cruiser *Charlestown* off the coast of Suriname. Major La Barré will coordinate with you concerning refueling and supply replenishment details. Make a list of the supplies that you have consumed or will need along the way and get it to the Major so he can get cracking on it. Now is there anything else I need to know before I sign off?"

"No, that about wraps it up, sir."

"Keep me apprised. I want your best ETA on the rendezvous with the cruiser once you have it figured out." Then the line went dead.

Buck flipped a switch, hooking his headset into the bridge's comm circuit, and gave Tadhg the latest orders. When he was done, he toggled to another channel and had Rampage meet him on it.

"That's one call I don't envy the colonel making," Buck started.

"Which one is that?" Rampage replied.

"The one where he tells the UN Secretary-General that we now have proof that one of the upstanding members of his esteemed organization and OPEC is trying to shape world policy and the global oil economy through assassination."

"I'm shocked, shocked I say," Rampage mocked, "that a country would resort to such means to further its position in the world. I'm sure this is the first time that has ever happened."

"I'm sure he's no stranger to this sort of thing," Buck

countered, "but I'm also sure this is the first time he's agreed to police the matter. On a brighter note, with the extended run to Suriname, we should be able to get in some fishing. Did our gear get packed?"

"I see fish in our future, my friend. Of course I packed it. But we'll need to get some bait the next time we put in for fuel. I'll put it on the list," as he turned away to get busy on his tasks.

"Good," Buck thought, *"It'll also give me time to give Lila a call to let her know who's been behind the killings. Fear of the unknown is always the worst. Maybe this will put her mind at ease."*

Or maybe he was just trying to put his mind at ease by creating an excuse to hear her voice?

53

"You're damn right I want to send that sonofabitch a message!" President Tillman said forcefully to the room. Sitting around the Oval Office were Senator Cyrus Templeton, Congressmen Anthony Castillas and UN Secretary-General Andrew McLaughlin, the original founders of Operation Neptune, and its biggest proponents, as well as his Chief of Staff, Clayton Biggs. "He and every other tin pot dictator that thinks they can assassinate whoever is convenient in order to further his political agendas. I want those OPEC pricks to understand, too, that I won't tolerate their manipulations of the global oil market like this either. If they want to play in the deep end of the pool, they had better be able to swim, and that means dealing with *me* when they kill my citizens; especially that yapping little Chihuahua, Hugo Chavez. He's been mouthing off for years about how evil America is, and now, *he's* the one assassinating U.S. citizens among others. I'm not going to put up with it. I don't give a rat's rear end if his Minister of Oil is cruising around the Caribbean with him on his presidential yacht or not. If Torres thinks he can hide behind the skirt of his OPEC *él jefe* or international opinion, he's got another thing coming. The only question is: can your guys pull it off? Because if they can't, I've got some Blackwater boys who can."

"Mr. President," Andrew McLaughlin cooed, "Colonel

Barrett, who heads Operation Neptune, has assured me that his strike team is ready, able, and willing to partake in this mission. The only area of assistance that they need is transportation of the prisoner, once acquired. To that end they have requested that the cruiser *Charlestown* be repositioned into international waters off Venezuela so that they can immediately transfer the prisoner to U.S. custody as soon as they clear Venezuelan territorial waters."

"Mr. President, if I may, I want to urge caution in this matter." Clayton Biggs tried to inject some restraint into his boss's enthusiasm. "All that this will accomplish is to provide credibility to Chavez's claims of America's bully tactics and imperialism. It will only prove to strengthen his position among his allies. At the very least, as a member of OPEC, this type of tactic could lead to an embargo; at the worst, taking a government official from his country could be considered an act of war."

"I don't think that Chavez is stupid enough to declare war, especially once our grievance is made known to the world. He only gets mileage when he can bad-mouth America. Declaring war would only provide us the excuse we need to affect a policy of regime change. Chavez is mouthy, not stupid."

"On the other hand," countered Congressmen Castillas, "it could have a positive effect. Taking the yapping dog analogy further, like all dogs, they behave better when they know their boundaries and position in the pack. This is just a little training session to help Chavez know what his limits are, is all. Think of Khadafi in the eighties; same yapping dog syndrome until he went too far and we put a couple of missiles up his ass in the middle of the desert where he was supposedly beyond our reach. His silence became deafening after that. Later, when we dismembered

Iraq in thirty days in Desert Storm II, one of the biggest militaries in the Arab constellation, he coughed up his nuclear program so fast, he became the picture image of projectile vomiting."

"By forcibly removing his oil minister from his yacht in the middle of his country's coast? You call that training?" Senator Templeton exclaimed indignantly. "I signed on to help bring pirating under control, not to provide fodder for reckless foreign policy decisions. This is a cabinet minister of a sovereign foreign country we're talking about. This is a State Department issue, not a military one."

"Cabinet minister or not, Cyrus," Tony offered calmly, "when they murdered Dr. Cadburess and the crew of the *Constellation*, they moved beyond the realm of words into reality of action. This wasn't a crime they perpetrated in their own territory to which they can claim sovereign rights. This was a crime commissioned on another country's front porch, Mexico. Despite our differences, Mexico is a good neighbor and friend to America. Dealing with this problem for them, a problem that they have neither the resources nor experience to handle, is a huge diplomatic win for us. Mexico would appreciate this problem being handled without their hands getting dirty. It sends the message to all those who would trifle with them that such transgressions against America's allies will be dealt with in one manner or another; and the perpetrator will not enjoy the benefits of their ill-gotten gains."

"But this sets a dangerous precedent," Cyrus countered, "interfering or assuming the authority to deal with neighbors' issues without invitation."

"I must disagree," President Tillman interjected. "America has a long and glorious history of fostering development in South America, starting with the Monroe Doctrine. We told Europe to keep hands off of South and Central America under President Monroe: interference and colonization would no longer be tolerated by European powers in South America. Under the Roosevelt Corollary, we furthered the Monroe Doctrine by telling Europe that we reserved the right to intervene in any monetary or fiscal crisis rather than let the Europeans seize countries as collateral for loans made to countries in Central America and the Caribbean if they defaulted. So we have plenty of precedent for taking such action. This is just another step in the progression to let South and Central America come into their own.

"Besides it's a likely and logical extension of the reasoning behind the North American Free Trade Agreement. In creating an economic union with Canada and Mexico, we declared to the world that these are our most important trading partners. If you mess with one of them, you are messing with the U.S. So we have every right to protect interest, theirs and ours."

"I see little difference between state-sponsored assassination and state-sponsored terrorism. Both are bloodlettings to further a political agenda. The only difference between the two seems to be focus. Terrorism is more or less random attacks, while assassination is selective. But dead is dead, whether it is random or specifically targeted persons. And America already has a doctrine for this put in place by President George W. Bush: if you sponsor terrorism by act or omission, we will deal with you directly. That's all the precedence that I need," President Tillman concluded.

"I agree, the precedent is more than adequately supported. But the real question is how conclusive is the evidence that we have against the Venezuelan oil minister? Will it stand up in a court of law?" Representative Castillas voiced the question that they were all feeling.

Secretary-General McLaughlin, who had remained silent during the exchanges, now jumped into the discussion. "We have apprehended the pirate responsible for killing crew of the *Constellation* on two occasions. The lone survivor of the first attack has positively identified him as being the leader of the first attack. Penny Hartwell has also identified him. The confession we obtained from this pirate led to the capture of Dolph von Buhl, a known international arms dealer and known consort to the drug cartels of South and Central America. We have his pilot, flight records and false identifications that can be traced directly back to von Buhl, placing him in the locations at the times that money was exchanged for murder. Von Buhl has also provided us a confession. Project Neptune's computer specialist, Yoshi, has documented the transfers and deposits claimed by von Buhl of the amounts described at the times detailed in the confessions. All in all, it paints a comprehensive portrait of murder-for-hire by a rogue nation."

Tony Castillas could not silence the attorney in him, "Yes, it paints a richly detailed scenario for the pirate Salterez and arms dealer von Buhl. However, the case against Torres is pretty thin. All we have is the word of an admitted murderer and arms dealer backed by a cancelled check that could have been received for legitimate purposes. I'm sure if we query Venezuela, they will miraculously be able to produce a documentation trail claiming that money was for legitimate purposes. All someone needs to conjure up 'proof' is a word processor, Venezuelan state stationary and half an hour. All of which they have in abundance in the oil minister's office, I'm sure."

The room went silent for a tick, before President Tillman spoke. "I think that's good enough, Tony. Von Buhl is a notorious middleman with no motive for involvement for the assassinations of oil scientists. The closest party to benefit from the crimes in Mexico is Venezuela and its OPEC brethren. And Chavez's own anti-American blustering and words are ample support of that government's aims and intents. The one murder that we can pin on the Salterez-von Buhl connection is Dr. Cadburess, an American citizen. Given that, combined with the circumstantial evidence and it's the smallest of leaps to conclude the actions of hiring killers came from a regime that spews anti-American venom and had everything to gain by stopping this research as a member of OPEC."

Looking directly at Secretary-General McLaughlin, President Tillman continued, "You'll get the cruiser *Charlestown*, Andrew. Now, tell your team to go get me that sonofabitch, Torres."

54

After three days of hard running, Buck and Strike Force Trident were ready to rendezvous with the cruiser *Charlestown* off the northern Venezuelan coast. The warm blue waters of the Caribbean were calm and inviting. The three days had allowed a constant stream of data and satellite images on the whereabouts of Miguel Torres to be fed to Buck, allowing him to put together a plan to capture him.

Right now, Torres was aboard the fifty-seven meter presidential yacht of Venezuela, *La Bolivariana*. It was a luxury craft that Hugo Chavez had recently received, a gift from the people of Venezuela, paid for with the proceeds of the country's oil sales. Of course, the people really had no say in the purchase of the luxury liner, more likely preferring the expansion of the electrical, communication or running water delivery infrastructures. But as far as President Chavez was concerned, there could never be enough statues or monuments built to express his people's gratitude for his benevolent leadership, nor was any gift too big.

Accompanying the *La Bolivariana* was the *La Tamanaco*, a Lupo class frigate built by Cantieri Navali Riuniti in Italy. This Anti-Surface Warfare/Anti-Submarine Warfare class frigate offered a compliment of eight anti-ship and eight anti-submarine missiles along with an adequate mid-1980's technology electronic suite of detection radar and sonar, as well as fire control systems to guide those weapons systems, making it a formidable ship to engage. In addition, the ship also packed triple tube torpedo launchers and forty-millimeter OTO Melara Twin 40l70 Dardo compact guns both starboard and port. The Dardo Twin compact guns mounted just above the helicopter deck were basically an updated version of the older Bofors anti-aircraft guns. These guns could throw three hundred rounds per minute from each one of the twin barrels in either high explosive or anti-aircraft rounds out over two miles. But the real punch for surface action came from the OTO Melara 127/54 gun mounted in the forward turret on the ship's forward deck and the torpedoes in the Mark 32 Torpedo Launching System. This gun could throw a one hundred twenty-seven millimeter round sixteen miles down range at forty rounds a minute. The one hundred thirteen meter frigate *La Tamanaco* was capable of controlling a battle space of over a hundred miles around it above water and the same amount underwater with the help of her anti-submarine helicopter.

Because the *La Tamanaco* would be lurking close by, it would be able to detect an attack from distance and speed to intercept any interloper. So Buck's plan called for the *Agrippa* to use her stealth capabilities to slip in under the frigate's search radars, placing her in the path of travel and let the *La Bolivariana* slip up on them before launching their attack. The plan was to get within nautical spitting distance before springing his trap, unnoticed by both ships. If things went according to plan, the occupants of the *La Bolivariana* wouldn't know that Strike Team Trident was even on board until it was too late.

******

"So tell me, Miguel, have you been able to halt the UN's research on the origins of oil?"

Hugo Chavez Frias, President of Venezuela, gestured for his old friend, Miguel Torres to sit in one of the overstuffed chairs in the smoking lounge on the third deck aft of the presidential yacht. President Chavez settled into one of the two chairs closest to the windows overlooking the teak wooden deck at the stern of the ship and commanded the lights to be turned off on the back deck so he could stargaze into the clear Caribbean night. As soon as Miguel settled into his seat, an attendant appeared from the direction of the large dining room from which they had just adjourned and placed two snifters of cognac on each man's table before offering a humidor full of fat Cuban cigars to each man, starting with the president. The conversation lulled as each man, having selected his preference, set about preparing his smoke for lighting.

Miguel Torres was thankful for the pause. The recent failure of Dolph von Buhl to kill the U.N. scientist using pirates had proven embarrassing for him. He now had to frame his response in the way that would best help rebuild his credibility.

"I received a copy of a U.S. newspaper two days ago, from Norfolk, Virginia, where the U.N.'s new chief scientist for petroleum research has been staying. The article went on to explain that the woman, our scientist, died along with a male companion in a car accident while driving in the countryside. It seems that every time it looks like the U.N. will be able to conduct their research, something bad happens to their personnel. Just recently, several more of their new crew died at sea in some sort of incident involving local fisherman. That bad luck seems to have followed them into port when another of their crew was killed in a mugging. Now their second lead scientist is dead in a car accident. After they lost their first crew in a mysterious attack upon their research vessel, it took six months before they were able to try to restart their research. I imagine that it might be getting hard to find a replacement scientist to lead their efforts. After all, there are only so many scientists with that particular skill set and professional interest. I would bet that it will take much longer than six months to restart the research this time. And when they do name someone to head the restart effort, who knows, maybe something dreadful may befall that person before he even gets a chance to get going."

"Excellent work, Miguel," President Chavez said between puffs on his cigar. "All of this keeps me at arms length from suspicion. I truly appreciate your loyalty and dedication old friend," he said raising his snifter in salute. "Now, tell me what the Arab bastards from the Middle East bloc of OPEC are thinking..."

55

"Grels," Tadhg asked, addressing the dark bridge of the *Agrippa*, his face darkly lit by the dimmed green light being cast from the computer screen that he did not take his eyes from, "any response from the frigate yet?"

"No, she continues to sweep with SPQ-2F surface search radar and SPN-748 navigational radar, but our returns remain minimal. They have not increased sweep rate or narrowed beam concentration in any direction. We remain undetected."

Tadhg eased on a little more power to the twin diesels. The tactical solution he was applying to the situation called for a steady hand on the wheel, a delicate touch on the throttles and total concentration on the computer screen that was slaved to the mid-turret's thermal vision laser sighting system. Through the computer, Tadhg could see *La Bolivariana* and *La Tamanaco* beyond. His challenge was to move the *Agrippa* to within EMP torpedo range while staying in the frigate's visual and radar shadow behind the *La Bolivariana*. In this way, he also should be able to hide the sound signature of the *Agrippa* in the clatter of the *La Bolivariana*'s sound signature.

With sweat rolling down his temple, Tadhg's concentration was total as he maneuvered his blacked-out vessel into a near collision with a much larger ship unaware of his presence. As Grels tracked the yacht with his weapons system's thermal imager, he continued to bring the *Agrippa* into collision proximity; tension filled the bridge. Finally, Tadhg cut the Super Mako's engines to idle and coasted. With such little leeway, she had no steerage-- the *Agrippa* was a sitting duck, vulnerable to ramming if the yacht unexpectedly veered from its course. Twenty seconds later, the yacht passed a hundred meters off the nose of the Super Mako. Tadhg blew out a sigh of relief and switched off the starboard diesel, hoping to fool the frigate into thinking they were a single engine fishing boat now that they were no longer being masked behind the presidential Yacht.

Grels had barely noticed Tadhg's reconfiguration, because now it was his turn for total concentration on his computer screen. He watched his weapons screen intently as the yacht's range increased. If the yacht did not change its course or speed, he had a good firing solution already processed by the torpedo's fire control system. Calculating firing solutions and shooting torpedoes was an old science to navies the world around. But Grels was firing an experimental weapon of unorthodox dimensions and design.

The EMP warhead of the torpedo was a relatively small electronic device that emitted an intense burst of an oscillating magnetic field that turned every pathway in an integrated circuit into a generator before overloading it with amperage that would melt silicon. Simply put, the EMP blast would fry any electronic circuit within range without anyone being the wiser. Because the burst of microwaves had to be placed in close proximity of the target, the torpedo had been fixed with homing devices from other torpedo systems to steer it directly under a target before detonating. Because the overall warhead was much smaller than conventional systems, the propulsion system had been scaled down from the Mk-34 aerial deployed torpedo system used by the U.S. Navy in the LAMPS helicopter submarine hunters. All these different subsystems had been cobbled together into a one off production run of torpedoes in a laboratory. They had been test-fired in laboratory test conditions only. To make matters more interesting, they only had one chance at this. If the first torpedo failed, the presidential yacht would be too far out of range for a second one to be launched. If the torpedo failed in any phase of its deployment, the *Agrippa* could not chase down the presidential yacht without its water-jet propulsion immediately being detected by the frigate's sonar.

Grels's palm began to sweat on his joystick, his finger poised over the trigger to launch the torpedo. "Target approaching minimal safe range launch point," he intoned into bridge's comm circuit.

"Unsafe torpedo locks. Arm torpedo firing system. Torpedo warhead master switch to ON," Tadhg commanded.

Grels repeated the order and then his nimble fingers danced across his touch screen monitor. After verifying that the torpedo's gyroscopes were spun up to speed, and that the acoustic tracking system had accepted the target data from the fire control system, he responded, "Torpedo armed and ready in all respects."

Another twenty seconds went by before Grels intoned again, "Target at minimal safe launch distance."

Tadhg waited another five seconds, "Fire torpedo!"

In the confines of the *Agrippa's* bridge, they neither felt nor heard the pop of the compressed air slug as it forced the torpedo from its tube, nor did they hear the slap as it hit the water. After a few moments though, Grels's screen began to display data streaming in from the torpedo, "Torpedo running hot and normal, range to target: seven hundred meters and closing."

Tadhg, whose hand had been poised over the lone running engine's throttle, his thumb hovered over the propane boost, removed his hand as the danger passed. It was not uncommon for a torpedo to be flipped by surface-wave action on launching, returning to detonate on the ship that launched it before it could obtain the proper running depth.

"Range to target: five hundred meters and closing," Grels intoned after another minute. The torpedo was slowly overhauling the fleeing ship. After another minute, Grels updated the progress, "Range to target: two hundred meters." As the torpedo closed in on fifty meters, Grels only hoped it could make it: the small, experimental weapon was close to exhausting its range.

56

Buck had been racing across the nearly moonless night for nearly twenty minutes now; his night vision goggles focused rearward on the gaily lit presidential yacht cutting through the light swells; a mile behind it looked like a floating carnival. His only companion, Sassy, sat at the rear of the CRRC, his hand gripping the outboard's tiller casually, as if he were out for an evening of sightseeing rather than an armed raid on the presidential yacht of a foreign leader. Occasionally, he would glance to his left to see Rampage and the rest of Strike Team Trident skimming along forty meters to the side and slightly behind.

Buck was just about to turn away to check on the other strike team boat when the presidential yacht vanished from the screen of his NVGs to be replaced by residual bright green dots where moments before the lights of the ship had burned brightly.

The EMP torpedo had done its job! Now it was time for the strike team to do its job.

Buck tapped Sassy on the shoulder, waved his fingertips across his throat then circled his index finger in the air to tell him to turn the boat around. As Sassy nodded, Buck threw his butt into the bottom of the CRRC, knowing what was coming.

Rather than cut his speed, Sassy threw the little inflatable into a hard left-hand turn at full speed. The little craft skidded around the corner, at one point sliding sideways down the backside of a swell. When it hit the swell trough, it felt for a moment like they were going to capsize. But the CRRC held its turn, pitched its nose up, and it was soon racing on an intercept course for the yacht. The big ship was still coasting at a good clip helping to close the distance quickly. In little over a minute, they were on top of the luxury yacht.

The plan called for simultaneous entry on both sides of the boat; Rampage and his boat peeled off to the opposite side of the ship and disappeared from view.

Sassy went wide, then turned into the ship that still had not bled off much speed. In the pitch black, aided by his NVGs, he angled the rubber craft's nose for the stern of the ship where a low railing ringed the aft leisure deck. With every piece of equipment and machinery dead on the boat, there was a chance that the outboard motor's sound would alert the company on the ship of Strike Team Trident's approach, but it was a risk that they would have to take.

He matched the speed of the big ship adjacent to the deck rails and then slowly angled in to its side. Just because the big ship was no longer under power did not mean that it wasn't creating turbulence, and those turbulences could easily flip the small boat if they weren't careful. When the boat was within a meter, Buck twirled a grappling hook on a knotted rope twice before letting it fly. After it nearly noiselessly dropped to the deck, Buck pulled it in, quickly taking in the slack until the line went taut as the hooks snagged on a ship fixture. He tested the hold with part of his weight. Satisfied, he tied the rope to the ring on the nose of the boat, and started to shimmy up the line as Sassy killed the engine and scrambled to the front of the boat.

At the top of the rail, Buck hesitated, peeking over the edge to see if anyone lay in wait for him. The only sight that greeted him was that of Rampage squatting on the deck having just cleared the rail moments before from the other side, Kriss in hand to provide covering fire as the rest of his insertion package scrambled over the rail. He slipped lightly over the rail to alight on the deck while he retrieved his own Kriss. Sassy appeared on the deck beside him seconds later.

Buck scanned the deck for the ship's crew but found none. Surely they were struggling with what seemed an inexplicable and unprecedented failure of everything on the ship. According to Major La Barré's intel, there should have been at least four security guards from the president's security detail on board. The wild card in all this was whether the crew would attribute the ship's shutdown as something threatening or be too busy trying to understand and fix their electrical casualties.

Rampage signaled all were on board, and they broke into three elements of two. Now, with their suppressed pistols drawn, each team would take a floor to clear. Their rules of engagement called only for them to sweep the boat until they found their target and to use deadly force only if threatened. Beyond that, it was pretty much Buck's call; Colonel Barrett was not much for micromanaging.

Buck and Sassy headed for doors at the end of the deck leading into the ship's spaces while Rampage and Bear moved to the port side of the boat and started down the ship's side deck, heading for the upper deck's exterior stairs. Rabbi and Coop moved down the starboard side in search of the lower deck's stairs.

Entering through an exercise room, Buck and Sassy made quick work of the next five rooms they expected to find empty. With each room, their anticipation heightened. Buck took a moment to check on the progress of the rest of his team. He called up their locations on his helmet's data screen and was able to see their positions overlaid on deck schematics obtained from the ship builder's computers by Yoshi. He watched for a moment, ascertaining that their sweeps had been proceeding so far without resistance yet.

Minimizing the screen he refocused on continuing his own sweep.

In the next port side room they detected a body lying on the bed when they slipped the door open. The stateroom had a large sitting area with the bed placed at the far wall, away from the door. It was an elaborate four poster bed with an elevated mattress and with matching wood steps placed next to the bed platform. Even if they could not see the body sleeping in the bed, the heavy breathing and snoring would have announced the person's presence to even the most casual observer. Buck motioned Sassy into the room, before following in quick succession. Sassy went to the far wall while Buck slid around the door and backed up to the wall. Buck and Sassy both stealthily advanced on the slumbering figure. A few feet from the bed, Buck holstered his suppressed weapon and produced a Taser. Taking quick aim, he squeezed the trigger and the nitrogen canisters discharged two electrodes into the sleeping figure's chest. Fifty thousand volts slammed into the sleeping form's body. No sound was made beyond the clicking of the Taser emitting its disruptive voltage and the rubbing sound of fabric from the twitching of the figure in the bed as the electrically induced convulsion racked the body.

Sassy dropped his weapon and slung it around his backside while producing flex cuffs and a small roll of duct tape. They rolled the figure facedown while they roughly placed flexi-cuffs on the wrists. By now both men were aware they were handling an older man. It was not until his arms were secure that they flipped him to his back. The drawn face below them, even through the NVGs, clearly was that of their target, Miguel Torres, Petroleum Minister for Venezuela. Buck gave a thumbs up while Sassy slapped a big strip of tape across his face, Buck broke radio silence. "Eagle one," he spoke quietly into the boom mic of his helmet. That two word code told the rest of the strike team that Element One had the package and it was time to retreat to the rally point to exfiltrate.

Buck and Sassy rolled the package and both men grabbed an arm, dragging the man between them to the door, where they roughly set him down. Buck pushed the door open and peeked outside. The hallway was clear. With a quick hand signal, they picked up the package and moved through the door into the hallway.

They hadn't taken two steps when a deep voice challenged them in Portuguese from behind. Instantly they dropped the package and knelt, reaching for their silenced pistols. The package's head made a horrible thumping sound as the stunned man's head bounced off the floor. Both Buck and Sassy spun to face the voice, both hands on the grips of the guns. Through his goggles, Buck could see a shorter man standing in the middle of the hallway. He was dressed in a silk robe with the emblem of the Venezuelan flag embroidered on the left chest, tailored pajama bottoms sticking out from under the robe. Leather slip-on slippers finished the ensemble of the man standing in front of double doors at the end of the hallway; one of them slightly ajar. Again the man challenged them, the confident authority of his voice apparent, even through the language he did not understand.

Standing before Buck, just over his gun sight, stood the President of Venezuela, Hugo Chavez. Buck's first thought was to wonder where the man's security detail was. He didn't have long to wait for an answer. From doors on either side of the hall from where the man stood, two uniformed men emerged carrying short machine pistols, either MAC IIs or Uzis, in their hands.

Buck targeted the man on his side and squeezed two rounds off at center mass; Sassy did the same to the man on the right. Both men tumbled back into their respective doorways.

This was now a hot operation. Buck keyed his mic, "One red."

As Buck scanned for another target, a security guard came flying out of the right hand door and tackled the President who stood still waiting for an answer, oblivious to the fact that two men had just been shot right next to him. However, the unknowing or ungrateful leader was now berating and striking the security guard that had knocked him to the ground and was attempting to drag him through the open door to Buck's left.

Buck and Sassy took that as their cue to get a move-on, turning and grabbing the package while the President's detail had their hands full securing their leader. They were counting that the guards would not risk gun fire until the president was safely out of the way. Lifting the bound man, they hustled him in a low run back to the French doors that led to the gymnasium. At the door, they had to set the package down again to free a hand to open the door. Buck had no sooner kicked the door open when a burst of automatic fire stitched across the wall to their left and swiped through the doors, shattering several of the door's glass panes. The noise of a firing automatic weapon in such confined quarters was thunderous, even through his headsets.

Buck threw himself to the ground next to the package as glass shards rained down from above. He pulled himself around to see from where the blast had come. The hallway was now clear. He assumed the shots had come from the room the president had been pulled into. As he eyed the doorway, he saw an arm holding a weapon project from the room and another burst of automatic weapons fire erupted.

This time, the stitch of bullets walked up the other side of the hallway floor through the left-hand door they had attempted to exit, raining down more glass fragments before walking back into the ceiling.

"I'm hit," Buck heard over his head set. For a moment his heart hung in his throat as he instinctively started crawling to Sassy's location on the other side of the package.

"I'm okay. I took a slug in my arm, but the body armor stopped it. Hurts like a bastard...," the Frenchman yelled over the package between them.

Buck realized they wouldn't last long exposed in the open. "You take the package. I'll provide covering fire," he commanded. *No need to be subtle*, he reasoned, with the first burst from the security guard's gun, their stealth was blown, announcing to the rest of the boat that there was trouble on board. He brought his Kriss to bear, flipping the fire selector to full auto. As soon as he pulled the weapon snug to his shoulder, he centered the red dot reticule on the open doorway to his left and pulled the trigger. The muzzle flash from weapon temporarily turned his NVG screen white when he emptied a thirty round clip into the door way.

When the bolt of his Kriss locked open after the last round, his support hand slapped his tactical vest and found a flash bang grenade. In one smooth motion, he pulled the pin with his other hand and lobbed it down the hallway towards the door he had just emptied a clip in.

As the first round from Buck's submachine gun fired, Sassy scrambled to his feet and lifted the package in a fireman's carry, kicking the shattered doors out of his way as he carried him out of the hallway and out of Buck's view.

The fuse on the grenade detonated as it was still rolling across on the floor. Even though he knew what was coming, the intensity of the blast and sound concussion froze him for a half second before he picked himself up from the floor, spun, and sprinted out the door after Sassy. As he ran, his finger found the magazine release button. Tugged by gravity, the magazine dropped away. His left hand extracted another clip from his tactical vest and in a smooth, practiced motion he slapped it home into his gun which released the bolt to chamber the first round of the new magazine.

As they exited, Buck ducked around the corner and smoothly turned to face the hall he had just left, bringing the Kriss to bear again. Blindly, he squeezed the trigger and held it as he emptied another magazine in the direction of the security guard, waving the muzzle to spray the bullets for effect before dashing to his next point of cover while reloading when the gun emptied again in the direction of the shooter. Ejecting, loading, emptying and dashing, he kept up an intense rate of fire until he approached the door of the workout room he had entered this deck from.

Five steps from the door, four gouts of flame erupted from both sides of the deck near the rails. Strike Team Trident had rallied to the boats for ex-filtration and was now giving him covering fire to withdraw. Bullets impacted and stitched across the entire backside of the yacht as the heavy .45 caliber slugs tore into everything, shattering glass and punching holes in the thin steel walls, small sparkles illuminating the impacts. The pristine lines of the luxury yacht were transformed into jagged holes, empty window panes with jagged shards and shredded lumber as the four Kriss sub machine guns chewed the beautiful yacht into something unrecognizable.

Buck reloaded as he ran to where his boat was tied. They knew the drill; they'd practiced finding the exit many times before while taking hostile fire. When he got the rail where his boat was tied, he took up a kneeling firing position. The rest of the team's guns were now empty. Buck squeezed his trigger and sprayed the back wall high and low to give his team covering fire.

Wraith-like, the team rose from their firing positions and in low runs to their boat on the opposite side of the yacht, reloading along the way, before disappearing over the rail.

When Buck's gun ran dry again, he threw himself over the rail. Landing on his feet in the boat, one of his feet hit a hard lump, which was accompanied by an "Oompf." He had landed on Torres knocking the wind out of him. He stumbled to his knees and scrambling forward, he whipped a knife out of his vest, and severed the bowline with one swipe, casting the boat adrift. Sheathing his knife, he reloaded his Kriss and brought it to bear in case he would need to give more covering fire.

Sassy threw the tiller over and gunned the engine. The CRRC peeled away from the still coasting yacht in a tight one-eighty and headed into the dark of the ship's wake.

As soon as Sassy settled on a course, Buck put his head on a swivel, trying to locate the rest of the team and the Super Mako. He found both. The *Agrippa* was cruising four hundred meters off the yacht's starboard, the other

CRRC already heading for it with a fifty meter lead. Sassy had already spotted it, too and was cutting across the big ship's wake, heading for the loading ramp.

Buck watched, as the first CRRC made a flawless slide up on the ramp. The strike team exited in quick and efficient manner, scrambling over the boat's nose and securing it to the deck as they went. The sky to the east had now started to brighten in the new day's dawn; with that light, Buck's NVGs were starting to lose definition and become a hindrance, so he flipped them out of the way. Sassy also steered a perfect approach, easing up on the throttle at the last second to coast their boat up the *Agrippa's* loading ramp, right next to the other CRRC.

Ready hands immediately helped make fast the boat and grabbed Torres as Buck lifted him forward. The man did not resist. He remained passive still partially paralyzed, drawn and wide-eyed with fear. The strike team hustled Torres, who was now able to stagger in a fashion, towards the deckhouse's rear door and the Team Room. Buck and Sassy were the last to leave the deck. As they dashed into the Team Room, they quickly stowed their weapons, peeled off their tactical vests and Land/Sea Warrior gear, tossing them into their lockers.

Rampage and Coop strapped Torres into one of the chairs as Buck donned on a mobile comm headset. Buck stepped up to Rampage, giving him commands as he worked. "After he's secured, strap yourselves in. That frigate has to know we're here by now. It might get dicey so let me know when everything is secure back here and we can get the hell out of here!"

"Roger that."

Buck moved quickly to the door to the bridge and passed through. As he strapped himself into the middle chair and pulled the monitor towards him, he spoke to

Tadhg. "What's our situation?"

"The frigate is bearing down on us at thirty-four knots off our starboard stern, range: three thousand yards," Tadhg responded. "All engines running and helm is answering."

"Weapons status?"

Grels responded this time, "Coil gun charged; all power units online; forward turret and central turret armed and ready. Ranging and targeting systems on standby. They are painting us with fire control radar, but so far, they have not got a lock on us yet."

Just then Rampage's voice broke in, "Bridge, Team Room secure."

"Let's get out of here, Tadhg," Buck commanded. "Take us on the shortest course to international waters."

"Aye, aye," Tadhg said, heeling over the Super Mako to a perpendicular course to coast and poured on power. The nose of the boat came around and up as the water-jets bit, driving the stern deeper into the water.

"Guns," Buck called to Grels, "I want a running report on what the frigate is doing. Keep the targeting system's optically slaved on the frigate, but do not bring any weapons to bear on the ship. I don't want to give them an excuse to fire on us. If we're lucky, we can get out of range before they figure out what we've been up to and start shooting.

"Aye, aye. Frigate is changing aspect; it is turning to follow us. They have spotted us. Range: two thousand eight hundred meters. Still no lock."

"Push it to the stops, Tadhg. I want to get out of range of their guns."

Tadhg slipped the throttles to full and the big diesels in the stern roared at maximum military power.

Buck was watching the weapons targeting sights on his

screen when he saw a bloom of smoke billow from in front of the frigates' bridge. A fiery tail emerged from the rolling white cloud with a thin white body atop it. "Missile launch! Missile launch!" Buck warned, tension filling his voice. "Guns, I thought you told me they did not have lock on us."

"They don't. They must be firing to coordinates," came his cool reply.

"If that's the way they want to play it, let's show them how we roll. Tadhg, commence evasive maneuvering. Guns, use the pig gun and knock that bird out of the sky."

"Evasive maneuvering, now," Tadhg replied, the boat started whipsawing first one way and then another as Tadhg started to yankng the rudder joystick control side-to-side.

"Aye, aye," Grels acknowledged.

The missile was now beginning to arc over in the *Agrippa's* direction. "I have a firing solution-- permission to shoot?" Grels calmly asked.

"Fire at will," Buck ordered.

Before Buck finished speaking, a tremendous ripping boom erupted overhead and the boat tilted heavily to port before righting itself. Through the lightening skies, Buck could see a vapor trail marking the flight path of the pig and terminated in a fiery explosion three hundred meters over the frigate, dropping flaming debris on the stern helicopter deck.

"Guns, fast charge the pig gun," Buck ordered.

"Ja," Grels answered in a Swedish accent, the tension starting to crack his cool demeanor.

As Buck monitored his screen, forty seconds later, another plume of smoke erupted from the frigate's bow.

Grels was on it instantly. "Missile launch. Calculating firing solution, now. Permission to fire?"

"Fire at will." Two seconds later, there was another ripping boom and explosion over the frigate.

"Fast charge, again," Buck ordered again.

La Bolivariana had been traveling parallel to the coast when they left her. And *La Tomanaco* was trailing to the seaward side. As the *Agrippa* was fleeing to the open sea, she was vulnerable only to the frigate's main gun by "Crossing the T," which was actually closing the distance between the ships. In addition, the frigate was now turning into the Super Mako's path cutting the distance even more. Buck could have chosen to run before the frigate and use his superior speed and lay a smoke screen to extend away from the fight, but that had problems of its own. By running close to the shore, he ran the risk of hitting other coastal shipping and he had to run without radar, lest he precisely mark his position for the frigate's fire control systems with his radar emission. Plus there were reefs, wrecks, and sandbars to worry about. So he opted for the open sea and maneuvering room, but in doing so, he had put himself in range of both of the frigate's gun systems.

"Guns, what's our range to the frigate now?"

"Twenty-five hundred meters."

Sure enough, as he watched the forward turret of the frigate came to life, the barrel depressed and started tracking the *Agrippa*, which had now cleared the frigate's bow. The frigate was unable to match its turn rate to the Super Mako's and it slid to the boat's starboard quarter as it raced for the open sea. As it did so, Buck saw two lights winking at him from the starboard mount of the OTO Melara Twin 40L70 Dardo compact gun. Small water gouts started to erupt wildly in the water between the two ships. *They must be firing manually using optic sights*, Buck thought. But this did not allay his fears -- even a blind squirrel finds a nut occasionally. "Guns," Buck interjected, "use the 25-mike-mike and put that twin mount above the helicopter pad out of action."

"Aye. Lasing target now."

Buck watched as Grels lased the gun mount for a distance and then locked on the Bushmaster chain gun on it. The Dardo mount continued to wink at them; plumes of water were erupting all around them, as Tadhg continued to rack the Super Mako all over the ocean at full speed. But the frigate's gunning was getting better with practice. He was just getting ready to urge Grels to fire when the chain gun barked to life. A ten-round burst of HE rounds impacted on and all around the gun mount before disappearing in an explosion. The back corner of the ship's superstructure next to the mount had disappeared -- flames and smoke were licking out of a blackened hole.

"Distance to international waters?" he asked.

"Five miles," Tadhg intoned over the comm circuit.

Eight more minutes, Buck thought, if they could just hold out. Just then, the frigate's forward fifty-four millimeter gun entered the fray, roaring to life with a three-round burst. Giant geysers of water erupted astride the Super Mako's path a hundred meters ahead.

"Steer for the spouts!" Buck commanded Tadhg, in the mistaken belief of many sailors, that it is impossible for a gunner to hit the same piece of sea twice.

"Guns, engage that forward mount with the coil gun!"

"Ja," Grels responded, immediately followed by "Buck...the frigate just launched two torpedoes from their starboard tubes," his voice half an octave higher.

Crap! This is getting out of control, Buck thought, before thinking, *Who the hell fires torpedoes at a small boat? That weapon is designed for large ships – they're throwing everything at us including the kitchen sink.* "We'll deal with the torpedoes later, focus on taking that gun mount out of action."

Then to Tadhg, "Hit the kick-a-poo juice. And keep it coming."

Buck did a quick calculation in his head, as he felt the propane boost kick in, spurring the Super Mako on another nine knots faster. The Mark 32 torpedo launchers on the frigate carried torpedoes that ran at close to forty plus knots and were designed to doggedly run their prey to ground. Unlike his little EMP torpedoes, these had plenty of leg to run him down if his engines faltered. With the boost that was coursing through the Super Mako's engines, he should be able to outrun them, even though the swells were keeping the Super Mako from making her top speed. But he'd overheat and burnout her engines if he stayed on the boost too long. He just needed to get enough of a head start to keep them from getting blown to hell.

Another salvo of fifty-seven millimeter rounds landed close by, close enough that the water gouts drenched the windshield, momentarily blinding everyone on the bridge.

The Super Mako was now powering directly into the off shore swells. What had been mild rollers at cruising speed were now pounding waves intent upon bending and breaking the *Agrippa's* hull. Even with the Super Mako's improved hull design, the boat was starting to pound into the rollers with astounding force as she leapt from roller top to roller top. The reactive shock absorbent cushions in their chairs were working overtime, and even then, it wasn't able to totally cancel out the shockwaves traveling through the boat. With the boost, he was pushing the boat beyond its design limits and speed.

A ripping crack emitted from overhead. Buck looked at his monitor to see if the forward turret was out of action. To his amazement, the normally stable picture was bouncing up and down. The gyrations of Tadhg's hair-on-fire maneuvering, combined with their speed in this sea state, had pushed the weapons stabilizers beyond their design limitations. "Did you get a hit?" Buck demanded.

"Negative, negative. Shot went over the bow."

"Charge and fire again. Keep firing until you put that gun out of commission," Buck instructed, *Or, until he hits us,* Buck thought grimly. It was taking forty-five seconds to recharge and fire their coil gun. In that time, the frigate's gun was getting off two or three salvos, each one getting closer to the *Agrippa.* Buck needed to change odds to his favor, but how?

Another salvo ripped across the stern of the *Agrippa,* one detonating so close that it kicked the boat's rear sideways, forcing Tadhg to fight for the slim thread of control he had on the boat's helm. *He had to act now.* "Tadhg, bring her to port ninety degrees on course two eighty and make smoke. We'll hide until we can charge the coil gun."

The *Agrippa* heeled hard to port as Tadhg brought her around and the smoke generators kicked a thick rolling blanket of smoke off the rear of the boat.

This is only prolonging the danger, Buck thought, *for Strike Team Trident. The longer they stayed in Venezuelan waters, the worse our predicament will get. By now, the frigate was bound to have called in for fighter support. We'll have to fight our way clear to the open sea and international waters. As long as I hold this course, it'll shorten the distance the two torpedoes had to cover to chase us down.*

Forty seconds later, Grels called he was ready to fire again. The frigate had changed course to pursue them on their new course, so Buck ordered Tadhg to bring her back to their original heading to get Grels a better firing angle and to cut the smoke generators. The *Agrippa's* weapon systems had been switched to infrared and could see through the smoke without difficulty. But Grels held his fire until Tadhg had steadied up on the new course and his target aspect improved.

The seconds scraped across Buck's nerves as he silently urged Grels to take the shot. After what seemed an eternity, he heard the ripping boom as the gun fired.

"I have a hit!" Grels said excitedly. Buck looked and saw that a major chunk of the frigate's bow had been removed, but the turret was still intact. Silently, Buck hoped that much damage to the bow would mess up their targeting systems, jam the gun or loading mechanism, or something even more disastrous.

Just as it seemed they had solved their frigate problem, the forward turret resumed firing, launching three more rounds at them. "Tadhg, come left again and make smoke." Then to Grels, "How many shots is that?"

"Four."

"How's the coil gun holding up?"

"System parameters aren't in the red, but will be after this shot. Capacitors are at near critical temperature."

"Roger. Keep firing."

"Buck, we may only have one shot left."

"Do you have a suggestion, Guns?"

"Ja, slow down."

"You know there are torpedoes in the water? We slow down, and they *will* find us."

"I know, but I cannot get a good shot at these speeds. We have to slow down to get the targeting systems back within parameters. It is that, or we risk wasting our last shot."

"There's more," Tadhg interjected. "The engines are over-heating. They're redlined right now. If I hold them in boost much longer, we'll burn out one or both engines. We've got to reduce speed."

Buck pondered his options for a second. None of them looked good.

57

"All right, here's what we're going to do: Tadhg, drop us out of boost for now but keep the engines at full power. We'll keep this tack until the pig gun is charged, then we'll make another break for the open sea under boost and start jinking. Thirty seconds after we make our break, Tadhg, I want you to drop us to two-thirds power and steady up on course long enough for Guns to take his shot. After that, we scoot like hell. Any questions?" There were none. "Let's do it."

Immediately, Buck felt the pounding ease as Tadhg throttled back the engines to a more sustainable power level. "Status on the pig gun?" Buck asked.

"Another twenty seconds. I'm already locked with the targeting system to the frigate's turret. All I need is a steady ride."

"You'll get it," Buck said confidently. Under his breath he added, "If the torpedoes don't get us first."

"Charge complete," Grels finally announced.

"You ready, Lieutenant?" Buck asked Tadhg.

"Aye."

Without hesitation, Buck spoke. "Execute."

"Roger," came the reply in unison.

Tadhg slammed the throttles forward one more time and hit the boost button, the acceleration shoving him back in his seat. As the Super Mako started to roll dangerously in the wave troughs and build to its top speed, he watched as the engine exhaust manifold and engine temperature indicators climbed back into the red. As soon as he had steady-up on the speed, he eased the boat into a starboard turn and headed back out to sea and international waters. He cut the smoke generator because now all it was doing was pinpointing their position as he cut across in front of the frigate one more time. The Super Mako started to pound then launch from every swell, the boat's speed bled down ten knots as it bucked and reared, trying to claw its way free of the Venezuelan waters and the frigate. Tadhgs started to jink the boat hard, helped by the unpredictable waves. The slamming was making it hard to hold his arm on his seat's armrest and control the boat's rudder joystick. He was holding onto control of the *Agrippa* by a razor's edge.

The seconds seemed to crawl on Buck's screen to the thirty second mark from the moment Tadhg initiated the turn. The instant the timer hit the mark, Tadhg chopped the throttle to two-thirds power and the boat decelerated, throwing everyone against their restraints. Just as his head snapped back into place from the deceleration, three giant water plumes exploded in the water fifty meters in front of the boat. Right where they would have been had they continued at full power. The Venezuelans had finally found their range.

"Hold… hold," Grels chanted unknowingly. Then, almost errantly, the *Agrippa* heeled over to port as the ripping explosion of the coil gun sounded overhead from the central weapons turret.

Buck eyed the monitor and was rewarded by seeing the frigate's fifty-seven millimeter forward unmanned turret go up in a huge ball explosion. The pig must have ignited the ammunition in the feeding racks to the gun.

"A hit! A hit!" Grels shouted into his microphone in a

heavily Swedish accented voice.

"Nice shooting, Guns," Buck congratulated him. "Now fast charge the gun again."

"What?! Why? The frigate is out of the fight--it can't hurt us anymore! The guns capacitors temperatures are critical. If I start charging them now, I could very well melt them and if the charging does not melt them, the discharge on firing certainly will. We need to let them cool before we shoot again."

"No can do, Guns. The frigate may be out of the fight, but her radios aren't. I'm sure she's vectoring in Venezuelan fighters right now while we're wasting time. Charge the guns and target the radio instrument shack at the base of the mast. Fire at will."

"Aye, aye, Boss."

"Tadhg, hold this speed and heading, until Guns takes his shot. What's our range to international waters?"

"Three miles."

"Damn!" Buck voiced his frustration. "I wish I knew where those torpedoes were."

He knew at the speeds they were traveling that the boat's sonar was useless. They would have to be traveling under fifteen knots to make that system functional. And there was no way in hell he was going to slow down to *that* speed with those killer fish in the water stalking him.

"Maybe there is a way to find out, Buck," Tadhg replied. "We could ask the *Charlestown*. I'm sure their sonar crew has been watching them since they were launched. Torpedoes in the water have a way of making everybody's butt pucker."

"Good idea. I'll make the call." Buck called up the radio controls on his screen and tuned a channel to the cruiser that was sitting fifteen miles off shore, awaiting the package they had on board. "This is U.N. vessel *Agrippa* calling U.S. Navy vessel *Charlestown*. Neptune. Neptune. Neptune. I say again, this is UN Navy vessel *Agrippa* calling the *Charlestown*. Neptune. Neptune. Neptune." The radio squawked briefly as he ended his transmission.

"This is U.S. cruiser *Charlestown* calling the *Agrippa*. Go ahead."

"*Charlestown*, we have a problem. A Venezuelan frigate has launched torpedoes at us, and we are trying to outrun them, but at this speed, we're blind here. Do you have a fix on their position relative to ours? Over."

"*Agrippa*, this is Captain Swinton of the *Charlestown*. Hold one while I bring sonar on the line with us." A short pause passed. "*Agrippa*, this is the *Charlestown*. Go ahead, sonar." Another voice chimed in, "We show both torpedoes tracking you at two thousand yards astern and gaining on your current speed and heading."

"Thank you, sonar. *Agrippa*, we launched our ASW helos the moment we heard those fish in the water. We weren't sure who the Venezuelans were shooting at. Our helo is holding at the twelve-mile international water marker right in front of you. If you can make it that far, our helo should be able to clean the torpedoes off your tail. Over."

"We should be able to hold this heading and improve our speed to hold the torpedoes at bay. Have your pilot ready to sweep our six the second we make the twelve mile marker. Let us know if the torpedoes start to gain on us."

"Roger. *Charlestown* out."

"Tadhg, you catch all that?"

"Yes, I did."

"Good. The moment Grels takes his shot, increase our speed to flank and steady up on the shortest course to the twelve mile marker."

"Roger."

No sooner had he finished when the ripping explosion of the coil gun sounded one more time. Buck switched his monitor to the weapons targeting system just in time to watch the frigate's radio mast crash into a heap on the remains of burning radio equipment shack. As he did so, he felt Tadhg ease on the power, and the *Agrippa* started pounding into the waves again, headed for the open sea.

"Well, that's it," Grels informed everyone on the comm circuit. "The coil gun is dead. It just went offline. I'm showing failures in multiple systems of the gun."

It was a risk that Buck had to take. The frigate could have easily vectored fighters onto their position. If they sent more than one fighter, and he was sure that they would, since their presidential yacht had been threatened, there was no way that they *Agrippa* could fight them off. The pig gun could have gotten one, but with its slow rate of fire, the other planes would destroy them before they could get off another shot. The same with the Stinger air-to-air missiles they carried on the rear deck. At least for now, they had a fighting chance to let their stealth qualities continue to work for them.

On cue, the *Charlestown* called. "*Charlestown* calling the *Agrippa*. We have air contacts. Be advised, we are showing five supersonic inbound bogies from the southwest, six minutes out."

"Roger, *Charlestown*," Buck acknowledged. *No problem,* he thought. *We'll be at the twelve mile marker in two and under the protection of the Charlestown's anti-aircraft umbrella. She could easily handle five Venezuelan fighters.*

A klaxon broke Buck's brief reverie. His eye was immediately drawn to the red flashing warning light on his monitor indicating a fire in the engine room.

Tadhg reacted first, already on the comm.. "Lenz, we

have a fire warning light in the engine room. Check it out and report back."

Buck heard Lenz's laconic reply through the bridge's comm channel on his headset, "Ya, I'm just arrived. The... set fire... the port...side near ..." his transmission was broken up by the sound of a fire extinguisher being discharged in the background. "But I should be able to get it under control.

"Say again. You're breaking up," Tadhg demanded.

Any reply Lenz started to give was overridden by the sound of a new warning bell. Buck's monitor showed the port engine was overheating.

"Buck, I'm losing the port engine! The engine performance computer is shutting it down," Tadhg exclaimed.

"Negative, negative. We need that engine. Override the computer, do whatever you have to. Run it 'til it blows up, but don't let it go offline," Buck directed.

"Bridge, this is Lenz. The coil gun capacitors melted and started a fire next to the port engine. I have the fire extinguished, but the port engine took some fire damage before I could get it under control."

"What about the port engine?" Tadhg asked Lenz.

Buck could hear and feel the *Agrippa* starting to lose speed as the port engine began to surge and stop, surge and stop. He could see Tadhg's hands fly all over his monitor, keyboard and mouse, fighting to keep the engine online.

"Some wire got burnt and the port engine cooling jacket is ruptured. It's pumping water into the engine room bilge, but the bilge pumps should be able to stay ahead of the it provided we shut it down."

The boat's surges were becoming more pronounced now as the power fell off from the port engine and their speed diminished.

"How long to repair the leak?" asked Tadhg.

"Three to four minutes."

"We don't have three minutes, Lenz. See what you can do with it."

"Aye."

The port engine was barely running now, so Tadhg cut it back to idle and it died immediately.

Tadhg was now feverishly fighting the helm. Every time the *Agrippa* pounded into a wave, the starboard water-jet, at full speed, bit into the water and its off-center thrust slewed the boat hard to starboard. So the only way the *Agrippa* could make forward progress was through a series of hard left jags and corrections, slowing the boat even more.

"This is the U.S. naval vessel *Charlestown* calling the *Agrippa*." A new voice sounded over Buck's headset.

"Go ahead, *Charlestown*," Buck replied.

"Be advised that torpedoes are still tracking you and are gaining. Range: seventeen hundred yards and closing fast. Inbound bogies are now five minutes out."

"Roger, *Charlestown*," Buck replied. *Torpedoes were designed for deep draft vessels, not the five foot shallow draft that the Agrippa drew. They shouldn't be able to track us in the swells,* Buck thought to himself. *They're probably acoustically homing in on our engine noise, which will only get them in the ballpark. Or was he wishful thinking…?*

"Roger, Charlestown," Buck replied. "Distance to the twelve-mile marker?"

Grels answered this time; since he had nothing to shoot at, so he had reconfigured his terminal for navigation. "Range is a mile and a half."

"What's our speed?"

"Thirty knots on the surface; actual speed is probably

less."

Buck did some quick mental calculations. The arithmetic didn't add up to his favor.

"Tadhg, we need more speed, put her into boost again"

"Negative, Buck… can't do it… I'm just barely holding on," Tadhg said through gritted teeth, straining to stay in control of the bucking *Agrippa*. "If I add more power…I'll lose the boat for sure… Plus, the starboard engine… is on the verge of overheating, too."

Buck knew he was right. They would just have to play the cards they were being dealt.

"*Agrippa*, this is the *Charlestown*. Torpedoes still closing; range now eleven hundred meters."

"Roger."

"Range to twelve-mile maker?" Nervous tension demanded he get up and pace, but the boat was lurching so violently making it impossible.

"Still over a mile."

"Copy." Seconds dragged on as the *Agrippa* fought for her life, trying to cover the distance between her and safety.

"*Agrippa*, this is the *Charlestown*. Torpedoes' range now six hundred meters. Torpedoes have gone active with targeting sonar."

"Copy."

"Range to twelve- mile marker?"

"Over half a mile, Buck."

There it was. They were going to go up in a fiery explosion just short of safety in full view of the *Charlestown* and her crew, Buck thought bitterly. *But I'm going to go down swinging*, he said to himself with newfound determination. *Those torpedoes may be hellhounds with a bone in their teeth, determined to run down and destroy his boat, but they had been designed for much larger prey. They were not designed for stalking a nimble little minx like the Agrippa*. A plan took root in his brain and blossomed into a desperate gambit.

"*Charlestown*, this is the *Agrippa*. Keep the mic open and give us a running feed on the torpedo's status."

"Wilco... range five hundred yards and closing..."

"Tadhg, when I give you the word, I want you to lay the boat over hard to port, and hit the boost."

"What are you going...to try?" asked Tadhg through clenched teeth.

"Four hundred yards..."

"I'm going to let our asymmetrical thrust work for us rather than fight it. If we can sheer away at the last second and make the torpedoes miss us, by the time they circle around and reacquire us, we'll be outside the twelve-mile marker and the ASW helo can take care of them."

"Three hundred yards..."

"Whatever you say, Buck. It should work on the first torpedo... it's the second one that I'm worried about."

"Two hundred yards..." A pause, then "Target merge! Target merge! They're too close to tell apart!"

Buck held his breath and counted to three. "Now!"

The *Agrippa* slammed hard to port and her steel skag on the port side bit deep into the ocean's green waters, nearly flipping the boat on its side. Buck was thrown against the padded right side of his chair, the restraints the only things keeping him from being launched from his chair and thrown across the bridge into a wall.

At that moment, he felt one, then two huge explosions pulse through the *Agrippa's* hull as the stern was lifted skyward.

58

Buck felt himself float in slow motion, weightless in his chair straps, as the *Agrippa's* stern was heaved skyward by the combination of the radical maneuver and the two powerful explosions that ripped the sea behind the boat. Time passed in agonizing slowness as he felt the boat tip to port past forty-five degrees and keep going. It seemed that the boat was going to flip and land turtle. In the background of his mind, the sounds of the *Agrippa's* lone remaining engine screamed at an unnerving pitch, having been plucked from the water and its water-jet pumps having nothing to work against. The thought was jarred from his mind as the *Agrippa* slammed into the sea on the port bow railing. The violent jolt caused his chin to bounce off his chest as his seat belts bit deep, preventing him from being ejected out the bridge's windows. His mind remotely registered the great gouts of water and sheets of spray seen through the bridge's window as the hull took the brunt of contact on surfaces never engineered for such punishment.

The *Agrippa* teetered precariously for a second before she started to roll back into the sea, righting herself. As the keel slammed into the sea, Buck was slammed into his seat. The high Gs being inflicted upon the *Agrippa* had never been envisioned by the boat's builders and engineers. Almost every circuit breaker popped, disrupting his seat's electronic dampening system. His head was driven into the seat with the force of a heavyweight contender's punch, his spine electrified with burning pain as it was slammed and compressed into the un-giving chair.

Stunned, Buck remained inert until some of his senses slowly started to reconnect with his consciousness. The first thing that registered was his hearing. It told him that every system alarm on the *Agrippa* was screaming for attention. His eyes confirmed this as they slowly started to refocus on a sea of red, flashing lights on the console before him.

He looked over to Tadhg's seat to see him slumped, unconscious in his chair.

"Tadhg!" Buck shouted with all the force he could muster, which wasn't much. Tadhg started to stir but didn't respond. "TADHG!" He tried again, noting that Tadhg's headset was sitting askew on his head. His own set had flown off and was dangling from his chair by its cord. He reached for the cord, but his hands were numb from the impact on his spine. He fumbled for what seemed hours before he was able to reel in his headset and get it placed on his head. "Tadhg! Do you read me?"

"Aye," came a mumbled reply.

Buck saw Tadhg's head raise and hold as he clumsily started to punch flashing red boxes on his screen.

"Report!"

A long pause followed. "Port engine offline, starboard engine idling, propulsion unknown, navigations offline, weapons offline, communications partial; we have FM and AM bands operating at this time; we're taking on water; automatic pumps offline. I'm switching to manual pump activation...."

The rest of what he said was momentarily drowned out

as a helicopter passed just a few feet overhead, then settled into a hover over the water on the boat's starboard side, its rotor downwash kicking up a pelting spray, coating the bridge's windows with droplets.

"This is US Navy helo calling the *Agrippa*, this is U.S. Navy helo calling the *Agrippa*. Do you require assistance?" came a voice over his head phones.

Glancing out the window at the squatting helicopter, Buck noticed for the first time that the Venezuelan frigate was visible on the other side of the helo and was closing fast.

"Standby, U.S. helo..." Buck responded numbly.

******

"Damn!" Captain Swinton swore from the *Charlestown's* bridge as he watched the *Agrippa* tumble and disappear in maelstrom of two explosions. "This is getting out of hand," he said lowering the glasses and looking at his Executive Officer. "Time to finish this little dust-up once and for all. Take us to battle stations," he said as he brought the binoculars to his eyes again. He was able to make out vague parts of the *Agrippa* still on the surface through the mist of spray as his orders were repeated on the ship's intercom, a klaxon starting to warble. "Have Helo One render assistance to the *Agrippa*. Tell them to put their bird between the *Agrippa* and the frigate. If they want the *Agrippa*, they're going to have to go through that aircraft first. And if they fire on our crew, we'll send her to the bottom so fast they won't have time to shit in their pants!"

Just as the helo did as ordered, one of the junior officers of the deck reported, "CIC manned and ready; all weapons manned, armed and ready; damage control parties – ready and reporting the ship is watertight; engine room manned and ready, reporting full power available on all turbines."

"Very good," the Captain replied tersely. "X.O."

"Aye, sir."

"I want firing a solution for Mounts One and Two on the Venezuelan frigate."

"Aye, sir. Are you going to fire one across her bow?"

"Sort of ... I want Mount One to put one across her bow and Mount Two to put one on her stern at the same time. And Mike," the captain said, smiling at his second-in-command as he lowered his glasses, "I want to wipe the smug look off that captain's face with the spray."

"Aye, aye, Skipper!" he said with enthusiasm. Twenty seconds after picking up a direct line to the ship's Combat Information Center and repeating the order, he reported back. "AN/SPQ-9 solutions acquired and locked. Mounts One and Two, tracking, ready to fire on command."

"Good. Give me an open channel on guard to the frigate's captain," Captain Swinton said as he lifted a communications handset to his ear.

"Guard on position two, sir," one of the enlisted men informed him after making some adjustments to a console.

Swinton turned a selector switch to the indicated position before speaking. "Calling the Venezuelan frigate, calling the Venezuelan frigate, this is Captain Swinton of the U.S. cruiser *Charlestown*. Do you read me?"

Ten seconds later, a heavily accented voiced responded. "This is Captain Herdez of the Bolivarian Armada of Venezuela Frigate *La Tamanaco*. Go ahead with your transmission."

******

"Tadhg," Buck called out, "throttle her up and see if we can get her moving."

"Aye, aye." Tadhg slowly moved the throttle handle gingerly forward. Both men held their breath, expecting the engine to stall, sputter or die. But it did not. The *Agrippa* started to move under her own power. Slowly, he kept adding power until she had steerage.

"Set course for the *Charlestown* at your best speed."

"Aye, Buck."

"This is the *Agrippa* calling U.S. helo, we are accessing our damage now. But we have propulsion and have set a course for the *Charlestown*, over." Just then, Grels started to moan and rouse himself. Buck could now see that he had a nasty gash on his forehead that was bleeding profusely.

"Do you require medical assistance?"

"Unknown, but probably." Buck wanted to go to Grel's aid but he couldn't. His ship wasn't safe, and he was still in a fight. Just then, the sounds of a conversation between the captains of the *Charlestown* and the *La Tamanaco* broke over his headset...

******

"We are currently rendering aid to a stricken vessel. Sheer away from your present course or you will endanger my helicopter and the vessel we are assisting."

"Who are you to tell me what to do in waters of my own country? We will do as we want. Besides, a member of our government's cabinet has been abducted and is on that vessel. We will board that pirate vessel and rescue our minister."

"You must be mistaken," Captain Swinton replied. "Both my helo and the stricken vessel are in international waters. You appear to have battle damage to your communications and navigational mast. Let me repeat; shear away or we will take your actions as hostile and will respond with any and all force necessary to destroy any threat to my ship, aircraft or the stricken vessel. Do you understand? Over."

"How dare you threaten me, you colonial imperialist!"

"It is you who has threatened me. You fired two homing torpedoes in my direction. If the stricken vessel had not veered in front of them, they would have locked onto my ship. That is an act of war! So, I repeat, sheer away or declare your intentions. I'll give you ten seconds before I sink your ship." Then, with his thumb still jammed on the transmit button he calmly said, "Weapons officer, target all Venezuelan navy vessels in within weapons range. Designate two anti-shipping missiles per target, including the vessel that went dark five miles north of the frigates position. Open silo doors when missiles are ready to launch. Launch on my command."

"I did not threaten your ship!" the captain of the *La Tamanaco* countered, "I fired those torpedoes at the escaping pirate vessel."

"Like hell you did! Nobody fires torpedoes at a small craft. Those weapons are designed to kill ships, and my ship was the only one in the vicinity." Then to the side, Captain Swinton looked at his XO and calmly stated, "Let's show this bastard we mean business, Mike. Fire Mounts One and Two."

The executive officer hit a large button on a console and simultaneously both five inch gun mounts fired.

******

Buck watched as the naval artillery shells landed ten

yards in front of the bow and the same distance from the stern and exploded. The explosion in the stern drenched the aft decks while the bow shell set up a great column of water as high as the frigate's bridge, soaking the foredecks and washing the bridge's windows as the ship sailed into the plume.

The frigate, battle damaged and outclassed, waited two seconds before she heeled hard-a-port as she sheared off to the *Charleston*'s starboard.

******

"That was nice shooting, Mike. Give my compliments to the gunnery officer," Captain Swinton said.

"Yes, sir!" his XO replied with a wolfish smile.

"Sir," another officer interrupted, "radar reports we are still tracking five inbound hostiles. They're sixty miles out and closing fast."

"They must not have gotten the message, yet," Captain Swinton pondered aloud. "Very well. Light them up with AN/SPG-62. Fire if they cross the forty-mile line."

"Yes, sir," the officer replied before repeating the order and communicating it to CIC.

"And give me a running account of the in-bound bogeys..."

"Yes, sir...

"Targets acquired...Ten VLM tubes designated...targets locked...data transfer set on all ten tubes...bogeys at forty-seven miles ...

"Forty –five miles... forty-three miles..." a slight edge entered his voice as they heard five VLM tube hatches opening to fire.

"Forty-one miles... wait! Radar reports that bogeys are changing course." After a few tense moments, he followed up: "Radar reports that the bogeys have reversed course."

A few audible sighs could be heard over the hum of the electronics of the bridge as the peril lifted. The captain, who had never even broken a sweat, mildly commented to the bridge at large, "Now, let's see what we can do to help the *Agrippa*."

59

The spectacular Manhattan view overlooking the gray morning held no interest for Buck. His mind, still fogged from the activities of the last week and hectic travel of the last three days in particular, latched on to nothing as he stared out the window. The wind swept cold rain past the window, serving only to remind him to be thankful that he was inside today, warm and snug.

"I've read the after action reports. Officially the U.S. Navy is saying that they lost a training torpedo off the Venezuelan coast, dropped by accident from an ASW helicopter in a routine exercise." Colonel Barrett paused to look over his reading glasses at Buck and Steve sitting across his desk from him. "Unofficially," he continued, "the U.S. is telling Venezuela to stick it in their ear. In no ambiguous terms, they've told the Venezuelans that next time they send two torpedoes in the direction of one of their cruisers, they will wipe the skies and sea, above and below, of anything with a Venezuelan military emblem in a two hundred-fifty mile circumference. They really should be thankful that it was not a carrier battle group, otherwise they would have taken the Venezuelans' actions as a declaration of war and dealt with it in a decidedly hostile manner."

"Who knows? Maybe, our last ditch maneuver might have worked," Buck said absently. "But the helo pilots were in the best position to know. Evidently, he had dropped a sonar buoy and were watching the tactical situation. I'm glad he took matters into his own hands and dropped their torpedo to hone in on the ones on our six. Technically, they *did* drop their torpedo in international waters, so there was no violation of Venezuelan sovereignty. The fact that they strayed into Venezuelan waters could be explained as mechanical error," he offered lamely.

"And one more question, were you actually in open seas when the *Charlestown* fired on the Venezuelan frigate?"

"I don't know," replied Buck. "Our navigation systems were down from battle damage. The frigate's navigational equipment was down or degraded from our last coil gun round. The only one with a working GPS fix was the American cruiser, and they insist we were in international waters."

"Either way, I'm sending those helo pilots and the captain of the *Charlestown* each a case of Scotch," Rampage announced, "for having a pair when action was needed but not politically ordained."

"When you do, expense it to my account," Colonel Barrett ordered.

"I already did," replied Rampage.

At that, the Colonel glanced over his glasses again at Rampage, who returned his stare with a Cheshire cat's grin. He started to say something to his subordinate and then thought better.

But Buck still had a niggling of doubt to which he gave voice, "I hope that their actions won't adversely affect their naval careers."

Colonel Barrett smiled slightly, "I doubt that very seriously. President Tillman is secretly delighted that we not only got him the petroleum minister, but also that the cruiser was able to foil the Venezuelans' attempts to get him back; or at the very least, it thwarted their attempts to stop you from succeeding. By doing so, the cruiser's actions allowed him to... I believe he used the phrase 'welcome Chavez to the deep end of the pool where the big boys play.' There will be an inquiry, of course, but I don't see how they will be disciplined for something that delighted their Commander-in-Chief. On the other hand, certainly, there will be no medals, but in the end, it will probably be a career enhancer."

"What about the petroleum minister? Have they decided what to do with him yet?" Rampage asked.

"No. U.S. Congress has yet to start wrangling over what to do about that issue. But the U.S. Justice System is ponderous and glacial in its movement. But like a glacier, their system crushes and grinds down all before it. So, too, will be the case of Miguel Torres. Just look how long it took them to try Manuel Noriega after they captured him.

"Now, on a completely different note, I want the both of you, and Strike Team Trident to take a week off. Go see family, hug a loved one, do a...what is it you Yanks call it...bar-b-cue? Point is: I don't want to see or hear from you for a week. Is that clear?"

"Yes sir," both answered.

"And when you get back, I want to talk to you about a little problem brewing up in the northeastern Mediterranean Sea. Now be gone with ya." He said the last sentence with a flick of his wrist, which Buck and Rampage took as their dismissal.

Arising from their chairs, they filed to the office door and exited. Outside, they were waylaid by Gloria Stienmetz, Colonel Barrett's secretary.

"Oh, there you are, Steve! Steve? I need to talk to you," the curvaceous middle aged beauty called, getting up from behind her desk, flashing a stunning smile that would have frozen a lesser man in his tracks. She was wearing a cream colored cashmere sweater with brown and tan prints of leaves over a light brown buttoned blouse with a V-neckline, cream pleated skirt and brown three inch heels that perfectly set off the ensemble. She was the picture of refinement and professionalism, the clothes accentuating all her attributes that started at her toes and pretty much ended at the top of her stylish bobbed ginger hair.

"I can't stop, love; orders from the boss. I must be on my way," he said without breaking stride, heading for the door. "Urgent business...just call me if you need me."

Rampage flew out the door followed by a bemused Buck. "What was that all about?" a smirking Buck asked, catching up with Rampage at the elevator doors, as if he didn't already know.

"I don't know. Either she wanted to make me go to a Sensitivity Training class or she was looking for another kissing. Either way, I wasn't about to find out."

"'Call me, if you need me?' Was that a Freudian slip or are you just planting the seed... uh hem... for future investigation?"

"Ah, c'mon!" he groaned.

"What, was she that bad of kisser?" Buck asked as they got on the elevator.

"Noooo...not bad for a *married* babe."

"Since when has marriage stopped you before?"

"Oh, I don't know...maybe since it involved my boss's secretary."

"I thought I was your boss."

"Now, don't go getting all technical on me; you know what I meant. I think I've created a monster."

"Monster is totally inappropriate for someone that attractive. I think you're looking at this all wrong. I'd like to think of it more as though you've awakened a new, burning passion inside her."

"God, no! But enough about me, what are you going to do with the rest of today before we fly out?"

"I've got to meet Lila in the lobby. She's meeting with her boss and then she's got to fly off back to Central America. I'm riding to the airport with her to see her off."

The elevator arrived at the ground floor, and they stepped out and started to part company. "Good luck...and give my love to Lila."

"That would require a round of antibiotics afterward, so I think I will pass. See you later..."

Buck made his way to the front door and found Lila waiting in the big, open glass atrium of the front door. As he approached, the clouds of the gray day parted ever so slightly, allowing a beam of sunshine to shoot through the windows, illuminating Lila. The effect made her glow; her face beamed as she caught sight of him and his heart fluttered for a moment.

She gave him a quick peck on the cheek as she grabbed his hand in one of hers; she babbled while Buck grabbed her rolling suitcase as he hustled her outside for a taxi. The ride to the airport was filled with pleasant small talk and smiles, both trying to ignore the unpleasant reality of the impending separation.

After checking in at her airline, they moved off for the airport's security-check station for international flights and stopped just short. Moving off to the side, Buck swept Lila into his arms so he could talk to her privately in the sea of humanity that swept by them on all sides.

Buck started, "Lila, I know the timings not right but I promise we'll finish that picnic someday if you want."

"Oh, Buck, don't say any more," she said, putting her finger to his lips. "It's such a nice illusion, one that I'd like to hold onto. I know our work will keep us from ever having a life together, because we're always going to be at the opposite ends of the world. But I'd like to dream every once in a while of your head in my lap while we read under a lazy Virginia summer day's quiet in the shade of a big oak tree. That dream can keep me happy for a long time."

"Better that than the nightmare of the drive home," he quipped. She just smiled beatifically at him as he continued, "I think a little separation might be a good thing, though. Being with you has stirred things in my heart that I haven't felt for a long time, things that I've been trying to ignore. When we kiss, I see dead people. I see my wife and child. My feelings for you are just as strong and fierce for you as it was for them. But I haven't let go of them yet, and I could not let myself be with you as long as the ghosts of my past are hanging around my neck. It wouldn't be fair to you. But when that time comes that I can let them go, I hope you'll be in a place in your life that has room for me."

For an answer, she kissed him tenderly. Then she grabbed the suitcase handle and started walking backwards towards the line with an enigmatic smile on her face before she waved and pirouetted, disappearing into the crowd.

60

The steaks, bratwursts, and hamburgers were sizzling on the grill, filling the air with a scent that made the primal man within everyone in range salivate with anticipation. It was a fine, late summer Sunday afternoon, the sun shining brightly above. Not that anyone would know, since Buck's warehouse ceiling prevented nature's beauty from penetrating.

Gathered on a massive piece of carpet that served as Buck's lawn were the members of Strike Force Trident and their dates. Buck was trying to instill within them an appreciation of two American institutions: the barbecue and football. At one end of the lawn was a table loaded with chips, dips, snacks, beans, salads, buns, condiments, etc., and at the other was a big screen TV in all its high-definition glory. From the barbecue, tongs in one hand, ice cold beer in the other, he was shouting out explanations to Tadhg, Coop, Sassy and Grels, who seemed utterly perplexed by random acts of violence and the capricious random starts and stops of the game. A few of their dates were trying to help out in explaining the game to men who believed real football should only be played with their feet.

The other women were more intent on doting on Bear's daughters and his splendid wife, who fascinated them with the lilting elegance of their accents.

Lenz had found a couch on the periphery that he and his

wife occupied. The oldest of the team, Lenz's children had long left the nest. He was more content to watch the proceedings rather than be part of them. He and his wife watched with bemused fondness over their new family.

Rampage had appointed himself as the "Brew Master" and "Chief Beverage Host." His duties consisted of fishing beers from the big galvanized metal bucket filled with ice water or topping off glasses of wine. The revelry had reached full bloom when Buck's cell phone started vibrating in his pocket. Setting his beer down, but still tending to the grilling meat, he flipped thumbed his cell phone to answer. "Hello?"

"Hi, this is..." Just then a spectacular hit on the TV that jarred the ball loose set the whole room to hoot'n and holler'n.

"I'm sorry, I couldn't hear that. Could you hold on a minute...?" Buck waved over Rampage and handed the tongs to him while he stepped off to the side and stuck a finger in his opposite ear "I'm sorry, I didn't catch that..."

"Hi, this is Chip Hartwell, Penny Hartwell's dad."

"Oh, hi..."

"I hope I'm not calling at a bad time. I'm Congressmen Castilla's chief of staff and I asked him for your number. I hope that was all right?"

"No, uh, that's fine. Just a few friends over watching football is all."

"I'm sure you're enjoying the Cowboys game-- everyone does."

"Well, not everyone...what can I do for you, Mr. Hartwell? How's your daughter?"

"She's recovering quite well. The doctors feel she'll make a complete physical recovery. Her psychological healing is another thing altogether, though..." he said, trailing off. "But I know my girl, she's tough, she'll bounce back, eventually. You remember Selena, the Mexican girl you rescued?"

"Yeah."

"Well, she's the best therapy we could've hoped for. We got one of the best surgeons in Texas to fix her hip. She's gettin' about with hardly a limp and the stitches have hardly been out a week. Penny is taking her out and getting her new clothes, getting her hair styled, teaching her to do make-up and to speak English, so she is finally getting to help someone, which is what she started to do in the first place. Helping Selena is letting Penny find her balance again. The boys are already starting to circle her. It won't be too long before we're going to have to beat them off with a stick. Those two are just thick as thieves. And we hope, between the two of them, they can help each other find a road to recovery and new lives."

Buck had wondered what had become of Penny, and he was glad to hear about her progress. "That's just great to hear Mr. Hartwell," the sincerity in his voice undisguised. "I'll let the rest of my team know. In fact, they're all here. It will make a great day even better."

"Listen, the other reason I called is that I feel that I owe you a debt of gratitude. My family is not without means...I would like to send you a token of my appreciation for what you did for my daughter. How does a check for fifty thousand dollars sound?"

"Sir, I appreciate the gesture and your heart is in the right place. But I do what I do because of a sense of duty and honor. I'm not a mercenary. The U.N. pays me adequately; I don't require remuneration."

"I'm sorry if I offended you. I just feel like it's only honorable to express my gratitude by doing something for you."

"I'm sorry, Mr. Hartwell, I did not mean to be rude. I

certainly can understand that..." Buck was about to continue when his eyes alighted upon the hydroplane racer sitting on saw horses out beyond his tools. Quickly an idea flashed into his head. "You know, there is a little something that I could use a hand with," he said, his gaze intensifying on the bright yellow boat. "I have this little aquatic project that could use your help...."

THE END

For information on this and upcoming books, go to:

scottwilliambooks.com

COMING SOON!!

"TOOTH"
By
Scott William

SPRING 2015